BROKEN WINGS

JIA PINGWA

Translated by
NICKY HARMAN

ACA PUBLISHING LTD

Paperback published by
ACA Publishing Ltd.

eBook published by
Sinoist Books (an imprint of ACA Publishing Ltd).

University House
11-13 Lower Grosvenor Place
London SW1W 0EX, UK
Tel: +44 (0)20 3289 3885
Fax: +44 (0)20 7973 0076
E-mail: info@alaincharlesasia.com
Web: www.alaincharlesasia.com

Beijing Office
Tel: +86 (0)10 8472 1250
Fax: +86 (0)10 5885 0639

Author: Jia Pingwa
Translator: Nicky Harman
Editor: David Lammie
Cover art: Daniel Li

Published by ACA Publishing Ltd in association with the People's Literature Publishing
House

Chinese language copyright © 2016, by People's Literature Publishing House, Beijing, China

English language translation copyright © 2019, Nicky Harman

Paperback ISBN: 978-1-910760-45-1
eBook ISBN: 978-1-910760-55-0

A catalogue record for *Broken Wings* is available from the National Bibliographic Service of
the British Library.

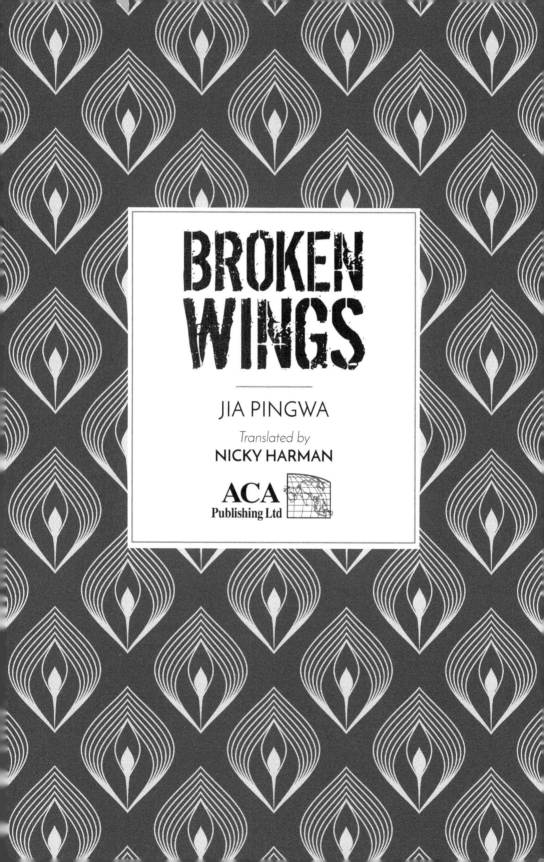

BROKEN WINGS

JIA PINGWA

Translated by
NICKY HARMAN

ACA
Publishing Ltd

Chapter 1

THE NIGHT SKY

Evening.

I made my one hundred and seventy-eighth scratch on the cave wall.

The roosting crows spattered shit all over the ground.

Good-Son's dad topped himself.

And I got to know Great-Grandad.

I knew all about Good-Son and his family. I'd overheard the gossip on the strip. The word was that Good-Son had not been a good son at all. At one time he used to go out with the rest of them to dig nonesuch flowers – though they were going on extinct and a fortnight's digging would only get you five or six specimens, but at least they were all doing it as a family. Then, after Padlock's wife got stung to death by hornets, Good-Son made up his mind to leave and get a labouring job in the city. He'd been out of sight and out of mind for four years when his left-behind wife had a baby. The villagers pointed the finger at his old dad:

Is the baby his grandchild or his own kid?... But the old man's seventy-three, there's no way he can get it up nowadays!... Hey, didn't Zhang the Prop from East Gully hot springs get a girl pregnant when he was eighty?... Still, Zhang used to eat blood onions, and Good-Son's dad had a stroke and his eyes and mouth are all pulled down on one side. Even if he's up for it, his daughter-in-law wouldn't be, would she? ...But if he isn't the father, who is?

Rumours swirled; there were plenty of men in the village and a dozen or more were wifeless, 'bare branches' as they were called, so everyone suspected someone else.

"You fucker, was it you?" they asked each other.

Finally, three days back, Good-Son's wife ran off with the man who'd come to buy up the nonesuch flowers, taking her baby. That proved the old man's innocence, and everyone stopped accusing each other too. They turned their fury on the village girls who refused to take village husbands and ran off to marry elsewhere. Like Good-Son's wife. She may have been abandoned, but she could have had her pick of the other village men. Instead, she rubbed their noses in the dirt by going off with an outsider!

Now, as soon as dawn broke, you could hear crying in two places. One was on a ridge to the east of the village, where Padlock sat weeping on his late wife's grave. He'd been off his head with grief for four years and swore she was still alive. The other place was Good-Son's dad's house below our strip, where he sat slapping himself around the face, wailing that he hadn't kept a watch on his son's wife.

No one paid much attention, until the old man drank pesticide and died, bleeding from his eyes, ears, nostrils and mouth.

Bright Black was with Three-Lobes, La-Ba and Running-Water on the strip, loading up his small tractor with blood onions that they'd go and flog in the township that evening. When they heard the news, they stopped what they were doing and went and buried the poor old man themselves, seeing as the son wasn't around to do the decent thing by his dad.

When they'd laid out the body and set up the spirit table, a man or a woman from every family went to pay their respects, with a bunch of incense sticks in one hand and a roll of hemp paper tucked under the other arm. Bright's dad and uncle went too, but the dog stayed lying outside the cave, and Great-Grandad didn't go either.

Great-Grandad sat on the millstone. In the branches of the four lacebark pines, the roosting crows cawed and splattered their crap down below. Every day at dusk they made this terrible din and dropped so much crap that the stink wafted into my cave.

There were rats in the cave, gnawing at the old chest. They never gave up even though there was no grain in it, only a heap of rags and some old cotton waste. They must have been using the chest to grind their teeth down, so their teeth didn't grow too long and stop them eating properly. I wasn't going to get up to scare them away, what the hell, they could carry on gnawing for all I cared, let them gnaw the chest into bits, let them gnaw the darkness to bits for me!

One night about six months ago, I made the first scratch on the cave wall with my fingernail. Since then, I'd added a scratch each day. There were two of us here in this cave: Bright's mum, but all that was left of her was a piece of cardboard hung on the wall, and me, and all I had to show for the last six months of my young life was a few scratches. When I made the one hundred and seventy-eighth scratch, I was so humiliated and furious and distressed and helpless that I dug my right index finger in too hard, broke the fingernail and made it bleed. I wiped the blood off on the poster girl.

The poster of the girl had been stuck to the wall with flour paste. She'd obviously been torn from a calendar and the date cut off, leaving just her picture. There were slashes that ran from her neck down to her feet, deep score marks that cut right into the wall.

I asked Bright: "Did you stick that up?"

He said: "I wanted her."

"You wanted her so you cut her up?"

"I was angry that she wasn't mine."

Pah! I spat at him: "You hate her that much because she isn't yours? Well, there's a lot that isn't yours in this world!"

A mosquito flew in through the crack in the door, whined past my ear, settled on the girl's face and proceeded to suck up the blood I'd wiped there. I looked at the girl and she looked back at me, and I suddenly got hysterical and shrieked and tried to rip her off the wall, but she wouldn't come off. I used both hands to rake the poster off, until flakes of paper and plaster dropped on the floor, and I slumped against the windowsill, panting for breath.

Great-Grandad was still out there sitting on the millstone.

"Hey you!" I shouted. "Aren't you going to the funeral? Or have they told you to keep an eye on me?"

"I'm not watching you," the old man said. "I'm stargazing. You see that streak of light? When Good-Son's dad died, one of those stars fell out of the sky."

"Let them fall, I hope they all fall out of the sky!" I wailed.

"Don't talk like that. If all the stars fell out of the sky, there wouldn't be any sky left. From the twelfth degree of the Eastern Well to the fifth degree of the Spirit, there's the Quail's Head and...'

But it all sounded like a lot of mumbo-jumbo to me. I couldn't make head or tail of what he was saying, especially with his accent, and I told him so.

He explained: "I'm talking about star-fields."

"What are star-fields?"

"The sky above is divided up according to the stars, and the earth below is divided into corresponding fields, they match each other, so together they're called star-fields. How come you don't know that?"

"I only know I want to go home!"

"Bright said you'd done middle school. And you don't know about star-fields?"

"They don't test you on them."

"Oh, well, no wonder...'

"I want to go home. Let me out! I want to go back to the city."

I had been shut up in this cave for the last six months, and it was beginning to smell quite ripe. There were plenty of visitors to the strip, the bit of tamped earth outside the row of caves. Villagers came to get Bright's dad to do stonework for them because he was a stone mason and could chisel doorsteps and stools, and make pig troughs and mortars too, and they'd swarm around the door and peer through the crack at me inside, and chatter about how Bright had got himself a young and pretty wife, who was educated too, and a city girl. I used to stand at the window so they could see my face, then turn around and show them the back of my head and shoulders, and say: "Want an eyeful, do you?"

"What a fine girl!" they'd exclaim.

And I'd yell back: "Get lost!"

But Great-Grandad was different: he lived nearby on the same strip, he was the Blacks' neighbour, but he never came to look at me, never even turned his head if he was passing by.

He was a dry old stick of a man, with slow movements and an impassive expression, not that you saw much of his face anyway because it was covered with a long white beard. I used to wonder if he even had a mouth. He spent his days either inside his cave or sitting under the gourd frame outside his door, sometimes writing with a calligraphy brush on cut-up pieces of red paper, one character on each bit, then stacking the paper together; sometimes braiding brightly coloured twine, completely absorbed, till he had a big ball of it. He'd do this for a whole day and then the next day too.

I'd asked Bright if he was really his Great-Grandad because that was what he called him and so did everyone else who came to the strip, and he said: "He's Great-Grandad to the whole village."

"Is he the clan head or the village boss?" I asked.

"No, he's just the most senior villager. He used to teach in the community school when he was young but he never got a transfer to a state school, so he came back to farm. He's got a bellyful of knowledge and he's a good man. When he was younger, he used to plough the first furrow in spring, and when the villagers made a lion for the lion dance, he was the one who painted the dots on the eyes. He was the one who discovered the nonesuch flower and named it, and now he's very old so everyone calls him Great-Grandad."

I was sceptical. I knew that this was a poor village; none of its elders had been able to marry till they were old and that meant that they'd had late families or very small ones. Being called Great-Grandad didn't mean he was an honoured patriarch. In fact, he was just a bumbling old fellow waiting for the Grim Reaper to come and get him. He never paid any attention to me shut up in my cave, so I treated him like he was a block of stone or wood.

Anyway, that night, with Bright and his dad and uncle at Good-Son's dad's funeral, I was racking my brains as to how I could get past the dog that was guarding the cave door and run away again. But Great-Grandad carried on sitting on the millstone. He was keeping an eye on me, I was sure, and that was really pissing me off. He was banging on and on about the stars, the Eastern Well and star-fields, stuff I'd never heard of, and I was sure he was doing it to wind me up. The Blacks, father and son, had my body shut up in this cave, but Great-Grandad was doing my head in. It didn't matter how I got to the village, he had no business being sarky about my education.

I scraped together the bits of wall plaster and threw them out of the window at him and one bit hit him on the shoulder. Without looking around, he struck a match and the flame leapt up and illuminated the sheet of paper resting on his knee and his face too. The half of it you could see wasn't much to look at, it was like a shrivelled-up aubergine buried in his beard and moustache. Then the flame went out, making things look darker than ever. Above us, the heavens were carpeted with stars and only half the moon was left.

"Go to sleep," he said.

But I couldn't sleep.

I looked at the cave walls. In the lamplight, they looked slimy, as if someone had flicked snot all over them. The dog outside must have been dreaming because every now and then it let out a yap. The crows were still crapping from their roosts, but you couldn't see them any more, they had merged into the darkness of the night, and the shadows from the pines shrouded the edge of the strip.

The day I arrived, dragged here kicking and struggling, I caught sight of those four pine trees rearing up tall against the undercliff. I was terrified. What kind of a place was this? All I could see was a steep slope pitted with holes, caves that were strewn higgledy-piggledy from top to bottom. I felt like a grub, injured but still wriggling, being carried into a hole by an army of ants. I shouted for Mr Wang, the man who had been with me up till now, but he had vanished. I heard someone say: "Blindfold her so she won't remember the way", and it flashed through my mind what my mum used to tell me, that when you went down into the underworld, little imps would force you to drink a potion so you would forget everything about where you came from.

They pulled my suit jacket over my head, but I struggled free and shouted again: "Mr Wang! Mr Wang!"

They roared with laughter: "Mr Wang's hit the jackpot! He's gone off to count his winnings!" Then I felt a punch on the chin and the next thing I knew, I was flat out on the ground. And then I was shut up in the cave.

I'd never lived in a cave, I didn't even know you could live in one. There wasn't a scrap of timber to hold this one up, and though there was a window, it only let in a small square of light. There was no back door either so no air circulated. It was stuffy, cramped and gloomy, and stank of a mixture of sweat and mildew. Bright boasted that they'd lived in caves for generations, they hardly needed timber or tiles, and they were rock-solid and long-lasting. Maybe so, but only snakes, scorpions, beetles, ghosts and ghouls lived in caves. Or humans who'd been buried alive.

That was me, a human buried alive.

I'd heard talk of the kidnapping of women and children for many years, but I'd never imagined it happening to me. It didn't bear thinking about, I mean I was a grown-up and educated, how could I have been kidnapped?

Locked up in the cave, the only thing connecting me to the outside world was that one window and its lattice of forty-eight squares, forty-eight beady eyes looking at me. Beyond the strip, I could see puffs of smoke and hear cocks crowing, dogs barking and people shouting and swearing, but I couldn't see their caves. I could see the yellow earth plateau rising and falling all the way to the horizon, like an immense leaf that had rotted away until only the ribs and veins remained. The ribs and veins were the ridges and gullies and flat-topped knolls that made up the plateau. Below the clouds that hung over it every day, the farmers ploughed the terraces with their donkeys. They worked from the edge of the knolls into the centre, and the furrows showed up dark against the yellow, as if they were ropes coiling round and round in ever-smaller circles, with the farmer and the donkey in the very centre. Sometimes, all of a sudden, the clouds drifted away, the sun shone, the wind got up, and then shadows swished across the strip like swiftly drawn curtains plunging the strip and the pine trees into gloom, and Bright's dad's eyebrows and eyes merged into his swarthy face.

Bright's dad spent his time either chiselling stone on the strip or sitting at the door of his cave, to the left of mine, sewing. He looked completed absorbed in whatever he was doing, whether it was the hardest or the gentlest kind of work, but a breeze only had to ruffle the grass for him to whip his head around and stare at my window. I could not see beyond his cave because the corner of the undercliff stuck out and got in the way. He would collect my piss bucket every day and take it around the corner, so maybe there was a shit-house there. The henhouse and the pigpen too. To the right of my cave were two more, the nearest of which housed the donkey. The donkey didn't lie across my door all day like the dog did but every time I shook the door or the window, the dog barked and whenever the dog barked, the donkey brayed. The second of the caves was where

Bright's uncle lived. He was busy whether it was day or night, working over the mule's bedding of dried earth and grass, or gathering armfuls of fuel. The first night I saw him, I thought I was seeing a ghost, then I realised he was blind so it made no difference to him whether it was light or dark. Beyond his cave, another bit of the undercliff stuck out, and that was where the gourd frame was, with half a dozen gourds hanging down, encased in little boxes of different shapes. I couldn't see round the corner but when there was a wind I could sometimes hear a flapping like a bird's wings, which I guessed was the Spring Festival couplets pasted around a doorway catching in the breeze. That was where Great-Grandad lived. I reckoned his surname must have been White. That's because the dog belonged to the Blacks and was called Blackie, and his gourd flowers were white when they opened, so that made him Mr White. I didn't know whether the crows that roosted in the pines every evening were Whites or Blacks. I gathered from what the villagers said that the pine trees had been there for a hundred years and only crows roosted in them. The pines gave the village good *feng shui*, and they regarded the crows as lucky birds. They were as black as a sooty cooking pot, but their shit was white, and they spattered the whole strip white every evening, so it looked like it had had a coat of whitewash.

Outside on the strip I could see a millstone on the right and a well on the left. The villagers used to say millstones and wells were mythological beasts, their White Tigers and Green Dragons. The millstone was huge, its bed stone and runner stone like a great big maw devouring the grain. It was the runner stone that got pushed around, and it had worn down over the years to half the thickness of the bed stone, so they had to put a big rock on top when they were milling the grain, to weight it down. The stone rim of the well was also very old, and was scored with grooves worn by the rope used to haul the bucket up. They used to unreel the spool of rope and let it down, which took half an hour, and then it took nearly another hour to wind it back up again, creaking and groaning, as if they were dragging a demon up by its neck, and then all they had to show for their efforts was half a bucket of silty water. Bright's dad kept muttering that there hadn't been any rain since the beginning of summer, that was eight months, and the water level was dropping every day.

"Heaven's really got it in for us, we're short of food and now there's not enough water to drink either."

Then there were the cave's doors and windows. A cave without doors and windows was just a hole in the earth, the way a head without ears, eyes and mouth was just a lump of flesh and bone. In this cave, apart from the window three feet away from the door, there was another one, half-moon-shaped, sitting on top of the door like a sort of cap. The whole thing looked like a mushroom to me, but Bright told me it was a "stone ancestor".

"What's a stone ancestor?"

"A penis, meaning life and strength."

I spat in his face then: "If everyone's got things like that over the door, no wonder there are so many wifeless men around here!"

"Motherfucker!" said Bright furiously.

"Are you calling me motherfucker?"

"No, the city! That's who I'm swearing at."

"What's the city done to you?"

"All these new cities the government's developing, they're like giant bloodsuckers, slurping up money and property from the village, sucking away the village girls."

I didn't know what to say to that. I'd been sucked away by the city too, after all. But if there weren't any girls left in the villages, the lads could have gone to the city to find themselves girls, couldn't they? Why did they have to act like bandits and kidnap them? Bright saw me scowling and changed the subject. He got some papercuts out of the trunk and said: "The door and windows could do with a bit of prettying up. I'm going to stick the papercuts around them, they look too plain as they are."

He stuck the papercuts onto the window lattice and on the half-moon window above the door.

Auntie Spotty-Face had brought the papercuts. She was a tiny little woman, always darting hither and thither, you never knew when she'd turn up on the strip or when she'd leave either. She'd arrived with a pile of papercuts for Bright and told him to stick them up, but he said: "Why would I do that? Last time, I stuck them on the tractor and look what happened! It overturned on the road."

"Well, maybe if you hadn't, you might not be here to tell the tale," she said.

Bright's dad had even less time for her than his son. If he was brewing some tea, he never offered her a cup. But Auntie Spotty-Face wasn't bothered. She asked Bright if he had any coloured paper for sale in his store, then started on a tirade about her husband: he was beating her, she'd be better off if he died of jaundice or 'dry cholera', stuff like that. Then it was as if her burst of temper had never happened and she came to peer in through my window.

"Is she being good?" she asked, but Bright's dad pulled her away and pushed her towards the exit. And, when she was already out in the alley: "Is she pregnant yet?"

I'd hardly seen any flowers around here, except the pathetic little white specimens on the gourd frame at the edge of the strip. But the flowers that Auntie Spotty-Face cut out with her scissors came in all shapes and sizes. When the moon shone in, they cast their shadows from the lattice onto the *kang*, the bed built of mud bricks, as if they'd been planted there. But then Bright said: "You're the prettiest flower on the *kang*!" and I jumped up and ripped all the papercuts off the window lattice.

After that, Bright didn't stick up any more papercuts. Sometimes during the day I used to press myself up against the window and peer outside. When I was bored of that, I'd bang it, which made a bell jangle. That bell used to hang around the donkey's neck, but Bright's dad took it off and strung it on a rope that he tied between the window and the door. The bell jangling set the dog barking and the chickens squawking and the donkey braying, and the old man would rush out of his cave to see what was going on.

If the bell jangled and Bright's dad didn't come out and the animals were quiet, then it was Bright, back from his store. He carried the key to the door padlock hung from his belt, and he used to say that hearing the jangling as he unlocked it made him happy. I just blanked him and carried on picking the cotton waste stuffing out of the pillow and dropping it all over the *kang*. He never got annoyed. The first thing he'd do was go out with my piss bucket and empty it in the shit-house, then go to the kitchen to finish making the dinner, or if the dinner was already made, he'd bring me some in a bowl. Whether or not I ate it, he always smiled: "You're here, so I'll be off to the store."

"You like living like this?" I challenged him.

"Well, at least I've got a wife."

There was a dimple at the corner of his lips when he smiled, but I couldn't stand dimples. "You've got a wife, have you? And who would that be?" I said.

Then he left again, locking the door behind him, and the cave became like the Bull Demon King from *Journey to the West*, and I was like Sun Wukong, trapped in the Bull Demon King's belly.

I started to freak out. I rampaged around, yelling and breaking everything I could get my hands on and throwing the bedding to the floor. Then I grabbed Bright's stinky shoes from under the *kang* and went to the back of the cave to whack things with them. I broke a jar of beans and all the beans spilled out, then I kicked the stool so hard I hurt my foot, so I smashed it against the edge of the *kang* and broke three of its four legs. In the gloom, the two picture frames hanging on the cave walls gleamed faintly. One had a dried pressed nonesuch flower in it, the other a picture of Bright's mother. I didn't know what the nonesuch flower was for, so I yelled at his mother instead. "It's your fault for giving birth to this bandit!"

I had got tired out by then, so I flung myself on my front on the *kang* and cried and cried. This cave wasn't the Bull Demon King's belly any more, it was a clam that had swallowed a grain of sand (that was me) that chafed on the clam flesh, which in turn chafed on the sand and turned it into a pearl that hung around Bright's neck and make him look good.

All of a sudden, I had a brainwave. Great-Grandad!

I hated the old boy, my face still burned whenever I remembered his teasing and I wanted to chuck all the bits of wall I had scraped off with my fingernails out at him. But snapping my fingers in delight at my own cleverness, I composed myself and called softly out of the window: "Great-Grandad!"

He looked startled when I called his name.

"Great-Grandad!" I called again.

"That's me. And what's your name?"

"Butterfly."

"Butterfly... With a name like that, you must have been a flower in a former life."

"Great-Grandad, did you say the heavens above match the earth below?"

"Well, the clouds in the sky are just like the ripples on water, on the earth, don't you think? And the birds in the sky are just fish with feathers on, and fish are featherless birds."

He spluttered a bit and I couldn't tell if he was coughing or laughing. I guessed he was paying me a compliment talking to me like this, but I couldn't help thinking that birds and fish were free and I was locked up in a cave. I felt the tears coming but forced them back and said: "And what matches human beings in the sky?"

"Each human being on earth has their star."

"Where's my star, then?"

I peered upwards out of the window. The sky was like a gigantic upturned wok studded with countless nails that glittered silver. I tried to count them, and then counted again and again, but each time the number came out different.

"You're not any of those stars, nor am I, nor's anyone in the village. Our stars don't shine until we die."

"I want to see my star!"

He spluttered again.

"I want to see it!" I repeated.

"Then you have to look at a bit of empty sky, fix your eyes on it, and if you can see a star it'll be yours."

The sky was dark above the lacebark pines and I started to look at it. Inwardly I was crying out: "If I'm a star, why am I so miserable?"

My eyes started to hurt from too much staring and I was getting a crick in my neck. The sky above was still pitch-black, there were no stars.

"Maybe I can only see my star from the city."

"But there are stars everywhere, Butterfly."

"Well, if that's the Eastern Well above us, then where's the star-field boundary and what's the village called and the township and the province?"

More spluttering.

I was suddenly apprehensive. What if he had rumbled me? I felt like a TV screen: completely dark when it was off, but as soon as you switched it on, everything was bright and clear. I began to sweat and found myself edging away from the window.

"Great-Grandad! Great-Grandad!" I cried.

I heard a sneeze. It was so loud, it sounded like an explosion. But it wasn't Great-Grandad. It came from the entrance to the strip, and it was Bright's dad.

He had just come back from Good-Son's house and had overheard me and Great-Grandad talking, so this was his way of putting a stop to it. I said nothing more and nor did Great-Grandad. All of a sudden, the night was dead quiet, except for the sound of Bright's dad who kept blowing his nose.

Finally, seemingly to spare Great-Grandad any embarrassment, he said: "Looking at the stars, were you? Any sign of rain?"

"There's no water vapour around the Eastern Well."

"If we don't get any rain soon, we'll all die of the heat... There used to be a temple where you could pray for rain."

Great-Grandad got off the millstone, stood up a little shakily, then bent to rub his knees. "Time for bed," he said, and he went back to his cave.

I hit the window furiously with my hand, which made the dog jump to its feet and snap. Bright's dad glanced at my window, then kicked the dog and shouted at it. Then he called to Great-Grandad: "Hang on a minute, I've got something to ask you. When we were laying out the corpse, I was putting a copper coin in his mouth so he'd have money to get himself to the underworld, and he scared the hell out of me – he sat upright, and I thought he'd come back from the dead, then he lay back down again, stiff as a board. It was weird. But killing himself like that, how can his soul rest in peace? We have no temples, no monks and no ceremonies any more."

"Sometimes a corpse jerks, and there are reasons. Did a cat get up on the bier?"

"No, the cat didn't come in."

"Was there anyone born in the year of the tiger standing nearby?"

"Good heavens! Yes, I was born in the year of the tiger." He slapped himself on the forehead.

Great-Grandad screwed up the piece of paper he had in his hand and flicked it quickly through my window lattice, where it landed silently inside.

Bright's dad hadn't finished his questions: "Does that mean I shouldn't go back there?"

But he got no answer. When he turned around, Great-Grandad had gone.

I saw a red glow below the strip, where they were burning spirit money for Good-Son's deceased dad. It was very bright. Bright's dad looked down on it and muttered to himself, then spat a few times and went back to his cave.

The wick in the kerosene lamp sparked and spat.

The village did not have electricity. I'd heard the village boss ranting about this and about the village alleys turning into a quagmire in the rain, but when he wanted to repair the alleys, he couldn't get people to do the work. I'd heard him cursing and swearing at Spring-Starts, La-Ba and Pillar for refusing to cough up any money so the villagers would always be like Old Man Two. Old Man Two was Bright's uncle Blindy, and Bright wasn't at all happy at hearing the village boss talking about his uncle like that: "My uncle's blind, so what if he puts his food in his nose instead of his mouth and ends up on the *kang* in the wrong house?"

The pair of them had a row. It was only afterwards that I found out the reason for the village boss being so angry with Bright: Bright had told everyone about the village boss forcing himself on some of the village widows. He had even done the same with Pillar's wife when Pillar was away from home. So Pillar was not on speaking terms with the village boss either. When it came time to get together the money to install electricity, Spring-Starts and La-Ba had just started their blood onion business and money was tight. None of the three paid up, so nor did any of the other villagers, and the electricity project never happened and everyone carried on using kerosene lamps.

When the price of kerosene went up, the Black family only lit the lamps when they were cooking their dinner and washing the pots, and then they sat in the darkness chatting until they went to bed. But I wasn't having that. I wanted the lamp lit day and night. I'd been in this cave for one hundred and seventy-eight days and apart from crying, swearing, breaking things and plotting how to make my escape, blowing the lamp out and lighting it again was my only form of entertainment.

Every time Bright refilled the reservoir, he said suspiciously: "How come it's out of oil already? Have you been keeping it on during the daytime?"

"Why shouldn't I have it lit in the cave?" I asked, staring at him. He said nothing, his lips just flapped a bit like loose tiles, and he passed me a handkerchief to wipe my nose. My nostrils must have been black with soot, but I refused to wipe them, I just re-lit the lamp and turned the flame up high: "I'll waste your kerosene if I feel like it!"

But every time I lit the lamp, its trembling pea-sized flame, burning red, then white-yellow, showed how frightened I was.

I flattened the scrap of paper under the lamp.

I thought that the reason why Great-Grandad had thrown it to me behind Bright's dad's back was because he pitied me, and maybe he'd written down where I was, the name of the village, the township and the county. Maybe he wanted me to know so that I could grab my chance to let my mum know where I'd been taken by the kidnappers, or was telling me the way so I could get out of here. But the scrap of paper had a different kind of diagram on it.

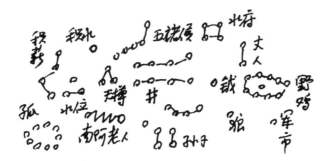

It was a map of the stars. I couldn't make head or tail of it, but no doubt Great-Grandad used it when he was star-gazing. I peered up at the sky again, through the window lattice. There were thousands of stars and I couldn't match them up with the drawing on the paper. I felt so let down and disappointed, I spat through the window in the direction of Bright's dad's cave.

To my surprise, I saw him come out and head towards the well, carrying a pair of high heels in his hands.

Chapter 2

THE VILLAGE

THEY WERE MY HIGH HEELS.

I'd bought them in the city and they were real leather. They'd cost me five hundred yuan, I'd had to sell two whole barrowloads of scrap my mum had collected to get the money. She'd been cross with me about that, told me that only city girls wore high heels, how could I go splashing out money on such things? I was furious: "But I'm a city girl! I'm just borrowing the money off you, I'll pay you back, five times over, two thousand five hundred yuan!"

Whenever I put them on, those high heels made me much taller, and made my bum stick out too. I couldn't sit still at home, I had to go tap-tapping down the street in them and then tap-tapping back again to our courtyard.

"You fly along in those! Ai-ya! No one would guess our Butterfly's from a village," said the landlord.

But my mum said: "Once a village girl, always a village girl. A black bantam's black right through to its bones."

"Butterfly was born to be a city girl," insisted the landlord. "City girls nowadays all want to look like westerners, they get their flat faces remodelled with plastic surgery, but Butterfly's got naturally angular features."

I had a small face, you could cover it with one hand, and I'd always hated it for not being nice and plump, but here I was with a naturally fashionable face! Whenever I went out to do the shopping, I squirrelled away the change so I could buy a mirror and any time I had a spare moment, I looked at myself in it, at my face and my high heels, and told it: "I'm a city girl now!"

"That mirror'll eat you up!" my mum yelled at me.

And now Bright's dad had those high heels in his keeping.

The day he brought me to the cave, Bright took my high heels away and gave me a pair of cloth shoes instead. He said his mum had made them for her future daughter-in-law, stitch by stitch, by the light of the kerosene lamp. I never wore them. I'd lost my identity the day I lost those high heels. I kicked the cloth shoes into a corner, I'd rather go barefoot.

"Put them on," Bright had said, retrieving them. "Make my mother smile in the underworld."

"Your mum can smile, but my mum's crying!"

We fought over the high heels in that cave. But no matter how furious I got, how loudly I wept and wailed and screamed and cried, I couldn't get my shoes back off Bright.

"I spent thirty-five thousand to get you," he'd said. "And five thousand yuan of that was extra."

"So did you pay the extra because you saw I was a city girl and young and pretty? Even if you'd paid a hundred thousand or a million, don't you think that's like putting a horse's saddle on a donkey, or sticking a flower in cow dung?"

That took the wind out of his sails. He stood there, a dark, scrawny figure, but he still wouldn't give back the shoes he was clutching to his chest. He put them in his dad's cave. After that, his dad used to tie my high heels to the rope and dangle them down the well every evening and draw them up again the next morning. Every night, without fail.

That was a village custom: if ever a villager disappeared, or went away and didn't come back for a long time, they would take the person's shoes and dangle them in the well, in the hope that would bring the person back. By now, I'd learnt quite a lot of village lore. For instance, you couldn't point at the sky with your middle finger, because that way, your mum's brother would die. You weren't supposed to pee in the road or your child would be born without a bum hole. If you went out at night, you had to keep spitting because that was the only thing that kept the demons away. You always had to lick your bowl clean when you'd finished your gruel or porridge because it was wasteful to leave anything edible uneaten. You always took a gift of food when it was an elderly person's birthday, and that was called a 'top-up'. Lots of top-ups, and the person would live to a ripe old age. It didn't matter how little, a dipper full of grain or even a few handfuls, but you had to say when you presented it: "I've brought you a stone in weight of grain, may you live ten thousand years."

If you had a bad tooth, you shaved your hair. Then you had to throw the tooth and the cut hair up onto a high place. If you were sick and wanted to borrow a pot to boil the herbs in, the family you borrowed it from would leave it at the top of their alley. When it came time to return it, that was where you left it too. When you were rearing a pig, if you discovered its tail had gone a bit thin and flat, you had to cut off that bit, because a tail like that attracted the wolves. Whether the cave had a walled yard outside or just an open strip of ground, you mustn't stick bare posts into the ground, because it meant that there would never be any more women in that family – men without wives were known as 'bare branches'.

There was so much lore that the villagers clung to and which regulated their lives. In this day and age, I could hardly credit it. I was a kidnap victim and kidnapping was a crime, and Bright's dad was hanging my shoes in the well, but that didn't mean I had to submit to being Bright's wife and die in this godforsaken village of wifeless men, who had only their digestive organs and their sex organs. I could fight back, I could run away.

The first time Bright hit me around the face was a warning not to say bad things about his family. It was a resounding slap, and my mouth bled. I felt a stabbing pain in my belly too and rolled around on the *kang* and wouldn't eat for two days. That scared Bright and he desperately tried to make it up to me. Actually, my period had come and that was the reason for the bellyache. Every time I got my period, I felt dizzy with the pain. But I didn't tell him that. He thought it was because I couldn't stomach their buckwheat noodles and potatoes, so he went to the township to get me steamed wheat buns. After that, every week he'd go into town for steamed buns made of wheat flour, a bag at a time, so that I'd have at least two to eat every day. He used to put them in a willow basket and string it up from the cave ceiling so the rats wouldn't get at them, and thread the string through a piece of wood to stop them climbing down and getting into the basket. Every time he came back with the buns, he'd talk to me about his family and village business. "Once you've been here a while, you'll get to like me, and you won't want to leave the village," he insisted.

Bright said he'd lost his mum eight years before. She was the best-looking woman in the village, and she was sweet-natured with it. One day when he was three years old, she had taken him to bathe at the hot springs in East Gully Bottom, and they met an official from the county tourist office come to check up on the state of the springs. The official saw her and pronounced: "A good woman is clean in body and placid in nature."

As a result of which, his mother became famous as the most beautiful woman for miles around. The reason she was so good-looking was that she burned incense to the masters of Heaven and Earth, King, Parents and Teachers every day before the family spirit tablet, and laid out offerings of potatoes and sometimes a perfectly-formed nonesuch flower she had dug out of the ground. His mother revered the nonesuch flower, his mother was beautiful, his mother used to say: "My future daughter-in-law will be beautiful too!"

Now his mother's words had come true, and since my arrival at the Blacks' home, the other villagers had begun to frame a nonesuch flower and place it on the offerings table too. But that was all they did. They knew nothing of all the preparations Bright's mum had made for her future daughter-in-law, sewing cloth shoes and buying ten *jin* of cotton wadding. She had bagged it up and stored it in the cave roof. That cotton wadding had gone to make the bedding on the *kang*, which was all new.

The villagers thought that his beautiful mother sat at home doing nothing, but she was a good cook, seamstress and farmer, and strangest of all, when she went digging for nonesuch flowers, she never came back empty-handed. She'd get to a cliff or a ravine and it was like they were there waiting for her.

One day at dinner, when everyone was sitting around the table, Bright's dad had said: "When you go looking for a wife, make sure you get one like your mum."

"Easier said than done," said Bright.

Then three months later, his mum was dead. She had gone out digging nonesuch flowers and had just found one on Southern Tip Ridge when a plane flew overhead. Spring-Starts happened to be passing, on his way back to the village with his new wife, Rice. Rice looked up and exclaimed: "Look, a plane! I've been on a plane." Bright's mum looked up, lost her footing and rolled down off the ridge. She was in a coma for three days, then she died.

After that, the family fell on hard times.

"Look at that picture frame," Bright said. "That dried flower is a nonesuch flower. It's like the caterpillar fungus on the Qinghai plateau, it grows from a grub. At that stage, the grubs look just like green caterpillars, only they're brown and have sixteen little hairy legs, so they're called 'woollies'. Come winter, they go underground and hibernate. Then in spring, when other kinds of caterpillars pupate and turn into moths, the woollies put a green shoot above ground, four or five fingers high, with a fat bud on top, round like a baby's fist. First of all, it's purple, then it opens blue. Fist-bud flowers, they used to be called. When the Qinghai caterpillar fungus became famous as a high-class nutritional supplement, and the price went through the roof, some of the folk around here said: 'But we've got our very own caterpillar fungus.' Dealers turned up and persuaded the villagers to dig up the grub underneath the stalk, pull off the woolly's sixteen legs and pass it off as a caterpillar fungus. But they diddled us, they sold each piece for twelve yuan and we locals only ever saw three yuan of that. So we decided to go it alone, sell this variety under a different name, and Great-Grandad chose it: the nonesuch flower. Great-Grandad said: 'Their grass grows in summer from a grub that overwinters underground, and Qinghai folk call their fungus the nonesuch grass. Our woollies do the same but they put out a flower, so we can call ours the nonesuch flower.'

"The local government promoted the nonesuch flowers as hard as it could, as an even more precious rarity than the Qinghai nonesuch grass. The county town and our township were plastered with advertisements and the township even had a billboard proclaiming, Capital of the Nonesuch Flower. Prices shot up, and companies were set up to market them. There were buyers in every village who bought up the harvest and sold it in town. I used to be the buyer in this village."

The nonesuch flower boom had lasted nearly ten years; almost everyone went out to dig and no one bothered to farm their fields, but nonesuch flowers were never plentiful. When the ridges and slopes around the village were pitted with diggings, the diggers moved further afield, until those cliffs were pitted with holes too. Finally, they went as far as Bear's Ear Peak, a long way away, where the mountains were infested with wild beasts and shrouded in mist all year round, but it was difficult finding the nonesuch flowers there. After a bit, if someone found a likely-looking grub, they'd stick a piece of grass in its head and dry it out so they could try and pass it off as the real thing, until even they became scarce. A few people carried on digging and dreaming of making their fortune, but most of the villagers gave it up and life went back to how it always had been. Bright started buying supplies in town and bringing them back to village to sell at a mark-up, and when he'd got enough money together, he set up his shop.

Bright said his dad hadn't had it easy either: his parents had died young and he had been left to fend for himself and his little brother, Bright's Uncle Blindy. For fifteen years, he agonised about finding a wife for his brother but no woman was willing to marry a blind man. There was the stonemason in Wang village with a half-witted daughter who didn't know her arse from her elbow, and Bright's dad agreed to be the man's apprentice in the hope that his brother could marry the girl. Blindy never did marry the girl but Bright's dad learned how to carve stone. When he was forty-five, he had a new worry, this time about how to get his son a wife. He looked everywhere for a match-maker. In those days you had to give a gift of a pair of shoes to a matchmaker, so for years he carried around a pair of rubber shoes in his breast pocket. After his wife died and the years passed, the old man practically went off his head with worry. He asked everyone he met: "Find someone for Bright to marry, will you? It doesn't matter what she's like so long as you lift her tail and check she's female!"

Bright's dad was scared stiff that his son would never marry, the way his brother hadn't, and the family would die out.

With Bright's dad being a stonemason, any of the villagers who needed rollers and millstones in the village came to him. He made new stone well-rims and doorsteps, and mortar and pestles for grinding rice flour, and the feeding troughs for pigs and donkeys as well. His dad could make anything with a bit of stone, it was like dough in his hands. These past years, the village population had been shrinking while the number of men without wives kept on growing. One day, Rake Zhang came and asked Bright's dad to make him a stone woman to stand at his door so he wouldn't feel so lonely when he went in and out. After that, Clan-Keeper Wang, Water-Come Liang, Delight Liu and the brothers La-Ba and Spring-Starts all wanted stone women too, and Bright's dad made them all for free. Any time the old man had a spare moment, he'd carve a stone woman and put it at the entrance to the village, then he'd make another and put it there too, so now there were dozens there. After they got their stone women, Spring-Starts and Delight Liu got themselves real wives, and so did Clan-Keeper Wang, even though his was paralysed. She had to get around by crawling on the floor, with her hands pushed into a pair of shoes, but she was a wife and she'd given him a son. The village men still without wives gave the stone women names; everyone could tell which statue was whose wife, by whether they were tall or short or fat or thin. There was so much stroking of the stone that each woman's face ended up all dark and shiny.

Bright said: "Look out of the window, as far as you can see. Can you make out those big ridges? There are four long ones to the east and the west that run straight up and down, and the south ridge runs crossways, that makes a rectangle. If you look to the south of the south ridge, where it's always covered in cloud, there's a circular ridge. Look at all six ridges together, don't they look to you like a woman lying with her arms and legs splayed, showing her breasts? For generations, all the folk around here believed this used to be the sea, and our ancestors used to make their living from fishing. But then a sea monster called Grab made the waters rise and caused a huge flood. The spirits killed Grab but the sea vanished after that, leaving just a wasteland. Grab's bones were left behind and they grew upwards and turned into these six ridges. To stop the ridges growing any higher and turning into snow-covered mountains like Bear's Ear Peak, a dozen *li* from here, they built a temple on each ridge. Great-Grandad says that they always had incense smoke rising from them. The villagers used to go there to pray for rain, or for someone who was sick, and if there was a fight between villagers and it couldn't be resolved, they'd go to the temple and each one would kneel and swear an oath: "If I've done you wrong, may I be struck by five bolts of lightning!" But after Liberation, the monks were chased out of the temples and went home to their families. Two of the buildings fell down. Then during the Cultural Revolution, the other four were destroyed. It was only on one of the west ridges that a few ruins remained, with a locust tree growing out from them. It had a hollow trunk and looked dead, but it came into leaf every year. Some of the locals still go and worship the tree, so its branches are covered with strips of red cloth.

Auntie Spotty-Face was outside her cave lying on her mat in the cool of the evening one day, when she fell asleep, and she dreamed a great monster was pressing down on her chest, so hard she couldn't cry out. After that, she got pregnant. The baby had one head and two bodies, so of course it was drowned in the piss bucket at birth, but after that Auntie Spotty-Face was so scared of becoming pregnant again that she used to pray to the tree once a month. She met an old woman there who knew how to do papercuts, and Auntie Spotty-Face learned too. She loves papercutting, she spends all her time cutting figures and shapes out of paper and giving them to the village households, and never does any housework. She's married to a stutterer, the pair of them are always arguing, and he beats her with anything he can lay his hands on. She goes around the village bruised black and blue, complaining that he beats her by day because she hasn't cooked his dinner and he beats her by night to force her to have another baby. The villagers take the piss out of her, they say Tongue-Trip's a real bull, he's not only doing it cos he wants a baby!

"'He can hump me all he wants but I'm barren ground,' she says.

"'All the same,' they tell her, 'you should stop spending so much time on papercuts.'

"'You ate this morning, but you'll eat again this evening. Just because you ate yesterday doesn't mean you've got fed up with eating, does it?' And she gets out the scissors she always has tucked away inside her jacket and snips another figure: 'Come evening, I wish I could give him the snip too!'"

Bright said there were always arguments between the villagers, and if they came to blows and the village boss couldn't sort it, he'd threaten to phone the township police. But then someone would grab him and say: "No, don't do that, we don't want all those cops here, it doesn't look good for the village, why not get them to swear an oath at the temple ruins on West Ridge? Or if that's too far away, they can swear it in front of Auntie Spotty-Face, she goes there so often, she can stand in for the spirits, can't she?"

But the village boss wasn't having it. "I'm supposed to uphold the law, not worship spirits. And even if she does worship the spirits, how can she stand in for them? She might be possessed but that's all!"

· · ·

Bright said his great-grandfather had built his cave. Just like if a wooden house has good *feng shui*, a *lingzhi* mushroom will grow on the cross-beam, if a cave has good *feng shui*, there'll be a spider's web on the ceiling. He didn't say 'spider's web' though, he said 'wa' web, pointing to a small mound thick with dust and shaped like a frog. A frog is 'wa', and Nü-wa is the name for the Great Goddess, so all that adds up to good luck: the year they got that 'wa' web on the cave ceiling, Bright passed the exam into the township middle school and his mum went digging nonesuch flowers and found twelve specimens all in one spot. And a weasel killed all the hens from thirteen of the village houses, but Bright's family didn't lose one, and their hens were good layers too. Dogs normally never got past ten years, but their dog was fourteen and still fierce as a jackal. But what made the villagers really envious was their donkey. It was more intelligent than a human. When he was a kid, Bright used to sleep over at the township school during the week, get home towards evening on a Saturday and leave again on Sunday evening. The donkey used to transport him and all his food for the week to the school entrance and then come back to the village on her own. She never dilly-dallied or got lost. When the donkey was big enough, they took her to the stud farm at Qingyang village ten *li* away to put her to a stallion. She dropped a little mule foal and they sold it, and Bright's dad took her back to the stallion again. Every time he took her to Qingyang, she trotted briskly along leaving the old man way behind.

Whenever she turned up, the stable lad would leer: "Why are you in such a hurry? This is a stud farm, not a brothel!"

The donkey gave birth to five mule foals in a row, and with the money from selling them, the Black family bought themselves a small tractor. When you mate a donkey with a horse, you get something that doesn't look anything like a donkey, but the Blacks' beast was a good mother to her foals and never rejected them. Just now, the Blacks' income came from two sources: the donkey mare and the store.

"You must have heard about the hot springs in East Gully Bottom," Bright said. "Well, if you're very good, I'll take you there for a bathe, or you can go with Rice and help her manage them. They're magical those hot springs, water spurts out from a crevice in the red rocks, and it's between fifty and sixty degrees all year round. They've dug out two trenches where people can bathe in the waters. The Tourism Bureau came and inspected, and they've said the water is full of minerals, so bathing in it can cure rheumatism and scabies and vitiligo, and it can even turn dark skin fair again. East Gully Bottom is part of our village, but people come and bathe in it from the villages around. It used to be that men bathed on the first to the tenth of the month, and double-digit days were only for women, but then Zhang the Prop started living there and charging a yuan per visit. He built a wall between the two pools and made one for women, one for men, so they could bathe at the same time. Zhang the Prop had no family, and when he went to live there he was already seventy-three.

"Apart from charging for entry to the hot springs, he also raised chickens and grew blood onions. Blood onions are special to this village, just like the lotus root with eleven eye-holes that grows in the pond in Qingyang village, where the stud farm is, is special to them. Blood onions don't grow as tall as other onions but they're bright red, that's why they're called blood onions. They're really strong too, just cutting off the flowers makes you cry and even a little bit in a mutton stew covers up the muttony taste and makes the meat tender and sweet. Blood onions keep you warm in winter, and if you boil them up, you can sweat out a cold. And there's something else, blood onions make a man more virile. There's an old saying in the village: 'One onion stalk and you're hard all winter.' Our blood onions were already known outside the village, but Zhang the Prop was the one who really made them famous. When he saw that blood onions grew really well near the hot springs, he planted his allotment with them, and he had no other vegetables to speak of, so he had blood onions and fried eggs for every meal and kept getting more robust and healthy. He lived there six years and then a thirty-year-old woman from Qinghai, who'd come in search of nonesuch flowers till they got too scarce, turned up. She started to help Zhang the Prop manage the hot springs, and in exchange she got somewhere to live and food to eat. No one thought anything of it, except that it seemed like a good arrangement, until two years later, Zhang the Prop was hacked to death one day, and when the police arrested the murderer, it turned out to be the husband of the young woman. He'd come from Qinghai in search of his wife and when he found her, she was pregnant. He beat it out of her that the father was Zhang the Prop, so he hacked the old man to death. When the news got out, no one believed it: could an eighty-two-year-old really have got a woman up the spout? Well, yes, he had, and the reason was that he was eating blood onions every day. After that, blood onions got known as a miracle food.

"After Zhang the Prop died, no one went to East Gully Bottom any more and the hot springs were abandoned. Word was that the rasping cry of a bird heard there at night was the unquiet ghost of Zhang the Prop, crying the name of the young woman.

"That same year, Spring-Starts came back from the county town where he was doing a labouring job, with a wife whose name was Rice. Rice was completely unlike a village woman in the way she dressed, spoke and behaved. Spring-Starts had a rough, swarthy-looking scar-face, and they made a weird couple. But when they arrived, Spring-Starts didn't keep her locked up. They used to go out walking together, hand in hand too. Clan-Keeper Wang went there for a drink one evening and reported back that the reason Rice was so rosy-cheeked by day was that she was plastered in rouge. After she'd washed her face at night, she looked like a ghost, plain ugly. Zhang the Rake said: 'Well, I dream of ghosts every night but I never get a visit.'

"She's a sharp one, that Rice. When she first heard about Zhang the Prop and his blood onion business, she kept telling the brothers, Spring-Starts and La-Ba, to go to East Gully Bottom and grow them. 'It's a business opportunity, grab it!' she used to say. 'After all, Zhang the Prop's done all the advertising for you.' So the brothers went and let off firecrackers to placate his spirit, and started planting. These days, Rice manages the hot springs herself, and even though not many people go there, the bottom of the gully where the hot springs water makes a pool is always wet, and blood onions do well. They've brought more and more land under cultivation, and they call it the Blood Onions Production Base."

Bright said he'd been running the store for three years, and it was the only one in the village. Any goods the villagers wanted, he would buy them in the township and stock his shop with them, like needles and thread, woks and bowls, kerosene, tobacco and cigarettes, buckets, kettles, flour-sifters, shovels, flails, rope, harrow nails, axes, umbrellas, sun visors, strainers, cooking ingredients like oil, salt and vinegar, and tea and white sugar. He could buy in herbal medicine, fertiliser and seeds too. And he bought the village produce, like potatoes, garlic and pumpkins, and sold it on in the township.

Potatoes were a staple crop all over the loess plateau, but in the village, their potatoes were special: purple-skinned, they were dense and floury and tasted like chestnuts. They were good for skin irritations too. Whether it was ringworm or eczema, even if the sores were ulcerated or pus-filled, all you had to do was lay slices of raw potato on the affected area, and in ten minutes the itching would have stopped. If you carried on the treatment for a week or so, you'd be completely cured. The garlic grew as a single clove and burned in the gullet. The pumpkins were small compared with elsewhere and slightly flattened at each end, and they would keep up to two years without going bad. In the past, diggers used to bring their nonesuch flowers to the store too, and when Bright had enough, he would put a mark-up on them and sell them to a buyer in the county town; he'd stopped that now but bought up blood onions instead. That all started with the brothers, Spring-Starts and La-Ba, who sold their blood onions to the township and the county town, and Bright helped out by transporting them on his tractor. Then other villagers, those who used to grow small quantities of blood onions for their own consumption, saw how well the brothers were doing and wanted to sell their produce too, so Bright collected their onions for reselling in town. Actually all he did was sell them to the brothers' buyers, at only three yuan a *jin*, thereby undercutting Spring-Starts and La-Ba.

The shop stood on a slope at the village entrance on the west side. "When you came to the village, that was where the car stopped," Bright told me. "Didn't you see the three-roomed building with a tiled roof, and STORE painted in whitewash on the gable end? The store faces onto the main road that passes the village so it gets passing trade too. And I always look after my customers, whether or not they buy anything, bring them into the shop to put their feet up and offer them a drink. It's hard to make a lot of money out of the store, but at least I'm better off than the rest of the villagers. I can't buy just anything I please, but if I really want something, I can usually afford it."

Bright said: "That's enough for now. The rest you'll find out afterwards."

"There isn't going to be an afterwards!" I shouted. "I'm not staying here."

"But wherever you are, it's all China, isn't it?"

"I want to go home. Let me go home!"

Bright shut up then. The chisel his dad was carving with stopped tapping away, and the hens, the dog and the donkey, who'd been making a racket because Blindy was swiping at them with the broom, all fell silent too.

A few crows flew up out of the pine trees and over the strip, then disappeared.

Chapter 3

CALLING BACK THE SOUL

WHEN THEY'D CARRIED me into the cave and dumped me down on the straw mat covering the *kang*, pain and shame made me curl up into a little ball. "This is your *kang*," Bright had said. Out in the courtyard the villagers were having a noisy celebration, wiping the soot from the wok bottom and the tar from their pipe bowls onto Bright's dad's face. That was the custom in the village: when a son got married, his dad came in for some roughing-up. They got his face as dirty as they could and ribbed him.

"The only good father-in-law is one who's had the snip! No having it off with your new daughter-in-law!" Then there were cries of: "Bring the booze! Where's the booze?"

"It's coming," said Bright's dad. "And I'll do some snacks too."

There were three pitchers of wine in this cave and Bright was on his way out with them when he stopped and leered at me: "Let's share a marriage cup, you and me." He filled a cup so it slopped over the brim and sat it on the low *kang* table, then lowered his mouth to the rim and slurped. The wine gleamed like amber in the lamplight. I reached out and grabbed Bright's face. I gripped so hard I could feel my fingernails digging into his flesh and got his blood and skin under my fingernails. He dodged out of reach but managed to set the cup down on the *kang* table without dropping it.

"You're just as pretty when you lose your temper," was all he said. He had scratches all down his face, one of them as red as an earthworm. I retreated back into the shadows so he couldn't see me. He went out carrying the pitcher, shutting the door behind him. Then I heard him shout: "Ai-ya!" as he was passing his dad's cave door, and crouch down and knock over a harrow that was leaning against the wall.

"What's up? Have you twisted your ankle?"

"Ai-ya! I just knocked into the harrow and got scratches all down my face, but I didn't drop the wine."

There were shouts of: "You should be popping her cherry tonight, not messing up your face! Pour some booze."

It seemed like a booze-up stood in for a proper wedding ceremony or wedding feast in this village. They were scrapping like a pack of wild dogs. It made me think that a lot of people in this world weren't really human at all, they were beasts. There were howls of protests that Bright had only brought one pitcher of wine.

"When Clan-Keeper Wang bought his crippled wife," someone said, "there were three pitchers of wine even though she had to crawl on all fours to get around!"

"There's plenty to go around," said Bright. "Drink all you want, in fact, no one's leaving till they're drunk!"

Clan-Keeper Wang was annoyed at the dig at his wife, and said: "All you've ever got your leg over is the edge of the *kang*, so I don't know how you've got the face to talk about other people!"

The other man said: "If I had to put up with what you have to, I'd cut it off!"

The quarrel got fiercer until Clan-Keeper rolled his sleeves up, and then Bright jumped in with: "Let's have a drinking game." And he started with Clan-Keeper's tormentor, pouring six cups and shouting a finger-guessing game. Bright was hopeless and lost four out of six goes but he downed his drink and tipped his cup upside down to show there wasn't a drop left in it. They were only half-way through the game when Bright started slurring his speech and asked his opponent to drink for him.

"Sure, if you can't hold your drink, I'll drink it for you. And I'll do the business with the girl if you're too tired for that too!"

More hoots of laughter. One man laughed so hard he was sick, right into the face of the man opposite him. He got a furious cussing for that: "Can't you fucking eat your noodles?"

I could see the other man had a strand of noodle hanging from his ear.

I'll never forget that evening. The villagers got so drunk that three of them toppled over onto the ground, puked and then lay still. The dog went to lick up the vomit, got drunk and lay still as well. The rest of them carried on drinking until they'd finished two pitchers and opened the third. Meantime, I was inspecting the cave, plotting how I could make my getaway.

It was a sizeable cave, five metres wide by fifteen metres deep. There was a large *kang* by the window, wide enough to sleep five or six people crosswise. On the wall above it, pegs had been banged in to support a shelf on which sat lots of pottery jars. I didn't know what was in them but they came in all shapes and sizes, and there were at least thirteen. Next to the *kang* stood a dresser. A screen sat on top, and some bottles on either side of it. They had a random collection of things stuck into them, and there was a feather duster too, which can't ever have been used because the place was thick with dust.

Next to the dresser lay a heap of sacks, stuffed with grain or clothes, I supposed, and tied tightly at the neck. A bit further on there was a chest. I reckoned that the centre of the cave was where guests sat because there was a square table, painted black, and two benches. A blue and white teapot that Bright had filled with cold water stood on the table, along with a blue and white jar.

"Drink the water if you're thirsty," he told me. "And there's sugar in the jar, so you can make yourself some sugar water."

Behind the table, two picture frames hung on the wall. One had a dried flower in it, the other had a bit of black cloth tied around it, and held a woman's photo. I didn't know why the flower had been framed or what flower it was, but as soon as I saw the photo I knew it must be Bright's mum. Dead, but still looking at me. I pulled the cloth off and covered her face with it. I looked up at the ceiling. No skylight. There was a smaller cave behind this one, and I went to have a look, bumping into the table and the chest on my way. It suddenly struck me that the furniture wood came from the corpses of trees and I was surrounded by piles of corpses. The back cave was full of crocks filled with maize, buckwheat, millet and beans, and there were sacks of mouli, cabbages and potatoes too. There was only one way in and out, and it was the cave door. I gave it a tug, but it was padlocked from the outside. I tried the window, it was one of those that would open half-way, but I was worried it would make a noise so I wetted the hinge with water from the teapot and slowly pushed it open.

I quickly blew out the lamp.

I looked around outside. They were still drinking. Some of them were sprawled out flat on the ground. One man was shooting his mouth off about stuff going on in the village, telling everyone what was what, then his neighbour said: "Get your hands off! Why are you whacking me like that?"

"Cos I'm talking to you!" Another whack.

"Hey! Stop that!"

Someone else said: "Monkey's just drunk, that's why he's gabbing!"

"I'm drunk, am I? But it's the truth, straight up," said Monkey.

Meantime, I had pushed the window open as far as it would go and propped it on the window stay. I took a deep breath and stuck my head out. There was no way I could get out head first, so I turned around and got my legs out. I was proud of my slender waist and long legs, but they still weren't long enough to touch the ground. I rested my chest on the windowsill, and lowered myself using all my strength. My bra strap snapped and I tore a hole in my jacket and my belly got jammed in the opening and it hurt, but finally there I was, crouching in the shadows at the foot of the window.

None of the drinkers saw me.

"Has Bright been watering down the booze? It tastes weaker the more I drink," said someone. Bright said nothing.

"When you're drunk, your mouth's not your mouth any more," said a man.

A woman yanked her lip down: "Of course it mother-fucking is!"

"What the fuck do you know, you're not drinking!"

The woman wasn't annoyed, she just said: "I can't drink because I've got to have a baby boy this year."

Someone else shouted: "Having a baby boy just means trouble. Don't you think we've got enough bare branches in the village already?"

"Maybe so, but at least we can grow blood onions and get hard enough to fuck a mousehole or a crow in mid-air!"

I started to move, creeping along to the right of the window. There was another cave coming up, and I didn't know what else beyond it. As I got to the next cave, I heard a snort and the donkey poked its head out. Suddenly my mum flashed into my mind, she had a long face too. I froze, not daring to move, and the donkey sniffed me.

"Don't bray, please!" I begged it.

It snorted again, but that was all. The tears came and ran down my face. That donkey felt like my mum, or maybe my mum was looking for me and her spirit had possessed the donkey.

There was another cave up ahead, with the millstone outside it. I had to move further from the caves so I decided to crawl over the millstone. But someone was asleep there on a straw mat. I got such a fright I nearly cried out. Whoever it was, I must surely have woken them up. I rushed back and pressed myself against the undercliff next to the cave and waited, but the sleeper didn't move. I looked up at the sky. There was thick cloud and only a faint glimmer of moonlight that came and went again. Just then, the sleeper sat up, grabbed a handful of straw from beside the millstone and threw it in my direction. I wondered who he was. He was asleep here, hadn't gone to join the drinking and the drinkers had left him alone too. He must have known I was there but he hadn't called out. Was he helping me on my way? But that was hard to believe. More likely, he'd chosen this place to sleep because it was nice and cool, and had half-woken up and in his befuddled state thought I was one of the drinkers going for a piss. The straw was for me to wipe myself. The villagers didn't use paper in the shit-house, just cleaned themselves with a stone or a clod of earth or leaves or straw.

I grabbed the straw and when everything was quiet again, I ran around the millstone as fast as I could, and away.

I found out later that the sleeper was Bright's uncle, and he was blind. I never asked why he hadn't called out, but after that I was always nice to him. Like, I never called Bright's father 'Dad', but I always called Blindy 'Uncle'. I felt warm towards the donkey too. Afterwards, when I was back locked up in the cave and banging at the window and door, making the dog bark and the donkey bray, I never held it against the beast. It had been my accomplice. Its face really did remind me of my mum, and it was always snorting just the way she used to witter on.

But I never forgave the cat. It didn't even belong to the Black family, but as I nipped past the millstone, it made a weird yowling noise, and all the drinkers heard it. There was shouting: "Are you on heat too, now Bright's got a woman?" Someone threw a shoe at the cat and caught sight of my shadow.

"Who's that?"

Bright rushed to his cave. The door was still padlocked but the window was open. "She's escaped!" he yelled.

I got as far as the four pine trees and felt a splat as a crow shat from the branches. I discovered the pines were at the edge of the strip and it was pitch-dark here. I didn't know how big the drop was or what lay beneath but I could hear the drinkers gaining on me so I jumped.

I bounced off something soft, and it didn't hurt at all, until I banged my chin and tasted blood in my mouth. I must have landed on a straw-stack. I jumped to the ground and was scrambling to my feet when the drinkers jumped from the strip too and someone got me by the scruff of the neck. Whoever it was got a handful of the crow shit that had splatted on my shoulder.

"Shit, you're covered in it! You're spattered in white!"

"You're just like the Blacks' tractor and everything else they own. White's the Black family colour!"

"There's no point you running away, now you're whited, you're a Black!"

I mustered all my strength to get away. My jacket was coming off, and then it was off, like a snake sloughing its skin. But someone grabbed me and lifted me up by my hair, then flung me to the ground.

I don't remember now how they got me back to the cave, whether I was dragged or whether they each got an arm and a leg and carried me. When they dropped me on the strip, I tried to scramble up again, but I was surrounded by drunk men who were laying into me with their boots. I wailed loudly. That was all I could do.

Someone was shouting at me: "Bitch! You think you can run away, do you? You think a woman we've bought can leave the village just like that?"

I glared at him and a gob of spit landed in my left eye and I couldn't see out of it. I screamed again and again, imagining that each scream was the swipe of a knife blade, making them back away from me.

"What a firebrand!" someone said and slapped me across the face.

It hurt like being splashed with chilli oil or branded with a red-hot iron.

"Go on, hit me! Beat me to death, then I'll haunt you!"

But the more I yelled, the more they seemed to enjoy it. A forest of hands reached out, someone was treading on my hair, and my hair clips were all gone, they were pinching and grabbing, twisting my ears till my earrings came out. I tried to protect my head but I was being punched on all sides. They were groping my breasts and my bra was pulled off so I didn't have a stitch of clothing left on top. Finally, I was too exhausted to cry or scream, and I just curled up in a ball on the ground. Still they grabbed at me, my back, my belly, my breasts, pulling, twisting and pinching my nipples, yanking my trousers down and exposing my bum. I felt like a potato thrust into the fire, its skin cracking and exploding in the heat, or a pottery jar left in a freezer till it shattered into smithereens.

Finally, I heard Bright shout: "Stop hitting her, stop hitting her!" He pulled the men off me and lay on me so he was covering me with his body, still yelling: "Hands off!" Most of them did, though I felt someone grab my breast really hard. Bright tried to pull me to my feet, but it was like he was scooping up porridge, I slid through his fingers. When he couldn't make me stand, he picked me up in his arms and carried me back into the cave. They were still talking away on the strip, about how I must be a virgin because my nipples were so small and my arse cheeks were so firm.

I'd never thought about my soul before now, and I had no idea it could leave my body, but that's what it did. That night I felt as if the top of my skull had gone numb, and there was a hole in it, and my soul had popped out. They must have beaten a hole in my head and I was going to die, I thought.

Then I found myself standing on the table, while Butterfly lay on the kang. *Body and soul, there were two of me. I was Butterfly but I wasn't her. I was in shock. I watched Bright pour some water into a cup and take it to Butterfly, then I jumped onto the frame with the flower in it. In the lamplight I saw Bright and Three-Lobes' wife, and their shadows expanded and retracted, as if they were ghosts.*

Butterfly clenched her teeth and refused the water. Bright pinched her cheeks, then pinched her nose to try to get her to open her mouth so he could pour some in. Finally he gave up and just said: "Next time you run away, I'll break your leg for you."

After that, he shackled Butterfly by the ankle. He used a chain that once belonged to the dog. Bright was worried that the chain would chafe Butterfly's soft white ankle and he wrapped a thick wad of cotton waste around it. He padlocked the chain around her ankle securely, then attached the other end to the door frame. The chain was long enough that Butterfly could roam all around the cave. The window he locked with an even bigger padlock, nailing it down tight and making a cross bar to fit the window frame on the outside with two stout posts.

The hours dragged by and I no longer knew who I was: I was a butterfly perched on the table or on the picture frame, looking down on Butterfly lying on the *kang* or with her face pressed against the window frame. Or I was Butterfly herself, and every time the door creaked open and Bright came in, I clenched my fists and opened my eyes, and got ready to fight him off. Hour after hour, I paced miserably up and down that cave, feeling like my head was full of ants or buzzing with bees.

Bright saw me massaging my legs and came over to rub them for me, but I quickly tucked them away. In summers past, I'd get back home tired out and fall asleep on the bed. When I woke up, my mum would be sitting next to me, stroking my legs.

"Look at those legs of yours," she'd say. "Like two roof beams!"

My legs were long, and so straight that I could clamp a bit of paper between them and you couldn't pull it out. But just now, they were battered and bruised all over, and swollen too – if I pressed my finger in, the dent stayed for ages.

I scowled at Bright: "What do you think you're doing?"

"I want to kiss you."

"I'm your mum!" I said loudly, pointing at the clothes he'd given me to wear. And he backed off.

He went to fetch food and water and put them down on the table. He added salt and vinegar to the spicy noodles and said: "You go ahead and eat."

I didn't touch them. I wasn't going to eat when he was there. Before he went to his store, he brought in the piss bucket.

"That's where you piss and shit," he said. "Here's a piece of wood to cover it, keep the lid on and it won't smell."

He went out, then came back in again to see me pacing up and down, my fringe sticking to my forehead with sweat, which I didn't bother to wipe away.

"If you're too hot, dip your nipples in water and that'll cool you down."

When I glared at him, he added: "And calm down. If you carry on like that, you'll only get thirstier." But I didn't calm down, I couldn't.

I watched as Butterfly paced up and down like a lioness, cracking her arms on the table top till they came up all purple, banging her head on the dresser, making the top shudder and knocking a bottle to the floor where it shattered. A bluebottle settled on the cave walls and she batted at it furiously, only it wasn't a bluebottle, it was a nail. It scratched her palm and bled, and she wiped the blood off on her face. Bright hurriedly picked up and took away anything that was hard or could easily be smashed. He brought in a sack with some old bedding in it: "If you want to take it out on anything, kick the sack." He sighed, padlocked the door again and went away with the key hanging from his trouser belt.

When Bright wasn't there, I was back with the other Butterfly in my body, kicking the sack, screaming and crying, throwing anything that I could pick up out through the latticed window: shoes, socks, the brush for sweeping the *kang*, and potatoes and moulis from the back cave. Bright's dad and his uncle, Blindy, were outside on the strip but they said nothing. The dog kept on barking and Blindy shouted at it, then picked up all the things I'd thrown out, one by one.

The days passed. Most mornings, things went like this: we were woken by the cawing from the crows roosting in the pines. Bright's dad got up and let the hens out. Then he put a scant ladleful of water into a plastic bowl, barely enough to cover the bottom, so he had to tip the bowl against the wall to scoop up enough to wash his face. Bright washed his face when his dad had finished, then shouted: "Uncle, come and wash your face."

Blindy fed the donkey, muttering to himself that she was off her food. He was worried that she was farting less than she used to, she used to let off great blasts of air but last night it was more like puffs, as if she was blowing out a lamp. He came to wash his face, but there wasn't enough water left, so he just wetted his towel and wiped his eyes.

He needn't have bothered with his eyes, it didn't make any difference, he could just have wiped his cheeks and forehead, but he obviously thought I didn't know he was blind, and he was doing it for my benefit, turning and smiling towards my cave. "Uncle, go and get some straw for the stove," Bright instructed him, and then he brought me some water to wash with. I refused.

"We're short of rain, this water's precious," he said.

"Precious, is it? I want a shower!"

"Leave it out, Butterfly. I can't do the impossible!"

Below the strip I could hear shouting and the clatter of footsteps, but no one appeared. They must have been standing in the alley that led up to the strip.

"Bright, Bright, when are you going to market?" said someone.

Bright's dad said: "Did you get tea yesterday?"

"One pack, but the price was up again."

Bright raised his voice: "The tractor's broken down, I'm not going."

"You never said that yesterday!" protested the speaker. "Why didn't you say yesterday? I washed my face and head specially!"

"If the price goes up, buy it anyway, we've still got to have tea," said Bright's dad.

"Well, it's broken down, what can I do? Do you know in advance when you're going to get sick?" said Bright.

"Mind your language!" said his dad.

Blindy came bustling back with an armful of pea sticks. Bright's dad pulled the high heels up from the well and put them back in his cave, then sat on his heels in the doorway peeling potatoes. Bright chased and caught one of the hens, and poked its arse: "How come you haven't laid in three days?"

Great-Grandad came out of his cave carrying a low table, and Bright wiped his fingers on his jacket front and went to take it off him and put it down under the gourd frame. "Are you going to write?" he asked.

"No, I'm pressing a nonesuch flower, Water-Come wants one."

Suddenly I heard a banging and Bright's dad said: "Bright, has the pig got out again?"

"So Water-Come wants a nonesuch flower, does he? They're all doing what I did but I haven't seen them with any wives!"

Then he answered his father: "I just put new stakes around the pigpen, and the little sod's jumped straight out!" Bright went around the corner of the undercliff and I heard a lot of squealing, then he came back, mixed up some pig swill in the bowl and carried it round the corner again. Great-Grandad had a nonesuch flower on the table and was carefully smoothing out the leaves and petals, then pressing it flat between two pieces of wood. Bright, back from feeding the pig, looked over his shoulder.

"You got a nonesuch flower framed and then you got Butterfly, so of course other men are going to want to do what you do... Have you heard Padlock's still weeping over his wife's grave?"

"I don't notice it any more," said Bright.

"I told him to come and I'd press a nonesuch flower for him, but he didn't, Water-Come came instead. You ought to get Padlock a wife."

"He's got ten *jin* of nonesuch flowers, but he won't sell them, he keeps going on about how they belong to his wife. And if he hasn't got any money, how can I find him someone?"

Bright's dad started up the bellows in his cave, and black smoke poured out of his chimney.

Breakfast was always 'bean-coin' gruel – so thin you see your reflection in it, with flattened soybeans floating on top. The villagers pounded the fresh soybeans flat, then cooked them and they looked like floating flowers. They called them bean-coins. Some money! Even if you had two or three bowls, you only had to piss and you'd be hungry again. Bright did steamed potatoes for me: he peeled and cooked them, and dipped them in salt. They smelled better than potatoes I'd had from other places, but they were dense and floury and stuck in my throat, making me burp, and I couldn't eat potatoes at every meal. Bright's dad tried to think of other ways of cooking them but they were still potatoes: stir-fried potato strips, stewed potatoes, mashed potato cakes, potato griddle cakes, and then there was hot-and-sour potato noodles.

After breakfast, if there was no farm work, Bright's dad went back to his chiselling, bare-chested if the weather was hot, and then I could see the two rows of raised dark circles from the cupping he'd had, running the length of his spine. With a lump of rock about up to his waist, it took him a morning or an afternoon for a woman's head to emerge, then her neck, then the shoulders until it looked like she was going to walk right out of the stone. Blindy brought out some grain that still had to be milled, not wheat but maize, buckwheat and a whole lot of beans in all sorts of colours. Blindy did all the heavy work on the homestead, and if there wasn't anything else to do, he pushed the millstone around. It seemed to be his reason for living. Bright brought the baskets of beans out of the cave for him. To his dad's back, he said: "Haven't you chiselled enough?"

"This is for you," his dad told him.

"But I've already got one in the cave, haven't I?"

"If I've got something on my mind, carving settles me down."

Blindy tipped a basketful of beans onto the runner stone and stuck three chopsticks in the eyehole, then took the driver stick in both hands and began to push it round. It made me dizzy to watch it going round and round, and the way the chopsticks bounced up and down made my heart flutter. It was the job I used to hate most when I was a girl in our village. After I'd done that, my mother used to sift the ground wheat flour, the thimble on her finger tapping rhythmically against the basket. My little brother and I used to doze off with our arms around the driver stick. Our mother would hear we'd stopped and say: "Get a move on! What are you stopping for?" We carried on pushing with our eyes shut. We could even dream while we were walking round and round too. Blindy didn't have a thimble, and he milled and sifted, milled and sifted, all without a sound.

There was a snail on the windowsill. It had probably started crawling from the left-hand corner during the night towards the right-hand corner, leaving a silvery trail in its wake, but it had only got half-way.

There was an argument going on below the strip, something about someone's hens stealing the grain that someone else had spread out to dry in the sun. The argument ratcheted up till they were trading obscenities about men's and women's sex organs. Then someone shouted from one end of the village to the other.

"The village boss has finished his new cave, are you coming to the roof-raising?"

"What do we take as a present?"

"Whatever you want, I bought him a bed cover, and I'll take a woman too!"

"Since when have you had a woman?"

"Just because I haven't got one of my own doesn't mean I can't take someone else's!"

"Same here!... Bright, Bright! Are you coming for some booze?"

"Is he standing us drinks or just cadging presents?" Bright's dad muttered.

Bright glanced down below the strip and didn't answer. "I'm off to the store," he said. "I need to talk to Spring-Starts and La-Ba about the commission they're paying me. They're crafty, that pair, I offered to be their agent but they wanted to cut me out as a middleman. Now they've changed their minds but I'm upping my commission to twelve per cent."

When his dad didn't answer, Bright carried him in half a bucket of water, then came into my cave for his straw hat. He gave me an odd look: "Do you know what that water was for?"

I couldn't be bothered to answer. He told me anyway: "Watering down the vinegar. But don't tell anyone."

Bright left after breakfast and didn't come back till evening. While he was out, his dad brought me two meals, leaving the bowl on the windowsill, then knocking on the window, stepping back and calling: "Time to eat!" This was directed at Blindy and me. The bowl often had a fly crawling around the edge, and he would bat it away. I'd better eat, my belly's been rumbling with hunger, I thought, and reached out for the bowl and wiped the rim.

"Forget it, it's only a food fly," the old man said. What was the difference between a fly that ate food and one that ate shit? But I let it go.

It was almost dark and the crows were roosting in the pines by the time Bright came staggering back carrying an empty bucket. He was plastered, I don't know whether he'd been drinking with the village boss, anyway he came into the cave, shut the door and flung a wad of notes down in front of me: "Here! Fucking look at this!"

Normally of an evening he sat down to count up the day's takings, cursing the village boss: "He's been getting stuff on tick again!" Once he'd counted the notes and coins, he turned his back on me, stashed them in the dresser and locked it. But today he was drunk and threw the money down in front of me.

I remembered my dad when he was alive doing the same thing to my mum, and she'd grab it, then go and get my dad a cup of soured vegetable water to drink, help him to bed, take his shoes off, and complain: "Why do you have to drink so much? Does it really taste that good?" I always despised my mum for grabbing the money like that, but she never minded him getting drunk. It was only when he was drinking that he was really himself, she used to say. But I wasn't going to do like she did, I just left the money lying right where it was. I was furious.

By day, I waited for night and by night, I looked at the stars, but I couldn't find a star that belonged to me in a starless part of the sky. The sky above the lacebark pines stayed as black as ever.

This particular day, as the sun dipped over the roofs in the west and the clouds were still rosy, Great-Grandad came and sat on the millstone, and I thought he was going to look at the Eastern Well but then two men turned up: Monkey first and then, on his heels, Water-Come Liang back again. Monkey came to tell Great-Grandad that he'd had a dream last night, that a snake got into his arsehole when he was cutting grass, and what kind of an omen was that? Great-Grandad looked at him and said nothing, so Water-

Come Liang picked up the pressed nonesuch flower and kissed it: "Nonesuch flower, nonesuch flower, I'll put you on the offerings table and pray to you, if only you'll give me a Butterfly too!" He turned and looked at the window of my cave and I jerked my head away and spat.

Then Monkey said: "Well if that works, I want one too."

"The offerings table belongs to the masters of Heaven and Earth, King, Parents and Teachers," said Great-Grandad.

Then I heard Bright's dad: "What's going on? All these people come to see Great-Grandad and all empty-handed!"

I looked out and saw four or five more people on the strip, one with a kid with a harelip in tow. The dad said: "Dog-Egg, kowtow to Great-Grandad, so he'll choose a name for you."

Someone said: "But your kid's already called Dog-Egg, isn't that a name?"

But Great-Grandad asked how old the child was and what time of day he was born. Then he flicked through his almanac, thought for a bit and said: "Loyalty-Wisdom. But mind you call him by that name, now I've chosen it."

"We will, we will," the dad said. "Dog-Egg, do another kowtow to Great-Grandad."

"Call him Loyalty-Wisdom," said the old man.

"Loyalty-Wisdom!" And the kid knocked his head three times on the ground to Great-Grandad, and father and son went away. All the villagers had had names chosen for them by Great-Grandad, but they all got called by their nicknames anyway. So Virtue Ma got called Monkey, Show-Humanity Wang was Snatch, Celebrate-Knowledge Yang was Spring-Starts, Celebrate-Virtue Yang was La-Ba, Righteousness Liang was Water-Come, Trust Li was Rake, Filial-Piety Liu was Padlock, Virtue-Wisdom Liu was Ladle, Truth Liang was Withy-Weave, Forever-Humane Wang was Full-Barn, and Nobly-Humane Wang was Flagstone.

"Best choose a humble name if you want your kid to grow up," commented Water-Come.

"You got to call me 'Virtue Ma' from now on," said Monkey. "Great-Grandad, if people don't use the names you choose for them, stop picking names in the first place."

But Great-Grandad said: "If I don't pick names for the villagers, there won't be any village left in a hundred years."

"Monkey! Monkey!" shouted Bright's dad.

"I'm called 'Virtue Ma'!"

"You think you deserve to be called Virtue? Monkey, that's who you are. Monkey, you go and bring me that stone that's sitting by the shit-house wall."

"Why should I bother?" said Monkey.

"We've got a flatbread left over," said Bright.

And Monkey went into the cave, took the flatbread and munched it as he headed for the shit-house.

So the villagers all had other names, I thought. I don't know if Great-Grandad had chosen one for Bright, but now I felt my name wasn't good enough. That first evening, when I told Great-Grandad I was called Butterfly, and he said a butterfly must have been a flower in a former life, was that what he meant? Maybe because any butterfly looking for the spirit of the flower it used to be, wouldn't find it here in these hard-scrabble, arid highlands. I used to daydream of the husband I was going to marry and where we would live, and somehow I'd got myself kidnapped by Bright. I wanted to ask Great-Grandad to choose a name for me, but there were too many people sitting around on the millstone for me to speak up.

More people were turning up by the minute. Probably because there were too many people in the village without enough to do, and when they saw something was going on at Great-Grandad's, they came along to join in the fun. There was a lot of noise and shouting and I saw Three-Lobes dragging with him a man who was digging his heels in like a donkey. When he got to the strip, the man threw his arms around the rock Great-Grandad had been chiselling and Three-Lobes couldn't prise him off it.

"Caterpillar, let's go and see Great-Grandad, you made the promise to him too, how could you leave your dad with nothing to eat or drink for two days?"

"I only went to the township," said Caterpillar. "I said I'd be back the same day, I didn't know I was going to get held up by a bit of business."

"A bit of business?" said Three-Lobes. "You were gambling! And did you give a thought to your old dad, stuck at home bed-ridden?"

"He's my dad, not your dad," said Caterpillar.

"If you're good to your dad," said Three-Lobes, "I'm happy even if you're not being good to my dad. But if you're bad to your dad, even though it's not my dad, I won't put up with it. Go and fess up to Great-Grandad."

"He's not a temple god," said Caterpillar.

"No, he's not, but he's Great-Grandad," said Three-Lobes.

"So? He won't give me food or cash. OK, so I respect him for being Great-Grandad, but what'll happen if I don't? Fuck-all!"

For that he got a clap across the face from Three-Lobes: "You stupid fucker! How can you say terrible stuff like that?"

Caterpillar was about to hit him back, but Three-Lobes kicked him to the ground at the entrance to the strip and was about to land a few more kicks on him but Caterpillar scrambled up and fled.

While Three-Lobes was laying into Caterpillar, the folk sitting on the millstone all sat silent, looking at one another in dismay, but once Caterpillar had run off, a chorus of curses followed him. Great-Grandad grunted something that sounded like "son-of-a-bitch".

Monkey said: "Anyone who makes Great-Grandad angry is a son-of-a-bitch for sure!"

"I didn't call him 'son-of-a-bitch'," said the old man, "I said he's forgotten the eight precepts."

"The eight precepts? What's that?"

"Virtue, filial piety, humanity, love, truth and justice, harmony and peace." And he turned his back on them and went into his cave.

"Time to go," they told each other, and then they were gone too.

I was surprised at how quickly the strip went quiet. The sky darkened and a gentle breeze got up, making the broom propped against the well wheel creak and groan. It sounded like it might have been crying or muttering to itself. I stood at the window for a while, scratched a new line on the wall, then went and lit the lamp.

I was still thinking about my name: what flower could a butterfly find? The only flower in the cave was the nonesuch flower, and the flower was dried and the grub was dead. Bright had framed the nonesuch flower and I'd turned up, and the village's wifeless men had followed suit and framed their own nonesuch flowers, so was it a nonesuch flower I was looking for? I took down the frame, pulled it open and took the flower out: "Was I you in a former life?" I asked it. "Have I come looking for you?"

I repeated the question a few times, not caring if Bright's dad was outside on the strip or not, or whether the dog barked or the donkey brayed, and there was a lump in my throat and all of a sudden the tears came. It was as if the nonesuch flower was listening to me and understood what I was saying. I held the nonesuch flower towards the window and commanded the wind: "Come and blow the nonesuch flower to life." And sure enough, the wind came in and blew the petals of the nonesuch flower, making them flutter.

Then I commanded the petals: "You go and tell my mum where I am, she's lost her daughter, she'll be sick with worry." And some of the petals really did drop off and fly out of the window with the wind, rising and dipping, over the millstone, towards the pines, as if they were in a hurry, like a dog after a bone, and all of a sudden they were gone from the strip.

I missed my mum.

Outside Yingpan village was a mountain with three peaks, which the villagers called Pen-Holders Peak. But the village had never produced any scholars, not even a college student.

My mum used to tell my brother and me: "You make sure you study hard, and maybe some of the village *feng shui* will rub off on you." But my mum had such a hard life after my dad died, she was busy at home, busy on the land, and her long face got longer and thinner than ever. At the beginning of every school year, she scrimped and saved to get the fees together. She sold one room of our house to the neighbour, then the trousseau chest she'd brought with her as a bride, plus a table and four chairs, then things that had been in the family for generations, like the copper washbowl, the pewter wine pot and a screen, they all went too.

I saw her crying as she lit our stove, and I wiped her tears for her. She just said the smoke was getting in her eyes.

"But the fire's not smoking," I said.

She told me to get on with my jobs. She was always criticising me for getting this or that wrong, until I started to get annoyed. The third of May was the anniversary of my dad's death, and she made a bowl of food to offer to his portrait: rice with a bit of beancurd and some fried egg. "I know you like pickled cabbage as well," she addressed the portrait, and added some of that on top.

Then she suddenly burst into tears: "You have it so easy, you have nothing to worry about, you went and left me on my own!" And she lashed out at the bowl and the portrait and knocked them off the table.

In winter, the stones turned icy cold, you just had to touch them and your hand got stuck.

One day, I was coming back from school with my brother and he said: "What are we having to eat today?"

"Rice porridge."

"We get rice porridge every meal, every day!"

"If you start getting picky about your food, you'll have Mum going on at you." I looked up at that moment and saw Mum by the pollarded willow, taking off her padded jacket and putting on her flowery one. It was six *li* from the village to the township, and you had to pass by this tree. It was pollarded every year, cut right back to the trunk, and every springtime it sprouted branches again. Willows like that one flourish with hard pruning, and the trunk was now so thick that it took three people to girdle it with their arms. That flowery jacket was Mum's best, she only wore it to town, and changed out of it when she came back. She had taken a big bag to the township and come back with exercise books, ballpoint pens, bags of salt and cooking soda, and a whole *jin* of mutton.

"It's not a holiday, is it?" I asked her.

"Can't we eat meat when it's not a holiday? I got it for you two, so you can have a good dinner."

That evening, dinner was stewed mutton and a big flatbread. When we'd eaten, Mum told us: "We can't go on like this. Even if we don't starve to death, there's no more money for your studies. Three of the villagers are moving to the city to get labouring jobs, and I'm going with them."

At first, I was happy with Mum's decision, because if she wasn't around, she couldn't go on at me all the time, but then I realised the task of looking after my little brother would fall to me. He was just a kid, in his first year at the village primary school and doing well – he was always in the top three in tests; I was five years older, near to graduating from lower middle school. The upper middle school was in the county town, fifteen *li* away.

"Butterfly," my mum asked me, "do you think you'll get good enough grades for upper middle school?"

"My maths marks aren't very good," I said, "but the teacher took one of my essays as a model and made the other children study it."

"So, you can't be sure of getting good enough grades, right? Then drop out of school, stay home and look after your little brother. He's the family's hope, and I'm going away to earn money so that I can pay for at least one of you to go to university, whatever it takes."

I burst into loud sobs, and she shouted back: "However good a girl is at school, she'll go to another family when she gets married." Then she added: "You won't get in anyway."

When I went to sleep that night, Mum was knocking back the drink. My dad used to like a drink when he was alive, and when he died there was half a crock left. Mum used to have a sip every now and then, it was a pity to waste it, and she developed a taste for it. By the end of the night, there was none left in the crock. She got out the cough medicine she'd got for my brother a few weeks before and drank all of that too.

The next day, Mum left and I dropped out of school for good.

The first evening when Bright wanted to sleep on the *kang*, I tore up a sheet and wound the strips round my trousers from waistband to my feet, and made the knots tight. Bright threw himself on top of me and tried to stick his wet tongue in my mouth, but I wrenched his head away and using all my strength turned over on my belly and gripped the strip of the *kang*. Bright tried to roll me over again but he couldn't, it was like I had suction pads on my hands and my feet and my belly. I'd struck root, and if he pulled up one root and went to pull up another, the first one rooted itself again.

Bright panted: "Don't you start yelling, my dad and my uncle will hear."

I was going to cry out anyway, but he clamped his hand over my mouth. I bit him so hard I felt like my top and bottom teeth were crunching together, my mouth tasted all salty, and Bright yelled and pulled his fingers out, and brought one of my teeth with them. Bright stopped trying to turn me over. He sat on the strip of the *kang*, panting.

"I won't try and turn you over, but don't yell." I didn't. I just kicked Bright off the *kang* and felt for the window latch. I didn't find it but I did put my hand on an empty liquor bottle on the windowsill.

I broke the neck off by smashing it against the *kang* and held it up: "If you dare make a move, I'll kill you!"

Bright was sitting on the floor: "I won't make a move." He got up and rolled out a mat next to the table and went to sleep on that. Then he came back for the pillow and, as he turned away, he grabbed my foot and held my toes in his mouth. I struggled to get my foot free, but he kissed the toes some more before he went back to his mat.

Not that he went to sleep straightaway. He kept repeating softly: "Butterfly, Butterfly."

For the first seven nights, I didn't dare close my eyes, I felt like there was a wolf crouching in the cave. I stared into the darkness, watching Bright for signs of movement. In all my twenty years, I'd thought that day was light and night was dark, but now I discovered that you could see anything by day or by night, after all, a cat could and rats could, and my eyes could too. I could see Bright's hand moving between his legs as he called my name, his voice urgent and trembling and strange, and then stuff spurted out and hit the cave wall and the table leg. Is that what men did? He was a creep, a jerk, he disgusted me. Every time I heard him whispering "Butterfly, Butterfly" I grabbed anything I could on the *kang*, the *kang* brush or a pillow, threw it at him and yelled: "Stop fucking calling my name!"

When it got light, Bright got up, rolled up the mat and put the pillow back on the bed, then he opened the cave door and went out and talked to his dad, who had been up a long time.

"Everything OK, Bright?"

"Fine, Dad."

"That's good. You treat her well, really well."

I started thinking about the room I'd shared with my mum.

We lived in a building at the end of Daxing Lane on the south side of the city, one of the five-storey blocks built around a courtyard and rented by migrant worker families. My mum and I lived on the ground floor on the east side of the north block. There was a pond outside our door with a fake mountain in it and the landlord used to sit there in a deckchair, playing Chinese opera on his radio and holding a small teapot in his hands. Apparently, it had Dragon Well tea in it.

Once my little brother got into the county middle school, he boarded there so I had nothing to do at home and I joined my mum in the city so I could help her out. My mum worked as a trash-picker and I pulled the cart. Once a woman asked: "Trash! Who's the girl?" I was furious that she'd called my mother 'Trash', and I told my mum to ignore her but she wasn't bothered, she was happy that someone was shouting "Trash!" because it meant they wanted her to go to their home, they had trash to sell. The woman wouldn't let her in, she brought the trash out. She watched my mum tie the trash in a bundle and hook it onto the balance scales, and check they were properly balanced.

"Your daughter? How could you have such a pretty daughter?"

Then she got out her daughter's old clothes and gave them to me, and asked: "Can you cook? If you can, you can come and be our housekeeper."

I didn't like the woman so no way was I going to be her housekeeper, but I wore the clothes, especially the suit jacket, which fitted me like a glove. But Mum told me not to wear it when we went trash-picking, it was too good and we wouldn't get any trash. I was annoyed and didn't go trash-picking again, just stayed in our rented room and cooked and washed for my mum.

I was a city girl now so I felt I should look like one. I stopped plaiting my hair and let it hang loose, and as soon as my mum had gone out, I heated some water and washed it in a bowl. Where I came from in the mountains, the roads were all potholed and you had to lift your feet up and walk with your toes splayed out, but city girls had skinny legs and walked pigeon-toed, so I started to do the same, taking small steps too. I even tied my legs together at night with a belt. I also learned how to talk proper, in standard Chinese. Once, I was supposed to take five hundred yuan from my mum's monthly earnings of two thousand yuan to post to my brother, and I pocketed an extra hundred for myself and got my hair dyed blond. Then I bought the high heels. My mum and I had a fight about them, but then she hugged me and burst into tears: "You're a big girl now, of course you should get what you want."

And the next day, she went out and bought me a pair of trousers. I stopped being angry with her when she gave them to me, in fact I washed her feet and cut her toenails that night. And I made up my mind then and there that I was going to earn money too. If I couldn't earn enough for my mum to live out the rest of her life in comfort, at least I could take some of the responsibility off her shoulders.

When I went to the market, I could see that the vegetables stall always had people around it, pulling the old leaves off the cabbages when the woman wasn't looking. I had a proper go at them, and the woman thanked me, and when it got dark, she gave me all the old leaves to take home.

There was a man I saw hanging around the market several days running. He came up to the vegetable seller and said: "That's a lovely girl you've got there!"

"She's not mine," said the woman.

So he asked me about my family situation and then: "Do you want to earn loads of money?"

Of course I did, but I asked him: "Doing what? I'm not working in any nightclubs."

"Come and work with us, and you can take home three thousand a month."

This was fantastic news, and I said yes. He told me to report to the Sheraton Hotel the next day. I never told my mum, I wanted to surprise her by earning a ton of money. The next day after she left to go trash-picking, I got ready. I took a lot of trouble over my appearance, putting on my suit jacket, my new trousers and high heels, and went to the Sheraton. It was only then that I found out his name was Mr Wang, and he was head of marketing in the company where he worked. He took me into a room, where there were half a dozen other girls, but none of them as pretty as me. They all had migrant worker parents too. They asked me where I was from and I said from the south side of the city. They were impressed with my high heels, and I let them try them on, but their feet were either too big or too fat. Definitely not born to be city girls.

That afternoon in the hotel, we all had showers and Mr Wang gave us two hundred yuan: "Get your hair permed tomorrow," he said. And we got some face powder each too. I wondered if I was going to be working in a posh hotel like this in my new job. But that evening, Mr Wang told us there was a sales exhibition in Lanzhou, and we'd be travelling there overnight.

"Where's Lanzhou, and how long are we going for?" I asked.

He said it was another big city and we'd be there four or five days, then we'd come back when the event was over. Four or five days? That made me worried about my mum, so before we left, I called our landlord, he was the only one with a landline in the building, and asked him to tell her I'd found a job and would be back in a few days with money.

We got on an overnight bus. It was rammed, and it was a really bumpy ride too. I had no idea where we were passing through or where we were headed. I started off looking out of the window: as it grew dark, I could see jagged mountain peaks against the night sky and, at the foot of them, dark clusters of village houses, some still with their lights on, and then I fell asleep. Around noon the next day, I finally woke up when the bus stopped. We must have arrived in a county town or township. We were pretty confused when Mr Wang took us into a small hotel. He wouldn't let us out either, he said the streets were dangerous, and the people weren't like us, so we weren't to go running around. He brought us some takeaway food to our room and then, when it was evening, it was time to set off again. Only this time it was a car, and in it, just Mr Wang and me, and a man I didn't know. He was very friendly and bought me loads of snacks and drinks, and pretty soon I was asleep again. It was the afternoon of the next day before I woke up.

"Why aren't we there yet?" I asked.

"Not long now."

My head felt heavy and I kept dropping off. "I'm sorry I'm so sleepy," I said. I realise now they must have spiked the drinks they gave me. Towards evening, we finally got out of the car. My legs had swelled up and my head swam. And that was how I got to this village.

Bright's dad put yet another stone woman down on the edge of the strip. They'd taken the chain off my ankles but the cave door was still padlocked, and the dog was still lying in front of it. The Blacks' dog was a wanderer and when it wasn't asleep, it was restless, chasing chickens or running off as soon as it heard someone somewhere in the village calling their dog with a "Yo, yo!" because the kid had crapped and there was shit to be eaten. Then it would be gone for the rest of the day. Bright's dad swore at it but he knew it was never going to change, so finally he attached a chain to the statue at one end and the cave door at the other end, and tied the dog to the chain with a long rope looped around it. It could have the run of the strip, but it wouldn't wander off again.

I was delighted to see the dog chained up just like I'd been. I pulled a face at it and said: "I'm not free, and you're not free either."

It got its revenge when I was pressed against the window looking out, by lifting its leg and pissing against the bottom of the window frame. The smell of dog's piss was horrible and Bright gave it a beating for that.

Bright was still going to the township every week or ten days to replenish his stock, and he brought me back a bagful of steamed buns each time. Once he actually bought a pork shoulder too. I thought he wanted it for red-cooked pork or for stuffing dumplings, but his dad boiled it, then minced the meat, potted it, and gave it to Bright to keep in our cave, insisting that every time we had buckwheat noodles or stewed potatoes and vermicelli, we should put a spoonful of mince in our bowls. He threw the big bone to the dog, telling it: "Do your duty!" The dog spent all day gnawing on the bone, though there was no meat on it, it was like a dry old stick of wood, but it still kept gnawing.

The evening of day two hundred and five, Bright had gone to Great-Grandad's cave, and Blindy was pushing the grindstone round, milling the corn. I made my daily mark on the cave wall and then Bright came back with a sheet of paper that he stuck on the wall. There was nothing on it except one character drawn with a brush, which I didn't recognise:

I counted the brush strokes – sixty four. "Why have you stuck that up?" I asked.

Bright was thrilled that I was actually asking him a question: "We've got a character of sixty-four strokes, amazing, eh? I bet you've never seen it before, and you don't know how it's pronounced, right?" He sat down cross-legged on the *kang* and told me it was pronounced '*biang*', and was a kind of wide ribbon noodle. It probably dated back before the language was unified under the Qin dynasty, and it carried on being used in this region after that too, right up until today. Great-Grandad used to write it on sheets of paper every New Year and gave it to the village families. His explanation was that this character contained elements of food, clothes and houses, carts and farm beasts, heart and soul and language, and beautiful scenery to go and see, so if you hung it in the house, the family would be lucky.

As Bright went on animatedly, I interrupted: "Me? Lucky?"

That stopped him in his tracks. He looked at me, then said: "Well, you could be, if you'd only go along with things."

"You mean, go along with it like the condemned man stretches out his neck on the chopping block?"

Before Bright could answer, we heard footsteps coming onto the strip, and the dog leapt to its feet, panting, and the rope loop swished along the chain. It had got as far as the well and was barking furiously. The newcomer grabbed a stick and brandished it. Bright's dad came out of his cave: "Hey! Hey! You know the village boss!"

The man walloped the dog hard with his stick and the dog howled in protest.

"You just want to bite me today because I'm not wearing my uniform?"

There was someone coming along behind: "It's me it wants to bite, I'm all in rags today."

The man (who really was in rags) took the stool Bright's dad had fetched from the cave and put it down for the village boss. The village boss sat down and asked: "Where's Bright?"

Bright's dad picked up a corn cob that had bounced off the millstone onto the ground and shouted: "Bright, Bright! The village boss is here!"

He went to throw the corn cob back in but then thought better of it and put it in his mouth and chomped it up instead: "What do you want Bright for?"

"Well, I have to worry about the whole village," said the village boss. "Your family's complete again, but Withy-Weave's still in a mess."

"What's up with you, Withy-Weave?" asked Bright's dad, looking at the man in rags.

"Wait till Bright comes, and the boss can tell you."

Bright's dad looked up: "Why haven't you harnessed the donkey?"

Blindy was pushing the millstone around, his forehead shiny with sweat: "She's been ploughing for three days straight, she needs a rest."

Bright's dad threw a face towel over, and as luck would have it, it landed on the millstone driver stick. "Bright, Bright!" he yelled into my cave again. A flock of crows came in to roost in the pine trees.

Bright said to me: "That's not what I meant." Then he went out. As the village boss spoke to him, Withy-Weave clasped his hands together and begged him for help. The story was this: another girl had arrived in the township and the village boss, who felt sorry for Withy-Weave, wanted to fix him up with her as a wife. The township people were keen to get rid of the girl no later than that night, so the boss asked Bright if he'd take his tractor and go and fetch her. Bright tried to wriggle out of it: it was late, his tractor had no lights, the road was bad and so on.

"What are you making such a fuss about?" said the village boss. "I've got a torch. You've got to go anyway, a man who's eaten his fill doesn't let a starving man go hungry."

Withy-Weave took a bundle of notes from his pocket and thrust them at Bright, who refused to accept the money.

"Go!" his dad commanded.

"OK," said Bright and went to sort out the tractor with the village boss.

"How much did you pay?" Bright asked Withy-Weave.

"Twenty thousand."

"Cheap."

"She's got one bad eye."

Withy-Weave made another attempt to pass the money over, this time pushing it inside Bright's dad's jacket. He glanced after the village boss and lowered his voice: "I'm giving Bright a thousand, I hope it's not too little. I had twenty-six thousand, I gave five thousand to the boss, and I've only got a thousand left."

"Don't say that, otherwise Bright won't go," said Bright's dad.

The tractor took its time but finally fired up.

"Bright, have you got any decent clothes to lend Withy-Weave?" the village boss was asking.

"What's wrong with what I've got on?" said Withy-Weave.

"Shit, you may not care how you look but it reflects badly on me," said the village boss. "Go and get some rope."

"Rope?"

"If you don't tie her up, she'll run away. You reckon the two of us can catch her? Wait for us at the village entrance with the rope."

Withy-Weave grunted and ran out and down the alley. Bright's dad pulled his son to one side and there was a lot of muttering, and then Bright came back into the cave and fetched some clothes.

"Off to kidnap someone else, are you?" I asked.

"We're going to buy her," said Bright.

"You can only buy her cos someone else kidnapped her! Look what you did to me, and now you're going to do it to someone else!" I retorted.

"I'm just helping Withy-Weave, he's a really sad case." Then he said: "Are you bleeding, can I have some?"

He told me that the villagers thought that, if you had your wife's blood on you, it warded off the evil spirits. He was a bit embarrassed and vague about it but I understood all right: he was asking me for a used sanitary towel. Where on earth would I get a sanitary towel? We didn't even have toilet paper in the cave, not even newspaper, I'd been using the cotton wadding out of the mattress. I pulled a little bit out of my knickers and he happily wrapped it in a maize leaf and stuffed it in an inside pocket.

"Right! Now I've got my wife's blood with me, there's nothing I can't do."

I waved him away. "Get out of here!"

I hoped he wouldn't crash the tractor.

They drove off. The cock crowed twice and it began to pelt with rain. A layer of water quickly covered the strip, and the raindrops looked like countless nails jumping up and down in it. Bright's dad was still standing in his doorway. "Where's all this rain come from?" he said.

Blindy echoed him, maybe standing at his own cave door, but I couldn't see him: "Where's all this rain come from?"

Bright was away the whole night. I didn't sleep, and nor did Bright's dad or Blindy. I didn't sleep because I was wondering where this girl with one bad eye had come from and how she'd got herself kidnapped. The two men didn't sleep because they were worried about whether the tractor was safe on the mountain roads in the rain. It suddenly occurred to me that an accident would be good for me: if Bright was killed then I could leave this place. Then I felt bad about having thoughts like that and gave myself a slap across the face.

At daybreak, the rain stopped, but the tractor still hadn't returned. Bright's dad did a bit of chiselling then started to pace back and forth until the strip was a sea of mud. When he got to the gourd frame, he asked Great-Grandad: "What could have happened?"

"Nothing's happened," said Great-Grandad, and Bright's dad went back to his chiselling.

I finally heard loud tooting. The tractor sounded like it had asthma, spluttering and choking, then coming back to life again. Bright's dad had been banging away with his chisel but now he stopped and said to Blindy, who had just fed the donkey and was propped in his doorway: "You reckon there's something wrong with its engine?"

"Maybe it's skidding on the wet road."

The engine was spluttering as if it had gravel or mud in the tank instead of petrol. Bang, bang, poop, poop, it sounded like it was farting. Bright's dad and Blindy grabbed an armful of straw mats and ran out and down the alley.

Bright was back, safe and sound, but they hadn't brought the girl. According to him, when they got to the inn in the township, the kidnapper had changed his mind and upped the price from twenty thousand to thirty thousand. They'd finally haggled him down to twenty-five thousand, and Withy-Weave had promised the village boss he'd pay him the extra five thousand when they got back, and begged him to pay up. The minute the village boss handed over the extra five thousand, they went to fetch the girl but when they opened the room door, she wasn't there. She must have got away through the back window while they were arguing. She'd torn up the bed sheet and made a rope with it, and it dangled from the window. It was three floors up, and there was a big patch of blood on the ground below, but the girl was nowhere to be seen.

I pulled the quilt over me and slept until noon. I was glad for the girl but I cried because I felt so stupid and powerless.

I remembered the pond.

There were three lotuses in the pond in summer, and a dozen frogs. I could see them from the window of our room. The frogs would jump onto a lotus leaf one by one. First one, then another joined it, then a third, and the leaf would tip over and land all three frogs in the water. At first on Sundays I shut the window because Qingwen would come and crouch down at the pond strip with his camera and take pictures. Qingwen was the landlord's younger son, he was good-looking and studying at university, so there was no chance he would take any notice of a girl who rented one of his father's rooms and was a trash-picker. So when he turned up at the pond, I shut the window and wouldn't open it even when the room filled with choking smoke from the stove and I started coughing.

One evening, not a Sunday, I needed to go out to the water tap to rinse the rice and Qingwen happened to be by the pond photographing the frogs, so I hung around at home picking over the leeks. Eventually, it began to get dark and I went to turn on the light but nothing happened. So I went outside to check the fuse box, to see if it had tripped and it hadn't.

"Mr Landlord!" I shouted, and Qingwen came running over to see what was up.

I blushed.

"The light's not working. Is it a power cut?"

He checked our line, checked the fuse box again, then finally got on a stool and took out the light bulb.

"The bulb's gone," he said. Something so simple and I hadn't even thought of it, I was a bit embarrassed. I went to his home and fetched a new bulb to put in, and suddenly the room was bright.

"Thank you," I said.

"What's your name?"

"Butterfly."

"I'm Qingwen."

"I know. You're at university and your hobby's photography, your dad's shown me some of your pictures."

"Has he really?" and Qingwen suddenly picked up his camera and took a picture of me. I didn't want him to, because I was still in the old clothes I'd brought from the countryside and my hair was in plaits that were coming undone.

"I'm ugly!" I protested.

"You're pure." He smiled and then he left.

That evening, I wondered if he'd keep me in his camera.

I never asked him if he'd printed the picture and he never mentioned it, I wondered if he'd gone home and deleted it.

I'd ignore him from now on, I decided. But how could I? Every Saturday afternoon I sat in the yard looking out to see if there was any sign of him. Often I didn't see him at all. I would wait through the afternoon until the next day, and I was so frantic that when my mum sent me to the market to buy a pumpkin, I came back with aubergine, and when she asked me to wash her shoes when she went to work, I forgot until she came home again and she was cross.

"How can a young girl like you be so forgetful?" But as soon as I caught a glimpse of Qingwen, I was in a really good mood. I would put on my suit jacket and cut my hair, and go and wash the greens at the water tap, and pop out with the rubbish to the bin in the yard, and all the while Qingwen would be at the pond photographing the frogs, completely absorbed. I didn't disturb him. But when I went back in, I felt stupid, why hadn't I made a sound to attract his attention?

Finally I got my chance and we met again. My mum had gone off trash-picking and I took three old manhole covers she had picked up and went to the depot to sell them, but the woman said that they were public property and the police had warned them not to buy them. I said my mum had been sold them, she hadn't stolen them, and anyway they were broken. The woman took them off me but she wouldn't give me any money. I said, pay me or give them back. She wouldn't pay but she wouldn't give them back either.

"I won't report this, isn't that enough for you?"

I went home in tears and bumped into Qingwen as I entered the yard.

"What's up?" he asked.

And I told him the story. He offered to take me to the depot. But first he went home to leave his camera, and when he came out, he had rolled his sleeves up to the elbows and undone his collar button.

"Are you really up for a fight?" I asked.

"I'm not afraid," he said.

"I don't want any fighting. My mum shouldn't have bought them."

"Well in that case, the depot shouldn't have taken them off you. Bullies!"

When we got to the depot, it turned out the woman knew Qingwen, and Qingwen only had to say a few words and she paid up good as gold.

"What's she to you, Qingwen," said the woman, looking at me.

"My cousin," he said.

On the way home, I said: "Thank you!"

"I'm only doing what a cousin should do!" he said, and laughed.

I laughed too. "I'll make you some noodles."

And I really did, I made them by hand, I didn't buy them in the market. I mixed the flour with water till finally it made a soft dough, kneaded it as hard as I could, rolled it out paper-thin and cut it into ribbons the width of a leek leaf. When I cooked them, the noodles came out firm and shiny, and I added salt, vinegar, chopped onion and chilli oil, and I thought I'd made the best noodles ever. But when I took the bowl over to his house, they said he'd been called back to the college urgently, so I gave the noodles to the landlord to eat.

I never saw Qingwen again. I wore my high-heeled shoes, and the other tenants in our yard saw them, the landlord saw them, nearly everyone in our alley saw them, but not Qingwen. When I was in the hotel and gave the landlord a call, it was Sunday and I hoped Qingwen would pick up, but he didn't, his father did.

Bright had been in the township for three days. When he got back and drove the tractor onto the strip, a swarm of villagers turned up too. The dog didn't bother barking, it just lay there gnawing its bone. They were making such a din, it sounded like a hive full of bees.

"What kept you so long?"

"That's a nice scarf! Can you get another one?"

"Very nice, but who's it for?"

"Don't scrape your muddy feet on the wheels!"

"Did you bring any salt? We can do without oil for a couple of weeks, but we can't do without salt!"

"I don't eat salt."

"Of course you don't, it's bad for your kidneys."

"Full-Barn's wife's about to have a baby and there was only white sugar in the store, no brown sugar, his mum's furious with me!"

"Ai-yaya!" That was Monkey. He went on: "So she's furious, what's that got to do with you, are you the father of the baby?"

Bright glanced at the window of my cave: "Don't talk rubbish!"

"Cut the tractor engine, or it might run away," said Blindy. Once, Bright had left the tractor engine running and an old hunchback woman got into an argument with Bright and kicked it, and the brake came off and it headed towards Great-Grandad's cave. Luckily, Bright was a quick mover, and he jumped on board and slammed on the brakes.

Three more people turned up on the strip. One of them wiped his snotty nose with his hand and went to clean his fingers on the tractor.

"What do you think you're doing?" said Bright.

"I've got a cold." The man wiped his hand on a stone instead.

Monkey carried on: "Are you worried that Butterfly will find out what you've been up to? How did it go?"

"Fine," said Bright.

"Don't overdo things," said Monkey. "Look at those dark circles under your eyes, too much poking and you'll do yourself an injury!" Suddenly a bird flew at my window, but it only dropped a leaf.

"The fuck you know," said Bright. "Let's get this unloaded."

A little guy, a head shorter than Bright, shouted: "You go and have a fag, Uncle, I'll do the unloading." He pulled a big bundle of brooms off the tractor and then a container of vinegar, which he gave to Blindy to take into the cave.

"I'll take a poke, any time, even if it does do me an injury."

Monkey gave Short-Arse a kick up the arse.

"You better sell all your blood onions, or you'll burst a blood vessel!"

The day I was bundled into the cave, Short-Arse had hold of my leg and he dug his fingernails in so hard, they left marks. He was so old, he had wrinkles like gullies crisscrossing his face, so why was he calling Bright 'Uncle'?

"You want a poke do you?" said someone. "Well, you buy a pair of shoes tomorrow and I'll be your match-maker. I'll talk to Triple-Edge about his big sister."

"Didn't she marry a man in South Gully village?" asked Short-Arse.

"He's dead, fell off the roof of the house he was building."

"Then I don't want her, her mouth's all twisted to one side, she dribbles, I don't want her."

"Then go and find a hole in the wall to poke!" said Monkey. "Hey Bright, this bag's full of steamed buns, why have you bought so many?"

Bright's dad snatched the bag out of his hand and took it into his cage.

"Not even a please or thank you," grumbled Monkey, and he aimed a kick at the dog, who leapt at him. Monkey grabbed a strainer from the tractor and threw it, but missed, and it landed on my windowsill instead. I threw it back again.

Bright was in discussion with an old guy, who asked: "Lighting papers have gone up in price, have they?"

"Yes, ten cents."

"How much is this enamel mug and lid? And these bowls?"

"The mug's the same price as before. The bowls are from Jingdezhen, three for ten yuan."

"Weren't they four for ten before? And did you buy thread for my wife?"

"Yes, it's three yuan a reel."

"Bright Black, you're as black as your name!"

"No I'm not, prices have gone up. I only make ten cents on a reel of cotton!"

There was a shout from Bright's dad: "Monkey! Monkey!"

"My name is Virtue," said Monkey.

"Cut the crap, come and give me a hand."

Bright's dad was shifting a gravestone he'd made.

Monkey read the characters: "'In memory of Liu Delin and Liang Maiye, beloved parents of...' Is that for White-Hair Liu?" he asked.

"Yup, his mum and dad have been gone three years at the end of last year."

"That's quick! Time flies by when someone's died! What a good boy your Bright is, all those steamed buns he's bought you."

"Shift that stone!" grunted Bright's dad. Monkey stuck his arse out to get a grip on the stone and farted.

"You've been fucking eating garlic chives!" complained the people nearest to him.

"Withy-Weave treated me to some garlic dumplings," said Monkey.

"Hey, where is Withy-Weave?" asked Bright. "He got me to buy him fertiliser and he hasn't come to fetch it."

"When we'd finished the dumplings, he went off to dig nonesuch flowers," said Monkey.

"Will he find any?"

"The village boss is after him for the five thousand, he said he wasn't paying up because he never got the woman, and they had a big fight. Withy-Weave said he'd try and dig some nonesuch flowers, he couldn't be sure of finding any but that was his only chance."

"Now what's going on?" said Bright's dad. From down below the strip they heard swearing and crying.

"They've been fighting all their lives, how do they do it?" said Snot-Nose. "Auntie Spotty-Face, come up here!"

Auntie Spotty-Face had appeared on the strip. I hadn't seen her for a long time. She'd got thinner. And she was crying her eyes out.

"Bright! Why didn't you bring me any of the lucky red paper I asked for?"

"Ai-ya! It went clean out of my head."

"You never forgot to buy steamed buns for your wife!" said Auntie Spotty-Face.

Short-Arse said: "Oh, so you bought the buns for your wife! She's got two lovely white buns of her own, and you're buying her more?"

Bright aimed a kick at him and Short-Arse yelped. Then he turned away and spoke to Auntie Spotty-Face: "What's cheered you up all of a sudden?"

"I'm still crying, aren't I?" And she came towards my cave. I was standing at the window, but she didn't see me. She banged the padlock and the dog, which had been lying at the edge of the strip, came bounding towards her, its loop of rope swishing along the chain.

"Down! Down!" Auntie Spotty-Face yelled. The dog didn't lie down but Blindy came over and grabbed hold of it.

"Tongue-Trip is on his way," he told her.

"So you've seen Tongue-Trip, have you? And is that a man or a donkey?" Loud laughter.

"I heard his footsteps," said Blindy. "He wears rubber shoes and they're split so the water gets in."

Auntie Spotty-Face turned to look, and sure enough, just at that moment, Tongue-Trip turned up at the entrance to the strip.

"Bright, have you got any wrapping paper I can have?" she asked.

Bright handed over a sheet, and she went over to the gourd frame and yelled: "Great-Grandad, why can't you keep Tongue-Trip under control?"

Tongue-Trip was on the strip by now, swearing at Bright for giving her the wrapping paper.

"If Auntie wants to do papercuts, let her," Bright said.

But Tongue-Trip was annoyed: "You... you... can't eat... or dr... drink pap... papercuts! Have I got to spend my whole life looking after this bitch?"

Bright's dad hurriedly got out his pipe and offered it to Tongue-Trip to shut him up: "Here, you sit down and stick that in your mouth."

I was thinking.

I was thinking how my mum can't have had a good night's sleep since I disappeared, and she must spend all the time crying. Surely she'd told the landlord all about it and he must be helping her, making suggestions about what to do, reporting it to the police. I was wondering whether the police would take the case and start searching for me. Before, when someone on the third floor of the south building was burgled, they reported it, and the police wrote up their notes and sent them home. The tenant asked when they were going to crack the case, and the answer was: "If we can nab a petty thief, then that's the case cracked."

And the tenant never heard a thing after that. The landlord would have known this, so he'd tell my mum: "Life's complicated these days, such a high crime rate, the police won't search unless she dies, they don't have the funds or the manpower. Best thing is, you print off a few thousand Missing Person posters."

And my mum would go and get them printed, and they'd ask for a picture but Mum didn't have a picture, all she could say was, I was twenty years old, taller than her, not fat but not skinny either, big eyes, long legs. The printers would just say there was no point printing a poster without a picture of me. I imagined my mum going home to tell the landlord and crying buckets, and maybe just then Qingwen would come back from college, and he'd find that picture of me in his camera. I was sure he hadn't deleted it, he'd get it out and go with Mum to the printers, and they'd get a few thousand posters printed. The whole of the alley would know by now that I'd disappeared.

"That trash-picker girl, the pretty one!" I could hear them gossiping. "Do you think she's been kidnapped and sold? Surely not, she's a big girl and she's done years of school too, so we heard. Surely no one could kidnap her? Or maybe she fell in love and ran away with a man because her mum didn't like him? But surely if the girl had a boyfriend, her mum would have said so? Or maybe she's gone to work in a nightclub and once a girl starts that kind of work, they don't let her out. Or maybe someone's done her harm, have they looked in derelict buildings, or in the river?"

Yes, they'd go on and on, but my mum wouldn't pay any attention, she'd be up in the middle of the night, taking her posters around the streets and back alleys, sticking them on lampposts. You had to look out for the Street Conditions Observation Unit, the SCOUT Patrols, if you were fly-posting, so maybe Qingwen would go with her, not to stick them up, just to stand some way away and keep an eye out for the patrols.

One night, Bright didn't come back until very late. I was lying on the *kang* and he must have thought I was asleep and wasting kerosene, so he blew the lamp out.

"Light it!" I said immediately.

"Aren't you asleep?" he said, but he lit it again. He sat on the edge of the *kang* and I turned my back on him, but I could feel his eyes on my feet, which were sticking out and freezing cold. I pulled them back under the quilt.

Bright went on: "I got some good news in the township, our village is getting electricity next year, and the telegraph poles will all be paid for by the government. When we've got it, I'll buy you a TV. His gaze shifted and I felt his hand slowly creeping towards me. I hurriedly sat up, grabbed his bedding roll and threw it on the floor. Then the pillow. He picked them up and took them to the table where he laid them out and lay down to sleep. There was a bit of steamed bun there and he picked it up and shoved it in his mouth.

"I left that for the rats!" I said.

"For the rats?"

"That's right, I'm rearing rats."

He looked astonished. "Butterfly, what's up with you?"

"I want to go home!" I yelled at him.

"Why are you yelling? It's the middle of the night!" He lay down and I heard a few sniffles.

I admit I'd been bad to him, but I couldn't be nice to him, not even a tiny bit nice.

After a while, Bright's sobs died away, and he fell asleep. He must be really tired. I got the picture frame down and started talking quietly to the nonesuch flower. By now I could communicate in all sorts of mysterious ways, like with the nonesuch flower, with the rats, with the pine trees and the birds in them, with the sun by day and the moon at night, the wind blowing across the strip, the rain and the rolling mist. When I'd had enough of talking to the nonesuch flower, I went to the window and looked out at the sky. I thought I could see a star but when I looked hard, it disappeared and there was nothing but blackness. I prayed before I looked: Please let me see a star, tonight I've got to see a star. But when I looked, the sky was pitch black, as black as if I was blind. I suddenly felt desperate.

Bright was snoring and I could hear the dog snoring on the strip too, and it occurred to me that I could try running away again. I slipped off the *kang* and went to open the door, carrying the picture frame with me, ready to use it to ward the dog off if it woke up and lunged at me. If I could just get to the entrance to the strip, he wouldn't be able to follow me because he was chained up. If Bright and his dad woke up, they'd still have to work out what was going on, then get their coats and shoes on, and I might just get away before they caught me.

I pulled open the door and someone tumbled in. He'd been hunkered down outside, propped against the doorframe.

"Who's that?" He sounded scared out of his wits.

"Who are you?" I asked. It was Bright's dad.

By now, Bright was awake. He threw himself at me, got me round the waist and bundled me back onto the *kang*. His dad hurriedly went out again and shut the door from the outside, and at the same time, the dog began to bark. Calmer now, he said: "Bright, I came to ask if you're going to buy more stock tomorrow?"

Bright answered from inside the cave: "Dad, go to bed." And he blew out the lamp and hunkered down propped against the door inside, still breathing hard.

Bright's dad never came to the cave when Bright was away from home, in fact he completely ignored me. Now that his son was home, I guessed that he was hunkered down outside in the small hours to check up on us. If we were either fighting or silent, that couldn't bode well for our relationship. He must have known that Bright was sleeping on the floor by the table, and that must be really, really upsetting him. A tiny thrill of excitement went through me: if he saw how things were, then maybe he'd give up hope and make Bright let me go.

I kept an eye on the old man the next morning. When Bright went out to fetch water for me to wash my face, his dad called him into his own cave. It was a long time before Bright brought me the water. His dad didn't appear, he was making breakfast and I heard the knocking of the bellows. When the food was ready, Bright brought me my bowl and sat down on the edge of the well with Blindy. Great-Grandad was watering the gourds.

"Great-Grandad, have you had your breakfast?" asked Blindy.

"Yup."

"Great-Grandad, my legs have been hurting me."

"Then smoke some wormwood."

"I did, but they still hurt."

"Then you've got demons. The Yellow Emperor's *Canon of Internal Medicine* tells us that the body's channels should be full of energy but if the energy's lacking, then you get demons moving in."

Blindy grunted. "Demons moving in? Then what am I supposed to do?" he asked.

"I can't get rid of demons," said the old man.

"Uncle Blindy," said Bright. "I'll get Auntie Spotty-Face to take you to the West Ridge temple."

"There's no temple there any more, is she going to take me to pray to the tree? Forget it. And your dad's run out of tea leaves," said Blindy.

"I'm going to buy some tomorrow, and while I'm in the township, I'll ask old Lu to get you some sunglasses from the county town," said Bright.

"Waste of money, what do I want sunglasses for?"

"Don't worry about the money," said Bright.

"Don't you go buying sunglasses. I won't wear them. Anyway, you won't have time to go and buy in more stock tomorrow, Ladle's dad's gone, you'll need to go and help them."

"Ladle's dad's gone? I only saw him a few days ago. He was pottering along, leaning on his crutch near the entrance to the village."

"A bleed on the brain, his third," said Blindy.

The pair of them chatted on as they ate. Bright's dad wasn't eating, he was working on a stone trough with his chisel, thwack, thwack, a sonorous, rhythmic sound.

When the meal was over, Bright went to the store again and Blindy loaded the big basket on his back and went out too. The village boss was issuing directions to half a dozen men who were hauling a large stone onto the strip. He had his jacket draped around his shoulders again.

Bright's dad muttered: "Flapping around all day with that jacket draped over his shoulders!"

The village boss wasn't meant to hear but he did: "You think I'm flapping around? I've brought you this stone to carve a stone ram!"

"It's the way you wear your jacket I'm talking about," said Bright's dad.

"But that's the way all village bosses wear their jackets."

When the men got the stone onto the strip, they started to argue, waving their arms around, and turned to consult Great-Grandad, who was sitting under the gourd frame, reading a book.

"You reading that almanac again?" exclaimed the boss. "What year is it this year, how come everyone's going down like ninepins, and we keep having to bury people?"

"The earth feeds us all our lives, the earth eats us when we're dead," said Great-Grandad.

"Does the almanac tell you how to carve a ram?"

"Auntie Spotty-Face can cut out sheep, get her to do one and you can use it as a model," said Great-Grandad.

Bright's dad offered the village boss a smoke: "I don't need her to cut out a sheep, I carve them year in year out, why can't I do it?"

"The one you did last year, it didn't have its legs bent," said Great-Grandad. "If you want it to take disease away with it, it has to be kneeling."

The village boss held the pipe between his lips and said to his men: "Go and bring more rocks, ones from the edge of the gully, there have been a lot of deaths and sickness this year, we need to carve more sheep!"

The men spent the whole morning hefting rocks of all sizes, big and small, onto the strip until they had ten all piled up. Bright's dad never asked if he was going to get paid for the carving, nor did he complain that there were too many, how was he going to carve them all? He just boiled them all some water for tea.

Before the tea was ready, there was a shout from below: "Baldy, Eight-Jin!"

Eight-Jin answered and the first man shouted again: "Is the village boss up there?"

"Someone for you, boss," said Eight-Jin.

'Tell 'em I'm busy."

"It's Griddle-Cake."

"She after me for a welfare payment again?" And the village boss put down his pipe and went off.

Eight-Jin said: "It's usually men looking for women, I've never seen Griddle-Cake so frantic!"

"So she wasn't looking for you!"

"I couldn't handle her, she's a restless sleeper!"

And they all laughed.

Bright's dad didn't stop at offering them tea. When they'd finished that, he got out some wine and invited them into his cave for a drink. They carried on drinking until Bright came back from the shop and then carried on some more, and got Bright drinking too, and it sounded like they were tearing him off a strip. Finally, when he was properly drunk, he came out of his dad's cave with three blood onions in his hand, chewing on them and muttering obscenities.

Someone shouted from inside the cave: "Are you up for it, Bright!"

"Yup!"

"You fucking go for it, you're a man, aren't you?"

I was thinking.

What was I thinking about? Suddenly there didn't seem to be any point in thinking about anything any more.

So that was day number three hundred and three. I felt numb, as if someone had tipped a basin of flour paste over me. All I could do was scratch a new mark on the cave wall.

Bright came over to the cave still chewing on his onions, the padlock rattled as he unlocked it and then the door opened wide and there was a blast of air which nearly blew the lamp out. The wine and the pungent blood onion had turned his face a flaming red.

I was sitting on the *kang*: "Why are you throwing the door wide open like that?"

"I've got to have you!"

And he lunged at me, grabbed hold of me and tore at my clothes. This was a side of Bright I'd never seen. In my panic, I curled up in a ball, my hands clasped across my chest. He suddenly seemed a hundred times stronger than before. He had me pinned down with one knee, so I couldn't kick him, and he gripped one arm so hard it felt numb, pulling it away from my chest. Then he ripped my jacket off, so that three out of the five buttons shot off and pinged against the cave wall. I managed to roll over and grip the edge of the *kang*, kicking him as hard as I could so he fell off the *kang*, but he came right back up again. He pulled one foot to the edge of the *kang*, I grabbed hold of the corner of the *kang* table, but he pushed it away and he got the rest of me to the edge of the *kang* and lay on me like a stone slab, pinning his bristly mouth to mine. I couldn't breathe, I felt like he was smothering me, I tried to push him away but I couldn't. He was biting my lips, pulling on them, I scratched his face, drawing blood. He let go for a second and I bounced upright like a leaping fish, and my head hit the shelf above the *kang*, and pots and bottles came cascading down with a crash, spilling rice, flour and beans all over the *kang*.

"Bright, you motherfucker!"

I screamed and cursed him, using the vilest language I could think of, the sort of swearwords I'd heard people at home use but never used myself, they came spewing out of my mouth. I thought my swearing might make him back off, but he just glared at me and cursed me right back. I grabbed one of the pots and hurled it against the window. The window wasn't damaged but the pot smashed, and some of the shards flew through the lattice and hit the dog, which yelped.

Just at that moment, I saw Bright's dad standing by the well. He was saying to the men in his cave: "Go on, all of you!" Six of them emerged and came running to my cave.

Just then, my soul left my body through my skull and I was perched on the frame with the nonesuch flower in it.

The men had red faces, red necks and their heads flamed like cockscombs. They flung themselves on the kang *and held Butterfly down. Her legs were pinned down, her arms were pinned down, but her head was still jerking and she was still swearing and spitting, so Eight-Jin got hold of her head. First he grabbed her by the ears but she jerked away so then he grabbed her chin too and that stopped her. They started by ripping her clothes off, then her bra, and her breasts popped out. Then they tried to remove the leg bindings, but they wouldn't come off so they searched frantically for scissors. They couldn't find any, and Monkey shouted: "Uncle, fetch a knife!"*

Bright's dad, who was outside the cave, was going: "No, no, that's too dangerous!"

But one of the men went into the old man's cave and fetched a knife anyway, and pushed him out of the way.

"We won't harm her. You shouldn't be here."

Bright's dad said: "Once you've got her under control, you lot leave."

And he went back to his cave and didn't come out again.

They cut the strips around Butterfly's legs with a knife and their hands were all trying to pull her trousers down, but they still had to tear the trouser legs to get them off.

"Let me do that!" Bright shouted, but no one took any notice of him, they ripped the trousers into four strips, and there were Butterfly's lily-white legs on show.

Someone said: "Her legs are so straight, hasn't she got any knees?"

They could see her bottom, she was wearing red knickers. Monkey reached out to rip them off, Butterfly couldn't move but all of her muscles strained like a leaping fish and she cried out in a hoarse voice that wasn't like hers at all: "Bright! Bright!"

Bright shoved Eight-Jin out of the way (Eight-Jin had one arm around Butterfly's head and the other hand pressing on her breasts), then he pushed Monkey away too. He held onto Butterfly's knickers: "OK, OK, time to go now."

The men had no sooner released their hold than Butterfly arched her back, pushed Bright off the kang *and rolled over onto her front, still swearing and screaming blue murder. Bright didn't get up immediately and his mates didn't make any effort to pull him up. Instead, they grabbed Butterfly and pulled her straight again.*

"You can't manage on your own!"

Butterfly lay splayed on her back, naked apart from her red knickers, while they taunted him: "Get up, you useless s.o.b, do it, do it! If you don't do it to her, she won't be yours, she'll never give you a child, you'll never keep a hold of her!"

Bright was practically begging them: "I will, I will, you just go!"

But the men said: "You've been trying for nearly a year and you still haven't popped her cherry!"

"I have, I have!" said Bright.

A fat-cheeked man said: "What? With little pink nipples like that? I don't believe you."

They got some rope to tie Butterfly's arms and legs down, but there wasn't anywhere to tie her to on the kang. *Eight-Jin went out of the cave, then came back again: "Haven't you got a ladder? Wait, I'll go and get our barrow."*

But Short-Arse pulled a bench out from the back of the cave: "This'll do."

Butterfly was dragged off the kang *and onto the bench, and Monkey started to rope her down. First, the top half (three hands pushed her breasts out of the way), then her arms were tied to the bench legs and her legs were splayed open, one tied to the table leg and the other to the window. Butterfly was spitting furiously, she got Fat-Cheeks in the face and he wiped the spittle off and onto Butterfly's bum: "City women are no different from country women when they're naked!"*

"She's got big tits but there's not a scrap of flesh on her anywhere else!" said Monkey.

As they left, one said: "And we didn't get a word of thanks!"

Another said: "If you still can't manage it, you just give us a shout!"

Bright shut the door after them. His face was still bleeding and he smeared it with one hand so he looked like Lord Guan. Then he ripped Butterfly's red knickers off and took off his own clothes. Butterfly gave a terrible shriek but Bright didn't stop, and the blood ran down over her bottom, staining the bench top red and running down its legs. His face contorted in a frightful grimace, Bright was working away with all his might, making croaks that might have been from pleasure or pain, and with each thrust, the bench creaked and slipped forward. Outside the window, the donkey brayed and it sounded like it was banging its head on the cave door.

"You're going at it hard, aren't you?" I heard someone shout.

The men hadn't gone away, they were still there outside, heads pressed to the window. Bright's neck was rigid, he gritted his teeth, and he was covered all over with a sheen of sweat. He was crazed, like a wild beast, the bench kept slipping forwards, leaving a long streak of dark red on the floor, and the room smelled of blood. It sounded like Bright's dad was trying to get rid of the men, shoving packs of cigarettes at them as he pushed them away.

"What a lot of blood! He's going to kill her!" exclaimed Monkey.

Then their footsteps faded away into the distance. The donkey brayed again and the dog dashed back and forth across the strip.

Finally, Bright collapsed on top of Butterfly like a bundle of firewood, then slipped down to the floor and lay there without moving.

"Wife, wife, I won't lock you up any more," he said.

Butterfly didn't cry. She lay on the bench in a faint.

I didn't get off the *kang* for five days. I couldn't move.

I hated Bright. He was a repulsive ghost, a cruel bandit. He didn't know where my door was but he wanted in anyway, the key didn't fit the lock but he was going to open it one way or another even if he had to smash it open, or kick it open or jemmy it, then he could push himself in, it didn't matter that I was bruised black and blue and bleeding. My whole body was dammed up, I could hardly breathe, my body's blood and water, even my internal organs, sucked out of me. I was like a soft persimmon and then I was an empty sac. Bright came for his bride armed, poking me over and over with his bayonet till he'd riddled me with holes, banged me as if he was pounding sticky rice with a pestle and mortar, bashed me like he was mashing potato to glue. Then there was the spittle, the snot and the piss and the shit that turned me into a human latrine, a rubbish tip.

That first night, I remembered a TV film I'd seen called *Animal World*: a pride of lions jump on a deer, gripping it hard and rolling over, biting its mouth so it can't breathe, ripping its belly open so its blood bubbles out and the entrails spill. The deer, its eyes staring wide, has its flesh devoured until only the legs are left, sticking up into the air, long graceful legs and little delicate hooves.

That night I was like a chicken with its head cut off, dropping off the chopping board and frantically fluttering in a desperate attempt to escape. They shouted, they laughed, countless eyes watched me, but no one came to my aid, no one told that chicken where the door was and finally she hit the wall and fell to the floor, and was cooked and eaten, and all that was left were a few feathers.

On the sixth day, the sun came out and lit up the cave. Sunlight shone on the *kang* and I could see there were bloodstains everywhere.

Bright said: "I'm not shutting you in any more, why don't you go out and sit in the sun?"

I felt like I'd died and been buried in his belly. I must have looked reluctant because Bright said: "It's always like that when a woman marries... you get some sleep then."

That changed my mind and I jumped off the *kang*, even though I was so unsteady on my feet I had to hold onto the edge and between my legs hurt like hell. He tried to make me lie down again but I insisted on going out. I was cold and hard as ice, sharp as glass shards, and I was going to go out with one of those shards and slash his tyres and let the air out.

It was the first time I had been out of the cave in nearly a year. It was like coming out of a tomb, like being re-born. I actually collapsed in the doorway, the rays of sunlight were sharp as needles, they dazzled me so I couldn't open my eyes. I pulled myself up onto my feet again, holding onto the door frame. Outside on the strip was air, wisps of air, spiralling upwards like water-weed in a pond. Great-Grandad was sitting under the gourd frame. The gourd vines had withered and dried by now, but they were still coiled around the supports like dark twine. Great-Grandad was tearing apart the wooden cases around the gourds, he must have fitted them on when they were small, so the gourds grew round or square, or with two or three 'bellies'. A character was written on top of each case.

"Great-Grandad! Great-Grandad!" I shouted, but he ignored me. He pulled a gourd towards him and looked to see what was written on the case. I saw it was the character for Virtue, 德. Then, still keeping his back to me, he returned to his cave.

I didn't blame him. Even if he had answered me, what could I have said to him?

From then on, there was no padlock on the door, and when I heard the donkey braying, I came out and sat on the strip. That day, the wind got up and blew one of the gourd frame supports askew, toppling one corner of the vine, but the gourds kept hanging on, they were dry and hard as bone. A crow flew down from the clifftop to perch in the pine trees, but before it got there, it suddenly plummeted out of the sky and smashed on the millstone. A couple of birds were fighting over a worm, pulling each end so it wasn't soft any more and went stiff as a twig. Blindy, on his way out with the big basket on his back, put his left foot down and heard a sharp crack. He jumped away and nearly fell over. It was a snail, shell and flesh mashed into the ground. The wind snatched at the smoke from Bright's dad's cave, and the sound of the bellows suddenly stopped, and the old man muttered something about rats getting into the bellows box. The smoke went from white to black, and belched out of the cave door and hung over the edge of the strip, where plastic bags and bits of paper fluttered from the crow-black thorn bushes. Carcasses and lost souls floating everywhere. I looked at the cave doors. They weren't the mushroom shape I had imagined them to be when I was indoors. They were giant erect penises, standing on end in a row.

More and more, every time I went back into the cave or to the shit-house, I had the feeling that someone was tailing me. I felt their breath and even the shuffling as they tiptoed behind me. I'd stiffen, lash out behind me, but I hit nothing and there was no one there. When I lay down to sleep, I heard noises everywhere, as if something was walking cautiously across the quilt on giant feet, and I would kick out, fling off the quilt, but there was nothing there. I was sure there were scorpions in the cave, and I moved every stick of furniture, table, dresser, sacks and crocks and looked all around, and then I sprinkled ash all over the floor around the *kang*, to see if any claw or other prints showed up. I was always worried that Bright's dad hadn't washed the vegetables properly before he cooked them, that they'd have eggs on them and I'd end up with parasites in my belly, sticking to my intestines, growing as long as they were. I worried that the crack down the east wall of the cave was growing wider and any day now, the cave would collapse. I got a pen and wrote my name on my arm, and the city where I'd been living, the address of the room we rented, my mum's name and the landlord's name and phone number. Then, if the cave collapsed, or the undercliff outside, and I was buried, I'd make sure to stick my arm out before I died, so the rescuers would find me and send my body back home.

I sat at the cave door, sat on the stone used for beating clothes on, to the left of the door, without moving, as the morning hours went by. At noon, I gazed at the hills and gullies and knolls far away. Distance seemed to soften them so they looked like watery billows. I longed to escape from this ocean and climb back on dry land again. But when the sun set and it turned chilly and the light left the strip, the sea suddenly died, and I was left like a stranded fish.

I heard Bright's dad talking. He stood propped against Great-Grandad's doorway and I could see his legs and feet, and the heels of his shoes worn right down on one side. I couldn't see Great-Grandad at all. Bright's dad had been talking in a low voice for some time, it sounded like he was getting something off his chest and asking the old man's advice. I heard smatterings of conversation.

"When you get the millet in, don't you take the straw too?"

"If you make a pot with a crack, it's always going to leak, isn't it…"

"A one-off achievement is down to strength. A lifetime's achievement comes from virtue…"

"Here, take a gourd for Auntie Spotty-Face, go and ask her if she can do anything."

The square-shaped gourd with the character 'virtue' on it hung at my door for three days and then Auntie Spotty-Face showed up.

Bright had just gone out. Earlier, I'd heard his dad talking to him, saying I was looking thin and sallow, and he ought to get me to eat more. Bright said I didn't like the food here, it was too hot and sour.

"But we've always cooked our maize and buckwheat hot and sour to make it go down, we like strong tastes," said his dad. "But if she won't eat hot and sour, go and get some sweet rice starter from Spring-Starts and La-Ba, and make her some sweet fermented rice."

So off Bright went. His dad was chipping away at a stone on the strip when Auntie Spotty-Face arrived.

"Have you eaten?" he greeted her and went to fetch her a stool from inside his cave. I came out of the shit-house and hadn't got as far as the cave door when Auntie Spotty-Face came fluttering over to me like a hen and grabbed my arm.

"Let me look at our Bright's wife!"

A cloud passed over the ridge above us and it was like a curtain being drawn and the strip was plunged into gloom. Auntie Spotty-Face examined me from head to foot, her eyes like gimlets, and exclaimed loudly that my face "shone", as she put it, "like glass". I wriggled out of her grip, muttered that I had a headache, and went into the cave and lay down.

Left on her own, she asked Bright's dad: "Have I got dirt in my hair?"

"No."

She blew into her palm and sniffed it.

"I haven't got dirt in my hair, my breath doesn't smell, what's wrong with me that you won't talk to me?" she called after me. "If your head hurts, it's a demon pinching it, I'll do you a papercut and that'll stop it."

She came in after me and sat herself down cross-legged on the edge of the *kang*.

There was no way I could sleep so I had to chat to her.

"It's not a demon, I've been beaten up," I told her.

"Who beat you up? And don't you go making up accusations. It was your father-in-law asked me to come."

"I've haven't got a father-in-law."

"That's as may be, but you've still got to call me Auntie. And your Auntie's telling you not to get it into your head to run away. If the Blacks don't treat you well, you just come and tell me and I'll sort them out. And even if you run from this strip, you'll never get out of this village, I can tell you that! You've seen a spider's web, haven't you? Once a moth or a fly gets entangled in it, they never get out, and the harder they struggle, the more entangled they get."

At that, I threw myself into her arms in floods of tears.

Once I'd started crying, I couldn't stop, I cried and I cried till the tears and snot puddled on my cheeks. Auntie Spotty-Face didn't stay long.

On her way out, Bright's dad asked her: "What's she crying like that for?"

"Let her cry it out," said Auntie Spotty-Face. "Better out than in. It's like when someone has water on the belly, tomato leaf tea gives them diarrhoea and that gets rid of it. Have you got something for me to eat?" She went into his cave but there was no cooked food, so she went off, munching on a mouli.

Auntie Spotty-Face came three days running. Bright bought ten sheets of red paper from the township and gave her one sheet by way of a thank you. She used all the other nine for her papercuts, or 'flower cuts' as she called them.

"Why do you call them 'flower cuts'?" I asked.

"Because that's what I'm cutting out," she said.

I figured out after a bit that around here was so arid that there weren't many real flowers, or much fruit either, so when someone died or you needed to make offerings to the ancestors at festivals, they used to go and buy wheat flour and make flat sheets of dough and cut them into fruit and flower shapes and deep-fry them for offerings. Then they started cutting the shapes from paper to save time and trouble. Then they started to cut them from cloth and cowhide and donkey hide, and as well as fruit and flowers, the shapes became birds and animals, mountains and rivers, and people, anything that could be cut out, but they still called them 'flower cuts'. They didn't use them as offerings any more, they were decorations, part of their everyday lives.

"It's like a husband and wife sleeping together," she told me. "First they do it to have a baby and carry on the family line. Then they do it because it gives them pleasure." She was very serious about it all. She gave me the spiel and she showed me the sort of shapes you stuck in different places: 'door flowers', 'window flowers', '*kang* flowers', 'cupboard flowers', 'crock flowers', 'pillow flowers', 'shoe flowers'... wherever you could find a space, you stuck a flower cut. Then she worked herself into a rage, cussing Tongue-Trip and the other villagers who didn't understand how important these flower cuts were. They were like prayers, and they brought the gods with them. She cut all nine sheets of paper into little red people, they had big heads, heads as big as the rest of their bodies, and each head had a little topknot on top.

She covered the whole *kang* with these figures, then stuck them up around the room: on the door, on the window and in neat little rows on the walls, then she fixed a stick over the *kang* and hung ten strings from it, and each string had four little figures on it.

She was completely absorbed in cutting out her figures: she took each sheet of paper and cut it into small squares. Then each square was folded and folded again. Then she made me sit beside her as she explained how to turn the scissors to cut a circle and how to scissor into sharp corners. I began to lose patience, my legs were going numb, and I got restless. I could hear a man outside, it must have been Tongue-Trip. He was talking to Bright's dad and he sounded annoyed: "I've got a cold hearth and no food at home, and she... she's here at your house, what's that all about?"

"I asked her to come and do flower cuts," said Bright's dad.

"But she's... she's g-got a sc-screw l-loose, she doesn't know... know wh... what she's doing, and you're just egg... egging her on!" Tongue-Trip stuttered.

"I'm paying her, so she's earning money for you, cheer up!" said Bright's dad. He got a coin out and gave it to Tongue-Trip, who bowed and went away. Auntie Spotty-Face bent her head over her cuttings, acting as if she hadn't heard what was going on outside the cave. I slipped off the *kang* and looked for my shoes. At the foot of the *kang* were my shoes, Bright's shoes and Auntie Spotty-Face's little pointy-toed cloth shoes. I picked up Bright's, thinking to throw them in a corner, but on an impulse threw them at Auntie Spotty-Face's back instead. That stopped her in her tracks.

"Why can't you sit still, you little monkey?" she said angrily.

"I'm fidgety."

"Your soul's gone walkabout."

"I'm just a walking corpse."

"These little people will call your soul back."

"I'm not coming back!"

She put her scissors down and made me get back on the *kang*. She searched me with her gaze, gimlet-eyed, and her eyes suddenly looked funny, the corners turned up and the pupils were enormous, and they had a weird gleam in them. She told me a story. About fifty years ago when she was just fourteen, her mum, who was a dressmaker, took her to a salt merchant's house to make clothes. One night, the salt merchant raped her and so she became his concubine. The man's wife was brutal, if Auntie Spotty-Face didn't do things to her liking, she made the girl kneel on a washboard. The salt merchant never intervened to protect her. She gave birth to a baby, and then she ran away. She got as far as Shanxi province and met a soldier, twenty years older than her, but a good man. He gave her all his earnings and she collected a whole jar of silver dollars. She had a child with him too. The war was still on and his unit moved south. For two years she didn't know if he was dead or alive. Famine struck, and she fled with the children. On the road, the children got typhoid and died. She married into this village. But three years later, the soldier turned up looking for her. When he learned that she had a new husband and couldn't go back to him, he slapped her around the face and left. He was right to hit her, she didn't take it amiss. Her third husband was a handsome man when he was young, though he was tongue-tied and had a foul temper. He beat her for every little thing, for not being able to cook, for laughing and talking too much and for not giving him a child. She did get pregnant once, but the baby was born deformed and didn't survive. She didn't conceive again. So here she was, living with Tongue-Trip and his temper was worse than ever now he was old. He still beat her all the time.

"So you see," she finished, "I've had three men in my life and I've realised that it doesn't make any difference how hard you try, you sleep where you sleep."

She finished her story and laughed so her face was all one big open mouth. The laugh made me think she was half-witted, but she was interesting, and I sat there after that, letting her talk and watching her cutting, helping her fold the paper and even trying a few cuts myself. But though I followed her instructions, my 'flowers' came out wonky. She yelled at me for being clumsy and set me to sticking up her figures on the walls with flour paste.

When we finished, I don't know why but I sneezed three times in a row, and then I felt so sleepy, my eyelids kept drooping and they felt like they were glued together, I just couldn't keep my eyes open. Finally, I lay down on the *kang* and began to doze. I sensed Auntie Spotty-Face gathering up the bits of paper, some as big as a coin, others as small as a thumbnail. Then she chuckled to herself and I heard her go out.

I opened my eyes enough to see her go out of the door and I tried to follow, but when I stood up, the door seemed very far away, I could see the light outside but I just couldn't get there. The walls were flickering and when I touched them they felt soft, like the walls were covered with a layer of sponge. I carried on trying to move towards the door and the walls on either side closed in on me, till they made a tunnel, and I was wedged in, the room got narrower and smaller till my shoulders were squashed together, really hard, and I was completely stuck and couldn't budge. I heard my bones begin to crack.

"Auntie Spotty-Face!" I cried out in fright. "Auntie Spotty-Face!"

I woke myself up shouting. I was breathing fast and covered in sweat. It was only a dream. I'd had a dream once before, about losing a foot falling out of an apricot tree, which I'd climbed to pick the only ripe fruit I could see. All the rest were green. This one was at the very top of the tree, yellow flecked with red. I put my foot on the branch, to test whether it would take my weight, then I reached out to pick the fruit. But the branch broke, and I found myself falling, down and down. The next day, I told my mum this dream. It means you're growing up, she said. But this dream wasn't anything like the apricot one. What did it mean?

Out on the strip, Bright's dad was paying Auntie Spotty-Face.

"I gave Tongue-Trip twenty," he said. "And here's fifty more for you."

Auntie Spotty-Face was furious: "Tongue-Trip's shameless! He beats me then he takes my money!"

"Has she quietened down?" asked Bright's dad.

"Yes, she fell asleep right after we stuck the little red people up. She's going to be tired for a bit longer, dog-tired, so you need to keep an eye on what she's eating for a few more days and make sure she doesn't go missing meals."

"It wouldn't matter if she was missing an arm or a leg, or a fool or a cripple, just so long as she's one of us and living in our cave, I'll make sure she's well-fed and well looked after."

"Don't say stuff like that!" exclaimed Auntie Spotty-Face, and Bright's dad laughed.

"Will she settle down, then?" he asked.

"For heaven's sake, stop worrying," said Auntie Spotty-Face. "I wasn't my mistress's pupil for nothing! I know what I'm doing."

I felt drained of every ounce of energy, I didn't even have the strength to cry or swear or throw things, not like I used to. Bright undid the dog chain, and he gave me back my high-heeled shoes too. But he refused to kip down by the table leg any more, he said we were husband and wife now, we knew everything about each other, so why shouldn't he get on the *kang*? Up he climbed and I didn't protest. I thought, so long as no more men came and tied me down hand and foot, Bright wouldn't do that to me again. So I just got a stick and laid it down the middle of the *kang*. "That's my side, on the inside," I said. "And you're on the outside."

One day around then, a big crowd turned up on the strip – Eight-Jin, Monkey, Full-Barn and Snatch among them – all griping about the monopoly that the brothers Spring-Starts and La-Ba had over the sales of blood onions. "They're a local speciality, they don't belong just to them. They can't just monopolise them!" They wanted Bright to set up a production company that they would all join in. Bright refused. In his view, setting up another company would mean that everyone's sales dropped and would destroy the blood onion brand. But his words had no effect, they were still furious.

"Just look at how those two are living it up now!"

"In the old days when times were really hard, you laughed at them," said Bright's dad. "Now they're doing a bit better, you're green with envy!"

Just then, some women, all in their fifties or sixties and looking dishevelled and dirty, turned up chattering loudly. ("What a bunch of twittering old hags," said Eight-Jin.) They'd come in search of Great-Grandad.

"We're going to dig for nonesuch flowers again, we know they're hard to find, but even if we only get a few and earn a few cents from them, it's still better than sitting at home with nothing to do. Great-Grandad, what's the weather going to do the next few days, is there going to be rain or wind? Will we have any luck?"

The men all jeered: "We men can't find nonesuch flowers, what makes you think women can piss higher than us?"

The women were outraged: "Eight-Jin, do you bleed?"

"I've got piles, how did you know?"

"And how many days do you bleed?"

"Days? I'd be dead if I bled for half a day!"

"Well, women bleed for seven days every month! Now who do you think are the stronger, men or women?"

The rowdy arguments and laughter continued, but Great-Grandad didn't say a word, just carried on sitting under the gourd frame writing characters on each gourd. The gourds had all been picked and lay in baskets, some round, some square, some as big as a plate, others small as a fist. Each one had characters written on the front like Virtue, Humanity and

Piety, and he was writing something on the back too. When he'd finished, everyone took one and he let them, just carried on sitting there, smoking. He used a pipe with a very long stem so he wouldn't set his beard on fire when he lit it. Eight-Jin took a gourd, and so did Full-Barn and Monkey. Bright wandered over to see what Great-Grandad had written on the gourds, but he couldn't read anything and got me to take a look. The gourds had three strange characters on them:

"I can only count the number of strokes, I can't read them, maybe they're more characters from before the Qin Emperor unified the writing system," I said.

"So you can have mine," said Eight-Jin.

"Don't you want one with Great-Grandad's writing on it?" I asked. But Full-Barn and Monkey gave me theirs too, and off they went.

That night, when we were on the *kang*, Bright asked me: "Could you really not read those three characters, or you just didn't want to say?"

"They weren't proper characters," I said. "No characters have that many strokes in them."

"I asked Great-Grandad," Bright said. "They mean good luck."

"Really?"

"And Monkey and Full-Barn and Eight-Jin gave theirs to you, so you've got all the good luck!"

"Then let me dream!" I said, and went right to sleep.

But Bright fidgeted all night, pawing me with his hand or reaching out with his leg, until I hit him with the *kang* brush.

"It's addictive, I want it after every meal. Don't you?"

I sat up at that, I'd stay awake the rest of the night.

I was so worried about nodding off that I sat at the window. Bright had hung curtains in front but I pulled them back, and let the breeze blow over me and the smell of bird droppings in the pines get up my nose. What a strange place this was, where men who couldn't find a woman ate blood onions, a woman got her period for seven days, where people were so poor that they couldn't afford good stuff like rice, and tried every which way to make the coarse grains they ate taste good, and hardly any of them had gone to school but they had characters with fifty or sixty strokes apiece. I looked up at the sky. What a lot of stars, except right above the pine tree, where it was pitch-black. I stared and stared, wondering if I was going to be lucky, but though I stared till daybreak, I couldn't find my star.

Chapter 4

THE MOUNTAIN WALKED

ONE MORNING AUNTIE Spotty-Face came by to ask if I wanted to go with her to the temple ruins on West Ridge. It was Buddha Washing Day and even though the temple and the Buddha weren't there any more, the place had spiritual power. Every year, a small cloud would hover over the ruins and a shower of rain would fall right onto the old locust tree, nowhere else. Bright's dad, who was sat there mending his clothes clutching the needle between his fingers, squinted at her and waved his hand in the air.

"What's the matter, won't the thread go through the eye?" she asked.

Bright's dad grunted and then said to me: "Isn't Bright taking you to the township with him?" Just then, the dog ran onto the strip and he yelled at it: "Why don't you stay at home like a good dog, and quit wandering off?"

He was obviously not happy that Auntie Spotty-Face had invited me to West Ridge, but she paid no attention.

"OK, then you go to town," she said with a laugh, and off she went.

In fact, there was no way Bright would ever take me with him to town. He'd left before dawn to buy supplies, and when he arrived back at the strip with the tractor, he brought three men with him: the village boss and Spring-Starts, and another man with a potbelly. I already knew that the village boss was an exhibitionist; if he ever had so much as a single banknote, he'd stick it to his forehead to make sure everyone knew about it. Today he was wearing tracksuit bottoms tied with string above the ankles so they ballooned like lanterns, and as soon as he was off the tractor, he began to pace up and down.

Bright's dad duly asked: "Bought new trousers again, did you?"

"You can't get trousers like this in the township!"

"They're a proper brand, are they?"

"I have to have branded gear, otherwise I itch all over."

"The meat's maggoty but he still keeps the meat rack," Bright's dad muttered.

Then he thought better of it, laughed and clapped the boss on the shoulder.

"Did Spring-Start buy them for you?"

"Well, yes, but he's tight-fisted, he got me the trousers but no shoes to go with them. Even though I helped them set up the blood onion company!"

Bright came into the cave with a bag of steamed buns and a bunch of blood onions. He got a bun out and offered it to me, but I was combing my hair and when I didn't take it, he put it down on the edge of the *kang*. "I brought you a treat!" he said. I still paid no attention. I looked at myself in the mirror. My face was thin and sallow, I wasn't my old self at all.

Outside, Spring-Starts was laughing loudly. I heard the village boss ask the fat man: "What brand are your shoes?"

"Nike," said the man, hitching his droopy trousers up over his big belly.

"Spring-Starts, they're Nike," said the village boss.

Spring-Starts' buck teeth seemed to be sticking out even more than usual, like spades. He was lighting the brazier for Bright's dad so they could have some tea.

"We zipped along today. The road's good, it's just that there's a lot of dust," he said.

The village boss spoke again: "I'm talking to you and you just play deaf!"

"I heard, you said Nike," said Spring Starts. "And you'll get a pair too just so long as business is good."

Blindy brought a bucket over and poured water into the kettle. "How are the blood onions going?" he asked.

"You're not getting any," said Spring-Starts. Blindy over-filled the kettle and the water spilled out.

"Go and sit down, Uncle," said Bright. He stacked some dried corn cobs in the brazier and lit them.

I eavesdropped: I heard that Spring-Starts had met Pot-Belly in the township. Pot-Belly was a businessman from out of town and was considering getting into blood onions, but he wanted to check out where and how they were produced. Just then, Bright happened to turn up on his tractor, so he brought them both back. Then they bumped into the village boss coming into the village, and now here they were at the Blacks.

"Mr Shi," said the village boss. "Speaking as the village boss, I'd like to say how awesome blood onions are!"

"They're just onions," said Pot-Belly.

"Not just onions! When the man eats them, the woman gets worn out. When the woman eats them, the man gets worn out. When they both eat them, the *kang*'s worn out!"

"That's what they say about all aphrodisiacs."

"Blood onions aren't aphrodisiacs," the village boss insisted, "they're ten times stronger. Plus they have no side-effects. Listen to this, an old villager, pushing eighty-two..."

"Yes," Pot-Belly interrupted. "Spring-Starts told me."

"Spring-Starts told you? Bright! Bright!"

Bright was adding tea leaves to the kettle on the brazier. "Just give it a moment to brew," he said.

"You're a newly-wed," the village boss told him. "Get Butterfly out here, get her to say what it feels like when you eat blood onions!"

I swore under my breath, stopped looking in the mirror, and went and pulled the curtains across the window. But Bright came in all the same.

"We've got a visitor, a businessman, come out and say hello."

I was furious: "Am I an escort girl now?"

Bright went out again.

"My wife's got a cold, she's in bed," he said.

"Hah! That's no cold, the blood onions have worn her out!" said the village boss. "That's the only thing with our blood onions, you mustn't eat too many."

"Spring-Starts, let's go and see your wife, she's eaten blood onions, show our friend here what kind of a woman she is!"

"Fine, fine," said Spring-Starts, and a small posse of them set off for his house.

"But the tea's just ready," Bright's dad protested, "and I was making a meal, and now they've all gone!"

When they'd disappeared, Bright said to me: "It's a good thing you didn't come out to talk to him. He may be rich, but he reeks of cologne, he must have terrible BO!"

I said: "You're all so foul-mouthed, you're like houseflies that can't stay away from the shit-house."

"The village boss's just doing propaganda, but it's true blood onions really do work, I ate three that first evening."

Bright went to wipe down his tractor, and I took the laundry-beating club to the blood onions he'd brought in, and pounded them to a pulp.

But then I got pregnant.

Not that I knew it at first. I realised my period hadn't come, they always used to last three days and then they were over and done with, but those three days I used to have terrible backache, so this time I was really happy to have no pain. But then I started getting dizzy and feeling sick. One day, I was sitting listlessly at the cave door, and I saw Great-Grandad talking to someone under the gourd frame. It sounded like the man was sick and was asking Great-Grandad to examine him.

"I'm not a doctor, I can't examine you."

"But you've got an almanac, that's got everything in it."

So Great-Grandad took a chopstick and pressed it down on his tongue.

"Say aaah...'

The man aaahed for a bit, then said: "I'll go and get some herbal medicine from Doctor Wu in Wang village, that'll see it off."

"Is it going to rain today?" Great-Grandad asked him.

The man emerged from under the frame, gave me a quick smile and looked up at the sky: "Probably. There are clouds over South Ridge."

"Then you've picked up something nasty, who've you been quarrelling with?"

"That simpleton son of mine, we're at loggerheads right now. He's been out of the village, and someone's been getting at him. Every day he comes back home and asks me to find him a wife. I told him, the fittest, healthiest men can't find a wife, how am I supposed to find a wife for a fool like you? And you know what he said? 'If you don't find me a wife, you'll never rest when you die, you'll be a ghost with no descendants to look after you!' Where does he get stuff like that from? Some fucker's been egging him on!"

Great-Grandad said: "When your tongue's better, maybe someone will find a daughter-in-law for you."

"This tongue's going to give Triple-Edge a tongue-lashing if he gives me trouble again!"

"What's Triple-Edge got to do with it?"

"Triple-Edge put a rock on his dad's grave, and it's facing my dad's grave, right in the way of our family's *feng shui.* What do you think, should I put a rock on my dad's grave too?"

"Why not? It sounds like his rock's really blocking your family's *feng shui,* so you put a stone on it."

"Triple-Edge is a mother-fucker!... And did you hear about Spring-Starts?"

"If you've been that sick, how come you're so busy sticking your nose into other people's affairs?"

"Well, it's like this, everyone's saying that Spring-Starts took Mr Shi to his home to sell him a big load of onions and fix a time for him to come and pick them up, and when Mr Shi clapped eyes on Rice, he knew right away who she was! Spring-Starts' wife used to be a prostitute in the township! How about that?"

Great-Grandad suddenly had a fit of coughing. The other man, a big guy with an under-sized head, really put me off. His eyes pulsated when he blinked, like a hen's arse crapping. And what gave him the right to call Rice a prostitute? If she really was and Mr Shi recognised her, then that meant he went with prostitutes. I felt too lazy to move, but then I picked up the broom and started to sweep a chicken out of the way – it scrambled to the left, I swept it to the right, and it squawked and fled to the gourd frame. Great-Grandad was still coughing and spluttering, and Big Guy said to me: "Why are you chasing that chicken away, you've made it lose a feather and the feather's got stuck in Great-Grandad's throat!"

"I'll chase you away next!" I said. And I gave him a prod.

Not that he budged, until Great-Grandad waved him away, and he reluctantly left, muttering curses at me as he went. Great-Grandad spat a gob of phlegm and stopped coughing.

"You're a firecracker, Butterfly!" he said.

"Was he having a go at Spring-Starts, or is he jealous of him?" I asked. "You said he'd picked up something nasty, but he's the one who's nasty!"

"All small animals have something nasty on them, they wouldn't exist otherwise," said Great-Grandad. "Butterfly, this is the first time you've been as far as my place, is your father-in-law out?"

"If I don't come out on the strip, then you can't help me run away from here."

He laughed but it was just a snort and his face was as impassive as ever.

"Haven't you seen your star yet?"

"Great-Grandad, you're pulling my leg. How can I see a star in a star-less bit of the sky?"

"You keep looking, you'll find it one day."

"Oh yeah? When?"

Great-Grandad stood up: "Butterfly, I've got to go to West Gully to catch scorpions. The sun's setting so they'll be coming out. When the scorpion wine's ready, you can come over and have some."

"Don't worry, Great-Grandad, I won't get you into trouble." I felt sick all of a sudden and screwed up my face.

"I'm not worried," he said. "I'm not afraid of anyone, they're afraid of me."

"Everyone in the village respects you," I said.

"Respect... you respect the gods, you've got to respect the demons too." I had no idea what he meant. Then he went on: "Butterfly, are you feeling all right?"

"No, I'm not, but there's no clinic round here and no medicine either."

"You're the medicine, you're the Black's medicine."

I didn't understand that either.

"Are you off your food?"

"Yes."

"Do you feel sick?"

"Yes, but nothing comes up."

"Put your hand over your mouth and breathe into it. What can you smell?"

"A weird sour smell."

"You're pregnant!"

I flushed scarlet, I didn't know what to say, everything looked fuzzy and the gourd frame started swaying, and the strip, and there were two Great-Grandads standing there. "I can't be! How can I be pregnant?" And I broke out into a cold sweat. "Great-Grandad! Great-Grandad! You've got to help me, I can't be pregnant! No way! Great-Grandad!"

"This child is your medicine too," he said.

"Great-Grandad!"

"Off you go now."

I went, walking like I was in a dream. I got to the cave and fell on the *kang*.

I didn't dare tell Bright I was pregnant. I grew more and more afraid and anxious, my forehead sprouted pimples, I got horribly constipated, and the moment Bright wasn't there, I'd start pressing my belly, jerking my legs and even jumping down from the *kang* and the table, hoping that this vile thing would drop out of me just like a turd. Me, a clean, untouched bit of soil, I didn't want to be buried in filth, I didn't want the seed of that hateful crime growing inside me. But I couldn't get rid of it. So I didn't go out onto the strip any more, I stayed shut up in the cave like I used to, peering mutely out of the window day in, day out.

A month before, Blindy had said he was going to build himself a new *kang*. He took the old one apart and piled the mud from the old one under the pine, it made the best fertiliser, he said. Then he asked Bright's dad whether he should grind up peas or black beans for the mule. Bright's dad said to leave the black beans because they'd sprout, grind some peas instead, and not many of them. "I'm feeding the old *kang* mud to the earth, to give the soil a good meal."

He harnessed the mule to the millstone but the beast wouldn't cooperate and the rope fell off. "Look where you're going!" Blindy yelled at it. "Haven't I given you enough peas to eat? Or is there too much *kang* mud?"

That made me look at the pile of *kang* mud, and suddenly I felt a pang of distress. Just the little bit of rain we'd had in the last few days had made three little sprouts appear. Were they grass, or beans, or tree seeds sprouting? They were so small and tender and green, what were they doing growing on the old *kang* earth? They were supposed to grow in the right kind of soil with enough water, then they could dream of growing into vegetables or flowers or trees, and here they were sprouting on a pile of old mud under the pines that would soon be cleared away and shovelled onto the fields. Poor little sprouts, other lives were wonderful, but theirs were destined to be nasty, brutish and short!

I stopped eating or drinking, or talking to anyone. I really was falling ill.

That scared the Blacks. Bright stayed home instead of going to his shop, asked me where I hurt and offered to take me to the doctor in Wang village. I didn't want the doctor to look at me so I said I had a cold, and I'd be fine if I had a good sleep. Black's dad made an effort with his cooking. He made stews of boiled millet, potatoes, bean vermicelli and pickled cabbage. He made buckwheat or cat's ears noodles, other times it was shredded potato and vegetables, or a casserole of pumpkin and green beans. Or he bought mutton and boiled it with red and white radishes. I got five meals a day and they watched every bit go down.

One day, as I was eating, Auntie Spotty-Face turned up. She was still at the entrance to the strip when she exclaimed: "That smells good!"

Bright's dad had been friendly when she came and cut out the little red figures, but the last time she arrived he was very curt, and it was the same this time too.

"Tea?" he offered.

"No, thanks, your tea's too strong for me."

"Have you had your dinner?"

"Yes, I had buckwheat noodles in soup."

"So you won't be sitting down then."

"Are you trying to get rid of me? Didn't I come and make papercuts for Butterfly?" She came into the cave, opened a cloth bundle and spread more paper cuttings on the *kang*. "He's so stingy, your father-in-law, he's got mutton in the pot and he won't give me a sup of it! Now, tell me, which is the prettiest."

But I wasn't in the mood for that. I shut the cave door and fell to my knees.

"Auntie, please save me!"

"That father-in-law of yours, he's an ungrateful so-and-so. Has Bright been beating you?"

"I'm pregnant! Can you help me get rid of it?" Auntie Spotty-Face didn't seem in the least surprised or put out. She told me to stand up and turn around so she could look at me, then she pulled back my eyelids and inspected my nipples. "You're just the same as I was, my first time."

And she told me her story: the first time she got pregnant, she didn't know, she was just horribly sick. The salt merchant's chief wife could see, however, and on the pretext of treating her nausea, gave her an infusion of chinaberry seeds, which made her lose the baby. After her miscarriage, she found out that the wife was worried that if she had a child, she would fight for a share in the inheritance. She got pregnant again after that and became the salt merchant's concubine.

"But you were different," I said. "I can't have a child, I'm begging you to give me some chinaberry seeds."

"But you're wanting me to do something wicked. A child's another life!"

"And don't you care about my life? If you don't give me chinaberry seeds, then I'll die and if I die, the child will die too!"

Auntie Spotty-Face thought for a bit, then she agreed.

"When you drink it, mind, you mustn't let anyone see, not even the chickens or the dog!"

True to her word, the next time Auntie Spotty-Face came, she had a pocketful of chinaberry seeds. She told me there was a tree at the village entrance. When no one was looking, I made the infusion and drank a cupful, putting the seeds in a hole in the *kang*. I'd make myself another later, to make sure it was going to work. When it came to the third cup, I mashed up the seeds, which made the tea horribly bitter and gave me a bellyache. I thought that would start the abortion, but all that happened was I got diarrhoea. I went to the shit-house five times that morning and eventually collapsed from dehydration.

When Bright's dad saw that as well as my 'cold', I had diarrhoea and was getting sicker, he went and talked to Great-Grandad, who was under the gourd frame making his scorpion wine. That was when Great-Grandad told him I was pregnant and advised against taking any medicine, even if I did have diarrhoea. When I overheard them talking from the window, I almost fainted from fright. Just then, Auntie Spotty-Face turned up with more chinaberry seeds. She had just walked onto the strip when Bright's dad hurried up and announced I was pregnant. He was over the moon. My heart was in my mouth because I was worried that Auntie Spotty-Face would give the game away. But she just laughed loudly, and Bright's dad laughed along with her.

"Did Butterfly tell you?" she asked.

"No."

"Did Bright tell you?"

"No, he doesn't know yet. It was Great-Grandad, he could tell by the way she looked."

Auntie Spotty-Face clapped her hands: "Well, I knew she was tinder to the flame, but I never imagined it would happen so quickly! You've got me to thank for that, it was my little red people who called down this new soul."

Bright's dad gave her ten yuan.

"You're being very generous all of a sudden!" she exclaimed.

"You're the first to know in the village, this is for good luck!"

"Well, if you want me to spread the good news, then I need a handout, don't I?"

Bright's dad took the hint and stuffed another ten yuan in her pocket. He felt the chinaberry seeds.

"What have you got those in there for?" he asked, but without much interest, and Auntie Spotty-Face just laughed and came in to see me.

Now that news of my pregnancy was out, I wanted rid of it as soon as possible. That afternoon, I mashed up all the remaining seeds and drank the infusion.

When Bright got back that evening, he came into the cave, put his arms around me and tried to kiss me, but I wouldn't let him.

"My breath doesn't smell!" he protested, and then: "How come you never told me the great news?"

I said nothing, and then his dad called us: "Come and get your dinner!"

I could hear them talking outside.

"What's for dinner?"

"Chicken stew."

"That noisy cockerel, you cooked that one?"

"I cooked the black hen."

"But it was still laying!"

"Never mind, black hen soup is very nutritious."

When we had had dinner, Bright went and sat on the *kang*.

"I've really made another human being!" he exclaimed, drumming his hands in excitement on the edge of the *kang*. "What shall we call it? Let's choose two names... if it's a boy, it can be Steel-Hard, and if it's a girl, Nonesuch-Flower."

"You can't call her 'Nonesuch-Flower'!" I said. I don't know why I said that, was it because a nonesuch flower was a plant and a grub or because it was special to me? Either way I sounded shrill, my voice sharp as a knife.

"All right, we won't then," said Bright. "We'll call her Heart's-Desire." And he got a thin mattress out of the trunk and laid it on the *kang*.

"You're important now," he added. "You need a good night's sleep and nothing's going to get in the way of that, not even a bean."

As he was arranging the mattress, he came across the chinaberry seeds I'd hidden under the matting and casually threw them out of the window. And that was my fate sealed. Great-Grandad happened to be passing by and picked them up.

Bright's dad, who had emerged to tip out the pot-washing water, spoke to him: "Hey, are you going out? Take Bright with you if you are."

Great-Grandad was still looking at the seeds: "What are these doing in your cave?"

And Bright's dad chimed in: "Why have you got chinaberry seeds?"

Great-Grandad muttered something to him in an undertone, and then Bright's dad called Bright out. When Bright came back, he had a face like thunder.

"Did you drink chinaberry seed tea?" he demanded. "Did you? Were you trying to hurt my baby, eh?"

I was defeated. I knew that now. I faced him, my nostrils flaring, my breath coming ragged, then wrapped myself in the quilt and lay down on the *kang*, with my back to him. Bright gave a howl and raised his fists to strike me, but stopped himself just in time. He kicked the bags, he kicked the stool over, and it creaked and groaned, he grabbed it and threw it at the door. The door flew open, the stool broke and one leg flew onto the strip.

Outside the cave, Bright's dad was shouting: "Bright, have you gone crazy? If you want to hit anyone, hit that wretched woman! All those spots on her face, I knew she was no good. She brought them, she brought the seeds."

Bright ran out of the cave and must have gone into his dad's cave for the vegetable knife because I heard: "Bright, put that knife down! Go and ask her about it if you want, but don't get into trouble." The dog was barking wildly and Blindy got up and came out and grabbed Bright, but he couldn't hold onto him.

"You go with him, stop him getting into trouble," Bright's dad urged Blindy. I heard footsteps. Blindy normally shuffled along in backless slippers during the daytime, you could hear them flapping as he walked. When he ran after Bright, I heard nothing so he must have gone barefoot.

I never found out whether Auntie Spotty-Face really got a beating from Bright and Blindy. The next morning, Tongue-Trip came to apologise to

Bright's dad, said he'd beaten that witch so hard he'd broken her bones and she was in bed, he was welcome to go and see if he didn't believe him. Bright's dad didn't say anything, and he didn't go either. I stayed in the cave crying. I was talking to Bright again, in fact I told him he shouldn't blame Auntie Spotty-Face, I'd got her to bring me the chinaberry seeds, and now she'd ended up with broken bones, maybe even paralysed. I begged him to go and see her. Bright told me that Tongue-Trip hadn't broken anything, he'd just knocked out her front teeth. But Auntie Spotty-Face didn't come to the Blacks' caves for a long time after that.

It was nearly winter and the corn cobs and pea stalks were piling up on the strip. The Blacks laid out the corn cobs and brought back bundles of pea stalks with the pea pods still on them. When the peas had dried in the sun, they beat the peas out of the pods with flails. Bright hardly ever went to the township or the county town to pick up supplies for his shop. Instead, he spent his days with his uncle Blindy digging up potatoes and harvesting pumpkins. They wouldn't let me go and help, and I couldn't be bothered to anyway, so instead I sat by the piles of peas, watching the ladybirds crawling in and out. There were plenty of them, all rusty red, the colour of my blouse, except that they had white spots on them too, like stars. If I poked them with a twig they flew away. They were luckier than me, I thought. Then a locust came crawling out from the peas. Before I could poke it, it bounced over to the edge of the strip, hop, hop, hop, then another four hops, then it keeled over, wiggled its four legs in the air, and died.

Three-Lobes came by one day. Great-Grandad muttered something to him and Three-Lobes went into Bright's dad's cave. The old man was busy cooking, enveloped in a cloud of smoke. There was more muttering, and the pair of them came out of the cave.

"Three-Lobes, I'm going to be grateful to you for this," said Bright's dad.

"When you hold your grandson in your arms, then you can thank me."

Three-Lobes made off in a great hurry, smiling at me as he passed. All this secretive muttering was getting me worried, but Three-Lobes' smile was genuinely kind. I couldn't work out what they were up to.

I sat there listlessly watching an ant. When it went to the left, I gouged out a channel with the twig on the left, and it turned and headed to the right instead. So I gouged out another channel. It went straight ahead.

Another deep channel in its way. Just then seven or eight people slipped onto the strip, some with corn cobs, others with pumpkins, potatoes and aubergines. Silently they went into my cave. "What are you doing?" I yelled at them. They came out empty-handed and slipped away as silently as they'd come. Bright's dad was standing at the door of his cave, seemingly not bothered. He threw me a meaningful look – but I had no idea what that meant. Then another half-dozen people turned up with corn, potatoes, aubergines, pumpkins, and even a big wax gourd carried between two of them, and deposited them in my cave. Once they'd all gone, I went to have a look... the *kang* was covered in the vegetables. Bright arrived.

"Did they bring the gifts for the baby?" he asked his dad.

"Don't say anything, just pull the quilt over them, then take them off at nightfall."

When Bright came into the cave and saw I'd thrown all the corn cobs onto the table, he hurriedly covered them up with the quilt.

"These are for our child to eat!" he said. "It's a village custom, when a newly-married woman doesn't get pregnant for a while, the villagers filch a few bits and pieces from someone's autumn harvest and leave them on the woman's *kang*. A dozen or so years ago, Tongue-Trip got them all to make offerings to his *kang*, but everyone argued he was just trying to get himself a bit of extra fruit and veg, so they stopped doing it. This time around, it's nothing to do with me and my dad, Great-Grandad got Three-Lobes to organise it. The villagers don't know you're pregnant yet, but Great-Grandad believes it'll help keep the baby inside, after all that chinaberry tea you've been drinking, so me and my dad have gone along with it."

I grunted and sat down at the table and looked at the nonesuch flower in its frame.

I didn't lose the baby and it kept on growing. Meantime, the old year finished, New Year came and went, springtime gusted along, every morning Padlock went and wept on his wife's grave, and my belly got bigger and bigger. My dizziness and nausea got worse, and every time I sat down, I had to spit saliva. I cursed this baby, it was a spawn of the village all right, giving me a hard time just like the rest of them. Sometimes I took a turn on the strip, but I soon got tired and went back to sleep on the *kang*. That was uncomfortable too, and I would get up and go out again. My legs started to swell. I took to sitting under Great-Grandad's gourd frame. The old vine tendrils were still there and new shoots were growing, putting out beard-like wisps that moved as if they were alive and then gripped the frame supports and strained upwards. Great-Grandad told me I ought to get up and move around more, instead of sitting down all the time. I'd lost all hope that the old man might help me, no one around here would.

I said to him: "You just don't want me sitting here, right?"

"No!" he said. "You belong right where you are."

"I don't belong anywhere," I told him. "Do I even belong to me?"

Great-Grandad looked at me and went back in his cave.

Maybe he wasn't going to come out of his cave again because I'd contradicted him. I took a stick and started poking a sour date bush that was growing out of a hole and up over the edge of the strip. There were still a few shrivelled dates from last year on it. But then Great-Grandad came out again with a bowl of water, and he sprinkled it on the vine roots. Without looking at me, he spoke: "When you can't see your way forward, fasten on a little thing to help you see the big thing. However big heaven and earth are, everything comes down to you, so then you take the big thing to help you see the little thing. You are the heavens and the earth."

When he'd finished watering, he added: "If you'd like a date, I've got a few left in the jar from last year." He brought three out of the cave and gave them to me. "Boy baby sour, girl baby spicy."

I threw them at the dog who swallowed them, then spat them out.

I didn't move. My mouth flooded with saliva and I spat. I spat wherever I felt like and the ground in front of me was covered in spittle. Great-Grandad sat down too and looked as if he was dozing off. That was something he often did, but now he spoke, even though he had his eyes shut:

"Are you upset with me, Butterfly?"

"No, you're just a villager."

"Now this child has come to you, you have to accept it."

"But it's come to hurt me."

"Some might say it's come to save you."

My mouth flooded again and I spat.

Blindy sat at his cave door plaiting straw. One end of the frame was hooked to the door frame, the other was attached to the rope tied around his waist, and he used both hands to rub the dried dragon's beard grass he used for the braiding. The donkey was having a good roll on the strip, three times it rolled over, making a cloud of dust, braying loudly. Blindy sometimes plaited home-made shoes but today he was weaving a rectangular straw mat. When he'd finished, he threw it over to us.

"Great-Grandad, I've made you a mat."

"He's made it for you," said Great-Grandad.

I sat on it. Blindy was a nice guy.

"Haven't you seen your star yet?" asked Great-Grandad.

"It's like you're drawing me a flatbread but I'd rather have a real potato."

"You've got a baby now, there might be two of them. Two stars to watch over you."

Two stars to watch over me. Was I waiting for stars to shine down on me? It sounded like a saying, but it wasn't one I'd heard before. Maybe Great-Grandad had made it up himself. I looked up at his gaunt figure sitting there, his eyes tight shut. His skin was the same colour as the undercliff, so he looked like a lump emerging from the exposed earth. What a strange man to live in this remote village, rough-hewn but sharp, ordinary but mysterious too. When I was with him, I felt as if I was made of glass.

"Great-Grandad. Great-Grandad," I began. I wanted to go on but I didn't know what else to say. I heard a gentle snoring. Now he really was asleep.

The eighteenth of the first lunar month was Great-Grandad's birthday. We were still celebrating the New Year when Bright said to the old man: "I'm going to town tomorrow to buy some meat. We can have a party!"

But Great-Grandad said: "Buy meat for your wife. What's there to celebrate?"

"It'll be for both of you!" Bright laughed. "You eat the meat, she can have the broth!"

But Great-Grandad was having none of it. "You tell them in the village, I'm not having a birthday this year, if anyone comes to wish me happy birthday, I'm not inviting them to dinner and I'm not accepting any invitations either."

On the morning of the eighteenth, the villagers trickled onto the strip, carrying not birthday cake but food of one sort or another: a scoop of buckwheat, a bag of corn cobs, a jar of rice or a *jin* of peas, all proclaiming loudly that Great-Grandad should eat more, and better. His birthday presents were extra food, something I'd never even heard of before. Maybe it was their way of helping someone in this hard-scrabble place, on the pretext that they were celebrating his birthday. The village boss was in charge, lining everyone up on the strip and preparing to make his speech.

"How long you live depends on how much you eat," he began. "The more you eat, the more years you live, so we're presenting Great-Grandad today with thirty thousand *dan* of grain."

"Three million litres?" I scoffed. "That's never three million litres of grain!"

"Don't say stuff like that!" said Bright, who was standing next to me and giving my jacket a tug.

"I can't tell lies!" I retorted. Everyone on the strip was looking at me, so I went back into my cave. Bright was close on my heels.

"A scoop here and a litre there is never going to make up three million!" I said.

But Bright just said: "You look so pretty when you smile."

I shoved him out of the cave and shut the door. The village boss was still speaking: "Yes, thirty thousand *dan*! We're giving Great-Grandad a whole thirty thousand *dan* of extra grain, to wish him a long and healthy life."

The villagers took up the cry enthusiastically: "Long life to Great-Grandad! Great-Grandad!" And they surged towards his cave.

But Great-Grandad's cave was padlocked. The old man wasn't there.

The sun had gone down by the time he came back, riding the mule and carrying a sack and a long staff. He was covered in dirt, he looked exhausted, and his clothes were torn, in fact his right sleeve had come completely off. Blindy was leading the donkey and he told Bright's dad that he had come across Great-Grandad in Back Gully. Great-Grandad had gone to catch scorpions and had slipped and fallen down the slope.

"Where are you hurt?" Bright's dad asked anxiously.

Great-Grandad drew himself up to his full height and threw the stick away: "I'm not dying. With the village in this state, King Yama won't let me leave."

"Why were you catching scorpions today?"

"I made a vow, but you seem to want me dead!"

"I don't want you dead, I want you to live forever!"

Great-Grandad smiled: "You know which year Delight Liu's dad died? The year Clan-Keeper Wang's mum died?"

"Of course I do. Delight's dad died the year after they built a new cave, and Clan-Keeper Wang's mum died the winter he took that cripple as his wife. Delight wanted a new cave his whole life and he did it when he was seventy-one, he got one year living in it. Clan-Keeper Wang's mum was pulling her hair out to try and find her son a wife, and she finally managed to find him a cripple. She said a load had fallen from her shoulders and now she wanted to enjoy life a bit, but the cripple hadn't cooked her mother-in-law many meals before Clan-Keeper Wang's mum upped and died."

"And you know the reason why?" said Great-Grandad.

"Why?"

"Because they were useless. The world doesn't keep you here if you're no use to anyone any longer."

Great-Grandad moved the grain piled up at his door inside the cave. He didn't complain, nor did he say thank you. He began to steep the scorpions he had caught in wine. He had no wine himself, but the villagers brought him jars and pots of wine, and he put three in this one, five in that one. Bright's dad told me that for more than a dozen years Great-Grandad had been the only one in the village who could catch scorpions. The wine he steeped them in was good for all sorts of things: treating rheumatism, relieving inflammation and ridding the body of toxins.

Great-Grandad made a pot of scorpion wine for the Blacks too, but Bright's dad wouldn't let me drink it in case it harmed the baby. Once Bright had gone out, I did my best to get at it; after all, scorpions could get rid of toxins and this baby inside me was the biggest toxin of all. But when I took the lid off and saw all those scorpions that looked as if they were still alive, I was too scared to drink it.

Great-Grandad was getting thinner, and he was unsteady on his feet nowadays. I guessed that his latest trip to collect scorpions had knocked him back a bit, or perhaps he had done himself an actual injury when he fell. But he didn't say anything more about it and Bright's dad didn't ask again. He didn't go out much any more, or stay in his cave. Instead, he spent the days sitting under the gourd frame, in the shade on the west side when the morning sun shone from the east, or in the shade on the east side when the sun was in the west. The villagers still came to see him, and they talked a lot but he spoke very little. His eyelids drooped and sometimes shut completely, and he just nodded. I used to go along and listen in, and I realised that when I was there, Great-Grandad's eyes opened and he would

speak a little more. He never looked at me, obviously, but he seemed to
want me to hear some things.

Here's a thing: one day, clouds gathered behind the ridge opposite, and they
looked like lots and lots of white peonies with their petals unfurling, and
while Get-Rich and Happy-Event and La-Ba were on the strip talking to
Great-Grandad about making scorpion wine, the clouds rolled over the
entire ridge and suddenly surged north like a roiling tide, until they hung
right over the village.

"Butterfly! Butterfly!" Bright called. "Come and look. It's amazing!"

I sat down on the cave doorstep and watched the clouds whirring over
the clifftop (you could almost hear them).

"Great-Grandad, why are there so many clouds? What do they mean?"
asked Happy-Event.

"It doesn't mean anything, it's just the earth breathing out *qi*."

"Clouds are the earth breathing out *qi*?" asked Happy-Event.

"And so are the birds and the beasts, and the trees and human beings
too, they're all the earth breathing out *qi*."

"Human beings come from a woman's belly, how can they be the earth's
qi? Where does *qi* come from?"

"Sogon Grass Ridge graveyard, to the west of the village, that's where we
villagers come from. When someone dies, the earth takes its *qi* back, and
wherever that person comes from, they go back to. Their grave is the eye of
the *qi*."

Bright's dad was patching his thin jacket. It was white and although the
patches were white too, they were a different white.

Great-Grandad went on: "Life comes through the eye of the *qi* and death
goes back through that eye. The women of the village marry in, they aren't
born here, but when they die, they're all buried on Sogon Grass Ridge."

"My nephew went to find work in Fujian and he died there, so that's
where he was buried," said Get-Rich. "Anyone who's born away has *qi* that
floated out from here, and if someone's buried away, they had the *qi* from
out there that floated here, but has to go back there in the end."

What kind of *qi* do I have? I thought. Where did I come from, was it
where my family came from, the lush land of fish and rice and mountains
and lakes, or was it the city with its reinforced concrete tower blocks and

streams of traffic, or was it this dirt-poor village on the endless loess plateau? How would I ever know? If I were to die here, did that mean my *qi* was from here, that it had just floated away but had to come back again? If I ran away, did that give me the *qi* of the countryside I came from or the city I'd moved to, or where? I got so agitated I took off one shoe and took a swipe at the hen with the fluffy top-knot that was pecking around my feet, making a '个' character in the dust with its claws. It scrabbled away with loud squawks as the shoe hit it. They all looked at me, and Happy-Event and Get-Rich muttered suspiciously: "Eh? Eh?"

I ignored them and chuckled to myself. My *qi* definitely wasn't from hereabouts, I decided, it was from my old village, from the city, it just happened to have floated here, like the way a petal falls on someone's shoulder as they're walking along, dandelion fluff floats upwards and lands in someone's hair, or foxtail seeds dart out like arrows and stick to a passing trouser leg, like snowflakes, like raindrops, like the wind or the moonlight. The Eastern Well stars might have shone on me and got me here by enchantment but my *qi* wasn't from this place, and one day I would leave.

And here's something else he wanted me to hear. After a few days' rain, the village alleys, normally four inches deep in dust, turned to a quagmire, and the shoes of anyone who went out turned into two clods of mud. When they got back to the strip, they'd use anything as a foot-scraper, a rock, the pine tree roots, the millstone base or the rim of the well, leaving mud everywhere. OK, so that made the strip dirty but the really annoying thing was that the maize stalks piled next to the shit-house got wet and so did the pea stalks. That Bright's dad had real problems cooking our meals, it took ages to get the fire going, and then billows of black and ochre smoke came out of the cave, like torrents of water except that, instead of rushing off downhill, the smoke-water rose up the undercliff that our caves were set into and hung over the clifftop in a great cloud.

One day, Monkey came shouting for Great-Grandad. He had an old strip of cloth wound around his forehead and sounded distraught. He had to stand outside the old man's cave so he wouldn't dirty it with the clods of mud on his feet, or maybe the old man wouldn't invite him in, so he squeezed under the gourd frame to tell Great-Grandad all his troubles. It was about Bear-Fruit Wang. Bear-Fruit had died ten years ago and had never managed to get a wife, even though he used to go on at his dad to get him one. Now Bear-Fruit's dad had dreamt three nights in a row that his son was still asking for a wife, so the old man wanted to get him a ghost-wife, and had asked Monkey to go around the nearby villages to find out if any young unmarried woman had died, and could he buy the corpse and bring it back to be buried alongside Bear-Fruit? Monkey did ask around but he couldn't find a suitable young woman anywhere. Then a couple of days ago, he happened to be passing the grave of Padlock's wife and there was a gust of wind and he felt like a goose was walking over his grave.

"Damn you!" he scolded her. "You ignored me when you were alive, why are you bothering me now you're a ghost?" Then he suddenly recalled what Bear-Fruit's dad had asked him to do and said: "If you come bothering me again, I'll dig you up and ghost-marry you to Bear-Fruit!"

Unfortunately, Padlock turned up and overheard him. They had a fight, and Monkey got a broken head. Great-Grandad looked like he wasn't following this tale of woe, but he did tell Monkey off for talking of digging up the corpse of someone else's wife. He deserved to get a broken head. Monkey had a fit of coughing and shouted: "Uncle Black! Uncle Black! Are you smoking badgers in there?"

Bright's dad came out of the cave wiping his eyes with his apron.

"Is it getting down your throat? Why don't you come and eat lunch with us, I'm steaming potatoes."

"I never scared any ghost, he had no reason to beat me up and give me a broken head!"

Great-Grandad came out of his cave and said: "I already heard what happened. Padlock threw a few punches, you kicked him, then you went to head-butt him, he dodged and you cracked your head against the tree, and you haven't got a broken head, it's just a bruise."

"But... Great-Grandad, Great-Grandad..."

"And I'm not only your Great-Grandad either."

Monkey stalked away at that, throwing off a clod of mud as he went, and losing his shoe with it.

"And take that bit of cloth off your head!" Great-Grandad called after him.

Monkey retrieved his shoe from where it had landed on the millstone, but he didn't stop to put it back on. The air was still thick with smoke. I sat at my door looking at it, feeling like I was burning up, only smouldering, without flames.

"The kindling was wet," Bright's dad said apologetically to Great-Grandad.

"No matter, the smoke just turns into clouds when it gets into the sky," the old man said.

And another thing. The Blacks had no mirror. After I broke the glass of the picture frame, I couldn't see myself any more. But one day I was leaning on the tractor and I suddenly caught sight of myself in the wing mirror. After that, I used that mirror all the time to look at myself. It didn't take long for all of them to find out what I was doing, Bright's dad, Great-Grandad and any of the villagers coming to our strip. I didn't care if they knew or not, but I did care about what I saw: I used to have fair skin, rosy lips, white teeth and bright eyes. Now my hair was dry as wild grass, and my skin was sallow and sunburnt, and I had a vengeful look about me. This wasn't me, that mirror was my ghost! The first time I saw myself, I grabbed a handful of dirt and smeared it over the wing mirror. But no matter how often I did it, the next time I went and looked, the mirror was bright and shiny again. I thought it was Bright who'd done it, but it can't have been, he hadn't been to the township or the county town to pick up supplies for a couple of weeks, he'd been hard at work repairing the store roof. He was out at crack of dawn and back late, he might not even have known what I'd done to the mirror. Then one day, I saw Great-Grandad: every time he went out he passed by the tractor, and his sleeve just happened to brush against the mirror.

Well, so be it. I leant against the tractor and peered into the mirror once more. Just then, Snatch turned up on the strip looking for Blindy to help them with moving some bricks – they were building up his father's tomb. Blindy said he would, but first he fed the pigs, tipped some fodder into the donkey's manger, then he stood motionless for a while in front of his cave, looking up.

"Have you turned to stone?" asked Snatch.

"Let him be," retorted Great-Grandad. "He's paying his respects to heaven."

"But I can't see any incense," said Snatch.

"No matter, you can still pay your respects to heaven just by looking up."

"Can he see heaven? He can't see anything!" said Snatch sarcastically.

"Well, heaven's looking at him," said Great-Grandad.

From then on, I stopped smearing mud on the mirror. Whenever I looked in it, it was actually the mirror that was looking at me.

So every day I went to see how the mirror was looking at me. Thing was, I didn't want it to see me so ugly, so I began to wash my face and comb my hair, and I got Bright to buy me lots of beauty products, and I put on some make-up.

And here's another thing: Bright brought me a basket of soy beans which he was going to sprout, and he asked me to pick them over if I had nothing else to do. They were all beans that had been picked up from the threshing floor after the harvest, and some were good, but there were a lot of shrivelled and mouldy ones, along with stones and bits of earth too. It took hours and I still wasn't done. Great-Grandad was sitting there reading his almanac, raising his head to look at the sky every so often.

"Are you looking at the Eastern Well again?" I asked him.

"You can't see the moonlit world in sunlight, can you?" he said.

Just then, the dog came charging across the strip after a sparrow, which flew off before he could catch it. The dog raised so much dust it got in my eyes, and I threw the basket down in annoyance.

"I'm not doing any more. Why am I bothering to pick out the bad beans, it's going to take me years!"

"Well, don't pick out the bad beans," Great-Grandad said. "Just pick out the good ones."

I picked up the basket and started again on the good ones, and sure enough I was soon finished. It started me thinking that morning: were there any good beans in the village, and if there were, was Bright a good or a bad bean?

And another thing: the gourd vines came into flower, and inside each flower a tiny gourd formed. They were a delicate green with hairs all over them, so that it looked like they had a white halo when the sun fell on them. Great-Grandad set to work making the gourd forms in all different shapes, and carved the usual characters on top: 德, virtue, 孝, filial piety,仁, humanity and和, harmony. He would put these forms over the gourds when they were about the diameter of a rice bowl. I went to have a look.

"Do you like them?" asked Great-Grandad.

"I like that one," I said, pointing to an oblong one.

"If you like it, then it likes you even more."

I went to look at it every day. It really was growing fast. But one day, I felt a bit faint and got up late, and heard Bright's dad cursing and swearing out on the strip. I rushed out, and it turned out that before daybreak, a thief had got onto the strip and nicked three of the young gourds. At that stage, they were tender enough for stir-frying but Great-Grandad didn't grow them for eating. Whoever the heartless thief was, they were never going to own up no matter how much Bright's dad cursed and swore.

That afternoon, Bright arrived from the township with a load of china, crocks, jars and bowls, big and small. As the tractor pulled up on the strip, the villagers came along to take their pick. The crocks went in sets of three, and some crudely-made black bowls were sold in lots of ten.

"Have you got any wooden bowls?" asked Bring-Silver. "We've got so many kids at home, wooden bowls don't get broken."

"No one uses wooden bowls nowadays," said Delight Liu. "You can get stone ones."

"Stone ones?"

"Yeah, what pigs eat out of, troughs."

He raised laughs for that but Bring-Silver didn't take offence, he just carried on asking Bright what other bowls he had. Bright pulled open a straw bag and took out ten plastic bowls, and one made of porcelain, a translucent white, which sounded like copper when you pinged it with your finger. He held it out but Bring-Silver didn't take it, he took one of the plastic bowls and threw it to the ground. It didn't suffer any damage.

"These are good," Bring-Silver said, and he bought all ten. There were so many villagers milling around that I got a chance to look each of them in the face. I was trying to work out which one was the gourd thief, but I couldn't tell.

Delight picked up the porcelain bowl and held it up to the light.

"Who ordered this, then?"

"No one."

"So who did you buy it for?"

"For anyone who fancies it."

Meanwhile, I was thinking about what Great-Grandad had said about the gourds: "If you like them, then they like you more." By the same token, they must hate the gourd thief.

I went and stood under the gourd frame and shouted: "Great-Grandad! Great-Grandad!"

I wanted to make sure that everyone on the strip could hear me, then I would check up on who was too embarrassed to look at the gourds, or if they did look, it was a shifty look. It was Monkey who looked most ill-at-ease, he looked at me, then looked away and pretended to be going through the crocks, clattering them against one another.

"Great-Grandad," I whispered, "it must have been Monkey who nicked the gourds."

"That's as may be, but they were nice and tender, so they'll be in his belly now."

"Why are there people like that in the village?"

"Well, you always get an even split of good and bad in any place."

The villagers were still arguing about the consignment of china, the shapes, colours, size and quality, and having digs at Bright for buying the porcelain bowl to get in his wife's good books.

"Butterfly, aren't you coming to look?" Delight shouted.

But I didn't go, I just said to Great-Grandad: "You could use that bowl."

"It's not the person who chooses the bowl, it's the bowl who chooses the person. It belongs to you."

Delight Liu was declaring in a loud voice: "Porcelain fragments are for building stoves, brick pieces are for building toilets, crocks hold more than bowls, plastic lasts longer than porcelain."

"Great-Grandad, you heard Delight, is he having a go at me?" I asked.

"Well, he's right in general, but if you treasure something precious, it'll last longer than plastic, wood or iron." So I went and picked up the porcelain bowl.

The bowl was mine, but I didn't use it so Bright put it on the shelf above the *kang*.

Another thing Great-Grandad taught me: one day, he was choosing an auspicious day for Rake Zhang to dismantle their old stove and build a new one. Then they got chatting about how his little boy hated having his head shaved, he screamed blue murder but you had to hold him down and do it anyway, otherwise it grew too long and got greasy and lousy.

"But you'd have thought that, after three or four times, any kid would let you do it, because otherwise he'd feel ill and get too much internal heat."

I watched a procession of ants marching down from the edge of the strip towards that pile of rubble, dragging with them a long-dead mosquito, carrying a bit of rice on their heads, most of them holding up bits of grass and leaves. They weren't making a sound, but you could feel how busy and alert and lively they were. It made me think of harvest-time back in my old village and going to work in the city and coming back home, and I sat hunkered down in my doorway, staring silently, looking for a young ant still pale yellow in colour to see if it looked like me. One morning, in a crack in the undercliff behind the shit-house, I had spotted a snake skin. When had it sloughed its skin? Surely it couldn't be as easy as taking off your clothes? Of the original six chickens, the five hens had been killed and stewed by Bright's dad. Only the cockerel was left and he didn't call cockcrow any more. He stalked past me silently glaring, splurting droppings. We were raising a dozen chicks, little yellow balls of fluff, always pecking each other over a worm or an insect, unaware of the eagle soaring over the clifftop above them. I rolled up the bedding and took it outside to air. Looking at the matting that covered the *kang* reminded me of the reed beds at the entrance to my old village. It rained that night, and I worried about the crows in the pine tree and the turtledoves in the brambles on the undercliff. When it stopped, a small frog appeared and hopped around on the strip, and that reminded me that Qingwen and his camera weren't here. When the wind got up, it howled from morning till night – didn't it get tired? In the depths of the night, in the gauzy moonlight, there were the nocturnal sounds. First, I could make out the dog, yapping in his sleep, Blindy snoring, sometimes rhythmically, other times erratically, the sound of water – Bright's dad peeing in the piss bucket, he'd go a couple of hours then have to get up. Then there were sounds that I couldn't quite make out, which might have been my mum pulling her barrow along the streets, its ungreased axle creaking and groaning, or maybe my little brother breathing when he stood in the corner of the classroom, waiting for the teacher to tell him off and punish him for being late, I could hear each breath. Each of these sounds were like shards of glass, knocking against each other. Until finally at daybreak, a gentle breeze would get up, shaking the broom that rested against the millstone so it made a *woo-woo* sound – like a litany of complaints from an abandoned wife. With the new day, new flowers came out on the gourds, paler and smaller than the earlier blossoms, making my heart ache.

Still no stars in the sky above the pine tree, though I looked hopefully every night, and when I couldn't see them, it made me wonder why the stars sometimes didn't shine.

The hunchback woman whose name I knew was Cassia-Fragrant – even though she was anything but fragrant – came to ask Bright's dad to lend her the carved wooden chicken. The Blacks had a carved chicken that lived in the kitchen and only got put on the table on high days and holidays. She said her cousin was coming today and she wanted to give him a good dinner. Bright's dad was not keen on lending it and she gave him a terrible telling-off: Why couldn't he lend it, it wasn't a real chicken, you couldn't eat the wings or the leg! Finally the old man agreed, but he kept telling her she had to give it a good wash afterwards because it needed to go back on our table. Cassia went away with the wooden chicken, but not before telling Bright's dad that there was a wolf in the village, it had come to her home last night and lay down at her door and didn't go away till daybreak. After she'd gone, I checked the strip carefully for wolf paw prints but there were none, just the imprint of something that looked like plum blossom next to the stone woman. Bright's dad saw it too.

"There are no leopards around here, it must be a fox," he said. But a fox would have taken away the cockerel or the chicks and they were still all here, and besides the dog hadn't barked all night. Bright's dad was puzzled. Maybe these weren't fox paw prints then. But I was sure they were, we'd had a visit from a fox and it had come to see me.

Truth be told, I'd never seen a fox in my life, but I knew some of villagers hunted foxes, especially the man called Bounty. I'd heard him on the strip talking about how he used to lay bait, explosives balled up in the skin and feathers of a chicken, on the mountain paths the foxes used. He'd blown up white foxes and black foxes. It was too bad he hadn't managed to kill any red foxes. He was always telling tall stories about how cunning some foxes were, they'd pick up the explosive 'balls' in their mouths and move them somewhere else and bury them, and then he boasted about how he'd upped his game, added the skin from under the chicken's wing and put glass shards in the balls, and when the fox picked it up, the slight movement would set off the explosives and blow the fox's whole jaw off. Once when Bounty was in full flow, he actually dislocated his own jaw. That stopped him, and all he could do was mew at Bright's dad to put it back again. The old man did it by gripping his chin in one hand and the crown of his head in the other, and pushing up hard, until it clicked into place.

"This is my mum's fault, it's been like this ever since I was born," Bounty complained.

"It's a punishment for sinning," countered Bright's dad. "You blow up a fox's jaw, what do you expect?"

"I'm not the only sinner," said Bounty. "I blow up foxes but you kidnap women!"

He'd struck home all right, but I still didn't like him, in fact I hoped that his jaw would get so badly dislocated it couldn't be put back again.

After we found the fox paw prints, I didn't sit by the window at night any more, just lay quietly next to Bright on the *kang* without making a fuss. Or rather he lay next to me and I kept the stick between us too. I waited for the fox to come, but Bright sometimes muttered, or tossed and turned, then fell asleep and started to snore, so I put a smelly sock in his mouth to keep the noise down. In the middle of the night I was half-awake, half-asleep, looking at the stars through the window when I was awake, then dropping off and dreaming. Suddenly there was a fox on the windowsill. It was a beauty, with long, slender eyes and a delicate muzzle. It was a red one too. Bounty never managed to catch a red fox, but now a red fox had appeared at my window. It smiled a beautiful smile at me and I smiled back. We carried on looking at each other, we didn't need to talk, we understood each other.

I was asking: "Have you come for the chickens?"

"No, I've come to see you."

"I'm a butterfly, butterflies go for flowers, foxes go for chickens."

"But it's you I've come for." And I had the strange feeling that this fox got inside me, or that I had its fur on me, I'd turned into a red fox. I jumped out of the window and ran across the strip and through the village to the place where the car had dropped me off that first day. The deep holes left where people's feet had sunk into the mud after the rain had become rock-hard ridges and furrows. I raced away from the village and up onto the plain, down into the gully, up onto the ridge, the next slope took me up onto a knoll, the roads split off into countless forks, and at each fork there was a wolf, and balls of explosives wrapped in chicken skin. In terror, I forced myself awake, to find I was still on the *kang* and it had only been a dream. But the road I took in my flight had been so clear.

I asked Bright: "Is there a stony gully to the east of the village, and is there a honey locust tree where there's a bend in the gully?"

"Yup."

"And then there are a couple of ridges you cross, and then on the left, are there a lot of abandoned caves, with no doors or windows?"

"Yup."

"And there used to be a village there, then there was a murder, one man accused his neighbour of stealing his nonesuch flowers, the neighbour said he hadn't, they came to blows, the neighbour was killed, then the murderer went home and killed his own family, then topped himself. Seven people died in one night, and after that the hamlet was abandoned."

Bright looked at me, puzzled.

"Further on, there's a long ridge with a small house on top of it, all tumbledown, there's just an old *kang* left."

"No."

"What do you mean, 'no'? If you go on and take the right-hand fork, there's an undercliff, vertical, too steep to climb, but there's a dead tree up there, with its roots exposed and hanging down the cliff like snakes."

"No. There's no cliff like that."

He could probably tell I was trying to work out an escape route. He must have been surprised that I knew so much about the way out of the village and he was flatly denying it. He could deny it all he liked, I knew my dream was telling me the truth.

But after that, there were no more plum-blossom-shaped paw prints on the strip. Someone said they had seen a wolf in Back Gully, and there were gazelles and roebuck in East Gully Bottom, outside the village. Someone had even seen wild horses and asses on Bear's Ear Ridge when they were digging for nonesuch flowers. But no one talked about foxes. I dreamed every night, but there were no more foxes, still less flights across the plateau in my dreams.

.   .   .

The long days dragged by. Bright's dad brewed tea on the strip and villagers turned up every now and then, either because the old man shouted to them or because they reckoned the Blacks were well-off and they could come and cadge a cuppa. The more I got to know the villagers, the more I felt they were like forest animals: there were tigers and lions, and centipedes and toads and weasels, then there were clouds of bluebottles and mosquitos. The bigger animals were taciturn, solitary and unfathomable, and could be combative too – like Great-Grandad, the village boss, Spring-Starts and Three-Lobes. The smaller animals were weak and had to fight for position, but they only had one weapon in their armoury, they could either run or bite or they had camouflage or they were venomous, they stuck together but they hated each other. Like La-Ba, Monkey Ma, Bring-Silver, Tongue-Trip, Clan-Keeper Wang and Delight Liu. They were usually into some dirty business or other, and always fighting, and if they came for a cuppa with Bright's dad, they were like a flock of sparrows, gossiping and arguing about who'd come out on top in a fight, like, in Dongwanli, one of the cliff-bottom valleys, two people had had such a brawl and they flattened a whole patch of lucerne. Like, who'd been knocking on which woman's door at night, and then found out she had a new lover with her, so he sat on her doorstep all night and saw the woman come out in the morning to empty the piss bucket, waddling along legs akimbo – and saw that the man in the room was his uncle. Like, whose wife had run off three times, and this time she got as far as Hougounao, but the thing was, she lost her bearings and spent so long wandering round in circles, she was caught and fetched back again. Like, who spent eight thousand yuan on buying himself a wife and reckoned he'd got a good bargain but after he'd brought her back and they'd spent one night together she ran off, and was one night really worth that much money?! Like, who hadn't paid his respects at the family grave for years because he had no son, and after he got a live-in husband for his daughter, she died and her husband took another wife, and a nephew was angry at him for taking his uncle's family property so the nephew chased him away and took the new woman as his own wife instead. Like, who was getting his rocks off with the family donkey, and the donkey brayed all night and made such a noise that the neighbours complained to the village boss. I got pissed off with the way they discussed all this with such gusto, laughing and shouting, that once I took the slops to feed the pigs, making sure to trip as I passed them and spill the dirty water over them, and then I started sweeping outside and raised a cloud of dust.

"Butterfly," they shouted at me, "why have you got it in for us? Can't we drink our tea in peace? Hey, Bright, if you and Butterfly ever set up home on your own, we won't come and drink tea even if you ask us!"

Bright glowered at me, grabbed the broom and threw it in the corner.

"We haven't got it in for you. The more visitors, the merrier! You carry on with your tea." Then he dragged me into the cave. But even though I couldn't get rid of folk like this, they often fell out among themselves after they'd had a fair amount to drink, and would go anyway.

This happened three times on the trot: they came for their tea, got very rowdy and had a furious row. Bright's dad reckoned people were too quick to take offence these days and that day when I embarrassed them, it added fuel to the flames and wound them up even more. Of course they didn't say anything to me, but their faces got longer than ever, not that I cared about that. One way or the other, I went ahead with putting up my washing line, knocking in two posts on the edge of the strip, hanging a rope between them and pegging my knickers out to dry. One pair vanished from the line, which surprised me.

Bright, meanwhile, wanted to make a flowerbed beside the stone woman. He started by trying to grow nonesuch flowers, but the nonesuch flower is parasitic, it grows from a grub, and once it puts out leaves and flowers, it's finished, it won't re-grow. Then he planted some wormwood and prunus cuttings and though he watered them every day, the pig got out of its pen one day and rooted them all up. There were more mishaps: the crows roosted in the pine trees and normally they only crapped from there, but a couple of times they crapped before they got there, once onto the millstone and another time onto the well rim, leaving white spatters all over the place. Then Bright was driving his tractor and hit a rock in the cliff, no great harm done, except that the mirror got broken. And the cockerel got ringworm, and lost all the feathers on his neck. And Blindy sprained his ankle. And Bright's dad smashed his hand with the hammer when he was working on a carving – he couldn't understand how a skilled workman like himself could have done that.

I had a feeling all these mishaps had something to do with me. I was sick of the villagers, they were such brutes, I hated it here, and that was making everything go haywire and topsy-turvy.

If I was in the cave, I lay curled up like the dog outside. When I went out on the strip, I sat there as immobile as the clothes-beating stone. I went five days without speaking, then another five, I felt like I had no mouth. I was a walking corpse. Finally, on the eleventh day, I spoke: "I miss Auntie Spotty-Face!"

I'd offended against Bright and his dad by trying to get rid of the pregnancy, which was why Auntie Spotty-Face couldn't come to the strip any more. When it happened, I'd sworn solemnly to Bright that they shouldn't blame her, I'd forced her to bring me the chinaberry seeds, and she didn't know what I was going to do with them. She'd done so many good things for the Blacks, they really shouldn't hold it against her!

"So you won't harm my child?" said Bright

"It's my child as well as yours," I reminded him.

Bright relayed my words to his dad and his uncle, and to his late mother in her picture frame too. That day was bright and sunny and Blindy got the donkey out and let it roam around, and it rolled on the strip, over and back, five times, kicking up a cloud of dust, until Bright's dad had a fit of coughing.

"I need a drink," he grumbled, and he downed a whole bottle and got drunk.

Bright wanted me to belong to him and to give him a child. I couldn't get away from him and his child was growing in my belly. Well, I'd have the child. Maybe once it was born, I'd no longer belong to Bright.

I carried on making scratches for the days on the cave wall but I didn't cry any more, or shriek, or throw things or kick the piss bucket and ladles down the hole in the shit-house, or kick the cave door and leave muddy footprints. A criminal had been shot in the village eleven years ago and he was supposed to haunt the place, so the villagers had driven a wooden peg into his grave and pasted a curse over his old cave entrance. I was afraid of turning into a malevolent ghost like him, and giving birth to a baby tainted by evil.

The atmosphere around the Blacks' caves relaxed, and the villagers started dropping in again. Black made me come out and meet them. "This is Uncle Seven-Jin, this is Auntie Heavenly-Princess, this is Uncle Baldy – even though he's young, he's a generation above us. This is People's-Kid, he's been on patrol at the county town building sites, he's just back." Bright greeted all of them by name. I took one look and turned my gaze away. They were leathery-skinned, with faces like dried persimmons and small eyes, as if they'd all been turned out of the same mould. The only difference was that some were tall, some short, some fat and others thinner.

I began to take on the cooking. The first time I said to Bright's dad: "I'll do the meal", he was sitting at the cave door smoking and he couldn't believe his ears. I was just stacking up the firewood inside the stove and he came hurrying in after me.

"Go and see if the pig has enough to eat," he said. I went to the pigpen and it had its snout buried in the trough. I went back to the cave and Bright's dad was sitting by the stove and the cave was full of black smoke. He pursed his lips and blew on the fire and with a pop the fire caught and the flames licked out of the stove top like chrysanthemum petals, and it began to crackle.

The meal was ready. Lunch was invariably maize porridge mixed with buckwheat noodles, and there were potatoes cut into cubes and sliced cabbage too. Bright's dad filled the bowls and put them on the edge of the stove. Then he went out and called Great-Grandad, who was sitting under the gourd frame.

"Don't bother with your stove today, come and eat with us."

Great-Grandad said: "I'm just having a sit-down here."

Bright's dad said to me: "Take Great-Grandad a bowlful."

But the old man came right over anyway and parted his moustache with his fingers, fastening it out of the way with elastic bands, so you could see his mouth.

"This meal should be eaten at a table!" he said.

Bright's dad grunted and hurried into my cave, brought out the *kang* table and rested it on the edge of the well. He put down saucers of salt, vinegar, chilli and chopped onion, and added the wooden chicken.

We brought out the bowls. Bright's dad ate a bit then lit up his long-stemmed pipe. He sucked so hard on it that not a wisp of smoke escaped from the pipe-bowl, then he breathed streams of smoke slowly out of his mouth and nostrils. There was what looked like dust all over his head and I gave the towel to Bright to wipe his father's head for him, but Bright said: "That's not dust." I took another look. He was right, it was his white hairs.

· · ·

One day Bright suggested that he and I go to the store together.

"You're not worried I'll run away?"

"No, my baby's too big now."

He was right. My belly had grown so big it looked as if I had a wok covering it, and I got breathless when I walked. There was no way I could run away. I did my hair and put on my high-heeled shoes.

"Your feet are too swollen to wear those," said Bright, but I wore them anyway. To get to the store, we had to walk through the village. The lanes and alleys were weird, they were like mouse runs. Bright kept saying: "Mind the potholes!" and, to the dog: "Lead the way!"

The dog ran in front waving its tail. We threaded our way through the maze of little streets, long and short, wide and narrow. They led us over the tops of other people's caves, or across their yards or strips. At first it seemed like a jumble, but there was order in the chaos.

Whenever we bumped into people, they'd look surprised and ask: "Are you showing your wife around the village, Bright?"

And Bright would make the introductions: "This is Crippled Uncle's home, say hello to him!" It was all "Say hello to Uncle This or Auntie That!" I did as I was told but in a very small voice.

"You're as quiet as a mosquito, speak up!" they'd exclaim. Then they'd laugh and give me a steamed potato to eat.

The store was at the southern entrance to the village. A river with a trickle of water in its bed ran past it, and a road followed its bank. The road ran east-west and was deeply pot-holed. This was the road I'd arrived on, I realised. I gazed along it: eastwards, it climbed a ridge and disappeared into the distance, while to the west, it descended into a gully, then went round the back of the undercliff. There were goats moving slowly up the undercliff. How could they get up such a steep slope? I imagined them getting stuck there, bleating.

"Come inside the shop and put your feet up," Bright said. The shop was not a cave, it was a three-roomed mudbrick building of two storeys. Bright explained that the building used to house the village theatre upstairs, while downstairs were communal rooms for meetings, but these fell out of use when the communes were abolished and individual families took back the land. So three years ago, he'd paid the village committee twenty thousand yuan to use the building as a shop. They'd cleared away the bits of wood

that were lying around in the communal rooms and the theatre props –
theatre lanterns, muskets, and gongs and drums – and stored them upstairs.

"There hasn't been a play or any entertainment for a dozen years, but
wait till the heir's born, then I'll get a troupe in and they can play for three
nights and three days for his birthday!" he said.

"What's 'the heir'?"

"The boy."

"Why are you so sure it's a boy?" I said.

"Because I'm sure!"

"But if it's a boy, that's another one you won't be able to find a wife for!"

I suddenly felt horribly sick and puked up not just bile but also that
morning's breakfast. That scared Bright out of his wits. He poured me some
water and wiped my mouth, then he rubbed my back and helped me to a
chair, and after quite a while, I felt better.

"Just look around you. Apart from the workers who go and get jobs in
town, I'm the best off of everyone in the village," Black boasted.

"Is there a map?" I flicked through some old almanacs. There was
no map.

"Is there a phone?"

"A phone?!"

"But if there's no phone, how do you make your orders from the
township or the county town?"

"There's only one phone in the village, the village boss has it."

Bright looked taken aback for a moment, but when he saw I was still
looking at him, he smiled: "I don't need to order in advance, if I need
anything, I just go into town and cut a deal."

It was the words "cut a deal' that got me, it reminded me that he'd cut a
deal for me, and I shivered. Bright realised he'd made a mistake talking
about cutting deals, and re-phrased it: if he saw anything in town that the
villagers could use, then he bought it for the store. He told me how hard it
was to get the stuff back: it took four hours to drive the tractor to the
township, and took two days to walk, and the county town was even further,
seven hours away, or a four-day walk. You had to get through Seven-Li
Gorge and go over Tiger Head Peak, then across Old Crow Gully and South
Luo River, up Lush Mountain, and through Black Fox Valley, up Fire Beacon
Hill and around Moonlight Rapids. There were hardly any houses on the
way, but there were plenty of snakes, hornets, jackals, wild boars and

demons. The summer sun was hot enough to crack your skin and in winter there were icicles. If you weren't careful, you'd fall off the edge of a cliff and they might never find your corpse. Twenty years ago, he added, there were a lot of prison camps around the township, and the convicts were taken to do hard labour in the surrounding countryside. They only ever had one soldier to guard dozens of them, they weren't worried anyone would run away because there was nowhere to run to. I could tell Bright was lying, or at the very least, exaggerating to scare me. I pretended not to understand and sat there flipping through his price lists.

"You should mark the stuff up eight or ten times," I exclaimed.

Three people came in.

They were from Xie Family Gully five *li* away, Bright told me, as he went to greet them. They had come to buy a brazier, and Bright enthusiastically got out all his stock for them to choose from. They inspected them closely, to check there weren't any bubbles in the casting, and pinged them to see whether they made a crisp sound, sneaking looks at me from time to time. They stared pretty hard and I kept my head down and went on flipping through the price list.

"How much?"

"Thirty yuan."

"Bright, you're ripping us off!"

"Check the weight, even that much scrap iron goes for more than ten yuan."

"Half price and we'll take three."

"Nope. I'd make a loss at that price."

"Twenty."

"Why would I take twenty!"

"Thirty yuan and you can throw her in too."

"Don't talk such crap, she's my wife."

"Your wife? A woman like that?"

"And why shouldn't I have a wife like her?"

The customers' eyes bored into me. "Where did you buy her from?"

"Just choose which brazier you want," said Bright. There was more loud arguing: the customers told Bright his braziers were too expensive, he was heartless, especially when he could afford a wife as good as me. Finally, they only bought one, at twenty-three yuan.

Once they'd gone, Bright said to me: "I'm good at sales."

"How much did you make on that?"

"Three yuan."

"Only three yuan? What's so good about that?"

"I don't want them to be envious of the amount of money I'm making. Besides, now they've got a brazier, they'll need to buy charcoal, and a kettle, and tea and tea cups, plus they'll need a stand to put the brazier on and fire tongs. They'll need to buy so many things, and I won't be dropping the price for them!"

More customers arrived, buying a basin, a hand towel, nails and a plastic bucket. Some fierce bargaining went on, but they couldn't keep their eyes off me either. I didn't feel good and kept spitting saliva. Bright certainly loved his customers, seeing them at the door with a big smile, then totting up his takings on the abacus. He tried to pass the money over to me but I refused to take it. "You'll be managing the household soon, you take the store money," he insisted.

"Why aren't there any cars on the road?" I asked.

"Take it," he repeated. "You'll be coming to buy things more often now, so you have it. There's no traffic hereabouts, only me and my tractor."

I rested my head on both hands and looked outside. There was a row of willow trees in the distance, the trunks were so thick it would take two people to get their arms around them, they were only as tall as an adult but their tops were covered in slender branches.

"Do you prune the willows around here?" I asked.

"Yes, you have to chop them down hard every year, otherwise they won't grow new branches, and they die."

"Like people like trees, slap 'em down into the dirt to make 'em grow," I said.

"What people?" he asked.

"People like me," I said.

A bluebottle landed on the counter and Bright picked up the fly whisk to swat it away, but the bluebottle just stood on the whisk. To the right of the row of willows, there was another tree that looked different.

"Is that a chinaberry?" I asked.

Bright grunted.

"No," he said.

But I could see it was a chinaberry. The seeds that Auntie Spotty-Face got me must have come from there. It looked old and seemed to have a completely hollowed-out trunk. I saw a bird fly out.

"That's not a chinaberry," Bright repeated. Just then, the village boss and Cassia-Fragrant popped out from behind the willows. They were walking in our direction. The village boss must have said something to her because Cassia-Fragrant veered off somewhere else. She had a pheasant in her hand. I turned my back on the village boss and examined the shelves, but it was my name he shouted: "Butterfly! Butterfly!"

"Good morning," Bright greeted him. "You shot a pheasant?"

"So Butterfly's turning shopkeeper!" said the village boss. "That's good, it'll help you settle down. You're the wife of a rich man now!"

"She's not feeling well," said Bright.

"I want her to look at me!" exclaimed the village boss in annoyance.

I turned to face him.

"You're a powerful man, Mister," I said.

"Powerful? What's so powerful about me?" he protested. "Everywhere else, weddings are held at midday. Do you know why we hold them in the evening hereabouts? It's because when China was under the Tatars, they had the right to deflower the bride, so the Chinese held their weddings under cover of darkness. And that's been the custom ever since."

"Would you like to have been a Tatar?" I asked.

He burst out laughing: "I'm a Communist Party man myself. But I'll tell you one thing: Bright has to call me 'Uncle' because I'm a generation senior to him, so you have to call me 'Uncle' too. You've got a big belly on you! Well, the seed was planted and it's sprouting, so you'd better be nice to me, because you and your child will need residency certificates, and it's me who has to sign them!"

The village boss had come to buy wine but he didn't take the whole bottle, he bought two fluid ounces.

"There are plenty of pheasants along the edge of the gully," he said. "Why don't you go and shoot some, they'll help Butterfly build up her strength."

"Sure, I'd love to," said Bright. "Only the government's made us hand in all our hunting rifles."

"Use a catapult," said the village boss. "I caught one yesterday, and another one today."

"I can't use a catapult."

And Bright pushed the red sand bag that covered the liquor jar, dipped the measure in twice and poured the wine into a cup.

"I can't get home without a drink, my legs will give way under me," said the village boss.

He stood there sipping, eyes screwed up and face puckered from the aroma, so all you could see was his nose.

"Good wine!" he said. "Put it on my tab."

"No, I won't," said Bright, getting a small notebook out from under the counter. "Why would I do that? Look, I'm tearing out your tab from before."

He really did tear some pages out of the notebook, and ripped them into small pieces. The village boss turned to me: "Butterfly, Bright's a good man but I can't drink for free. If you're ever short of food or tea, I can slip you some extra."

It was getting dark and I wanted to get back to cook, but Bright was still busy in the store, so he sent the dog with me. On the way over, the dog had led the way, but on the way home, he walked at my heels so he could protect me from strangers. There were no strangers, but when we got to the entrance to the alley I hesitated, until the dog nipped my trouser leg. "Damn you, you really are a Black!" I said. Actually the dog was white. We got to the stone woman, and the dog cocked its leg against her and pissed.

One day after lunch, Bright and his uncle were repairing the pigpen walls when Bright's dad came up: "When you've finished that, we're going to Spring-Starts, take a pen and paper with you. Spring-Starts says he and his brother are going to split up the family property, and he wants you to go and draw up the contract."

Bright finished the wall and set off with his pen and paper.

"You're going like that?"

"If I don't go, no one else can write the contract for them."

"But your clothes are covered in mud, that's not respectful!"

Bright looked taken aback, then he came over and dropped a kiss on my cheek: "Ah, now I've got a wife to keep me in order!"

Blindy was standing there and he must have seen, because he walked off.

"But the village boss should take care of that, why does he want you and your dad to go?"

"Spring-Starts and La-Ba don't trust him, he's been flirting with Rice."

"Then I'm going with you."

Bright thought for a moment, then agreed, and gave me a stick to walk with.

Spring-Starts and La-Ba and their family lived on the south-west corner of the village. We had just got to Second Alley when I heard a shrill squealing and Rake came towards us carrying a piglet in his arms.

"What's up?" asked Bright.

"The Xie village castrator is here."

"Come to cut you, has he?" said Bright.

"Come to cut my pig!"

"You're the one who needs cutting!" said Bright with a laugh.

"Just because you've got a wife! I've talked to the village boss and the next time there's news, I'll be the one to get her. I'll spend fifty thousand yuan on her."

I spun on my heel and walked away. Bright didn't hang around either but led me through the alley out to the west and up a slope where, after two hundred metres, we turned a corner and at the foot of the undercliff came on two caves. A dog barked furiously and I got my stick ready but before I had time to hit it, Spring-Starts came out of the left-hand cave.

"What are you making such a racket for? Can't you see who it is?"

Someone raised the curtain of the other cave and a woman came out. She gave an astonished cry: "Is this Butterfly?" Then she ran over to grab me by the hand and looked me up and down. "What a pretty girl you are!"

She reached for a lock of hair on my forehead and tucked it behind my ear.

"You remind me of myself when I was young!"

So this was Rice. I'd imagined her as being flashy, with a bit of a mouth on her, but this woman was older, still attractive, but with frizzy hair and dark circles around her eyes. Spring-Starts took Bright and me to the left-hand cave to sit down. Bright's dad was already there, with another man who must have been La-Ba. He looked very serious and worried, and they had probably been talking for a long time because there was a pile of cigarette butts in front of them. I didn't want to go in and Rice said: "Let them do the divvying-up. Come into mine for a chat."

The right-hand cave was hers. It was dark and gloomy inside, but she pulled back the curtain and opened the window. The setting sun's rosy glow caught three mirrors on the walls, suddenly brightening the cave and making countless dust motes glint as they danced in the air. Rice grabbed hold of my hand and exclaimed how soft it was, like cotton wool, the harder you squeezed, the smaller it got. Then she told me my eyebrows were too thick and she cackled with laughter.

"Every true beauty has a flaw! I'll fix them for you."

Her cave was cramped but laid out pretty much like the Blacks', with a large mud-brick *kang* down one side, with one rolled-up quilt on the inner side and one on the outside. She obviously slept nearest the wall because the quilt had a satin cover, and a soft pillow with a cotton square laid out on it. A row of wooden pegs had been banged into the wall and hung with clothes in all styles and colours, and for all seasons too. Underneath sat pairs of shoes – pumps, wedgies and high heels. In the middle of the *kang* was a low table, with five small saucers laid out on it and, instead of a wooden chicken, a fish. There was a bowl too, with half a poached egg floating in some broth. She explained they'd just had their dinner and offered to do me a poached egg, but I quickly said I didn't eat them. Ever since I got pregnant, they made me sick.

"Really? I've never had a baby, can an egg make you sick?"

She finished the egg herself, then looked at the dark broth. She must have thought it looked strange, and said: "I put soy sauce in it. The villagers don't use soy sauce. When I asked for some when I first got here, Spring-Starts said: 'Why would you want that? We've got castor oil and sesame oil.' He actually thought that soy sauce was a kind of oil."

She laughed again and her breasts jiggled.

The Blacks didn't have any soy sauce at all.

"You're living the good life," I said.

"The good life, here? The only good life is in the city. When I was there, I ate what I wanted, wore the clothes I wanted and met any men I wanted to meet."

I stared at her and jerked my chin towards the door.

"I'm not worried they'll overhear," she said. "When I first came here, I married a master but I married a beggar too. I made it clear to Spring-Starts: 'Don't tie me up and don't dog my heels all day. If I really wanted to run away, you could nail me to the door and I'd just run away with the door on my back. But I won't run away.' I told Spring-Starts: 'If you want it, you got to pay me for it, it doesn't matter how little.' And he gives me one yuan each time, so I'm not complaining!"

She really had been a hooker. I began to regret coming with Bright.

"I heard that Bright had married a city girl, and I've been wanting to pay you a visit, but I've been at the hot springs for a few months, running around like a blue-arsed fly! Which city are you from?"

"The provincial capital."

"What did you do?"

"My mum and dad have a shop," I lied.

"Oh, so you're really a city girl, not like me, born in a village, back in a village now. I'm glad you're here, though, it doesn't matter whether we're from the country or the city, the city is one big millstone grinding us all to little bits!"

I was fed-up with this conversation and looked around to see how many of the crocks they had, and how much grain was in them, but they didn't have many. What they did have was bundles and bundles of blood onions stacked right up the back wall as high as me. Rice was still chatting away: "The brothers can't get on, they've sold a lot of blood onions but they're gamblers, if they've got two cents to rub together, they're out the door and not back till all hours. I told him: 'Sex is at eight at night, whether you're back or not, I've got to have sex at eight.'"

She took off her jacket and put on a pink cotton top. Her body was even scrawnier than her face, you could see all her ribs but her breasts were like bags of milk.

"Are you going to stay here for the rest of your life?" I asked.

"With my past, I'm lucky just to have somewhere to live."

Outside the cave, Spring-Starts and La-Ba suddenly started an argument, and we heard Bright's dad yelling at them to shut up. When they'd quietened down, he muttered something, and La-Ba called out: "Rice, come out here!"

Rice got out a pair of white trainers to put on so she could see me out. They were clean but had gone yellow in the wash, so she got a piece of chalk to rub over them: "Don't shout at me! You divide your belongings up the way you want, it's your family!"

She lowered her voice and said to me: "Bright never has any blusher or lipstick or eye make-up in his shop. The first year I felt like I had no eyebrows because I had no eyebrow pencil, it took another year to get used to it. There's no shoe cleaner either, I started rubbing flour into them but Spring-Starts beat me, so La-Ba got me some chalk from the township primary school."

Spring-Starts, La-Ba and Bright began to carry everything out of La-Ba's cave, furniture, tools and grain, then came into Rice's cave and fetched out the *kang* table, sacks, chairs, a screen, baskets and a pair of iron-mesh lanterns. Bright came over to take the bedding off the bed, but when he got to the wooden chest in the corner of the *kang*, Rice said: "Don't touch that box, or the pillow or the clothes, they're mine, they don't belong to the Yangs."

She passed him the spirit tablet from on top of the cupboard to take outside, but Bright said: "That's not going in for divvying up."

Rice pulled down the door curtain and threw it out. It landed on Bright's head.

Rice sat on the edge of the *kang* and pulled me up with her.

"Do you like sweets?" she said.

"No thanks."

Then she opened her wooden chest, which was full of her bras, knickers, tights, hair pieces, earrings and necklaces, and lumps of brown sugar in a pot too.

"I have low blood sugar," she said, and put a bit of the sugar in her mouth.

I felt my gorge rise again and spat out saliva on the floor.

I looked out of the window where Bright's dad was shifting the cupboard to one side: "The eldest gets this."

Bright jotted it down in his notebook. A flat basket was next.

"The younger." Bright made another note. And so they went through everything, piece by piece, big and small.

"What about the spirit tablet, everything's got to come out. Don't you want it?"

Spring-Starts came in to get it and said to me: "That child you and Bright are making for us, it's going to be our main beam."

"What do you mean 'making for us', did you have anything to do with it?" said Rice.

"I gave Bright the blood onions," said Spring-Starts.

"If they're so great, why haven't you made a baby?"

"My seed's fallen on barren soil."

Rice kicked him, and he went out carrying the spirit tablet.

"How dare he fucking call me barren soil!" said Rice. "Other people are tools but I'm a work of art."

She chortled again, then said more quietly: "He might think I can't get pregnant, but I got pregnant three times back then. I'm just refusing to have a baby, you get a baby from making love but I don't love him so I got myself a coil."

If only I'd known Rice before, I wouldn't be in the situation I was now.

"Rice! Sis!" I almost yelped. And that was the first time I called her 'sis'.

"I don't want this baby, what can I do?" I said.

"What can you do? Nothing!" she said. "There's nowhere to get a D and C around here. You just have to let it grow in your belly."

There was more shouting outside the cave, first Spring-Starts, then La-Ba, it sounded like they were shooting each other, the bullets coming thick and fast. Bright's dad was trying to calm them down, but it didn't seem to be having any effect. Rice started to listen and then she went pale.

"They're fucking going to come to blows!"

"Do they argue often?" I asked.

"They've never got on, that's why they're splitting up," she said.

Bright's dad called again: "Spring-Starts' wife! Come out here!"

Rice took her time, combing her fringe in front of the mirror, until there was another call, and she pulled me outside with her.

To my astonishment, the crux of the disagreement about whether the divvying up was fair and square was Rice. La-Ba was saying that their belongings had been brought outside but Rice was a big piece of their property and she hadn't come outside. When they bought her, they'd spent 30,000 yuan, and the money had come from both brothers' earnings. La-Ba had originally agreed that Spring-Starts should get a wife first because he was the eldest, but now they were dividing up the family property, and Rice was part of the division. In his view, whoever got Rice should not get the cupboard, the chest, the *kang* table and the five crocks, and vice versa. At this point, Bright's dad said he wanted nothing more to do with the divvying up, he'd never heard anything like this in his life. He fell silent, his lips trembling, and spread his hands helplessly.

"La-Ba," said Bright. "Even if your brother agrees, it's illegal, the Marriage Law doesn't allow it!"

"So the Marriage Law allows kidnapping?" La-Ba retorted.

Bright glanced at me and said nothing more. I looked at Rice. I thought she must be seething, I expected her to yell at Spring-Starts for not protecting his wife, why didn't he beat La-Ba around the ears for saying stuff like that? And yell at La-Ba for talking such rubbish. No matter where she had come from, she was his sister-in-law, how could he treat his sister-in-law like that? But Rice was still smiling, as if none of this had anything to do with her. She picked up a pipe that was lying on the ground and began to smoke.

Finally Bright spoke: "Well, let's hear what your sister-in-law has to say about this."

"I've nothing to say," said Rice.

"Nothing to say?" I cried. "You're a human being, not someone's property!"

"I just look like a human."

Rice's words suddenly made me aware that there really were non-human people in this village. It wasn't a view imposed on them by others, it was how they saw themselves. The other day, Monkey got into an argument with a man called Lion-Dance. Lion-Dance was telling Monkey off for pissing in the alley in broad daylight: "So many people around, and you wave it around right in front of them. Can't you behave like a decent human being?"

"So I'm not human, so what?" was Monkey's response.

And now Rice was saying that she only looked human. It made me think that I shouldn't rely on her, because if I had anything more to do with her, I'd end up just like her, in fact I didn't even have her character, so I'd just sink to the bottom and wouldn't even look human any more.

"Let's go back," I said to Bright.

"I've got to write down the contract."

"There's nothing to write! Come on, let's go. If you don't want to go, I'll go on my own."

I set off but Bright caught up with me.

"You're better than Rice," he said. And we left the Yangs' caves.

The next day at breakfast, Bright's dad said to his son that it had taken him until the early hours to complete the division of Spring-Starts and La-Ba's property. First of all, Spring-Starts felt that it wasn't fair that, just because he had Rice, two-thirds of the property should go to his brother. So La-Ba suggested that he should give him Rice and of course they'd carry on managing the blood onion business jointly and split the proceeds equally, but he didn't want any more of the family's belongings, apart from a crock of grain, a wok and two bowls.

"You want to screw her, you go ahead!" said Spring-Starts. "But you've got to swear your promise to the spirit tablet."

So La-Ba fell to his knees in front of the tablet and said: "Dad! Mum! I'll make sure Rice gives you a whole *kang*-ful of grandchildren!"

And with that, Rice packed her things and moved into La-Ba's cave.

That day, a fierce blast of wind came whistling in from the plains to the north-west, without any warning or apparent reason, and suddenly a mixture of black and yellow dust and dirt spiralled up into the sky, there was a pitter-pattering, and someone's shit-house roof blew off, and someone else's chairs, and a pile of pea stalks blew away, the dogs howled, and it was as if the earth's skin had been flayed. On our strip, the harrow crashed down on the millstone, bouncing the baskets of peas drying on its edge into the well, the broom was sent scurrying, the chicks rolled around like balls of fluff, three birds' nests fell out of the pine trees, and the gourd frame suddenly inflated like a tent then collapsed inward, and tipped over on one side. We all ran into the caves, our bowls in our hands, and my chopsticks were snatched away by the wind.

"Great-Grandad! Great-Grandad!" Bright's dad yelled. "Make sure your door's properly shut!"

However, it was Three-Lobes who emerged from Great-Grandad's cave. He had arrived earlier that morning to talk to the old man about something, and now the pair of them held on tight to the gourd frame supports and tried to tie them down with rope, but before they could fasten the rope to the cave door frame, the frame keeled over. The vine dropped too, then leapt into the air like a frenzied snake.

"Great-Grandad! Why's this wind so strong? Where did it come from?" yelled Three-Lobes.

Bright ran over to help. "Maybe it's come from Bear's Ear Ridge," he said.

"We've never had a wind like this from Bear's Ear Ridge before now. This is a devil wind! A fucking devil! Do you think it's come from the city, Great-Grandad? Motherfucker of a wind!"

Great-Grandad was clutching three gourds, standing in the heap of vine tendrils, his moustache blowing across his face and covering it, revealing his toothless mouth. He said nothing.

From East Slope Ridge came the sound of Padlock crying over his wife's grave, and the storm snatched his weeping and shredded the sounds, and scattered them to the winds.

My body was growing clumsy, and the clumsier I got, the more stupid I felt. My feet and legs swelled up, my reactions slowed down, I had hiccups all the time and was horribly constipated. Bright told me to move around more, to go for a walk around the village. He'd completely stopped worrying about me, but I had no energy to go for a walk anyway, I spent all day sitting on the strip, shifting my position every now and then, but every position was uncomfortable. My legs twitched, my cheeks twitched, I twitched all over, and that scared me so much I broke out in a sweat. If the village women came to see Great-Grandad or borrow something from the Blacks, they'd take one look at me and say to Bright: "Your dad needs to feed that wife of yours up."

"He does," said Bright. "Every day's like New Year!"

"Then how come she's so thin?"

"I don't feel like eating," I'd tell them. "Whatever I eat, I puke it up."

They sympathised but told me I had to force the food down anyway, and keep eating even if I puked, so I'd be strong enough for the birth. After they'd gone, I took a look at myself in the tractor mirror. My cheeks were hollow and my eyes bulged, and worst of all my face was covered in freckles so dense it looked as if I'd acquired a new layer of dark skin.

One evening, Snatch's wife turned up with her three-year-old. She'd brought me a jar of honey, which she insisted came from her own bees and hadn't had anything added to it. She told me to dilute some in water every morning and evening and drink it, and it would help relieve the constipation. I thanked her, but the child really pissed me off, he was curious about my belly and kept coming up to me and feeling it. I moved away but he came back for another feel so I gave him a telling-off and Snatch's wife was mortified. Bright asked what had happened when we were eating dinner, then he said I should be friendlier towards the villagers, when a kid came to pat your pregnant belly that was a good thing.

"What's so good about it?" I demanded. He explained that his dad had told him that when they were building a new cave, if a kid came in and was happy playing there, that meant the *feng shui* was good. And the opposite, if the kid cried and made a fuss, that was a bad omen. If someone was going to die, you couldn't get a kid into the cave however hard you dragged it. At that moment, the village boss turned up, his jacket draped over his shoulders as usual.

"The way that jacket flaps, anyone would think you were going to heaven!" said Bright's dad.

"You're dead right, so long as the township secretary goes up to be deputy chair of the county-level CCPCC, then I can go up too, to be deputy township head!"

Bright's dad ignored his comment and asked: "Have you had your dinner?"

"I'm not hungry."

"In other words, you haven't. Bright, bring a bowl for the village boss!"

Bright filled a bowl and the village boss took it, saying to me: "Such a friendly man, your father-in-law, I'd feel embarrassed to refuse it. You're going to have a baby boy!"

"Are you just saying nice things because he's given you dinner?"

Bright said: "You really will have a baby boy, and he'll have a square mouth, and a square mouth will travel!"

The village boss opened his mouth wide, but it wasn't square. "You don't want me to eat your food?" he asked.

Bright smiled: "It's an honour for us if you eat our food. Butterfly, go and fry us another dish of garlic chives!"

I pretended I hadn't heard, and got up and headed towards Great-Grandad's cave.

Bright asked the boss: "How can you tell it's a boy?"

"Because of the way she looks. Carrying a girl makes a woman beautiful, carrying a boy makes her ugly."

The village boss had three helpings and kept saying the Blacks need never worry about not having a man to hang the lanterns at the cave door on New Year's Eve, or burn paper offerings at the family graves on the fifteenth of the first month. That certainly cheered Bright's dad up. He got out the wine and shouted for another four or five men to come and join the party. The village boss started to hold forth about how the village had changed over the last few years, everyone was much better off and better-off people were so much more hospitable, wherever he went there was wine on offer.

"Are you talking about the years you've been village boss?" asked one of the drinkers.

"When Pillar's dad was village boss, he was so poor himself, he never got his leg over anything but the edge of the *kang*, forget about making anyone rich! Did you ever see him get offered wine, or tea? No one even gave him a ladle of cold water when he went visiting!" said the village boss.

Bring-Silver said: "And how much richer are we under you, then? We still eat potatoes at every meal, and have to borrow clothes when we go and see relatives, right?"

"You're out of order, Bring-Silver," said the village boss. "Who was it fixed you up with a wife? You know how many bachelors there used to be in the village, six have got married in the last couple of years, and Bright's soon going to have a baby! What's that if not change?"

"But we've had to fork out and buy our wives," said Bring-Silver.

"Yes, you bought them and you had the money to buy them, didn't you? And where did you get that money from, you ungrateful fucker!" said the village boss.

The gourd frame, when it was re-built, was much smaller and lower than before because so many of the vines had been broken in the storm, and the dog took to squeezing in underneath and lying in the shade. Great-Grandad picked up a book that had been lying on the door pier and made me sit down.

"Still reading your almanac?" I asked.

"You think that's all I read? Those are the county annals. Today's Autumn-Starts in the lunar calendar, and I was looking up anything unusual that happened in years past on this date."

"Today's Autumn-Starts?" I echoed. "Then how come it's still so hot?"

"It's hot all right. Last summer was the hottest on record, but the day of Autumn-Starts was cold and damp. This year is unusual."

"Why don't you look at your Eastern Well?"

"It's not my Eastern Well! Anyway, I'm waiting till it gets completely dark and I'll take a look at it. Have you seen your star yet?"

I was finding the pier too low to sit on and pulled myself upright with the help of the gourd frame. The dog underneath started licking my toes.

"Go away," I told it. "Go on, go and find somewhere else to lie."

I kicked it away.

"I'm not looking any more," I told Great-Grandad angrily.

No sooner were the words out of my mouth than I felt a thud-thud-thud and suddenly felt horribly sick. I retched and retched but nothing came up. For the last couple of weeks my belly did that sometimes, it was happening more often, and getting stronger. I knew it was the baby having a temper tantrum, flailing with its arms and kicking me.

"Great-Grandad, have I got a baby or a monster in here, why won't it let me rest?"

All he said was: "You haven't been looking hard enough."

Bright was shouting for me. I didn't answer, just slumped down on the stone pier. Very soon, it had grown completely dark.

That evening, the sky seemed especially full of stars. Great-Grandad was looking at the Eastern Well and I was looking at Great-Grandad. He was sat on a low stool, propped against the high-backed chair in front of him, with his head and neck tipped back. He looked quite funny.

"Great-Grandad, you look like a fish coming up for a breath of air!" I told him.

"A fish that raises its head to the heavens is a dragon!" he said.

"You're a dragon, an old dragon," I laughed.

"You look for your star," he told me.

But I didn't look, the sky above the pine tree was pitch-black and no matter how hard I looked it stayed black, so there was no point. I started to count all the stars in the sky carefully: from the sky over the undercliff where Great-Grandad's cave was, to our own cave, right the way to the sky over the ridges to the east, west and south, I made it seven hundred and thirty eight stars. Then I counted again and got seven hundred and forty two, then again and again, and it kept coming out different.

Eventually, Great-Grandad said: "Let me teach you to recognise the Eastern Well."

He pointed to four stars that made a square, in the sky above our strip: "That's the Irrigation Official. Look at the string of four stars slanting towards the east, on top of them there's one star, they make up the Five Feudal Kings, got them? Under the Five Feudal Kings and the Irrigation

Official, there are eight stars in two parallel lines, four in each line, that's the Well, and on the left, next to the Five Feudal Kings, there's a very faint star, right? That's Accumulated Water, and under that one there are three stars in a triangle called the Celestial Goblet and, under them, another triangle called the Water Level."

He paused, then started again: "Butterfly, look to the right of the Well, there's the Battleaxe star, leaning towards the Pheasant. Can you see the big circle of stars, the Pheasant, actually it's not round, it's an oblong, look..."

But I had a crick in my neck by that time.

"I'm not looking any more, I don't understand what I'm looking at," I said.

He turned his head and his eyes were like two stars: "Aren't I teaching you what you're looking at? Those stars there are the Eastern Well and the Eastern Well shines down on us, can't you see?"

Then he waved me away: "You go to bed."

And he looked up at the sky again, muttering under his breath.

I carried on sitting there thinking I didn't care what or where the Eastern Well was. I looked at the patch of sky above the pine trees. Nothing. I looked again, still no stars. Great-Grandad was inspecting the Eastern Well tonight to see if there'd been any changes and what they might mean. I didn't care about that. What I did want to ask was, if I still couldn't see my star, did that mean that I didn't belong in this village? But he seemed to have lost interest in me. He sat quite still, not making a sound, his whole attention focused on the sky. I felt there was no point in asking my question, so I got up and went to bed.

As I walked back along the strip and passed the pine trees, I looked up, worried I might get droppings on me from the birds shitting down from their roost. And just then, between two of the branches, I suddenly saw a star in the patch of sky that had never had any stars before. I was so startled, I felt like hot liquid was rushing from my belly to my head, beads of sweat rolled down from my forehead, and my arms and legs trembled. Good heavens, there really was a star there, I rubbed my eyes, it still glimmered very faintly. I shut my eyes and took a deep breath to calm myself. A little voice said: Is it really a star? Maybe I'm going cross-eyed! Then I looked up again and there really were two of them, not flickering any more, one big and one small, very close to each other. It looked as if the small one was behind the big one, so if you didn't look carefully, it might look like one star.

The bird droppings plopped down, splashing first on my feet then on my shoulder, but I didn't move. Another dropping fell on my head, and a big bit slopped into my right ear.

My next feeling was panic. Was I really that tiny dim star? And if so, did that mean we – me and this child in my belly – belonged to this village? Would we belong here for ever and ever? I stared bitterly up at the sky for a long time. That's what it was looking like.

It had never occurred to me that seeing my star would plunge me into such low spirits, and I didn't understand either why I had longed to see it for such a long time. It was like when I was taking exams at school, I wasn't a good student and deep inside I knew I wasn't going to get good marks, but still I couldn't wait for the day when the results were announced, only to discover that I had done badly. I hated myself tonight for being so confused about everything. Why had I longed to see my star, what was I thinking of? I was angry at Great-Grandad too, because he had made me look for it. Was he trying to give me hope or shut me up? It was as if he had tricked me into a swamp by covering it with grass and flowers, or into a pot of cold water that was starting to heat up, and I was a frog that couldn't get out! I was so mortified that I didn't make a sound, not a cry or even a gasp of surprise, and I certainly didn't tell Great-Grandad that I had seen the star. I just crept back to my cave.

The village boss and his cronies had gone, but Bright was still awake, sitting in his uncle Blindy's cave learning how to plait shoes and waiting for me. I went indoors and he followed me and shut the door. The stars disappeared, invisible through the opaque window paper.

"Your trousers must be wet from the dew," he said. "Shall I heat some water so you can warm your feet?"

I couldn't see the expression on his face and I didn't answer. He groped for the quilts on the *kang* and rolled them into a sleeping bag shape, one for me and one for him, then got the stick and laid it down the middle of the *kang*.

"Leave the stick off," I said.

Bright threw it away and leapt like a cat onto the *kang*. But then he just sat beside me without budging. I unbuttoned my jacket and took off my socks and trousers. "I want it," I said, and put my arms around his neck. I could feel him smile in the darkness. He held me in his arms, kissed my mouth, my breasts and all down my body, but he didn't go any further.

"I don't dare, Snatch's mum keeps telling me it could harm the baby."

"I don't care!"

I lay flat on the *kang*.

Bright's breathing grew hoarse and ragged. He couldn't hold back any more, he uncoiled like a spring, he inflated like a sponge soaking up water, he rolled on top of me then jumped off the *kang* and raised my legs in the air. I held them there, vertical like a flagpole, or the mast on a boat. Ever so carefully he entered me, breathing hard, muttering something I couldn't make out. I pulled myself against him as hard as I could, he pushed into me then withdrew immediately, it hurt but I pressed myself to him anyway, chasing him, it was all so urgent, like a summer storm hitting the strip, the rain drops smashing to the ground and bouncing off again. After that, I had no idea what was going on, it was like my face was being pulled into weird grimaces, Bright was licking my legs and my toes, and I put my own thumb in my mouth, clamped my lips tightly around it, and sucked hard.

Bright seemed to be saying something like: "You were so scared of it even though you'd never had it, now you know how good it is!"

But I didn't know anything any more.

For the first time, I understood what sex really was. I sat up and rested against Bright's chest. He was saying: "Do you think it harmed the baby?"

I looked at my body. In the dim light coming through the window paper, it seemed very white. It shone, and Bright's body reflected the brightness, even the jars on the shelf seemed to gleam, and the *kang* table, and the sacks and the crocks too, and even a rat lurking under the stool at the back of the cave.

I put my arms around Bright. I wanted it again. He chuckled and poked me in the face: "Now you're having a laugh!"

But I did want it again, and I pushed him back on the *kang* and tried to ride him, but I couldn't get it in.

"Eat some blood onions!" I said.

That made him hard again and I got him inside me but somehow I couldn't keep my balance, I was rocking from side to side and up and down, and I began to feel dizzy.

He was shouting: "Ah! Ah! You're going to break me!"

I leaned forward to grab his chest but lost my grip, he suddenly had superhuman strength, he flipped me backwards, and my head hit the shelf and all the jars went crashing to the ground. I tumbled off him and landed on the *kang*, and he fell off onto the floor. At that point, the *kang* collapsed, and I found myself lying in a heap of rubble. Bright hurriedly went to pick me up, but stumbled and we nearly landed back down on the floor in among the mud bricks together.

"What's got into you, you been eating blood onions?" exclaimed Bright.

Out on the strip, Great-Grandad was yelling: "Earthquake! Earthquake!"

Then we heard Bright's dad shout: "Bright, Bright! Get outside! Get out!"

He banged on our door, then on Blindy's door. Blindy echoed: "Earthquake! Earthquake!"

The donkey brayed and the dog barked, and the birds circled in the air over the village, screeching and cawing.

Can a mountain really walk?

It did last night.

It walked?

Was it the one in the gully on the far riverbank?

It was the one at East Gully Bottom.

How far did it walk?

Ten *li*.

It walked ten *li*?!

In that night's earthquake, three of the caves in the village collapsed, though luckily no one was injured. The caves were dilapidated anyway, one had been used for keeping a sow in and she and two of her piglets were crushed to death, and the other two had stuff stored in them and some jars and crocks and farm tools were broken. A lot of inhabited caves got cracks in the walls, and doors and window frames were pushed askew, and some of the shit-house and pigpen walls collapsed. Where there were walled-in yards, the tiles along the tops of the walls all fell off. We heard about the mountain walking after breakfast. When a mountain walked, it meant a slope, a ridge, a knoll or a cliff had fallen into the gully below. It had happened in a lot of places but the most serious collapse was at East Gully Bottom, where the cliff had come down for a whole ten *li* stretch, on both sides of the gully, and the road through it was blocked in three places. Luckily, the streams running through the gully were dry so no quake lakes had formed. I hadn't been to East Gully Bottom, but from the strip I could see the opening to it, which was flanked by a knoll to the left

and the right. It was a beautiful view, and I said we ought to call our place
Bellavista. I'd planned to go and look at the hot springs and the blood
onion fields one day. But now that the mountain had walked ten *li,* the
knoll to the right of the gully entrance wasn't there any more, there was
just a huge chasm.

When the news broke about the disaster at East Gully Bottom, the call
went out for rescuers, and Bright was in the first group to leave. As soon as it
was light, he'd got up to go and check his store. Dozens of the edging tiles
had fallen off and a wide crack had opened up in the east wall, but the
building itself was still standing. Inside, everything had fallen down, goods
were lying all over the place, a few bottles of wine and seven or eight china
bowls had broken.

As he was cleaning up, Monkey came running: "The mountain's walked
at East Gully Bottom!"

"The mountain's walked at East Gully Bottom?" Bright repeated.

"Someone up there's got it in for Spring-Starts and La-Ba!" said Monkey.

Bright went to tell the village boss, then checked the brothers' caves. It
was true, they weren't there. Fearing the worst, Bright grabbed a saucepan
lid and beat it to call the villagers. Meantime, Rice set off for East Gully
Bottom, weeping and wailing.

I heard Rice crying and I wanted to go along with Bright, but he didn't
want me to, he said I was so slow and clumsy I'd find it really hard-going,
and they had no idea yet just how bad it was. But I insisted and finally he
said: "Well, just take your time." He took off at a run but then came back to
give the dog an order, and the animal tagged along with me, glued to
my heels.

The road through East Gully Bottom swung between clinging to the east
cliff and then the west cliff. It was almost blocked now, and clods of earth
and rocks still rolled down from time to time. Where it was really
impassable, the dog led me down to the gully bottom, and when that was
blocked we went back up to the road again. Finally we made it as far as the
blood onion fields. The cliff face on the left hand side had come down for a
whole three or four kilometres. This used to be the widest bend in the road
through the gully but now it was narrower than the opening. Rice and the
other villagers were already there, Delight Liu, Bounty, Rake Zhang,
Respect Wang, Tongue-Trip and Monkey too. They were all trying to move
a rock, but it was as big as a millstone and they couldn't budge it.

Rice, tears streaming down her face, cried: "Harder! Monkey, call a work chant! Everybody, harder!"

Monkey began to chant: "One – two...!" and everyone heaved together but still the rock didn't budge. "Water-Bring! Get a mattock!" shouted Monkey.

Water-Bring and Three-Lobes scraped a depression in the soil with their mattock, then passed it to Monkey who pushed it under the rock as far as he could and shouted again: "One – two...!" Everyone put their backs into it but there was still no movement. Rice fell to her knees and began scraping away the earth under the rock with her hands until her fingers bled.

"Get up, Rice!" the village boss told her. "You can scrape all you like, but even if we can push this rock away, it's only one rock, and the whole cliff has come down on them, and even if we worked away for ten years, we'd never clear it all!"

Someone was pulling Rice to her feet: "You go home now. The living have to live, and let the dead lie. Let this be their grave, the biggest-ever grave, bigger than an emperor's!"

But Rice was still screaming like a madwoman: "Spring-Starts – La-Ba! Spring-Starts – La-Ba!"

It was such a desolate sound that terror clutched at me, and my legs turned to jelly. I sat down on the ground. Bright saw me and told me to spit at the heavens.

"But I don't feel sick any more, how can I spit?"

Bright whispered: "Keep your voice down, Spring-Starts and La-Ba died violently, and their ghosts are powerful. You spit at them and they'll keep away from you." I still couldn't spit but tears ran down my cheeks.

"You go and calm Rice down," the village boss told me.

As I reached her, she flung her arms around me and said: "Sis, I've lost them both!" And she burst into sobs again, wetting my shoulder with her tears and runny nose.

Rice was speaking again: "Butterfly, when they split the house up, they kept fighting and arguing. I don't understand how they died together!"

"Sis, sis, please don't get so upset...' I said, though really I didn't know how to comfort her.

"It's all my fault. I've never been able to keep a man, and now they've both left me!"

As I was talking to Rice, people were walking over the landslip.

Suddenly there were yells from Bright's dad and Six-Fingers on the valley road, and just where the cliff fall had come to a halt, they had found a basket and a pair of scissors, and the body of Auntie Spotty-Face.

Everyone came running. It really was Auntie Spotty-Face, apparently lifeless, and Tongue-Trip stumbled over to her. I waited for the tears, but to my shock, he exclaimed: "You f-fucking ran... ran away! You f-fucking went and d-died on me here!" He put his arms around her and his fingers under her nostrils. She was still breathing, and he slapped her around the face, pressed the philtrum acupressure point and massaged her heart.

"Isn't there any water? Splash her with some water!" someone shouted. They looked for the hot springs but they had been completely buried, so Tongue-Trip undid his trousers and pissed on Auntie Spotty-Face's face. But her eyes remained tightly closed and she didn't come to. Tongue-Trip picked her up and started off for the village with her slung over his shoulder.

"Carry her in your arms! In your arms!" shouted Bright's dad, and some people ran up to help. But Tongue-Trip was too fast for them and left them behind.

It was anyone's guess what Auntie Spotty-Face was doing here when she was knocked out. Maybe she'd come to stick her papercuts around Spring-Starts and La-Ba's blood onion shed, and got caught in the landslip on her way back, not buried but knocked out by the air blast and the stones that rolled down afterwards. But the mountain had walked in the middle of the night, why was she sticking papercuts up then? So maybe she had gone to the site of the old temple during the day to pay her respects to the old locust tree, and was late coming back and was just on the rough track at the top of the cliff when the mountain walked and knocked her downwards. The force would have been huge so she'd landed right where the landslip had stopped.

"She's a born survivor," was the verdict.

The villagers were making their way out of the gully but Rice refused to go and I stayed with her. Bright was worried – there was usually rain after a mountain walked, and the wind was getting up in the gully. He insisted I leave, and so did Rice. But she asked Bright to come back with some hemp paper, because she wanted to burn funeral money for Spring-Starts and La-Ba. Bright took me home and gathered together paper, bunches of incense sticks and bottles of wine, two of everything because the brothers had fallen out before they died so they should have separate memorials. Then he left and didn't come back all night.

There were a lot of people around the Blacks' caves that night drinking tea and waiting for Bright to come back. They were talking about the mountain walking. That was when I learnt that it had happened several times before in these parts: twenty years ago, the township was hit when the mountain walked five *li*, destroyed three villages in its path and killed fifteen. You could still see people in the township who had lost limbs back then. Thirteen years ago, at West Gully Bottom, the mountain walked, killed only four people but destroyed a large number of fields. Three people had been ploughing with a donkey, and the animal survived unscathed but the three farmers were literally paralysed with fear. This time round, at East Gully Bottom, no one yet knew the extent of the damage, but it was clear that the village had suffered: Spring-Starts and La-Ba dead, and Auntie Spotty-Face unlikely to survive either. No one understood why the brothers were in the shed they'd built by the hot springs, because they only used it when they were harvesting blood onions. Why had they been there last night? Some of the villagers blamed Rice for making trouble between the brothers. When I asked why, they said that when they'd divided up the household, Rice had gone and married La-Ba, and that had ratcheted up the tension between the two men. But none of that was down to Rice. She was living in a cave on her own and she didn't bolt the door at night, so whichever brother turned up was fine by her.

"Like cattle," suggested someone.

"Right, like cattle, and bulls fight over their cows, don't they? I reckon they were there together because Rice went to the hot springs shed in the afternoon, and each of the brothers followed her, but then Rice went back to her cave and wouldn't let either of them go with her. The brothers stayed where they were and that was how they got caught when the mountain walked."

They were all talking at once. I boiled water for their tea at first, but then I got fed up with their gossip and stopped.

"It was lucky that it was the East Gully mountain that walked," said Pillar. "Any nearer the village and we would all have been buried in our sleep. We should drink a toast."

There were shouts of "Bright's dad! Bring the wine out!" But the old man said there wasn't any, they'd have to wait till Bright came back and fetched some from the store. They waited until midnight but Bright never showed.

"You think someone's got hold of Bright?" said Delight.

"Bullshit," I said. "Spring-Starts and La-Ba will get hold of you!"

"The brothers got on well with Bright, their ghosts will leave him alone," someone said.

But then Six Fingers put in: "There's only Bright and Rice out there. What are they doing so late, shouldn't you go and look for them, Butterfly?"

"Go fuck yourself!" I went into my cave, furious.

After Tongue-Trip got Auntie Spotty-Face back home, some of the older villagers came to try folk remedies – acupressure under the nose and on the top of her head, making a bleed between her eyebrows with a shard of glass and moxibustion to the soles of her feet – but Auntie Spotty-Face lay unresponsive on the *kang*. I dropped by three times to see her.

The Blacks weren't keeping us apart any more. Now Auntie Spotty-Face was in a coma, Bright didn't object, and his dad gave me a bag of potatoes to take: "You can make your uncle Tongue-Trip a hot meal with them, I don't know how he's been getting anything to eat these last few days."

Their home was on a slope at the west end of the village. They'd levelled a strip of ground and dug out a cave but it was dilapidated now, and the earthquake had made cracks so wide it looked as if a tree was growing inside it. But everywhere was covered in papercuts in all possible colours, they were on the door, on the window, anywhere there was a bit of space. Tongue-Trip was excavating a hole next to the cave; the entrance was small but he'd gone three or four feet in.

"Uncle, are you making a pigpen?" I asked.

The villagers often dug small holes in the undercliff to keep chickens and pigs in.

"I'm digging a grave f-for Aunt... Auntie Spotty-Face."

That really pissed me off. I felt like saying: But she's not dead yet, what are you doing digging a grave for her? Instead, I turned my back on him and went into the cave to see Auntie. Inside, it stank so badly I could hardly breathe, and it was pitch-dark too. I had to wait quite a while before I could make anything out. There was so much stuff piled on the floor that there was nowhere to put your feet, and the stove was covered in dirty pots and bowls, they hadn't even been put to soak and they were crawling with flies. The chopping board was even dirtier, a salt pot and a vinegar bottle and a tobacco box, plus an old hat, dirty socks, some steamed potatoes and a bit of buckwheat pancake were all jumbled up together. Auntie Spotty-Face was on the *kang*, her eyes tight shut and her face wrinkled like a walnut so you could hardly see her pockmarks any more. She looked like a skeleton lying there covered with papercuts. Nearby there was a wooden box with the lid open, maybe Tongue-Trip had picked it up and tipped them all over her.

There were flies crawling all over Auntie Spotty-Face's face, and mosquitos around the corners of her eyes. I brushed them away and gave the papercuts a closer look. I'd never seen so many before, and I tried to tell which ones were for windows, which were for above the pillow, or around the *kang*, or for sticking on curtains, and then I turned up a load of little people holding hands. It was ones like these that Auntie Spotty-Face had laid all over me the first time she came to call my soul back. I laid some on her head, in the hope she would regain consciousness. That was what she'd done to me, but she'd also muttered a long spell, that was the only way to call the soul back, so she said. I didn't remember any of what she'd said, so I just called her: "Auntie! Auntie Spotty-Face!"

I thought I saw her eyelids flutter, and shouted: "Uncle, Auntie's waking up!"

He came running in, but all he said was: "She... she c-can't have!" And he went out again.

I was sure that Auntie Spotty-Face sensed that I'd come to see her and that it was me shouting her name, and to prove it, I talked to her: "Auntie, if you know it's me, flutter your eyelids again."

I stared at them but they didn't move. Instead, a spider as big as a mung bean scooted out of a cranny onto her face, and squatted there, very still. I burst into tears and said silently: Spider, spider, that means she's telling me she does know it's me, she just can't move her eyelids, she's too weak to move them.

Tongue-Trip was making the whole cave judder, banging away with his mattock but he must have heard me call her name because the noise stopped and he came back.

"The... the wife of the b-brothers, w-why hasn't she... she come?"

He meant Rice. "Maybe because she's still mourning them," I said.

"It's all b-because of the stuff they were do-doing that this happened to

her. And that w-woman hasn't even been over to see... see if she's dead
or alive!"

I didn't know what to say to that. I stroked Auntie Spotty-Face's face:
"Haven't you called her soul back?"

"I'm no... no g-good at that st-stuff," he said. "She'd b-been do-doing it...
all h-her life, and n-now she's... she's ended up with h-her own s-soul gone."

"Haven't you had any lunch, Uncle?" I asked.

"I-I've been d-digging a... a cave."

"Oh, Uncle."

"How... how am I going to g-go on living all alone? I'm digging that c-
cave so when she pegs out, she can s-sleep in there, and she'll... she'll be a
bit nearer to me."

I looked at this fierce old man and suddenly felt sorry for him. "I'll cook
you a meal," I said.

I looked in the flour bin but there was only half a bowl of buckwheat
flour left. I mixed it to a dough and made some cat's-ear noodles for him. He
waited, hunkered down on the floor and watched me. Then he lit his pipe,
propped himself against the wall and opened his mouth wide enough to get
your fist in, groaning loudly. It was the kind of groaning that Bright's dad
did too, it was like they were so bone-tired that this was the only way they
could bring their exhaustion out from their joints. When the meal was
ready, I served it for him and he took the bowl and put it next to Auntie
Spotty-Face.

"Eat... eat some," he said. "Then I'll have mine."

After a little while, he took the bowl back and ate the noodles.

A couple of weeks after the mountain walked, more of the knoll on the left
of East Gully Bottom came down, injuring Blindy and his donkey. Blindy
had loaded his donkey with the grave marker that the villagers wanted to
put in place by the hot springs for Spring-Starts and La-Ba, but as soon as
he'd dropped it off, he turned to go home. The villagers who were putting
the grave marker in place tried to persuade him to stay and help.

"The brothers will be annoyed if you don't!"

But Blindy just said: "I brought the grave marker, how can they be
angry? And my donkey needs a rest."

Blindy and the donkey had just got to the gully entrance when the knoll came down. Blindy had sharp ears, and when he heard it start to go, he ran forward. The clods of earth struck them anyway. He got a big bruise on the back of his head, and the donkey hurt its leg.

When the second collapse happened, Bright's dad was standing on the strip and reckoned the collapse looked like a tiger's angry maw, coming to eat us up. He shouted at some people to bring a large rock so he could carve a stone lion to face down the tiger. But he'd never carved a stone lion before, in fact he'd never seen a lion, so he went to Auntie Spotty-Face's house to look at one of her papercut lions. He found a beast with a head a third as big as the body, and eyes a third as big as the head, and thought it must be a lion. He took it to Great-Grandad for confirmation.

Great-Grandad was talking to the village boss. He had sent me to fetch the man while Bright's dad was out looking for his papercut lion. All I knew was that the village boss lived in Third Alley, so I stood in the alley about to shout his name when he appeared from Second Alley with Bounty carrying the dynamited corpse of a fox.

"Great-Grandad's looking for you," I told him.

He said: "Bounty, let me present this fox to the old man."

"He won't want a fox," said Bounty, "and I need to sell it so I can buy new shoes. If you really want one, I'll give you the next one I kill."

"Huh, well, go and kill another one then. Great-Grandad's a fox and so is Butterfly!" '

"What?" I exclaimed.

The village boss smiled: "Great-Grandad's an old fox and you're a beautiful fox. You need a special spirit if you're going to be beautiful or long-lived!"

I turned, slapped the dirt off my bottom contemptuously and stalked off.

When the village boss arrived to see Great-Grandad, the old man said he'd only sent me to fetch him because, for a month now, his legs felt so terribly heavy, otherwise he would have gone to the boss's house.

"If you need me, I'll come even if I have to crawl on all fours! Your legs feel heavy? You must have had a premonition of the earthquake."

"When you get old, the heaviest thing in the world's your legs," said Great-Grandad.

I came out carrying the water bucket, and Blindy took it off me to lower it into the well. "The heaviest thing in the world is a heart, a selfish heart!" I said.

"Who are you talking about?" asked the village boss.

"You ask Great-Grandad, he's got a special spirit, he knows."

There was a loud clanking as Blindy began to turn the well wheel. "Why do you have to do that now?" demanded the village boss. "Can't you see I'm trying to talk to Great-Grandad?"

Blindy hauled the bucket up and took it into the cave. I sat down on the stone pier by the door. I was feeling a bit peckish, but there was nothing that took my fancy, so I took a deep breath and took in some air instead. Great-Grandad was talking to the village boss and he didn't sound happy.

"You're the village boss, can't you get people to clean up the theatre room?"

"Stuff from the village used to be stored downstairs, but now Bright's using the ground floor as his store, everything got bunged upstairs. Are you thinking of moving in?"

"Why would I want to live up there? You should be inviting theatre troupes, that's what I'm saying."

"You want to watch operas, is that it? Ai-ya, Great-Grandad, we'd never get the county troupe here. Even if they agreed, it's too far and there are dozens of them, too many to fit on Bright's tractor!"

"But there's a shadow theatre in the township, isn't there?"

"Why do you suddenly want to see a play? It's been ages since we had any events in our village. How about I talk to Bright and Rice? Rice has to do the brothers' funeral and she ought to invite a troupe, and Bright's baby will be born soon, so he'll want to invite them too."

"This has nothing to do with them. Opera isn't for entertainment or a thank-you for people's help, opera is sung for the spirits, to calm them down, so they protect our village."

"For the spirits? Which spirits? Where?"

"Don't you think there have been some strange happenings in the village in the last few years?"

"Well, anyone who's died has died of natural causes, and the mountain walking was a natural disaster, and I've asked the county for disaster funds and Rice will get welfare benefits too. East Gully Bottom never had many fields, so if we get some disaster funds then we'll be quids in!"

"I'm worried sick about it all."

"Don't worry, Great-Grandad, I'm in charge of village affairs, that's why the township government appointed me."

The old man's face fell and he said nothing more. The village boss got up to go. As he passed me, he spread his hands and smiled: "If we get the shadow players, then you and Bright can clear the stock out of the shop, can't you? Otherwise, where will we put the upstairs stuff?"

I ignored him and went into my cave to get a bowl of water to take to Great-Grandad. The old man drank some then choked, and the water went all over his chest. Bright and his dad had not heard anything that passed between the two of them, only Blindy and me were there, and we never mentioned it to anyone.

Later on, Bright's dad came back from Auntie Spotty-Face's with a papercut of a lion. He asked Great-Grandad: "Has Auntie Spotty-Face ever seen a lion? Where did she see one? Have you seen one?"

"Nope."

"Is this a lion? It looks scary enough to be one."

Bright's dad spent a few days carving his lion. First the head appeared in the rock, with a round face, big eyes and an open maw as big as a washbowl. Then the claws emerged, looking like the tines of a rake, and finally the lion's rump. In the afternoon he put the final touches, painting the eyes red. Padlock was back weeping at his late wife's grave, and the sounds carried to us on the wind, but no one took any notice any more. What they did notice was Rice setting off for East Gully Bottom with a bundle of offerings paper tucked under her arm to burn for Spring-Starts and La-Ba. So today must be the Seven Sevens. How quickly the days had gone by, forty-nine of them since their deaths.

I went with Rice to keep her company, but when I got to the village entrance I began to get pains in my belly. Rice asked me if I was near my due date but I didn't know. She had never given birth so she didn't either. Were they labour pains or had I eaten something that disagreed with me? She yelled for Bright, who emerged from his store and told Rice off for taking me with her.

"It was nothing to do with Rice," I said. "I wanted to."

But Bright wasn't letting it go: "You shouldn't have, Rice, look at her condition, and you're taking her to a place like East Gully Bottom?"

Rice by this time was thoroughly embarrassed and I got furious. Bright took me by the arm and led me to the store. Rake and Three-Lobes were there, a pile of cigarette butts in front of them, so they must have been chatting for a while. Bright wanted to shut up shop and give me a piggy-back home, but I told him not to bother, it was nothing, it would pass. And I went and lay down on the bunk bed inside. Bright brought me some water and carried on talking to Rake and Three-Lobes.

It sounded like they were talking about the blood onions: now that Spring-Starts and La-Ba were gone and the fields destroyed, the three of them could start up in business. They had a long argument about whether the best place was near the hot springs or in Back Gully, but they didn't come to any agreement. Bright was dead against the hot springs site, first because the ground would be too dry, and second because the brothers had only just died. What would the villagers think, and Rice?

The other two looked gloomy at that, then Three-Lobes said: "It depends how you look at it. We're grabbing our chances, and who cares what other people think? Rice can go in with us because she's got the sales set up. And she's a widow now, so Rake, if you play your cards right, you can take her home with you."

"You'll have to be matchmaker then," said Rake.

"You've just got to be firm," Three-Lobes advised him.

"I'm scared of her. Feelings take time to grow."

Delight spoke: "There are quite a few men in the village who'll have their eyes on her. By the time you've got around to growing feelings, someone else will have eaten up the bowl of red-cooked pork."

"Help me out, Bright," said Rake.

"But you're not her type."

"Who is then?"

"Bring-Silver, that's who."

"Why am I less good than Bring-Silver and Padlock? If you help me out, I'll buy you matchmaker's shoes, all leather!"

I sat up and interrupted: "That's enough of that! Aren't you afraid the brothers' ghosts will come after you?" Their faces fell. I got to my feet and set off for home.

Bright came running out after me: "Are you OK? Has your belly stopped hurting?"

Someone was doing their washing on the river bank at the entrance to the village, banging away with a wooden club, Clan-Keeper's wife passed me climbing up the steep alley, a dog scooted by with someone in pursuit, panicked and fell head-first into a large hole. My belly still hurt, in fact I felt like the whole world hurt.

I'd got as far as Third Alley when I came across a woman standing there eating. After a few mouthfuls she let loose a string of curses, really foul language, and another woman appeared from the alley above: "Hasn't that food stopped your gob? Now who are you swearing at?"

"I don't need to tell you that!"

"What is it, you've been fucked or you've got no one to fuck?"

The other woman bridled at that and the insults ricocheted back and forth like exploding popcorn. The alleys above and below were suddenly crowded with people, but no one tried to calm them down or pull them apart, they just whispered and snickered among themselves. I hurried back to the cave and lay down.

These villagers were a quarrelsome lot. No one ever kept their windows shut, and people were always talking about someone else behind their backs. There were arguments from morning till night. Bright had always told me: "If anyone badmouths someone to you, never say anything back. If you don't agree with them, they'll be there haranguing you forever. If you do agree, then the next day they'll make it up with the person they were badmouthing and you'll have made an enemy."

"Why are they so quarrelsome?" I asked him.

"It's like they're growing thorn bushes in front of them to keep other people away," he said.

"So how come they make it up again the next day?"

"Well, they all live in the same village, people can't avoid each other. Right and wrong don't come into it."

I lay on the *kang* going over all this until I couldn't think straight any more. My belly still hurt, I'd better go to the doctor. So I got on the donkey and rode to Xie Gully, where Bright had told me there was a small clinic. The donkey had recovered from the injury to its leg, but the beast was old and stumbled along and when we'd got over one ridge, I felt something slip out of me, I felt down there and there was something red on my hand, a pale, peachy sort of red. I was terrified.

"Mum! Mum!" I shouted, and there she was, coming towards me over another ridge, not far away from me but there was a gully between us. The sun had just risen and all I could see was her silhouette but it was definitely her.

I yelled again: "Mum!" but she wasn't listening. I yelled again, woke myself up and realised I'd been dreaming. My hair was damp with sweat, and my belly was still hurting a bit. What did that dream mean? I wondered. I hadn't dreamt about my mum for a long time. And why had she ignored me? If you believed that dreams were reality upside-down, then did that mean she was missing me? The thought made me panicky, and panic seemed to make me ill. Like, last month I had a panic attack and sprained my ankle; two months ago, the same thing and I got headaches, and now I had a bellyache. Maybe my mum was still angry that I hadn't gone home, or she knew something had happened to me and was looking all over for me. But the world was so big, how would she ever find me? I couldn't escape from the village, only the village boss had a phone and I'd never get a chance to use it. Just then, something made me break out in a cold sweat, and I sat up with a jerk.

I had just remembered the phone number in the courtyard where we rented a room. Though I couldn't quite remember whether the fifth digit was an eight or a five. If I got that wrong, I'd have lost contact with the outside world forever, and I'd never see my mum again. I racked my brains and punched myself in the head, and said a prayer to the nonesuch flower in its frame. Finally I settled on the five, not the eight. So I wouldn't get it wrong next time, I got up to scratch the number on the wall. Then I got worried that Bright might see and scrape the number off or whitewash over it so I divided the eleven digits up and scratched them in different places: zero on the shit-house wall, two on the pigpen wall, nine on the undercliff where it bent around the corner, and the rest of the numbers in a line going east to west, on the kitchen wall, the cave door, and inside the cave, behind the table, behind the sacks and crocks, behind the jars, until I had scratched the area code and our landlord's number, 88225761.

Then I addressed the nonesuch flower: "I'm not going to disappear, I'm still in the land of the living, and one day my mum will find me."

Chapter 5

THE EMPTY TREE

THE POTATO HARVEST HAD STARTED.

Potatoes – 'earth beans', the villagers called them – were the staple crop hereabouts. They believed they were clods of earth that turned into beans underground and had to be dug as soon as they were ready. If you didn't get to them in time, they might run away, the way buried gold runs away. So this was the busiest time in the farming year and everyone pitched in. Migrant workers, people who'd gone away digging on the off-chance they might find a nonesuch flower, and even the gamblers, thieves and scroungers who roamed the local villages, they all came back home. The village felt like a shrivelled, deflated balloon suddenly pumped full of air. Bright shut the store and stuck a notice on the door: 'Digging potatoes, shout if you want something.'

The Blacks' land consisted of five fields in South Gully and Back Gully. Once the potatoes were dug, Blindy packed them into sacks and onto the donkey, and then he brought them back. The donkey made so many trips, it went lame in its injured leg so Blindy loaded it with two sacks at a time and carried one sack himself.

On their first trip back, Blindy picked three potatoes as big as rice bowls, and he laid them reverently before the spirit tablet in the cave.

They wouldn't let me go and dig, or even prepare food to send to them. Bright did that: as soon as they arrived in the field, he dug a hole, put in a layer of potatoes, then a layer of firewood, then repeated this, then lit the firewood and covered it up with clods of earth, leaving just a small hole for the smoke to escape. By midday, when the hole had stopped smoking and they scraped the earth off, the potatoes were ready. Bright's dad and his two sons ate them, then carried on working. Alone in the cave, I made myself some porridge to eat, then chopped up the potato tops to feed to the pigs. As I chopped and chopped, it occurred to me that there was no one here so I could make my escape, but immediately I felt a thudding in my belly so fierce that it actually knocked me sideways onto the ground. I thought: Fucking kid! Your dad's not here to keep an eye on me so you've turned cop instead! I smiled grimly, stopped chopping and flung the knife outdoors. It landed right in front of the dog, and it sat up, ears pricked, and glared at me.

I'd stopped thinking about ways to escape, what was the point? It was as hopeless as this arid plateau yearning for water or the moon trying to shine on a moonless night.

I told the dog: "You can carry on sleeping, I'm not running anywhere."

And I went to the kitchen to heat some water to take down to the fields.

But before the water boiled, I got pains in my belly again, not a dull ache like before or stabbing pains, but cramps, as if a hand was pulling at my guts, or turning a knife in them. I'd been sitting on the little stool feeding the stove, but now I pulled myself upright and leaned against it. My legs trembled, and beads of sweat rolled down my face and pattered on the stove top. First, I gritted my teeth but soon I couldn't stand it any more. I thought I was going to die. I told the dog to fetch Bright. It hadn't been gone long when I heard it on the strip, barking frantically. I looked out: it was Blindy back from the fields. He unloaded the sacks from the donkey, then suddenly stood still and said in the direction of the cave door: "The pot's boiled dry!"

By that time, I could smell something too, but he'd already come in and taken the lid off the pot. The base was red-hot and the rim of the lid was burned black. He hurriedly ladled in some water.

I said: "Ai-ya, I was just boiling some water."

"That doesn't mean boiling the pot dry... Hey, are you sick?"

I let go of the stove and slumped to the ground. Blindy stood beside me, looking helpless, then rushed for the door and hit his head against the lintel.

He got Great-Grandad in, and the old man exclaimed: "What's up? What's up?"

He tried to pull me to my feet but couldn't shift me, so he yelled at Blindy to carry me to the *kang*.

"I'll go and get a sheet," said Blindy.

"She's in a bad way," said Great-Grandad. "Never mind the sheet!"

So Blindy picked me up, holding me out in front of him, his arms as rigid as iron bars. He actually managed to keep me level but he turned his face away. He took me back to my cave and placed me on the *kang*.

"What's the pain like?" asked Great-Grandad.

"Like I'm going to die," I said.

"You're having the baby," he said.

He gave me a chopstick and told me to bite down on it.

"I'm going to shout for Bright," said Blindy, rushing out the door and losing one shoe as he went.

Bright came running back, dripping with sweat, and he put his arms around me.

"Does it still hurt? Does it still hurt?" he kept asking.

The crotch of my trousers was wet and some blood was oozing out. I was thrashing around from the pain, and Bright couldn't hold onto me though he tried his best. I grabbed his arm with both hands and twisted it as if I was going to twist a lump of flesh off.

"Go ahead and twist," he told me.

But I let go and fell back and started banging my head on the edge of the *kang*. Bright was so scared, he ran out of the cave to where his dad was kneeling on the strip, praying to the heavens. "Dad! Dad! Her pains are so bad, I'm really scared!"

"Giving birth is a scary business."

"Is she really giving birth?"

"Get Full-Barn's mum, quick as you can, give her a piggyback!"

The dog went with him, and Bright gave it a telling-off it as he ran: "I trained you to bark when something happened. Why didn't you bark for me?"

Full-Barn's mum trotted along on her own two feet, bringing her grandson with her. She came into my cave but wouldn't let the boy in with her.

"Give him something to eat," she told Bright. Bright gave the child a raw potato.

"There was only the two of them, and he didn't want to be left behind," he told his dad. The old man swapped the raw potato for a cooked one.

"He's a good omen," he said.

"How come?"

"Having a boy here will mean she'll give birth to a boy!"

Full-Barn's mum was very short, and her arms hung below her knees. She came and had a look at me.

"Yes, you're having the baby," she said without a trace of concern. She picked up a pipe and sat down in the doorway for a smoke, sucking on the pipe like she hadn't had a smoke in years, head down, then finally letting out an endless stream of smoke from her mouth. Bright's dad sat down, then stood up, sat down then stood up again, keeping his eyes fixed on Full-Barn's mum.

"Are you trying to panic me?" she demanded. "Go and boil a knife in water."

Bright's dad grunted and went off.

"And bring some cloth," she added.

"What cloth?"

"To swaddle the baby in when it's born."

"We haven't got that yet," said Bright's dad.

"Haven't got it? Why didn't you get it ready before now?"

Bright said he'd go to the store for some cloth.

"And bring some brown sugar lumps," she instructed. Then she carried on smoking.

By the time Bright got back, I was shrieking with the pain. He came and put his arms round me again and told me to hang on, but I cursed and swore at him.

"How can I hang on? It was you who did this to me!"

That put him off and he let go of me, but then I started screaming so he came and put his arms round me again: "I won't say anything, you scream and swear all you like if it makes it hurt less."

Finally Full-Barn's mum finished her pipe.

"Off you go, Bright," she said. "This isn't your business. Go and keep an eye on my grandson, stop him running around like that."

"Why does she hurt so much?" asked Bright.

"Because having a baby does hurt!" said Full-Barn's mum.

Once he was out of the cave, the woman took off my clothes and propped me up on the rolled-up quilt. She went to the doorway and brought back the bowl of hot water and the scissors.

"If you carry on screaming like that, you won't have any strength left when you need it, and then what'll we do?" she said.

"Bring me half a basket of stove ash," she called outside to Bright.

"Stove ash?"

"To soak up the blood in a bit. And three poached eggs for her to eat. We don't want her collapsing before the baby's born."

"She's still screaming!" said Bright.

"So now you know how hard it is to be a woman, don't you?"

She shut the door and sat on the edge of the *kang* smoking.

"It happens to all women the same, there's nothing to be afraid of. When I had my first, Full-Barn, I was out hoeing the fields, he was born on the bare earth and I had to break the cord by smashing it with a stone."

She examined me again, sticking her fingers inside and muttering: "It's open." I was just going to ask what was open, when I felt an excruciating pain and I was gone.

I was up on the third bar of the window lattice, looking down on Full-Barn's mum.

Still sucking on her pipe, she parted Butterfly's legs and propped her bottom on a pillow. Some liquid oozed out, and a piece of flesh appeared then immediately disappeared again. "It's breech!" exclaimed Full-Barn's mum. The tiny foot appeared again. She threw the pipe down and half-knelt on the kang.

Bright poked his head through the door: "Eh? Why's it not crying?"

"It's a crab."

"She's having a crab?"

"The baby's stuck. The head always comes out first but for this one it's the foot."

"Eh?"

"Come in, Bright, come and give me a hand!"

Bright came in but he was too frightened to look down below. He moved to Butterfly's head, looked at her and said: "She's fainted."

Full-Barn's mum pressed hard on the point beneath Butterfly's nose and slapped her cheeks: "Wake up! Wake up!"

"Butterfly!" Bright shouted, through his sobs.

Full-Barn's mum said: "She's only fainted from the pain, what are you crying about?"

She bent down and picked up the bowl of water, swished it around a bit to cool it down and splashed some on Butterfly's face. Butterfly woke up.

I opened my eyes but the pain was even worse than before, and I shrieked again.

Full-Barn's mum began to push me into different positions. Bright tried to help but she wouldn't let him. Six times, then another six times. She pushed me onto my side, onto my back, then made me turn onto my belly but I couldn't so she made me get my knees underneath me, then she pushed on my back.

"Bright," she said, "you've got better eyesight than me, is her backbone straight?"

"I can't see."

"Turn her over, turn her over."

Bright turned me over and held me tightly to his chest, and I was back in the same position I'd been in before. The woman was kneading my belly, her face pouring with sweat. Then she bent down to look at me again: "That's better. You've got a little emperor in there, and it's causing me grief!"

Then she sat down for another smoke: "Have you done the eggs?"

"Yup," said Bright. "And one for you and one for the kid."

"Get down off there and feed her an egg," she told him.

But I was bleeding all over the *kang* and I fainted again.

I was up on the window lattice, looking at Bright pinching Butterfly under her nose, while Full-Barn's mum looked like she was getting annoyed. She grabbed Butterfly's hand and pressed the hukou *point between her thumb and forefinger.*

"You're a lazybones! I need you to make an effort and you just faint on me!"

Bright's dad was out on the strip, kowtowing to the heavens again. He asked Great-Grandad: "Nothing's going to go wrong is it? Is it?"

"Of course not," Great-Grandad reassured him. "Look how the sun is, look how the birds are roosting so peacefully."

Full-Barn's mum bent over Butterfly's legs again, strands of her hair hanging loose, and sprinkled a handful of ashes between them to soak up the blood, and when she scooped the ashes up, the blood on her hands got on her head too. "My hair, my hair!" she exclaimed.

Bright was propped against the wall, as white as a sheet, sweat pouring off

him, not daring to look. "Go and warm up the eggs!" Full-Barn's mum told him.
But as soon as he was out of the door, his legs gave way under him.

"Dad, dad, heat up the eggs, they've gone cold," he said. But his dad was off to
the shit-house.

Butterfly must have opened her eyes because I heard: "Are you awake?"
Butterfly breathed out a long breath.

Full-Barn's mum said: "Now you're awake, hold your breath, and push, push
as hard as you can!"

Butterfly gritted her teeth and pushed.

"You're not trying, push! Harder, harder!"

Bright's dad came out of the shit-house, took the eggs into the kitchen and a
little while later came back with them. He gave them to Bright and went back into
the shit-house.

"What's up with you?" asked Bright.

"I dunno. I had the runs, I went but I couldn't crap anything out."

Butterfly was puffing and panting, like the donkey climbing up the hill, or a
bellows with a leak. Suddenly, her waters burst with a whoosh, splashing the
midwife all over her face, and at the same moment, the baby leapt out like a fish,
and landed on the kang *mat, naked and slippery, then slithered off and fell into the*
basket of ash at the foot of the kang.

"You're a dirty little thing!" exclaimed Full-Barn's mum. She hurriedly picked it
out of the ash, held it up by the legs and slapped its bottom. There was a loud wail.

A little while later, Bright came out onto the strip with the afterbirth
and announced to his dad, Great-Grandad and Blindy: "It's a boy!"

They buried the afterbirth under the stone lion.

I had a child and his name was One Black. Bright chose the name because,
as he said: "I want there to be Two and Three, Seven or Eight even! You and
me together, we can build a whole new village with them."

"A village of wifeless men?" I spat a gob of phlegm.

Flies and mozzies never stopped breeding maggots, the lower the form
of life, they more they bred, so that made Bright a real low-life.

When One was born, I didn't want to look at him. I remembered Auntie
Spotty-Face saying that, once you set eyes on your new-born, you were
bound to it forever, so I decided not to. But as soon as I heard Full-Barn's
mum say: "You're a dirty little thing!" and realised he'd fallen into the ash

basket, I got such a fright I sat up for a look. He was a skinny, tiny thing, like a hairless rat, and his little face was all wrinkled, he was so ugly and dirty, and apart from the ash, his body was covered in sticky white stuff.

"A pregnant woman shouldn't have sex, or the baby will be unclean," Full-Barn's mum had said.

I lay down, wordless, a sudden flush on my cheeks. Was this really my baby? And so ugly! Had I given birth to a monster because I'd been raped? What with the long, hard pregnancy and then the breech birth, this baby had nearly cost me my life! Fine, I said to myself, I've given birth to you now, and that's taken away from me all the shame, the loathing and the suffering. From now on, you're you and I'm me, you're no son of mine and you can forget I'm your mother.

But at night, when the cave was plunged in darkness, and One started to cry, he had such a loud, clear voice, it was as if a lamp had been lit and the flames leapt up and spirits awakened in everything in the cave – the table, the chairs, the flagons and jars, the bedding and pillows, and all the papercuts stuck to the window and walls – seemed to come to joyous life. I'd never felt like that before, I was filled with a nameless happiness.

"Bring him to me," I told Bright.

One lay on my breast, and he stopped whimpering and went back to sleep. I touched him all over, kissing his head, his bottom, and his tiny hands and feet. His skin was like snow and his body was soft like jade. This is my son, I thought to myself, flesh dropped from my body. Bright was going back to sleep but I pushed him away and told him to sleep on the floor, I didn't want him to stink out the baby with his smelly feet, and he was a restless sleeper, I didn't want him to fling out an arm or a leg and squash him either. So it was just the baby and me on the *kang*.

"It's Heaven's will," Bright burst out from his bed mat on the floor. "My first child, and Heaven's given me you and a son."

It's Heaven's will, I repeated silently. Heaven's given me a son to keep me company.

It suddenly occurred to me that my baby should be called Rabbit, because when the goddess Chang'e was all alone on the moon, she had a rabbit to keep her company. I cuddled him and kissed him: "Rabbit, Rabbit."

"Are you calling One, 'Rabbit'?" Bright said.

"He's not 'One', he's Rabbit."

"Fine, 'Rabbit' it is then," Bright conceded. "That's a good name too. How long before Rabbit says 'Dad'?"

He'll only say 'Mum', I said silently. I looked at the ceiling of the cave, though I couldn't see it, only blackness. I popped Rabbit's little foot into my mouth again, it was like a sugar lump, ready to dissolve, then I took it out of my mouth. Rabbit, you listen to your mum, one day Mum'll take you to the big city, we're not staying in this desperate place.

I had the feeling that the world had shrunk around me till the world was only me, and I was a spirit here in this village, in this cave.

For ten days, I sat on the *kang*, yellow earth spread out under me. That was the custom in this village: they would dig some pure yellow earth out of the ridge, dry it in the sun and toast it, then spread it on the *kang* and put a sheet of hemp paper on top, and the woman who had given birth sat on that for the first month. The yellow earth soaked up the impurities from the woman's body and she healed quicker. After ten days, I got off the *kang* and began to move around. That evening after dinner Rabbit fussed and cried – from his fifth day he'd started to sleep during the day and cry in the evenings – and Great-Grandad wrote out a little rhyme for him:

> Heaven's up there,
> Mum's down here,
> We've got a cry-baby at home.
> Read this rhyme, ye passers-by,
> And baby'll sleep soundly till dawn.

The old man told us to paste the slip of paper on a tree in the village, so we went out and stuck it up. On the way back, I spotted the two stars I'd seen before, one big and one small, shining not white but red. I pointed up at it: "That's mine and Rabbit's."

To my astonishment, Bright said: "What do you mean, I can't see them."

"You can't see anything?"

"There's no star there, you've got something in your eye."

I didn't say anything more to him.

When Rabbit was a month old, the Blacks prepared a feast and invited the villagers. The sun was rising over the cliff when they started to arrive on the strip. Some had brought baby clothes and shoes, but most turned up carrying a pumpkin, or a basket of potatoes, or a litre of ground maize or haricot beans. Tongue-Trip came as well, bringing a *kang* tiger with him. Almost every family had a *kang* tiger, they were stone figurines about as big as your fist. Bright told me that when there was an infant in the family, until it was two years old, it would be tethered to the tiger by a rope, so it could play on the *kang* without falling off. After the child turned two, if the mother went out with it or took it to her parents' home, she would take the *kang* tiger too, to ward off evil. The Blacks had had one and Bright had been tied to it as a baby, but he couldn't find it. The one Tongue-Trip brought had been stroked so much by sweaty hands that it shone. He told us his mum had used it for him when he was a small boy. I liked it very much and was delighted to accept it. I put it next to Rabbit, but then Bright decided to take it out of the cave again.

"You can't use his *kang* tiger," he said. The reason was that Auntie Spotty-Face was still in a coma. Also, she'd had one baby but it had died, so it would be unlucky to use their *kang* tiger.

"I'll make One a new one," he said.

"His name's Rabbit!" I said.

"Right, Rabbit, he can have a new one."

When the sun was high overhead, Rice came. She was in one of her showy outfits, and her voice carried from the strip entrance: "This is a great day for our village!"

She sashayed over to my cave, hips swaying, and I heard someone ask: "What have you brought for the baby?"

"I've brought a nonesuch flower for my godson!" Rice announced.

She took out a roll of paper and opened it. There really was a nonesuch flower inside. But calling Rabbit her godson was nonsense.

"Godson?" someone said. "So you're related to Bright now, are you? You know what they say, you take on the child and you're half in bed with the dad!"

Rice just laughed and came into the cave.

She put the nonesuch flower down by Rabbit, bent down and dropped a kiss on his face. It left a red lipstick mark.

"I haven't come before because I was still in mourning and it might have been bad for the baby. But last night, I went to East Gully Bottom and burned paper offerings to Spring-Starts and La-Ba. I told them this was my last visit, I wanted to live again. And when I got home, I took off my mourning clothes and tore the white paper couplets off the door. How do you like my red jacket? Nice, eh?"

As she showed it off to me, she whispered: "My bra and knickers are red too."

"Did you dig up the nonesuch flower yourself?" I asked.

"No, I was coming back from East Gully Bottom last night and I met someone digging. I took a look to see it was all there, the grub and the flower, then I bought it. When there was only one nonesuch flower in your home, there was only you. You get Bright to dry this one and put it in the frame with the other one. Now you've got a baby there are two of you and two nonesuch flowers, isn't that nice?"

She picked up Rabbit and kissed his bottom. That woke him up and he started to cry.

"Butterfly, you've put down roots now, but I'm still floating weed. Let me be his godmother?" she said.

"But haven't you already told everyone you are?"

"I was worried you might not agree, so I got in first!"

Rabbit peed all over her chest.

The eating and drinking began. Bright's dad had done all the cooking and there were three tables of guests. Of course, there were potato dishes: cold shredded potato, hot stir-fried potato slices, beancurd stewed with cubed potatoes, potato cakes, potato flour noodles, and although there was red-cooked pork slices, and a chicken stew and stewed tripe, they all had potatoes in them too. But the guests were happy enough.

"It's good, we've got three main dishes, though one more would have been better," said someone.

"Well, there was going to be mutton too," Bright's Dad said. "Bright went to the Wang village slaughterhouse to buy it but the head butcher, old Zhang, is in hospital, and the slaughterhouse was shut. But the wine's good today, the bottles cost twenty yuan each. Bright, bring the wine!"

The food was soon eaten, but the drinking carried on. Every time a bottle got emptied, Blindy removed it, drained the dregs, then put it with the other empties. By now there was a pile of a dozen or more on the edge of the strip. Tongue-Trip was the first to get drunk, he got Bright's dad to drink with him, and the old man knocked back three cups in a row. Then

Tongue-Trip wanted to play drinking games with him and Bright's dad won six times.

"You got-got to take on everyone at the table!" Tongue-Trip insisted.

But Bright's dad said: "You carry on drinking, I've got to look after the other guests." Tongue-Trip was not happy, and he grabbed Bright's dad by the scruff of the neck.

Great-Grandad, who was sitting at the top table and sticking to water, said to Bright: "Go and stop them drinking, don't let your dad get drunk, he's got high blood pressure." Bright didn't want to get into an argument, so he came into the cave for Rabbit and took him out.

"You haven't met my son. Let me introduce him to all the grannies and grandads, aunties and uncles in the village."

The drinking stopped, and Rabbit, wrapped in his little quilt, was generally agreed to be a beautiful, chubby baby.

Tongue-Trip, sprawled across the table, said: "He looks... looks like his d-dad, and his d-dad looks... like his g-grandad!"

Just then a woman appeared at the entrance to the strip. Her old man had been bedridden for some years now, and Bright's dad filled a bowl with food and placed a piece of meat on top for her to take home. When the woman came back with the empty bowl, she asked Tongue-Trip: "Has Auntie Spotty-Face woken up yet?"

"She'd be... be here if sh-she had, w-wouldn't she?"

"Then how come I've just seen her picking pumpkin flowers outside your door?"

"Then you must ... have s-seen a g-ghost in broad daylight!"

"It was her, and she was wearing a long gown!"

Tongue-Trip jumped to his feet and staggered off home to see. Someone ran after him in case he fell over.

A short time later, the man was back. It was true. Auntie Spotty-Face really had come back to life, he insisted.

"You're having us on!"

"I could see smoke coming out of the chimney of Tongue-Trip's cave and there was Auntie Spotty-Face in the kitchen cooking a meal, wearing embroidered shoes and a long gown. Tongue-Trip went in and threw his arms around her. He said: 'When did you... you c-come back to life?!' And Auntie Spotty-Face said: 'I'm starving hungry.'"

With his wife in a coma, Tongue-Trip had been sure she was going to die so he got a coffin made for her. Then he washed her, dressed her in burial clothes and put her in her coffin in their cave. He left the lid off.

"You have a good sleep," he told her. "And when there's no more breath in you, I'll bury you." Auntie Spotty-Face lay there and lay there, until the day of Rabbit's feast, when she suddenly opened her eyes and tried to turn over.

"What am I doing in here? Come and pull me out!" she cried.

But there was no sound in the cave and she finally hauled herself out. When she realised the cave door was closed but not locked, she swore: "Dammit, you went out without locking the door! Are you trying to let thieves in?"

She felt hungry so she searched in the pot and on the chopping board for something to eat, but the pot only had leftovers in it, the board was in a terrible mess and there was nothing to eat. Finally she found some cornmeal in one of the jars, mixed it with water and was going to make porridge. She wanted to add vegetables to the porridge but there were no vegetables in the cave. So she stumbled outside and picked herself some fresh green leaves from the pumpkin vine growing on the bank outside their door. But then she thought that pumpkin leaves were too bitter-tasting, so she threw them away and picked three pumpkin flowers instead.

The man finished his story, and Bright's dad told him to run back and stop Auntie Spotty-Face eating, come what may. She hadn't had anything, even liquids, for so long that eating solid food would make her ill.

"Bring her here on your back and I'll make her some gruel."

Auntie Spotty-Face was brought and drank a bowl of gruel.

"Why are there so many people here?" she asked.

I carried Rabbit over to show her.

"You had the baby! Such a big event and no one told me!" She parted Rabbit's legs and cried: "A little bull! Other families had better watch out for their daughters!"

There was loud laughter.

Then she cried frantically: "Scissors! Where's the scissors?"

"W-what are you l-looking for... scissors for?" asked her husband.

"I'm doing him a Zhong Kui papercut, to keep the demons away."

That day, Tongue-Trip went home three times: to get the scissors, to fetch red and green paper, and then, when Auntie Spotty-Face demanded yellow paper, to get that too. He got a lot of teasing for obediently running back and forth but he just said: "I've got... got a new w-wife, haven't I?"

Auntie Spotty-Face came to see me often after that, and the Blacks didn't mind. She used to sit on my *kang* making papercuts, and when it was dinnertime, she would share our meals. Tongue-Trip was embarrassed about that, and he brought over a bag of cornmeal and a big basket of potatoes. Sometimes she never went home at all and slept the night with me on the *kang*, so Bright spread his mat on the floor, of course. He felt it was a bit odd, with the four of us sharing one cave, so he said he'd go and sleep in the store, but Auntie Spotty-Face said: "You stay in your home, no need to leave, treat me like your Auntie!"

She was even more chatty and cheerful than before, and eccentric too. She would wake up in the early hours, saying God had taught her a new papercut, light the lamp and sit there scissoring away. She used to mix up plants and flowers and animals and people, and make people with the bodies of trees, and dogs and donkeys and rats with human faces. Once, she pointed at the cave wall: "What can you see there?"

I looked and saw nothing.

"There's a frog crawling up it."

And the next minute, she'd cut out a dozen frogs.

One afternoon, the clouds above us went as red as if they were on fire, and Auntie Spotty-Face made a papercut of a tree. It was a dead tree, with branches that reached out symmetrically at right-angles to the trunk, and the root bole was in the shape of a human head, complete with nose. It looked weird and primitive. The branches had swirling chrysanthemum designs on them, and birds fluttering and hopping. Even weirder were the hundreds of yellow wasps' clustered on every branch and flying around in the hollow trunk like blood circulating. I could almost hear the buzzing and the bird calls.

"What's this tree, Auntie Spotty-Face?" I asked.

"It's the empty tree."

She stared intently at me and the look in her eyes spooked me. The empty tree?

She began to sing:

> In the first month, in the second,
> I heap up earth round the blood onions,
> There's an empty tree there,
> Empty tree, tree hollow, a wasps nest in the hollow,
> The wasps sting me, I sting the wasps,
> And the stings make us fluffy-headed.

This was the first time she'd sung a song when she was making paper cuts, but after that, she sang a little ditty every time. For instance, when she cut out a man leading a donkey with his wife riding it, she sang:

> Bustard bird, tree bark, Padlock leads the donkey,
> Plum-Scent rides, Padlock whips Plum-Scent's toes
>   with his whip:
> 'Ai-ya! Ai-ya! That hurts! Is that because I'm flirty?'

"Is that Padlock?" I asked.
"That's right."
"Was Padlock good to his wife?"
"He was."
If she cut out a nonesuch flower, she'd sing:

> Diggers of medicine wear their towels in strings,
> Drinkers of medicine groan and cry,
> Dealers in medicine dress in silk and satin,
> Sellers of medicine tot up the figures.

"What do you mean, wear towels in strings?" I asked.
"Haven't you seen the diggers coming back with their jackets in tatters?"
Or she would cut out a figure holding a bowl of maize porridge and sing:

> Heaven's dark, the earth's dark, the clouds are dark,
> The tiller planting buckwheat yells at the donkey,
> He's uncovered the earth, and turned three corners,
> Three times and he's turned nine corners,

He holds down the plough-share, stills the whip and
    looks for his wife bringing his food.
A bamboo basket in her left hand, a two-handled pot
    in her right,
She stands in the field looking at her man.
What's for lunch? It's maize porridge. Maize porridge
    again?
The fuel's wet and the fire's smoking,
Two pot-stands and a pot of four hand-spans,
The strainer has no head and the spoon no handle,
I'm carrying your baby tucked into my jacket,
What are you going to eat if not maize porridge?

I burst out laughing and she said: "I'll cut another one and you tell me what it is."

As she cut, she sang an old folk rhyme:

He's a fixer for everything,
He ploughs his furrow far and wide,
He blows his trumpet loud and clear,
He fills a donkey muzzle with piss.

When the figure emerged, I said: "It's the village boss."

"You said it, not me," she said.

Then she cut out a cave with a woman sitting at the door, a tree full of birds nearby and a dog chasing chickens.

"As soon as the sun rises, it hits the west wall, the foot of the east wall is always in shade, the wine cup is smaller than old rice bowls, chopsticks are shorter than carrying poles, one sock has no mate, two socks make one pair, the child calls mum's brother Uncle, big brother's wife calls his mother-in-law Mum, there's rain in the seventh month, frost in the ninth, the fifth and sixth months are hot and busy, you don't believe what I'm saying, the girl grows up to be an old hag." She finished cutting and singing.

"You've cut me," I said, and the tears ran down my cheeks.

"I cut out myself," she said quickly.

The villagers all believed that, after Auntie Spotty-Face woke up, she was no longer human but had turned into a witch or a spirit. The rumour went around that her papercuts had souls, so whenever they had family festivities or were anxious about something, they went and asked her for a papercut, instead of consulting Great-Grandad like they used to.

I heard Three-Lobes grumbling to Great-Grandad about Auntie's sudden popularity. These days, Great-Grandad could barely walk anywhere without his stick, and he was sitting under the gourd frame. "How many times has it rained this month?" he asked Three-Lobes.

"Three times."

"Ah, there are always rainy days every month."

Auntie Spotty-Face spent seven days in my cave and made nearly twenty large papercuts in that time, all of a woman with a garland around her head. The garland was made of different coloured paper, and she wore an old-fashioned wedding cape with geometric patterns on it, and a black skirt with red-patterned borders, and she sat on a brilliantly-coloured lotus seat.

She sang:

> Mother Papercuts has no home,
> She roams through gullies and climbs over ridges,
> She blows cold and things dry out.
> Since she came into the cave, she's comfy and cosy.
> She calls her boy, takes her scissors and keeps on
>   making papercut figures.
> She cuts the four arts and the eight treasures of good
>   fortune.
> I make Mother Papercuts in red paper and green
>   circles.

"Auntie Spotty-Face, what have you made?" I asked.

"Mother Papercuts."

"She actually came to your house?"

"Mother Papercuts is me!"

She hung one of them on my wall.

"Auntie Spotty-Face's going round the bend," was Bright's comment.

But I didn't think she was round the bend. I respected her, and learned from her how to make papercuts.

. . .

What with looking after the baby and practising papercuts, I hadn't scratched the days on the wall for a long time. Bright's dad had begun to snore very loudly at night, louder than he'd ever done before, his snores were thunderous. The dog had stopped sleeping at the cave door, and when I went in and out during the day, he didn't follow me. Instead, he spent all his days out, only coming back to scavenge for food in the donkey's cave or have a slurp of the pig swill, or overturn the chicken feed bowl and rummage around underneath. Blindy said to Great-Grandad that the dog didn't behave like a dog any more.

"He's turned into a pair of chopsticks," the old man laughed, "he'll try anything."

Bright had developed quite a paunch, and a double chin too. "You'll turn into a pig soon," I said.

He waggled his hands in front of each ear: "A blessed piggy," he said, and went and watered his fleeceflowers.

Bright had planted up the edge of the strip with cosmos plants, but after they were rootled out by the pig, he sowed fleeceflowers there instead. At first, nothing came up, he might as well have planted pebbles. We forgot all about them. But suddenly one day, I went to hang out Rabbit's nappies on the washing line strung up along the edge of the strip, and I looked down and saw a haze of green. Bright was delighted. It must be the fleeceflowers coming up, he told me He put a stone down, attached a string to it and tied the other end of the string to the washing line, for the plants to grow up. Two shoots shot up with the speed of Jack's beanstalk, and within a month or two they had entwined themselves around the washing line.

All I knew about fleeceflowers was that they were used in herbal medicine and were supposed to make your hair grow and stop it turning grey. I didn't expect them to be so vigorous. Every day Bright watered them, and when I had time, I used to take Rabbit to look at them. The leaves were pale one day, then darker the next, fingernail-sized one day, then a day later the size of a copper coin. What amazed me was that there were only the two stalks and they went their separate ways by day, pointing east and west, or north and south, but as night drew in, they huddled together head to head, tail to tail, entwined and trembling slightly in the breeze. Bright told me that they were 'yang' by day and 'yin' by night, and their roots could grow into human shape. Did I want to scrape away the earth and have a look, he asked? But I was worried that might damage the roots so I didn't, and I wouldn't let Bright either.

"You know why I planted fleeceflowers?" Bright said, very pleased with himself. I had no idea.

"Because the plant is like a family, isn't it? The root is the child and the stalks are you and me."

I was taken aback, looked at him and he was smiling.

"I never imagined they would grow," he said. "And so fast!"

I don't know what expression showed on my face. I looked out towards the west, to where there was a patch of flaming red like coral lilies in flower all along the ridge. Was that all there was around here, fleeceflowers and coral lilies, and had the lilies come out now? Then I looked more closely – they weren't lilies, it was a small tree with its leaves turning red. I took Rabbit back into the cave.

After dinner, I was out on the strip with Rabbit in my arms and Blindy was mucking out the donkey's stable and piling the dung under the pine tree.

"You and Rabbit better go inside," he said. "The muck will stop smelling once the wind's blown over it for a night."

I laughed.

"I don't think it smells bad," I said.

As soon as the words were out of my mouth, I was surprised at what I'd said. Of course the muck stank, so how come I couldn't smell it? Maybe it was because the birds shat from the trees every day so I was used to it. I looked up at the sky. There were the two stars, right above the pine trees. Stars appeared randomly in the night sky, and two of them used to look down on my mum and me. For some reason, I didn't want to look up again. I just took the baby back into the cave, and hurriedly wrapped him in his quilt and got ready for bed myself.

I was talking to Rabbit, the words tumbling out of my mouth: "Rabbit, Rabbit, I'm your mum. You came out of my belly, you're my son, Rabbit. There's not much else I can say, about me or about you. Oh, Rabbit, Rabbit. Here I am in the village, here you are, needing me to protect you. Is this what fate means? Did we do something to deserve living in this place? Why can't my mum come here? She went from a village to a city, why can't she come back to a village, eh, Rabbit? Who do you take after? You're not as fair as me. Your dad's Bright, how could it not be him? When your mum was a little girl, your granny went to work in the fields and left her behind in the yard, with the pigs and the chickens and the dog, so she played with them and fought over their food with them. So I had it coming to me, didn't I, to be with your dad? Are you listening to me, Rabbit, is my heart too big, is that why I'm suffering so much? Do I count as a human being? I was poor in the countryside, and I was poor when I went to the city, and no one ever treated me as a human being. And here I am in this village and all I know is that it's somewhere in China. I've married into the Blacks now, Rabbit, talk to me, Rabbit!'

But my baby didn't answer, not even with a gurgle, just sucked at my nipple.

The tears rolled down my cheeks and dripped on my breast. Rabbit carried on suckling.

Rabbit and I went to sleep. I have no idea what time it was when we dropped off, and that made me realise that, when someone dies, it's like they're going to sleep. A dying person probably knows they're sick, and they take medicine, and have a drip, but then suddenly they lose consciousness, so they can't know what time they actually die, or that they are dead.

After that, I was so busy during the daytime that I didn't know whether I was coming or going. As soon as it got dark, Rabbit and I went to sleep, deaf to the spattering of bird droppings from the pine tree, or the dog barking or the donkey sneezing.

Once I went to the store, and took Rabbit to look at the little stream that gurgled past the entrance to the village, I told him: "River, Rabbit, this is a river."

I went back to the strip from where I could see the stream, such a slender thread, glinting in the sunshine. I stood quite still.

"Look, someone left their belt there," I told Rabbit.

I made dog papercuts. I couldn't get them lifelike but I carried on trying, though they looked like pigs. I called our dog over and had a good look at his shape and the way he walked. Bright had gone to the township to buy a few pounds of pig's trotters – stewed, they would give me lots of milk. I kept the trotter bones for the dog, every time I called him over, I gave him a bone. I kept practising the dog papercuts and slowly my technique got better. Auntie Spotty-Face dropped in and I got them out to show her.

But she said: "You mustn't make them too lifelike, the person looking at them must see it's a certain thing but also feel it's not. They should look hard and not be sure whether it's one thing or another."

Her comments put me off my papercutting.

"Watch me," she said, and in a few snips she'd cut out a tractor, with a person on it with a pointy head and jug ears. I could see it was Bright. A bird had settled on his head and the tractor was resting on two clouds. She was mumbling as she snipped: "Black Bright Black, Black Bright Black, compare your colour to a crow, there's a big beautiful woman on your *kang*, and your tractor flies like a cloud."

Then she cut out a donkey lying on the ground with its hooves in the air, and someone drinking tea next to it, with a big head and round face, and just slits for eyes, and behind them the window to a cave with a small child at the window.

She was crooning:

> Son's cradling grandson at the window,
> My son watches him kissing his son,
> When his son grows up, he'll do my son an injury.

The person she'd cut out was Bright's dad, but we neither of us said so.

"Right?" she said.

"Right," I said.

Bright's dad was sweeping the strip and appeared at the door, so we quietened down and just giggled.

"Stay for lunch, Auntie Spotty-Face," he said. "I've made some sweet potato noodles."

"You better put lots of horseradish in!" she said. "Listen," she told me. "You've got to capture the outline of the thing you're cutting, and then the scissors will know how to cut."

She wanted to cut a papercut of the five poisons to stick on a tummy wrapper for Rabbit, but she needed red cloth for the wrapper so I went to the store for some cloth. As I went out, I called to the dog to come with me, but he refused.

I said: "So you're not obeying my orders?"

And the dog did come. On the way back, I felt my breasts engorge and leak all over my front, so I nipped around the end of a house with my back to the alley so I could express some milk and ease them. I was standing by someone's mud-brick cookhouse with a tiny window, sure that there was no one inside because it was dark, and squirting milk out, when I suddenly heard a voice: "Give me your mouth!"

Startled, I pulled my jacket down and peeked through the window. There was the village boss with Cassia-Fragrant hanging around his neck, her legs tight around his waist. She was saying: "I'm going to rebuild this cookhouse. You must let me have the wood from the theatre stage cheap!"

"Yes, yes, I will," and he tried to push her back onto the work surface.

But she was a hunchback so she couldn't lie flat. "Put it in from behind," she said.

The village boss didn't say anything, just turned her around and leaned her over a crock and pulled her legs open. My heart was hammering and I fled. When I turned the corner at the T-junction, I was at the village boss's house and the door was open. I spat, and the dog slipped in through the door. I went after it to call it back, and as I got to the door, I saw a phone on the table inside. I stared blankly at it. Meantime, the dog came out and stood outside the door.

It all happened so quickly. I flung myself at the table, grabbed the phone, knocked it onto the floor, then crouched down and dialled the number of our landlord. The first time, I didn't get through, I dialled again, it rang but no one answered. Why didn't anyone answer? Maybe I'd dialled the number wrong, I tried again and this time someone picked up.

"Uncle, Uncle, it's Butterfly!" I said urgently.

But it wasn't the landlord, it was a woman.

I was about to put the phone down when I heard the woman shout: "Uncle, it's for you!"

"Who is it?" It was the landlord, I recognised his voice.

"It's Butterfly!" I said again.

"She says it's Butterfly," the woman repeated.

"Who? Who? Butterfly?"

That was Uncle again. I heard footsteps, as if he was running in from the courtyard. But the dog outside began to bark frantically, I had to leave. I could see Monkey at the entrance to the alley with a load of earth on a carrying pole. I turned and banged on the cave door: "Village boss! Village boss!"

Monkey came up to me. I was covered in sweat and dared not look him in the eye, just jerked my head in the direction of the cave.

"How come the village boss's not answering?"

"Maybe he's out," said Monkey.

"Well, he went out and left the door unlocked," I said and hurried away, still feeling like I was in a dream.

As I waited for the dog to catch up, I said to it: "Bite me! Bite me!"

The dog clamped its teeth around my calf, which hurt, then let go again. I slumped to the ground: "It's not a dream, it's real, and I made a phone call!"

I'd phoned but I hadn't managed to speak to the landlord. How I hated Monkey! Well, I'd look for another chance and one day I'd manage to speak to him and let him know I was still alive. At least this time he knew I'd phoned, and maybe the number had displayed, and even if he didn't know which province, or county or village I was in, if he was on the ball he'd make a note of the number and go with my mum to report it at the local police station, and they could look it up and see where I was. Even if Mum didn't know, Uncle would know what to do.

On my way back to the strip with the dog, I met Rice leading a goat.

"I was just on my way to see you," she announced brightly. "You must have sensed I was bringing you this goat and come out to meet me!"

"You're giving me this goat as a present?" I asked.

"Don't sound so surprised! I've struck it lucky today! There's a Mr Wan in the township who owed Spring-Starts and La-Ba thirty thousand yuan and when they died, he conveniently forgot to pay up. But I wasn't going to let him get away with it. I went and asked for the money. The fucker really couldn't pay, but I spotted his goat, it's a nanny, so I brought it away to give my godson."

I pointed to the front of my jacket: "Look, I'm overflowing with the stuff, why would I give him goat's milk?"

"I've seen Bright buying you pig's trotters to keep your milk supply up, well, you won't need to if you have a goat."

She paused, then said: "What's up, Butterfly, why don't you express some milk?"

I didn't dare mention the phone call, so I told her what the village boss had been doing with Cassia-Fragrance and she picked up a bit of brick and said: "Come on! I'll chuck this at the window and that'll fucking scare him off!"

I grabbed hold of her arm and took the goat's leading rope: "But the village boss's always so proper, what's got into him?"

"He just has to look at a woman's crotch and he gets a hard-on!" said Rice. "He even tried it on with me, even though Spring-Starts and La-Ba were his uncles!"

I stood still.

"Tried it on with you?"

"It was when I was in mourning for Spring-Starts and La-Ba, the first day of the Seven Sevens, and I was coming back from the gully. My shoes were all covered with mud so I was changing them at home, and he came in with a cat in his arms. 'For you!' he said, and I said: 'Why?' 'Because you're all on your own,' he said. I thought he was really concerned about me so I said thank you. Just then, someone passed by outside, and he lowered his voice: 'Leave the door on the latch tonight.' And he really did come by that night!"

"Cheating bastard," I said.

"I told him I had to tell Spring-Starts and La-Ba about it, otherwise they might come and haunt me, and I got their spirit tablets out and put them on the *kang*. He went away without another word."

The two of us burst out laughing.

It started to rain, drops as big as soybeans spattering down, then it got heavier, and the drops were as big as copper coins, and puddles formed instantly around our feet. We must have frightened the clouds, or else there was a rent in the sky. It didn't stop raining for three days, so Auntie Spotty-Face stayed with me, and I was so anxious, I spoiled lots of papercuts.

Over the next few days, I imagined every possible scenario: if Uncle had noted the phone number and reported it to the local police and they'd found out where the call had come from, then they'd be coming to get me. That might take less than a couple of weeks. If Uncle had tried calling the number back, the village boss was often not at home so maybe he wouldn't pick up. If he did pick up and Uncle started asking about me, then the head would realise that I'd been in his cave and made the call, and got a message out, and in that case, he might tell the Blacks, and I didn't want to think what the consequences of that might be.

I fretted myself to a shadow, taking note of every movement in the village by day and not letting myself drop off to sleep at night. If no one was around, I'd sit in the cave or outside on the strip and shut my eyes so it was all dark, but I realised that I could see even with my eyes shut and what I was seeing was a hole, like a tunnel spinning in front of me, like when you watch a film, I didn't go into the tunnel, but it kept getting deeper and deeper. Where would it end up? I didn't know but I sensed that it might be showing me what this whole thing was leading to. The tunnel shot away from me, twisting and turning, and I could see the rocks of the cave walls interlocking like the teeth of a dog. I looked into the tunnel and said to myself: Whatever happens, I'm going to get to the bottom of this. But I kept being interrupted by someone passing by or speaking to me, or else I dropped off to sleep.

Rice came once more. She was sick with something, her hands and feet were icy cold while she poured with sweat every night, so she came and cadged a ride on Bright's tractor to the township clinic. She came back with more than a dozen doses of herbal medicine, said they had to be mixed with baby's urine. It had to be a boy baby, she said: "My birthday's the same day as the Earth Store Bodhisattva, do you think that Rabbit could have been sent to me by the Coloured Light Medicine Buddha?"

"What are you talking about? I never heard of any such thing," I told her.

"Don't you know about them? The Earth Store Bodhisattva is the one who declared, 'I won't become a Buddha until there are no demons left in Hell', and the Coloured Light Medicine Buddha is spotless and radiant and sent especially to cure sickness!"

"I don't have a clue what you're on about," I said. "But if you want Rabbit's urine, you get him to pee for you."

The funny thing was that Rabbit used to pee when she wasn't there but as soon as she turned up, he wouldn't pee any more. Every time she'd bring a little pot, give it to me, then go off and talk to Great-Grandad and wait for me to collect the urine and give her a shout.

One day I'd just taken the pot from her when the village boss turned up on the strip. He had a face like thunder and was cursing and swearing. My hand shook so much that I couldn't catch the pee, I just carried Rabbit back into the cave.

"Where's Bright, Butterfly?" he shouted.

"He's not here, what's up?" I asked in a shaky voice.

He didn't answer, just carried straight on to Great-Grandad's. I stood at the window, straining to hear what he was saying to the old man. But it was nothing to do with the phone call, and I calmed down. I guessed Uncle hadn't called the number back, or if he had, the village boss hadn't picked up. Great-Grandad and Rice were sitting by the gourd frame and Rice was asking about nonesuch flowers.

"You going to dig nonesuch flowers, are you? And how are you going to thank Great-Grandad for sharing his wisdom with you?" the village boss said nastily.

"There's more than one way of showing respect and appreciation," said Rice. "Like, bringing someone food, waiting on them, spending time chatting to them. And what have you brought to give Great-Grandad?"

"Strange we both had the same idea!" the village boss said.

At that moment, I came out of the cave and called to Rice: "I've only collected half a pot of pee, come and see if it's enough."

Rice took a look at the pot and sighed: "Rabbit, Rabbit, your pee's like gold-dust!"

It obviously wasn't enough, and she gave his willy a playful tweak. "So big already and you haven't eaten any blood onions yet! Those village girls had better watch out!"

I changed the subject. "Come inside and have a look at my cuttings, and see if he pees again."

We hadn't finished looking through the heap of papercuts when we heard the village boss over by Great-Grandad's, yelling at the top of his voice, cursing Three-Lobes and Rake. These two and Bright had planned to carry on the blood onion business but when the village boss found out, he wanted to get his oar in too, in fact he wanted to be in charge. The other three didn't want him involved at all, and they were still at loggerheads. The village boss had come to consult Great-Grandad: could he run a blood onion business on his own and make a success of it? If he did go it alone, would the other three still go ahead? He worked himself up into a rage, but it was all directed at Three-Lobes and Rake, he didn't mention Bright.

Just then, Rabbit had another pee. Rice filled her pot and said: "I don't want to see the head when he's sounding off like that."

She left, carrying the pot in both hands. I had just seen her to the alley when the dog came loafing back and, as soon as it saw the village boss, set up a furious barking. The boss aimed a kick at the dog and it dodged, but carried on barking. I hurriedly got hold of it. That dog knew what the boss got up to with Cassia, and it knew about my phone call too.

The village boss stopped talking to Great-Grandad and said to the dog: "What are you barking about? Are you telling me off or trying to tell me something?"

Thank heavens the dog couldn't talk.

In the alley below the strip, I could see Rice tripping along, slopping the pee over her hands.

Bright's dad was coming back from the fields with the hoe over his shoulder and he looked at her pot: "You gave Rabbit a goat, and he gave you pee, now you're quits!"

Rice seemed lonely so I told her to come and do some papercuts with Auntie Spotty-Face but she said one Auntie Spotty-Face in Spur village, Gaoba county, was quite enough. If we had more people making those papercuts, everyone would turn into crazies. That was the first time I'd heard that I was in Spur village, Gaoba county. What a weird name. I was delighted but also sad I'd found out too late, otherwise that would have been the very first thing I said to the landlord on the phone. I wanted to ask Rice what province we were in, and what the name of the township was, but I let it drop. I put my arms round her and gave her a kiss.

"What's all that about?" she exclaimed.

"You're right, forget Auntie Spotty-Face and papercuts, just come and see me and the two of us can have a chat."

"I never get a moment's peace at my place," she said. I thought she meant that the wifeless villagers had been pestering her.

"Well, at least there's safety in numbers!"

But she said: "It's the bought-in wives, they come by whenever they've got a minute."

"How many are there?"

She ticked them off: "Three-Lobes bought himself a wife, and Horse-Horn, and Peace, and Good-Luck, and Triple-Edge and Eight-Jin..."

"What a lot!" I exclaimed.

I only knew about Good-Luck's wife because she came to borrow the flail one day.

"Good-Luck's is the one who's doing the best. Three-Lobes' wife ran away three times, and each time she got caught and brought back, but with two kids in three years, she's settled down now. Horse-Horn broke his wife's leg after he bought her, so now she walks with a stick."

I'd been to Rice's house a few times and the first time, the bought-in wives were all there, gambling. The men in the village played mah-jong, but the women played with cards, long thin ones with pictures on them, and you counted up the pictures to get the number of each card. They had no money to play with so they brought a bag of potatoes each and gambled with those. The loser gave the winner a potato as big as a fist and at the same time put a little potato in a basket. The ones in the basket were Rice's rake-off, and she washed and scraped them and steamed them for everyone to eat. They were a noisy bunch, all talking over each other to explain the rules of the game to me, but I said I'd just come to see what was going on and I had to get back to feed the baby. I went to the kitchen with Rice to do the potatoes.

"Are they all older than you?" I asked her.

"They're only a bit older than you," she said.

"But they all look worn-out!"

"They've been here seven or eight years, so what do you expect!"

I felt a pang of distress and said nothing more.

The next time I went to see Rice, I took Rabbit with me, because it meant I could stay longer, but there were only a couple of bought-in wives there, and four or five others who I didn't know, all sitting around drinking wine. They wanted me to join them but I said I couldn't because I was breast-feeding.

One of the ones I hadn't met before said: "You must be Butterfly, we've heard all about you."

I looked at Rice, annoyed that she'd been telling them what had happened to me, when all I wanted to do was forget it. What had she been shooting her mouth off for?

"I don't know you," I said.

"Oh, right, let me introduce you." said Rice. "This is Cloud from Henan province, and these four are Duckweed, Jade, Grace and Plum, all from Gansu province."

All five reached out to shake my hand but I kept my hands to myself.

"Did you know each other before?" I asked. What I meant was, had they been working as hookers in the city with Rice? "Did Rice fix up for you to come here?" I asked again.

But Rice said: "What are you on about? Cloud came to dig nonesuch flowers and I was coming from Back Gully and found her lying in the road, she'd got her period and had terrible cramps so I brought her back here. When she was digging again, she met these four and brought them back with her. They were all dirt-poor where they came from, so they settled down here."

"That's right," said Cloud. "We heard you could earn money digging nonesuch flowers, but we didn't know how hard it was, and there are barely any left."

I was thoroughly embarrassed that I'd implied they were hookers.

"Rice is very kind," I said, and to smooth things over, I handed Rabbit to Cloud, and they passed him around, exclaiming how cute he was, kissing and cuddling and tickling him under the armpits.

"I'm not being kind," Rice said, "it's that I owe them from a previous life."

"What do you owe us?" came a voice from outside.

I turned to see Monkey come in, and Bounty and Bring-Silver, carrying between them a pumpkin, a sack of potatoes and a bowl full of mung beans. Behind them came Six-Fingers, his left hand bandaged, carrying a goat's stomach in his right hand.

"Butterfly, you're here too?" he said.

"Where are you taking that smelly stomach?" I said. "The flies got here before you did!"

Six-Fingers batted the flies off: "We've come to make Rice some goat tripe soup and cat's ear noodles."

I picked up Rabbit and left.

I heard Monkey say: "Jade, Six-Fingers has chopped his extra finger off just because you didn't like it!"

Rice came after me. "Are you really going?" she asked.

"You've too many people already," I said.

"I don't care, they can come if they want," she said.

"What, you'd let a wolf come and eat with you?"

"It wouldn't dare."

But I left anyway and didn't get another chance to visit her after that.

"Bright's dad!" I called. Or rather, "Dad!... dinner!" It was the first time I'd called him "Dad!" and he was so startled, he went bright pink. When I brought the food out to him, he said "Eh?", and his hand trembled as he took the bowl.

Although the Blacks were not badly off by comparison with others in Spur village – at least we never went hungry – still, there wasn't a lot of cash to spare. I told Bright to stop buying me wheat buns. We had steamed potatoes and Bright took one out for me, but Bright's dad grabbed it off him and fished around in the pot for an especially big round potato and gave it to his son.

"This is a really pretty one."

Bright passed the "pretty" potato to me and I was happy to accept it. As I munched away, I said to Great-Grandad: "Pretty potatoes are really good to eat, is pretty pork good to eat too? And do pretty flowers bear good fruit?"

"Of course," he said. "And a well-built cave that's sunny and airy bears fruit too. And a person who's good-looking is intelligent and wise."

I knew Great-Grandad was complimenting me.

When Bright's dad made *huhu*, ground-up cornmeal cooked to a thin porridge with soybeans added, he always spooned a few extra into the bottom of my bowl, and Bright always pretended to be jealous.

"He treats you like his own daughter, so that makes me just a live-in husband."

But when he got near the bottom of his bowl, he'd put it in front of me: "I've had enough, I'm off to feed the donkey."

There were always plenty of soybeans left, and I knew he'd saved them for me.

After I learned papercutting from Auntie Spotty-Face, I made some and stuck them on Bright's dad's door and window frame, and on the wall above his *kang* and on his jars and storage box and cupboard. The old man scrounged bits of paper when he went on visits, or picked them up from the side of the road. He smoothed out the creases and stored each piece inside the brim of his hat, then asked Bright when he got back: "Are these good for papercuts?"

"Your head's made them all greasy, don't flatten them in your hat," said Bright.

When he cuddled his baby, Bright was all fingers and thumbs. He either tickled him with his whiskers, or threw him up in the air and caught him.

"Mind what you're doing," said his dad. "Make sure you catch him around the waist."

"He's too little to have a waist," said Bright, and he rolled a mat out on the strip and held Rabbit standing upright.

Rabbit wasn't steady enough to stand, but he could crawl – backwards. I sat in the doorway, picking over some lucerne. Blindy had gone out at crack of dawn and brought back a basket full of mare's eggs from his trip up the mountain. I was amazed that he'd managed to find them in among the clumps of grass, but he'd gathered them piece by piece. Now, I was picking out the soil and leaves from the mare's eggs and wasn't watching Bright, who was playing with Rabbit. Rabbit was happy with his dad, and he made his dad happy too. But then Bright got the pillow out from the cave, and the ladle, and the abacus, and a pen, scissors and a pink one-hundred yuan note, and put them all on the mat and made Rabbit grab them. I was still bent over the basket, when Bright shouted: "Look! Look! Quick!"

I looked up to see my high-heel shoes on the mat. Rabbit had a firm grip on one and was about to put it in his mouth.

"You do nothing but eat," I said, and I brought the mare's eggs basket outside.

But I felt sad, all the same.

By now, all the villagers knew I was Auntie Spotty-Face's pupil and could make papercuts, and they could all see how much more relaxed and friendly I was after the baby was born. But there were things they didn't know I knew: I'd learned to swim breast-stroke as a child and although there was no water around here, I used to go through the motions with my arms, swimming through the air, when I was walking along. I knew that certain things belonged to the night-time: the moon and the stars, dreams, certain animals and plants, my own sleepiness. I knew and enjoyed the crows and their endless chattering when they roosted in the pine trees; and the same went for the fleeceflowers, their intertwining stalks and their fragrant flowers. I knew that, when you built a house, you threw up bricks and tiles for those above to catch, and the less willing those above were to catch them, the more they hurt their hands; it was only by meeting people halfway that you could grab an opportunity and gain some momentum from it, and then everything became easy. I knew that you used a rock to chisel a lion, and paper to cut out a tiger, and when you had finished them, they might frighten you. I knew that a healthy body depended on having a healthy mind, and that your state of mind could change how you looked and how things were around you.

It rained that night.

At dawn, a deluge fell on the strip and bounced deafeningly off the millstone and the well rim. The dog lay curled up at the cave door. The crows came back to their nests. The stones anchoring the fleeceflower root stayed put – they couldn't grow roots or wings, they just got covered in muddy water but they didn't complain, did they? A fox turned up at Great-Grandad's gourd frame, made a noise halfway between a chuckle and a sob, then jumped down off the strip and disappeared.

On the *kang*, Rabbit began to cry, and I picked him up. He had a wet nappy so I changed it. I heard a clatter – the pig jumping out of the pigpen and going to rootle around in the earth at the entrance to the strip with its cucumber-shaped snout, in search of food. Once I'd changed Rabbit, I put on a pair of Bright's straw sandals over my cloth shoes and started on the day's chores.

By now, I'd learned how to look after the chickens. The Blacks had started with one cockerel and three hens, but Bright's dad had killed one hen and cooked it for me. He was trying to keep me here by feeding me well. As soon as the other two hens and the cock saw me, they used to come and peck at my feet, and if they couldn't get at the front of my feet, they went around and pecked at my heels. But then Bright's dad killed another hen, which made the cock and the remaining hen flee when they saw me. If running was too slow, they'd take wing – they could get as high as the top of the gourd frame, scattering feathers all over the ground. I knew they blamed me so I told them: "I didn't kill the others, and I don't want to kill you."

I refused to let Bright's dad slaughter these two, and raised six more hens and two more cocks, so the Brights had ten altogether. The chickens and the dog didn't get on. No matter how much the dog tried to chase them off, the chickens carried on pecking and pooping all over the strip till it was covered in droppings. But their constant clucking made me feel less lonely and they were good company. The cocks had combs that kept getting bigger, blood red in colour and so fleshy that they flopped over. Great-Grandad always said humans had a yellow aura around their heads, and the bigger the aura, the healthier they were and the longer they lived. If your yellow aura got smaller, you would get sick or die. Great-Grandad said Tongue-Trip had a red aura, and that meant that he was fuming with internal heat. The cocks' combs were like a red aura and they fumed plenty – they used to mob the dog, pecking it so badly that it stopped chasing the hens and they crowed in triumph, so loudly you could hear them from the shop. The seven hens were altogether gentler. They each had downy crests on top of their heads, like little bouquets. Every morning at breakfast, I'd cluck and they'd come running and watch my chopsticks. Then I'd throw a bit of rice on the ground for them. As they pecked, I was able to grab hold of one and push my finger up its bum and feel if there were any soft-shelled eggs inside, and if the hen was going to lay right away or in the afternoon.

I berated the dog: "You get your meals every day, the hens eat anything, grubs, vegetable leaves, grass, even sand, and they lay eggs too and you don't!"

"If a hen doesn't lay, it gets constipated," Bright had said.

I sorted out nests for the hens so they'd have somewhere comfortable to lay, putting dried grass in the bottom of a basket and adding some corn cob bristles. When one laid, the egg came out all warm, and the hen went around bright-eyed for the rest of the day. Sometimes I held the new-laid eggs up to the light, to see if I could see a faint shadow inside, which meant the cock had mated with the hen and the egg was fertile. I kept those eggs in a separate jar because they could be incubated and we'd have chicks. There was one hen, an all-over black one, who I'd had a feel of but she hadn't laid for a long time. Still she used to spend all morning from breakfast onwards in the nest until around noon I'd chase her out of it: "Piss off, you little layabout!"

With her occupying the nest, the other hens had to find somewhere else to lay and I had to go and search for the eggs in the tussocks below the strip or in the firewood stack behind the shit-house, carrying Rabbit in my arms.

By now I'd learned how to make corn pudding. If you got it wrong, it just came out as a slurry. It was made out of cornmeal and was especially good when you used freshly milled meal just after the autumn harvest, with a texture that was smooth but chewy. Actually it was eaten all year round, but you couldn't always get the freshly-milled cornmeal. Meal milled from older corn was all right but it had to be used within a week of milling, or the porridge wouldn't be good. First, you mixed a ladleful of the cornmeal with enough cold water to make a paste, not too thin, just thick enough to stand a chopstick upright in. Then you boiled some water in a pot and tipped in the mixture and kept pounding with a rolling pin, adding more cornmeal as you stirred and pounded, and making sure it was well mixed-in and there weren't any lumps. Lumpy corn pudding didn't taste good, or look good. You had to keep stirring in one direction, not first to the left and then to the right, otherwise it would lose its chewiness. The pounding was hard work, you had to give it as many as eight hundred, or even thirteen hundred turns. At first the mixture would come to a rolling boil, then you'd get bubbles, and finally the bubbles would burst and spatter with a plop-plop. The best fuel to use when you were making corn pudding was not firewood but buckwheat or some other straw. When the rolling pin stayed standing upright in the pot for a second, then you were done. You took the pot off the fire, covered it and let it sit for a couple of hours. In the meantime, you could fry some onion, garlic sprouts and chillies in another pot, take them out and set them on one side, then fill it half full of water, bring it to the boil, and add salt, vinegar, soy paste, Sichuan and black pepper, star anise and fennel seeds. When the water was boiling you added garlic and fresh ginger, and tipped the fried onion, garlic shoots and chillies back in, and your broth was ready. Corn pudding without a good broth was just porridge. You served it in a bowl with a portion of the pudding in the centre, then poured some broth over, castle-and-moat-style. You picked up a mouthful of pudding with your chopsticks, then had a mouthful of broth. You had to eat at the right pace too: not too slowly or you'd find the pudding coming out of the corners of your mouth, and not too fast or you'd burn your throat (if you hadn't swallowed it) or all the way down your windpipe, if you had. Corn pudding was good but it didn't stave off the hunger for long. The locals called it 'half-way up the hill' because no matter how much you ate, that was how far it would get you before you were hungry again. When it was the busy farming season, they didn't eat corn pudding, it was a meal for rainy days when you had nothing much to do but fancied a bite to eat.

I learned to make buckwheat noodles too. The buckwheat didn't contain much gluten so it was hard to make noodles from. You needed a special noodle press. Most of the village homes lacked one or other household utensil so everything got shared around. But every household had a noodle press. They were simple enough: two flat pieces of elm wood hinged together like clappers. The top piece was longer, with a pestle fitted to it, and acted a lever; the lower one had a round disk pierced by dozens of eyelets. After the buckwheat dough was mixed, you heated some water in a pot and when the water had come to the boil, you rested the press on top of the pot, rolled some of the dough into a sausage shape, put it into the hole and lowered the lever, pressing it down hard so that the pestle squeezed the dough through the eyelets into the water as noodles. You had to use all your strength to operate the lever, leaning your whole body over it, sometimes even jumping up and sitting on it. The noodles could be eaten cold, flavoured with chilli, mashed garlic, vinegar and horseradish (that was a crucial ingredient). Or you could eat them stir-fried or in a broth. If family came to visit, you usually ate them seasoned and cold, as a main dish. If it was a wedding or other big village event with a lot of guests, then they were eaten in a hot broth. People would use their chopsticks to fish the noodles out, then pour the broth back into the pot for boiling more noodles in, so the same broth could be used for twenty or thirty servings. When the noodles were eaten, then everyone got a share of the broth to drink. The villagers called this 'spittle noodles'. I was afraid of picking up other people's germs so I steered clear of events where 'spittle noodles' were served. When I made them at home, we used big bowls, and everyone got two servings of broth and noodles each: Bright, his dad and his uncle Blindy.

And I learned how to cook potatoes. You could steam or boil them, slice or cube them, stir-fry or stew them. You could also cut them into matchsticks and serve them stir-fried hot or as a cold dish. You had to cut them very finely for that. At the start, Bright said I cut them like bench legs, but I got better, and faster, and I cut my fingers on a few occasions too. Now I could do it and hold a conversation at the same time, even in the gloom without lighting the lamp, and produce a nest of silky threads. For stir-frying potato slices or matchsticks as a hot dish, you didn't add water, but to serve them cold, you had to add water, otherwise you'd end up with a lump of gluey paste, which looked nasty and didn't have that fresh taste to it.

When you fried slices, you could add soy sauce, but for the matchsticks served cold, it was only vinegar, plain vinegar. The water used to cook slices or matchsticks could be set aside and when the starch settled, you could make pancakes, which were called 'stickers', and babies and old people loved them. If you fried the stickers with pork slices and shredded chilli peppers, that made a main meal dish. You could also thread string through potatoes and hang them on the wall to dry. They had quite a different flavour, and you could stew dried potato slices with string beans and pumpkins. There were other ways of cooking the matchsticks too: mixed with buckwheat flour to make steamed buns; mixed with cornmeal to make pancakes; mixed with wheat flour to make fried balls; and as a filling for dumplings. Or you could mix the potato matchsticks with buckwheat or bean flour and cook them in a basket steamer, and you flavoured them with chillies and garlic paste diluted with water. Then there were sticky potato cakes: you steamed potatoes and then put them in a mortar and pounded them with a pestle until they went gluey. The gluey mass had chilli oil, mashed garlic, vinegar and soy paste sprinkled on it, and a drop or two of sesame oil made it taste even better. It took a lot of hard pounding to make them, and ten *jin* of potatoes would only make half that weight in cakes, so you would only prepare them for special guests. The easiest way to cook potatoes was to steam them, or boil them in a thin gruel, because you didn't need to slice them, you cooked and ate them whole. The villagers had them like this for at least one meal a day, and you could see their cheeks bulging and their eyes popping as they pushed them into their mouths.

I learned to ride the donkey. You had to ride it bare-back and without even a rein to guide it. Going down the slope from our strip to the village, and through the maze of alleys, and even along the field dykes, I'd direct the donkey left or right by squeezing my left or right leg into its flanks. If I squeezed with both legs, it would trot. I also used to ride it carrying Rabbit in my arms.

I learned to pick capillary wormwood. The young plant was difficult to tell apart from stinking wormwood, you had to look at the back of the leaves, which were white and smelled pungent when you picked them. Obviously, it was a medicinal herb, which cleansed the liver and lowered a fever, but it also tasted good if you gathered and cooked the plant when it had just three or four leaves. Once mature, the plant couldn't be eaten and was only good for drying for fuel. I could recognise pepper grass now too. It was a kind of thyme, and you could add the seeds when you cooked pork and would take away any gamey taste. I learned to make straw over-shoes, which the villagers wore when it rained. I learned to sew belts – the older villagers liked to belt their jackets, Bright's dad used to take his arms out of his jacket when it was really hot and go bare-chested, but he always kept it belted round his waist, to keep him standing straight, he said. And I learned how to make millet cakes and millet wine, and bind bunches of wormwood sticks to make brooms, and make a pot-washing brush from a kind of straw.

The Spur village folk had nothing on me, I'd learned to do everything they could do. They couldn't pull my leg or take the piss any more. According to Bright, the most important thing I'd learned was to be a Spur wife. It pissed me off when he said that. In the mornings, if I heard Padlock weeping over his wife's grave as I was sweeping the strip, I'd stop and go and put my high-heeled shoes on, then carry on sweeping.

By this time, Bright had such a big paunch he couldn't see his toes when he stood up, and his trousers hung around his crotch, making him look like he had a very long torso and short legs. He tucked his food away at every meal, three times a day, and liked an evening snack too, after which he used to burst into song. I tried to make him lose weight, but Great-Grandad used to say that a man should be stout, and if you didn't have a bit of paunch by the time you were forty, you'd never do well.

Bright was keen to do well, he wasn't satisfied with running the store. After a big argument with the village boss and much discussion with Rake and Three-Lobes, they agreed to go into the blood onion business: the village boss would be the nominal head but the start-up money would be put in by the other three equally and they would share out the proceeds between themselves too. After much scouting around for a suitable site, they settled on Wild Cat Gully, behind the ridge that the village backed onto. The problem was that the land in Wild Cat Gully had been parcelled out to a number of different families, and forty *mu* needed to be aggregated for the blood onion business so Bright, Rake and Three-Lobes would have to swop their other fields. When the dozen or so families currently farming there heard their land was going to be turned into a blood onion business, they wanted in too. The three partners refused, so the families refused to budge, or only if they got two *mu* elsewhere for every one *mu* in Wild Cat Gully. The only way to break the stalemate was for the village boss to weigh in, which he would only do on condition that when the business began to make money, he took forty per cent and the others sixty per cent. Bright, Rake and Three-Lobes eventually agreed to this, but Bright had a condition of his own: he told the village boss about the crack in his cave from the last earthquake. Now he wanted to build a big new cave two or three hundred metres to the left of our current one, and the village boss had to sign a chitty to take to the township authorities for permission.

Bright had raised it with his dad at dinner. His dad had said: "The only reason he wants in is because he's got some dirty trick up his sleeve. When it really starts to make money, he'll get a whole portion for himself."

"Well, when we really start raking it in, maybe we can boot him out. Otherwise, why would I be asking him to get planning permission now?"

"Have you got the money to build a new cave?"

"Let me get the permission first, and we'll have money from the blood onions."

His dad looked at him then bent his head over his bowl. Then he got up and went to serve himself a second helping, but he didn't come out for a long time.

Bright said to me: "A man's got to do at least three things in his life: one, get a wife and a child, two, bury the old folks with proper respect, and three, build a new cave. I never thought of that till you came, but since Rabbit was born, I've been really keen. People always say that other people's wives and your own kids are the best, but for me, Rabbit and you are the best, and I want to give both of you the best cave in the village to live in."

He got so carried away that he stopped eating and dragged me off to see the site he'd chosen.

Just then, his dad came out of the cave: "Bright, sit down and finish your dinner! Calm down, it never does any good to go crazy. A crazy dog gets hit by a brick."

"I'm not crazy!" protested Bright.

"But you think there's nothing you can't do now you've got a wife and a child!"

"Butterfly and Rabbit have made me feel so much better about myself. I want to...' he suddenly stopped, and asked Blindy: "Isn't that a motorbike?"

"It's got as far as Second Alley," said Blindy. The put-puttering got louder and Bright had just climbed up onto the well edge to take a look, when a three-wheeler arrived at the entrance to the strip.

The three-wheeler was very dirty, and the man who jumped off was covered in dust. I wondered if this was a relative of the village boss but it can't have been because Bright said: "Are you looking for the village boss?"

"Fuck it, I just followed the tractor tracks, I thought only the village boss would have a tractor. Who are you?" asked the man.

"I'm Bright... hah! I recognise you now. I didn't before, because you're in plain clothes, we've met once, I remember you but you don't remember me."

"Get the village boss for me!"

Bright headed down from the strip.

"Get a move on!" the man shouted and Bright began to jog. What a bully. I took my bowl back into the cave. Bright's dad offered him some food but he refused, so the old man gave him a chair and a cigarette, and brought him some tea. Before he'd finished his tea, the village boss came hurrying along.

"What's been happening in Spur village?" the man demanded.

"Nothing."

"Nothing? Then what's this about Filial-Piety Liu?"

"Filial-Piety Liu? There's no such person."

From his seat under the gourd frame, Great-Grandad gave a cough: "Filial-Piety Liu is Padlock."

"Oh, right, right," said the village boss. "Of course, Filial-Piety Liu is his proper name, but we don't use proper names in the village, we call him by his nickname, Padlock. Yes, Padlock lives here."

"And Padlock's been going around the countryside buying up scrap metal?"

"How did you know?"

"Because in the township, someone's nicked five hundred metres of telephone cable. I need to go and search his house."

"He spends his whole time weeping for his dead wife. I only told him to get himself a job to take his mind off her, and then he goes and does something stupid like this," said the village boss.

"What he did is a crime." And the man left his three-wheeler parked on our strip and said to Bright: "What a place! My bike's covered in dust, you can rub it down with a dry cloth."

Once the village boss had taken him to Padlock's house, Bright got onto the three-wheeler, pulling at this, having a feel of that, then called to me to bring Rabbit and sit on it too. When I came out of the cave, he was giving it a wipe.

"Who's that?" I asked.

"The local police chief."

"There's a police station round here?"

"The Communist Party has police stations everywhere!"

"Oh," I said.

Suddenly on his guard, Bright said: "After Three-Lobes' wife came from Gansu, she brought two more girls from her village here, one married Withy-Weave, and the other married White-Hair Liu. Liu invited the police chief to his wedding feast."

I knew exactly what Bright was getting at, so I said nothing.

The village boss and the police chief didn't find any telephone cable at Padlock's. They did find two bicycles that they suspected were stolen, but when they asked Padlock, he said they were scrap, he was planning to repair them, and he would ride one and the other he'd bury alongside the grave for his wife to ride. She'd always wanted one but they never had enough money, and it made him want to cry just thinking about it. So the police chief dropped the matter of the bicycles – after all, they hadn't found any cable – and just issued Padlock with a warning.

"You make sure that any copper or iron you pick up is genuine scrap. If you ever receive any stolen goods that are state property, you might not get shot for it but you'll do a spell in prison."

Then they came back for the three-wheeler.

"Make the police chief some dinner," the village boss ordered Bright's dad.

"No, there's no need, I'm not hungry," protested the chief.

"Well, at least have a little soup," the boss said, and he turned to Bright's dad: "Do some fried eggs!"

Then: "Butterfly! Butterfly! Come and meet the police chief!"

I came out and said hello.

"Are you from Spur village too?" he asked.

"She's my daughter-in-law," Bright's dad answered for me.

"I never knew there were such pretty girls in the village! What's your name? Butterfly! Where did you get that name from?"

Rabbit set up a wail in the cave, and Bright shouted: "The baby's done a crap!"

I knew what he was up to: he didn't want me talking to the police chief. I went back in, to find that Rabbit didn't have a dirty nappy, but there was a red pinch-mark on his bottom.

"Don't you trust me? You've given him a terrible pinch!" I said.

The police chief ate up his four fried eggs and then left. There was a cicada on the fleeceflower vine that had been chirping loudly since noon, the village boss tried to shut it up so it wouldn't deafen their guest so he jabbed it with a stick. The cicada shed its skin and flew away, leaving the skin behind on the vine. I stayed right where I was, inside the cave.

About a month passed and at noon one day, when the sky was white and the clouds were blue like blue-and-white porcelain, Rabbit and I went to the store. Bright wasn't there. I sold some salt, some shoes and some washing powder to three customers, and then there was nothing to do. I pointed out the chinaberry tree in the distance to Rabbit.

"Do you remember how bitter the chinaberry seed tea was?" I said. "But don't go blaming your mum. You should be asking me where I come from and what I'm doing here with you."

Of course, Rabbit didn't say anything back, or even understand me, he just did a puddle of pee on the counter. Just then I caught sight of Auntie Spotty-Face, dressed in a long tunic, hurrying out of the village onto the road. As I watched, she pottered around a bit then headed back towards the village again.

"Auntie Spotty-Face! Auntie Spotty-Face!" I shouted, and she came over.

"Why are you still calling me Auntie Spotty-Face? My name's Mother Papercuts!"

I tried again: "Mother Papercuts, where are you off to?"

"Wherever the wind takes me. It was blowing towards the east and I decided to follow it and see my teacher, but now it's changed direction so I'm going back home."

But then she came into the shop and sat down: "Are you on your own?"

"Bright and his dad and uncle have taken the shoulder poles to fetch a load of muck," I said.

"So the Blacks have stopped worrying about you now, they're leaving you on your own."

"Well, there's still Rabbit and the dog."

Rabbit was sitting on the bunk bed behind the counter, in the process of pulling the pillow cloth into his mouth, while the dog lay at the edge of the bed, scrabbling at the cloth with its front claws. Rabbit was completely absorbed in his game, but the dog stopped scrabbling and raised its head to look at Auntie Spotty-Face. It gave a half-hearted wag of its tail. Auntie Spotty-Face grabbed some sheets of white paper from the counter and folding them up very small, stuffed them in her breast pocket.

"Don't tell Bright, I need paper," she said.

I picked up a whole pile more and gave it to her. She looked a bit awkward and offered to teach me something new: "What would you like to learn?"

"Whatever you like."

She didn't use the paper I'd given her but took her scissors out of her pocket, and picked up an empty carton from the floor and opened it out flat. She could turn her wrist a whole three hundred and sixty degrees, so she scissored the whole thing in one continuous movement. She began to croon: "Short tongue, mumbles nonsense, farts when he sleeps, rattle-rattle, no use to anyone in this world, leads me on the horse and the stirrup falls off."

When she'd cut out the head, I cried: "You're bad-mouthing Uncle Tongue-Trip!"

"Butterfly, tell me, if I left him, could he look after himself?"

I laughed.

"I'm worried that, if you left him, you couldn't look after yourself!"

Suddenly we heard shouts coming from the village. The language was pretty ripe.

"Fuck your mother!"

"Fuck your mother!"

"My mother's dead, fuck you!"

"Water-Come and Rice having a row," said Auntie Spotty-Face.

"Can Rice really swear like that?"

I went out of the store, and sure enough, I could see the pair of them, Rice Zi and Water-Come Liang, shouting at each other at the entrance to Second Alley.

"Boss! Boss!" Rice yelled. "Don't skulk in there pretending you've got cloth ears! If you won't sort it out, I'll get a bunch of people to give this bastard a slashing!"

"Slash all you like, but I'll cut your head off first!" retorted Water-Come. It looked like they were going to come to blows. Water-Come was built like a horse, and Rice would clearly be no match for him. I left Auntie Spotty-Face looking after Rabbit and ran back the village to see what was going on.

A crowd of people were standing in the alley where the village boss and his family lived, and he finally emerged.

"What's up?"

"I've got some girls living with me and every time they use the shit-house, there's someone peeping over the wall at them. First of all, they ignored it, but this morning they decided to go and dig nonesuch flowers, so Cloud Wang went to the shit-house and she was just squatting there when someone poked a stick along the channel and stuck it up her arse. She shouted and ran outside and saw someone running away. Rice chased after him and when she got here, she caught up with Water-Come."

She started yelling at Water-Come again: "What did you think you were doing poking her like that? Weren't you afraid of getting diarrhoea all over your face?"

"Whatever they were doing, looking, poking or gold-leafing her bum, you've no proof it was me," said Water-Come.

"We chased you and caught you, that's proof!"

"There are plenty of people in the village, who knows who you were chasing?"

"I sprinkled ash outside the shit-house and this morning there's a rubber boot print in it. You've got rubber boots on, haven't you?" It was true, he did.

"But I'm not the only person in the village with rubber boots!"

"Rubber boots come in different sizes, let's go and measure yours against the prints, and take your boots off so we can see if there's ash in the cracks!" said Rice.

"You're not the government, or the police, what right have you got to make me take my boots off? If you took your trousers off and told me to put them on, would I do it? I don't have time for this!"

With the two of them shouting and swearing, it was impossible to get a word in edgeways. More and more people crowded around to see the fun and in the crush, I got shoved out. Then Tongue-Trip turned up, his hands tucked into his sleeves, and someone shouted: "Uncle Tongue-Trip's wearing rubber boots too!"

"Wh-what do you m-mean?" stuttered Tongue-Trip, "I bought these... these boots, I... I didn't borrow them." There were shouts of laughter from the onlookers.

With the village boss around, there wasn't going to be an actual fight, so I turned to leave, but when I'd gone a few paces, I looked up and saw the village boss's door was wide open and the phone was on the table. My heart gave a thump: did I have time to get in and make a call? If I could, the first thing I'd say was I'd been sold to a place called Spur village in Gaoba county. I hurriedly repeated the landlord's phone number to myself and waited for a chance to sneak inside, but then I heard the village boss shout: "Water-Come, I want the truth, was it you?"

"No it wasn't."

"Well, if it wasn't you, go on home. Men shouldn't get into arguments with women, no more arguing with Rice."

Water-Come headed towards me down the alley and there were shouts from the crowd. Rice wasn't giving up either. She ran after him, shouting: "Where do you think you're going? Why are you letting him go?"

Others joined her in the chase, and now there were people standing outside the boss's cave, so I had no chance to slip inside.

The village boss grabbed hold of Rice and said: "So he took a peep, that's all."

"He poked her with a stick," said Rice.

"Even if he did poke her, he's a big man, he couldn't see what he was doing. And if I don't let him go, you're all going to beat him to death, aren't you?"

"Water-Come," said Rice, "I'm telling you, I hope your eyes turn into blind slits, and your hands curl up into chicken claws, so what if you didn't see this time, you'll never see for the whole of the rest of your life!"

Water-Come was some way down the alley, but he came running back to shout and swear at Rice again. There was more uproar. I couldn't use the phone so I went and grabbed Rice by the arm and said if she wanted to sort it out, she should go and ask Great-Grandad. But just then, Auntie Spotty-Face turned up.

"Where's Rabbit?" I said.

"At the store. He was crying so hard, I couldn't do anything with him."
So I ran back to him as fast as I could.

Rice and her girlfriends had been planning on setting off to dig nonesuch flowers first thing in the morning, but because of the argument with Water-Come, they didn't set off till the afternoon. They wanted to go to the north-facing slope of Bear's Ear Ridge because there was snow there all year round so not many people went, and they might find more nonesuch flowers. They planned on camping out a few days, so they went with a tent and some bedding, an aluminium pot, a bag of buckwheat flour and two baskets of potatoes. Four other women from the village went with them, including Three-Lobes' wife. Three-Lobes was on edge about running the blood onions business and when he was home, he drank and turned violent. When his wife had words with him, he yelled at her that she was less useful than a pig, at least you could make money from a pig: "All you do is stuff your mouth!"

So Three-Lobes' wife went to Rice and said she was coming along to dig nonesuch flowers: "I want to earn some money and then I can throw it in his face!" Since she was lame, she brought along their little donkey mare, so she could ride it and they could load their stuff on it too.

Rice rubbed the donkey's nose affectionately: "If only I could change my round face into a long one like yours!" And she got a small bronze bell from her cave and hung it around the beast's neck.

Five days later, they were back, dishevelled and dirty. They had dug up twenty nonesuch flowers, but they'd lost the donkey.

It was such an odd tale, it almost became a Spur village joke. I finally got the whole story out of Rice: they had climbed up to Bear's Ear Ridge and got to the north slope, which really was covered in snow. It was fiendishly cold and the weather changed from minute to minute – a glimpse of sun, then a gale, then rain, and even hailstones as big as walnuts. They put the tent up and went off to dig for nonesuch flowers, leaving the donkey tethered to a stone nearby. The first two days passed uneventfully, but on the third day, they were returning to the tent as the sun was setting when far in the distance, they spied five wild asses coming down off Bear's Ear Ridge. They were surprised because, though they'd heard about them, they hadn't seen any. The beasts were a lot taller than Three-Lobes' little donkey mare, with such glossy rounded rumps that Three-Lobes' wife went and pinched all the other women's rumps, and sure enough they didn't compare, they were all skinny and slack. The wild asses clustered around the donkey, braying loudly, then bit through her rope and drove her off with them. One of the asses brought up the rear, kicking her into a gallop, while the other four flanked her, two on each side, so the mare was forced to go with them. The women reckoned the wild asses must have taken her for a bit of fun and games ("They're jack asses, for sure," said Cloud) but half-way up the ridge, they began to realise that their donkey had been kidnapped. They took off in pursuit but couldn't catch them. They saw the six animals reach the top of the ridge, but then the mist came down and they couldn't see anything at all. They spent the whole night searching and all the next day, but there was no trace of the donkey mare.

Three-Lobes had been frantically busy planting blood onions and the last thing he expected was to lose their donkey mare. He gave his wife a terrible beating and she wept and wailed, but she dared not raise a hand, or even her voice, in protest. She was already lame in one leg, and by the time he'd whacked them with a stick this time, she couldn't walk at all. Anyone in the village who had it in for Three-Lobes had a good joke at his expense: there surely must be a wild ass encampment up the ridge, and his mare had gone to be the chief's wife. His friends tried to console him: "Well, at least your wife's here, what's the loss of a donkey?"

But Three-Lobes fretted that it was an ill omen for his blood onion business and went to ask Great-Grandad: "Will my donkey ever come back?"

His mates told him to stop fretting: "You bought your wife and you've fetched her back every time she's done a runner!"

Chapter 6

COLOURED TWINE

EARLY THAT MORNING there was a sudden roll of thunder, not a crack but a low rumbling, as if the millstone was rolling over the roof above our heads. Bright and Rabbit didn't wake, but I did. I sat up with a jerk and went to look outside. I could see Great-Grandad outside too, standing under the gourd frame. The vine had long ago withered, leaving the bare tendrils hanging like a skeleton from the supports, the dead leaves rustling in the wind.

"Why have we got thunder when the sky's so clear?" I asked him.

"It's the second day of the second month. I wondered if you'd be the first out of bed, and here you are."

"The second day of the second month? What's that got to do with getting up early?"

"This is the day the dragon raises its head, the earth starts to warm up, things come back to life, and intelligent beings are up early."

I felt quite pleased with myself then. My baby and his dad were still sleeping like pigs.

"Well, the first up had better start sweeping the strip," I said with a smile, and I got the broom.

The second day of the second month come round again! That was the day bugs and moths of all kinds came out from the earth, and some of them wished us ill, so we drank realgar wine and hung fragrant sachets around.

That had been a custom in the village where I came from, and we did it in the city so it must be the same everywhere I supposed, but the folk of Spur village carried it one step further: they fried five kinds of beans. Bright's dad toasted a mixture of soybeans, black beans, green beans, red beans and white beans, poured them into a bowl and brought them out. Bright got a handful to put in his pocket, and so did Blindy, Great-Grandad and I. Bright and Blindy munched theirs noisily but Great-Grandad said his teeth weren't up to it. He gave his to me but I didn't eat them.

"What does it mean, toasting beans of five different colours?" I asked.

Bright explained: "It's like this, the five kinds of beans represent snakes, scorpions, toads, spiders and centipedes, and they're all harmful. Eat them up and they can't do you any harm!"

"But you eat the poison and it's all in your body!" I objected.

"Spur village has been toasting five beans for centuries."

"Well, maybe the whole village is poisonous," I burst out. "Just look around you, people get robbed, there's bare-faced cheating, there's trouble-stirring, greed, jealousy, quarrelling and scamming. When it suits them, they store it all up, other times they let it blow sky-high, and if it lands on you, it sticks so your skin peels off with it, and if they really want to eat you up, there's not a bone left!"

I felt completely out of control by the time I'd finished. Bright listened to my outburst but said nothing, just stared at me.

His dad came out of his cave.

"Go and fetch some firewood," he told him. Bright fetched an armful of pea sticks from the pile behind the shit-house and put them down by the stove.

When he came back, he said: "I should give you a beating for what you just said."

I looked at him. "You're poisonous!"

He looked so foolish I had to suppress a smile. I thrust Rabbit at him and went to scrape the potatoes.

The tension passed, and after our meal, Bright went off to the store. There was a stream of villagers coming to the strip the whole morning, some of them with their entire families. I had never seen so many people before. But they weren't coming to see us, they were on their way to visit Great-Grandad and left straightaway, smiling at us as they went. I remembered the landlord back in the city inviting an old monk one day.

The alley filled with people coming to pay their respects, and the old man put his hand on their heads in blessing. The landlord told me that he was a Tibetan Living Buddha, and if he laid a hand on your head, it brought you good luck. I wondered if Great-Grandad was laying his hands on his visitors' heads too, so when White-Hair Liu brought his kid to the gourd frame and told her to kneel and do a kowtow, I asked him: "What's Great-Grandad doing with you all?"

"Haven't you seen the coloured twine that everyone's tied around their wrists?"

I looked and sure enough, I saw brightly-coloured twine on everyone's wrists. Snatch's and Three-Lobes' wives turned up, the latter hobbling on a pair of crutches.

"Why have you come all this way?" I asked her.

"Because nothing's worked out for me this year." She explained that every second day of the second month, Great-Grandad gave out these lengths of knotted twine, to 'knot in the luck', so that they and their animals and poultry would thrive.

"Does it work?" I asked her.

"If there's a chance it does, I'll take it," she said.

After she'd been in and got her bracelet, Great-Grandad shouted for me. I took Rabbit with me, and Great-Grandad picked a twine off the pile on the *kang* and knotted it around Rabbit's wrist and snipped off the ends, then did the same to me.

"I need a break," he said, and sat down for a breather.

"Where did you get all this twine from?" I asked him.

"I wove it myself from different coloured threads."

"I never saw you do that."

"I do a bit every night. It takes me all year... How many people are left outside?"

"No one."

"How come there's so much twine left and no one waiting?"

I loved the twine and when I got back to the cave, I took it off my wrist to admire it. It was made of seven different coloured threads. It would make a pretty hairband, I thought, and I tied my hair back with it and looked in the mirror.

Outside the cave, Bright's dad was saying: "Where's the sieve, I can't find it."

I knew he wanted me to bring it out of the cave and give it to him. He never came inside, just stood outside and asked where something was if he wanted it. I put the mirror down and took him the sieve. Then I got back on the *kang* again and took the hairband off. Only young girls tied their hair back with coloured bands, and I was a mother now, the twine was too bright for me. I went to tie it around my wrist again, then changed my mind. All the villagers had theirs on their wrists, I'd tie mine around my ankle, just to be different from them.

It was lunchtime and Bright wasn't back from the store. "Why's Bright being so long?" asked his dad.

"I'll go and call him," I said and came out of the cave. I turned my ankle this way and that, admiring the twine anklet.

Bright was talking to Monkey, Success and Baldy, but as soon as I turned up at the store, they stopped talking. They were all scowling. I looked hard at the three of them.

"Why are you staring at me?" Monkey demanded.

"It's just that she's got big eyes," said Bright.

They left in a hurry after that, and I asked Bright: "What's got them so wound up?"

"The blood onion business."

"You're in business with Rake and Three-Lobes, what's it got to do with them? You're having me on!"

"They want me to help them."

"Help them?"

Bright only muttered a whole load of stuff I didn't catch.

"Have they stolen something and they want you to be the fence?" I said angrily.

Bright finally said that Monkey and his mates wanted me to invite Rice over to us, so that they could kidnap Cloud, Jade and Grace. Once they'd got hold of the women, they'd shut them up in their caves, and keep them there for a year or two until they'd made them their wives.

I was furious: "How could you do such a thing, Bright? You've kidnapped me, you've kidnapped so many other women, and now you're planning to snatch these three in broad daylight!"

Bright hurriedly shut the door.

"What are you yelling like that for? Everyone will hear! Just listen to me."

"And how are you going to talk your way out of this one?" I demanded.

"They won't be harmed, just made to marry the guys. Besides, they're your friends, and after this they'll all be in the same village, you'll have company."

"You may not set out to hurt them, but if they put up a fight, they'll be hurt anyway, even killed. Did you agree?"

"No, I'm not joining in."

"Getting Rice over under false pretences, that's not joining in?"

"I don't care if we get Rice over or not, but they helped me, so what am I to do?"

I was panting in fury.

After a while, Bright said: "What shall I do then?"

"Go to the township for supplies and don't come back for three or four days."

"OK," he agreed.

The next morning, Bright really did leave for the township with his tractor. As soon as he'd gone, I set off for Rice's house with Rabbit in my arms. I let the dog come too, to allay Bright's dad's suspicions. I found the women there, carefully laying out their nonesuch flowers to dry in the sunshine. They'd harvested dozens of them. When they saw me, they came running, passed Rabbit between them and teased him till he chuckled and laughed.

"Why have you stayed away so long, were you worried we'd get you into trouble too?" Rice asked. "But it was only one lost donkey mare, and we paid Three-Lobes back, we gave him all the nonesuch flowers we gathered on that trip."

"It wasn't you who stole it, why bother paying him back?" I said. And I grabbed Rice's arm and hustled her into another cave and shut the door.

"What are you being so mysterious about?" she asked.

"I need to tell you something, don't be angry."

And I told her about the kidnap plot. To my astonishment, Rice burst out laughing.

"What's so funny?" I said.

"Just let them fucking dare!"

"They'd do anything," I said. "It happened to me, after all. I was kidnapped and sold here and shut in the cave for months."

"A couple of days ago, the village boss came and wanted me to persuade

Cloud to marry Padlock, but she refused. Padlock at least has something going for him, there's not a cat's chance she'd go with ugly mugs like Monkey, Success or Baldy! And the fuckers are planning to kidnap them?"

The women shouted through the door: "Hey, what are you cooking up in there?"

"You better not tell them, they'll be scared half to death," I warned Rice.

"I won't go anywhere for a few days, I'll stay right here and keep an eye on them," she said, then she shouted back: "Coming, coming!" and opened the cave door with a bright smile.

As we emerged, she caught sight of my twine anklet: "What have you got that on for?" she asked. "It's sexy, I bet Bright tied it on for you."

I grunted.

The next day, Blindy brought a shoulder-load of earth and tipped it out on the strip to make mud bricks. He had just added water and sogon chaff to the mix when Monkey, Success and Baldy turned up looking for Bright. I told them he'd gone to the township the night before.

"He said he wasn't going to buy supplies today," said Monkey.

"Well, if he doesn't run his business, we'll have nothing to eat but crap and farts!" I told him.

"Don't you stare at me," Monkey said. "He'll be back before lunch, so we'll wait."

"You do that. You can sit and watch his uncle make mud bricks," I said.

"I'll give you a hand," said Success, and he took off his shoes and waded in.

Adding sogon chaff made stronger bricks, but you had to tread it well with your feet to get a smooth mix. Baldy joined in too, but Monkey said: "I've got corns, I'll just smoke a pipe." And he clamped Bright's dad's pipe between his teeth.

"You crafty sod!" yelled Baldy and flung a shovelful of the slurry over him.

So Monkey had to join in too. When they had been treading a while, Blindy started to shape the bricks: he laid out the forms on the strip, and shouted at the three men to shovel the mud into them, while he pressed it down firmly with his hands. When that was done, he removed the forms, so that the two rows of neatly-formed rectangular bricks could dry in the sun.

Monkey started to complain; his back was hurting, so he wasn't shovelling any more. Instead he helped Blindy pressing and smoothing.

"What do you want so many bricks for?" Monkey asked.

"Bright's *kang* got damaged in the earthquake, we built it up again but it's no good. And I haven't had a new *kang* for ten years either."

"So Bright's worn his *kang* out, but what do you need a new one for?" said Monkey.

"You're an arsehole," said Blindy.

By the time the sun was directly overhead and the bricks had all been shaped, the men were covered from head to foot in mud. I fetched them some water from the well so they could wash their hands, but Monkey wouldn't wash his, said he was going to cool down first, and he sat in the shade of the pine trees. There weren't usually any birds in the trees during the day, but there just happened to be a crow perched above him and it just happened to let drop a load of poop that splattered all over Monkey's shoulders. Monkey was so angry, he grabbed a stick and began to beat the branches until Great-Grandad came to his cave door and shouted at him.

He turned to me instead: "Why's Bright not back?"

"I've no idea."

"Then why did you make us do all that work when you didn't know when he was coming back?"

"Nothing to do with me. We didn't force you to work, did we?"

"We only helped a bit, drop it," Success said to him.

"Success, if there's something you want done, tell me and I'll do my best to do it or I'll tell Bright when he's back," I offered.

"Forget it!" said Monkey, waving his hand at me. "We'll come back this afternoon." And he stalked off, puffing with annoyance.

I got Rabbit to sleep that afternoon and was taking a nap myself, when I was woken by Bright's dad and the village boss sitting chatting over cups of tea on the well rim. They seemed to be talking about moving some of the village families. Six families had agreed, but some were putting up a fight, and the main problem was Tongue-Trip. I went out to milk the goat.

Bright's dad was saying: "You mean he won't agree even if you talk to him as the village boss?"

"He fucking disrespects cadres!" said the village boss.

"He's older than you, you should mind your language," said Bright's dad.

"Well, he says if they have to move, he wants that piece of land of yours at the entrance to East Gully."

"His land in Wild Cat Gully is rubbish! What makes him think he can take over my land? That's our best land! What are we going to live on if we lose it? His wife's got a screw loose and he's completely off his head."

"But he's insisting," said the village boss. "He says they won't move otherwise."

I finished the milking, went to the kitchen to heat it up and was giving it to Rabbit when Monkey, Success and Baldy came back. When they saw the village boss, they beat a hasty retreat. I wasn't going to let them off that easily.

"Come and have some tea, boys!" I shouted after them.

And the village boss said: "Success, I hear you've been gambling."

"What with? You give me the money and I might."

"Don't try and deny it. The local police chief called me. Come here, Success!"

But Success stayed right where he was.

"Bright not back yet?" asked Monkey.

"No," I said. Monkey swore to himself.

"A lad with a full belly doesn't know what it's like to be hungry!" And he turned on his heel and went.

"A dog never stops eating crap," said Bright's dad. "Sooner or later, someone's going to end up in jail. It's not just Tongue-Trip's tongue that ties him in knots, he's completely useless."

"I've got an idea," said the village boss. "You Blacks and Rice relocate first and Rice gives up growing blood onions and gives her patch of ground at the entrance to East Gully to Tongue-Trip, and you give her your patch on West Slope instead."

"Would she agree?" asked Bright's dad.

"She's no good at farming, she can't farm even good land. Butterfly! You've finished feeding Rabbit, haven't you? You're close to Rice, you go and talk to her."

"But that's your business, what would I say to her?" I said.

I took Rabbit for a walk around the strip, pointing out the pine trees, and calling the chickens to me so he could stroke their feathers. Then we stood at the entrance to the strip and watched two sparrows perched on the dyke, one preening its feathers, the other's head raised as it chirped.

"Rabbit, listen!" I said. "The sparrow's singing you a song. Oh, it's gone."

The bird flew off and I saw Rice coming down the slope towards us.

I shot Rice a warning glance, but she didn't get it, just shouted: "Rabbit! Have you been missing your godmother?"

"Ah! Talk of the devil!" said the village boss.

Rice walked onto the strip with my baby in her arms.

"Why are my ears burning? The thing I most hate is arguments over land behind people's backs!"

Bright's dad offered her a seat and poured some tea, which she grabbed and drank without waiting to be asked.

"Who's talking about arguing?" said the village boss. "This is a big deal for the village! And we can't push it through without you."

"What deal?" demanded Rice. The village boss told her about the proposed field swops.

"Fine, swop my land, I declare I'm going to stop planting blood onions. But there's one condition: you get the village to dig out the hot springs and put me in as manager, and then I don't want any land at all."

"Are you going to dig up Spring-Starts and La-Ba?" asked the village boss.

"No way, there's half the undercliff on top of them, I can't do that, and I won't let you do it either, that won't bring them back to life."

"I couldn't put it better myself. If we can dig out the hot springs, I can plant blood onions there, there shouldn't be any need to swop fields!"

"Fine, then I won't swop. Butterfly, let's go to your cave."

Once we got inside and I shut the door, I whispered to her: "What are you doing running around like this? What if they're snatched while you're out?"

"I told them to scarper before daybreak."

"That's good. I was worried. As soon as I saw you, I tried to catch your eye, so you'd go home, but you went and talked to them."

"I've got something to tell you, I'm not going anywhere."

And she told me something so amazing, I was pinned to my chair in shock.

Rice told me that she'd told Cloud and the other women about the plot to kidnap them last night. They were scared to death and spent the night talking about it before deciding to leave. Before it got light, Rice led them out of the village, in fact she took them as far as Wang village to make sure they were going to be safe. On the way back, a car overtook her and stopped and two men and a woman got out and asked where she was from.

"Spur village, I told them, then they asked if the village phone numbers began with an eight. I said I didn't have a phone but I thought the village boss's number began with an eight. They asked me how far away Spur was, and I said not far, about four or five *li*. They asked if there was a woman called Butterfly there but I didn't trust them and I asked them who they were. The woman burst into tears and said she was your mum."

My mum? I slumped back into the chair: "Can you say that again? She said she was my mum?"

"That's right. She said she was your mum."

"You're making it up!"

I bounced out of the chair and clutched Rice. She was taking the piss! She was re-opening old wounds! Maybe she didn't mean to, but that was what she was doing. I pressed her head back against the edge of the *kang* and she rolled onto it, still with Rabbit in her arms.

"I don't care what you joke about, but don't you mention my mum!"

Rice sat up panting: "It's not a joke, she said she was your mum."

I looked at Rice, and she looked like she was telling the truth. I stood there for a long time. Was I dreaming? I pinched my leg and it hurt, plus Rabbit was lying on the *kang* wailing and a fly buzzed past me. "You're not pulling my leg?"

"Has your mum got white hair?"

"No."

"High cheekbones?"

"Yes."

"Shorter than you, comes about up to your earlobes?"

"No."

"A bit bandy-legged, gap between her front teeth, got a wart on the bridge of her nose?"

"Yes."

The tears rolled down my cheeks. "It's my mum, she always had black hair but it must have gone white, and she was the same height as me, how come she's shrunk like that? And she must have come to find me, my mum, my mum!"

"She said she was your mum, and I figured she was looking for you too. I remember once, when Dragon-Boat's wife's family came looking for her, and they asked when they got near, and someone must have told Dragon-Boat because he hid her away and when her family turned up in the village, there was a huge rumpus and the villagers all armed themselves with sledgehammers and shovels, and chased them away. So I told your mum absolutely not to tell anyone she was looking for you, that I was your friend, they should come to my house and I'd fetch you over. Your mum said yes to that but the two men refused, they muttered to your mum about needing to prove whether you really were in the village, and if so, they wanted to contact the local police and make preparations, and then they'd go into the village. Then they asked me lots of questions, how you looked, how you were living, and then they said: 'Some of what you said doesn't fit her description, can you get this Butterfly to go to the village entrance after dark so we can take a look?'"

"What did these men look like, was one quite old and the other young with glasses? If it's really my mum, then the other two must be the landlord and his son, there's no one else it could be."

"Yes, one did wear glasses. The big fellow interrogating me, was he your dad?"

"I haven't got a dad, he died a long time ago." I burst into loud sobs.

"Rice! Rice! Come out and drink your tea!" Bright's dad shouted.

He had obviously heard me crying and wanted to know what was up. I hurriedly grabbed the pillow and stuffed it into my mouth.

"It's OK," Rice shouted back. "She caught her leg on the edge of the table, I'm giving it a rub for her."

"She's a big girl, she should be careful," I heard him say.

Then the village boss spoke: "Are you and Tongue-Trip related?"

"Our mothers were cousins, we saw a lot of each other when the old folks were still alive," said Bright's dad.

"So why won't he have anything to do with you?"

"He's nursing old grudges. My mother died before her time, and his mother died ten years ago, and we were dirt-poor back then, and when we went to pay our respects at the graves, it so happened that it was exactly three years since my wife's father died, and there were all sorts of offerings heaped around his grave. There was a large wheat flour flatbread, a bit dried up by then, but anyway my brother and I took it to offer at his mum's grave. But Tongue-Tied caught us out and said we were disrespecting her. He hasn't forgiven us and didn't come and see us for years. It was only when Auntie Spotty-Face started teaching Butterfly to do papercuts that we started to see more of them again. But Tongue-Tied is still nursing a grudge."

I'd stopped crying but I gave Rabbit a pinch on his bottom and he set up a wail.

"What happened then?" I asked Rice.

"The big guy isn't your dad? He seemed scary and wouldn't let your mum speak. I even wondered if they really had come looking for you. But you can judge for yourself, if you go and see them."

"I'll go, I want to go."

"Why can't you stop that baby crying?" Bright's dad yelled again.

"So, go to the village entrance after dark. Do you want me to come with you?"

"No, I'll go alone."

"Well, wipe your eyes and take Rabbit outside," said Rice.

I petted him to calm him down and went out, but I was so frantic that I nearly tripped over the threshold.

"Hush, hush now, I'll do some nice warm milk for you," I said.

"You quieten him, I'll warm the milk," Bright's dad said.

But Rabbit was inconsolable no matter what I did. I sat down on the millstone, opened my jacket and pushed my nipple into his mouth, but he spat it out and cried even harder. The village boss was eye-balling me: "Rabbit – what a name to give a child – Rabbit, you drink your mummy's nice breastmilk, why don't you want it?"

Rice came and stood in front of me. "You drink your tea up!" she said to him.

When the goat's milk was warm, I gave it to Rabbit. Rice was going home and I stood up to see her off. I said loudly: "That piece of red flannel you've got, you go and look it out and I'll pop over this evening for it."

"Oh, right... I bought it to make a pillowcase, it'll do nicely for my godson."

My mum had come to find me.

I couldn't settle to anything all afternoon. I sat down on the *kang* and changed Rabbit's nappy, thinking to myself: I've been longing for my mum to come and get me, and she never did, I thought she'd never come and I've been so discouraged, and now here she is! It didn't seem real, it was all too sudden. As I mixed up the pig feed and went and tipped it into the trough, I thought, Rice couldn't be lying, could she? But she'd described my mum: high cheekbones, a gap between her front teeth, a wart on the bridge of her nose, and bandy legs. I'd never told anyone about my mum so Rice couldn't have known but she'd described her to a tee. I went to the shit-house and as I squatted down, I thought, it's got to be her. She'd asked whether the phone numbers in Spur village began with an 'eight'. No one could have known that if they hadn't been here or had a call from here. The landlord must have reported me missing, and the police must have done a search and she'd tracked me here. I had made that phone call such a long time ago, why had it taken her so long to get here?

I got the nonesuch flower in its frame down from the wall and said to it: "My mum's come to get me, did you tell her where I was?"

I went to the donkey's cave, looked it in the eyes, rubbed its nose and fed it a cooked potato. I went out on the strip and gazed up at the clouds in the sky and felt the breeze blowing on me. Suddenly the tears were rolling down my face. I felt so sorry for my poor mum, going with the landlord to report my disappearance to the police, how she must have suffered before she got here. Had it really made her hunched over? Did her hair go white overnight when I disappeared, or did it go white as she searched for me? The chickens ran over squawking, and I thought of those two men, who were they? The landlord wasn't a big guy, nor was his son, Qingwen, but he did wear glasses. I chased the chickens away and went to collect the new-laid eggs. But when I got to the nest, I found the shoe frame that Blindy used to plait his straw shoes in there. I took it out and hung it on the wall. I took the bucket to the well for some water, and as I cranked it up, I thought I really should go and get the eggs, so I did that and forgot all about the water bucket. I held the eggs up and looked at them against the light. They were cold by now, and there was no shadow inside them. The sun still hung over the undercliff – how come it hadn't moved? How could I make it go down and the darkness come more quickly? Rabbit was crying, again! He'd only just gone to sleep. My mum didn't know I had a baby, how would I explain that to her? I got Rabbit off to sleep again. I felt drowsy. I never went to sleep though. The donkey brayed outside and I heard Blindy say:

"Don't beat it, feed it some black beans. It's gone a good few *li*, it needs a rest."

I knew it was Full-Barn come to borrow the donkey to take some bricks to the Wang village brick kiln, and I was worried the noise would wake Rabbit. I didn't sit up but I knew the dog had come into the cave. It stood on its hind legs with its fore paws on the edge of the *kang* looking at Rabbit and me, then padded out again. I shut my eyes, and as soon as I did that, there was the tunnel again, not spinning this time or pulsating like the neck of a croaking frog, and I seemed to be going inside, and its walls were receding away from me rapidly. I had the feeling that going in would take me beyond the afternoon, that it was a short-cut to night-time. And so it was, as soon as I got out of the tunnel, there was the village entrance.

The sky was dark, with no moon. The noon sunshine had been so brilliant, the contrast seemed strange. I looked up at the sky to my left, just above where the pine trees must be, and there were the two stars I had seen. Even on a moonless night like this one, I could make out the store and the pollarded willow and the chinaberry tree a little way beyond it. I heard a low murmuring from the stream, it was noticeable by night, though you didn't hear it during the daytime. A cat strolled by. I couldn't see my mum.

"Mum," I called softly. "Mum! Mum!"

Under the chinaberry tree I saw what I thought were three mushrooms, but then they turned into three figures, mum and two men. But they weren't the landlord and Qingwen. My mother was as thin as a rake. I was rooted to the spot and so was she. Maybe she was as surprised at the change in me as I was at her. Neither of us said a word.

"Butterfly?" said the taller of the men. "Are you Butterfly?"

And I ran to them and threw my arms around my mother: "Mum! Mum!" Her hair really had turned white, white as snow, as if she'd wrapped it in a white cloth, and she was so frail that when I put my arms around her, she crumpled to the ground.

The man sounded annoyed: "This your daughter, right?" he said.

"Yes, it is," she said. "Butterfly, Butterfly, what are you doing here? Why didn't you come back to me?"

"Mum, oh Mum! You finally found me."

She started laughing. She laughed and laughed until she almost choked, and then she burst into tears. I patted her on the chest and wiped her tears dry, and then she introduced me, the tall one was the chief from the police station where we lived, and the one with the glasses was a reporter.

"Mr Gong, from the *City Evening News*, we wanted to come along as soon as we heard the police were sending someone to rescue you," he added.

"Butterfly, kowtow to them. If it weren't for them, we'd never have set eyes on each other again for our whole lives," said Mum.

I did as she asked, and then she told me what had happened. Once she found out I'd gone to earn money, she wasn't worried when I didn't come back for three days. In fact, she'd said to the landlord: "Butterfly's a big girl and she loves her old mum, that's why she's gone to earn some money."

But three days passed, and then five, and there was no phone call and she began to panic. She kept waking up, maybe four or five times a night, with her heart pounding. She told the landlord and he thought it was serious enough to take her to the police station and report me as missing. It was the big man who took the report.

"There's a lot of trafficking going on nowadays," he said. "She's been kidnapped, for sure."

"What do you mean?" my mother asked. "She's an educated adult, not a toddler."

"Kidnapped women get lured into it, then they're bundled off out of the province, sold to some family where they keep her under lock and key, it doesn't matter how educated they are. A year or so ago, a college student was going from the train station to the university and was tricked into getting into an unlicensed taxi, and the driver killed her."

My mum burst into tears: "Do you think my daughter's been killed?"

"No, I'm not saying she's dead, that's just an example." And he wrote some notes on my case.

"When can you get her back?" asked my mother.

"Who's talking about getting her back? We don't have the resources for that, and our funding's stretched. And even if we did, we'd need conclusive evidence of her whereabouts first."

"So where are you going to look for her?"

"You have to do that and give us the information."

So my mum began to search for me, with the help of the landlord and his son and his classmates. They put a small ad in the paper, got it put out on the radio, and printed posters that they stuck all over town, but I'd vanished without trace. She got plenty of phone calls, one saying I'd been found in the county town, but when she went there, it was a conman – he took her money and said he'd take her to me that evening, and then he never showed up. She got taken in like that ten times, but she carried on searching till all her savings were used up and she was down to dry flatbread and a bit of pickle at every meal. When there was no more money even for flatbread, she was forced to go back to picking up rubbish. Every time she grubbed together five thousand yuan, she started looking for me again, and then the money ran out, so it was back to trash-picking.

I burst into tears listening to her story, and she cried too, and beat me with her fists: "Why didn't you come back? Why?"

I told her, I couldn't, I couldn't get out of the cave, or the village, I had no money, and I had no idea where I was.

"Why did you only call once? How much does a phone call cost? And you didn't make any sense when you did call!"

"I only got the chance to make one phone call, and say one thing."

"Well, it was lucky the landlord wrote down the phone number and told the police. The chief did a fantastic job tracking you down from that number. You get down on your knees and kowtow to him again."

The police chief pulled me to my feet: "This is our fifth rescue of kidnapped women and children. Up till now, the victims' families paid up, but your case was different, we've shouldered the costs ourselves."

"The police chief's a hero in the city, he took charge personally the first four times, so this time when we heard he was going to rescue another woman, my newspaper sent me along too," the reporter added.

"We shouldn't be standing around talking," said the chief, "we'd better get going."

And my mum pulled me away.

"But Rabbit's back at the cave, I need to take him with me," I said.

"Pig, cat, rabbit... they don't cost much, you can get another one!"

'Rabbit's my child.'

"You've got a child? What are you doing with a child? You're big enough to know better!"

And she slapped me hard across the face. I didn't know what to say to her, I just stood with the tears running down my face and she kept slapping me till the tears ran into my mouth.

"You can't go back, we have to go," said the policeman.

"But I've got to get Rabbit, wait for me, I'll be right back," I insisted.

I'd just turned to go when I heard footsteps, so I hurriedly opened the store door and pulled the three of them inside. The footsteps were coming closer and sounded like they were heading for us. I turned the lights on so I could pretend I was checking the stock. There was a loud banging on the door. I opened it, it was Monkey, Baldy and Success.

"We thought it was Bright, isn't he back yet?"

"No, no, he's not, maybe tomorrow, I was just checking the stock."

I was about to shut the door when Monkey said: "Give me a packet of fags."

I fetched them for him, in such a rush that I forgot his money.

"Off you go, I'm shutting up," I said.

My mum piped up: "He hasn't paid you."

Monkey looked at her: "Who are you?"

"You haven't paid my daughter," Mum repeated.

Monkey, Baldy and Success looked suspiciously at the newcomers.

"Who are you? Are you Butterfly's family?"

"Come on, time to go!" said the police chief, pulling me along with him.

But Monkey grabbed me by my jacket and shouted for reinforcements: "Butterfly's running away!"

"I'm a policeman!" the tall guy yelled back and shoved Monkey hard. Monkey fell to the ground and grabbed my leg. Baldy tackled the police chief, who kicked him. Baldy lowered his head and charged but the chief dodged and Baldy crashed to the ground. Success hared off in the direction of the village, shouting at the top of his voice. Immediately, a dozen or so figures materialised. The police chief tried to pull me out of the store, dragging Monkey along with me. Then my mum threw herself on Monkey and bit him. He let go. The chief broke into a run, pulling me along, and the reporter followed, dragging Mum with him. Then we came face to face with a crowd of villagers. I could see Bright's dad, brandishing a shovel over his head.

He came running towards us, shouting: "Butterfly! Butterfly!" He kicked the reporter to the ground, the man's glasses fell off, and he scrambled around for them.

"I'm a policeman! We've come to rescue a kidnap victim!" shouted the chief. "Don't you dare obstruct a police operation!"

But the men were still advancing, and Rake Zhang, Water-Come Liang, White-Hair Liu and Full-Barn Wang all set on the chief. He lashed out with fists and boots, and they couldn't get near him, but Bright's dad came up behind and whacked him with the shovel, and he staggered and fell. Tongue-Tied hurled himself on top of him, but the chief jumped out from under and trod on Tongue-Trip's face. Tongue-Trip wriggled away and jumped to his feet. The village boss was shouting: "Grab Butterfly back! Grab her!"

Rake, Three-Lobes, Water-Come, Monkey and Baldy rushed at me, but the police chief got out a can of something and squirted it at them. Bright's dad was the first to clutch his face, then the others all fell to their knees with cries of pain.

"Fucking pepper spray!"

"Get to the car!" shouted the chief.

The reporter still hadn't found his glasses, but he grabbed my mum and they started running towards the village.

"Butterfly! Butterfly!" my mum cried desperately, but my eyes were burning with pepper spray and I couldn't open them. When I did, I saw they were running in the wrong direction.

"Run away from the village! Run the other way!" I shouted at them.

The village men were almost on me, and Three-Lobes took a flying leap and grabbed my legs: "You're not going, Butterfly!"

The chief gave him another squirt of pepper spray, and Three-Lobes clutched his face. The chief grabbed hold of me, then spun around, squirting the can as he went.

My pursuers fell back, then Monkey shouted: "Get a long stick to poke him with!"

But the chief was running out of the village with me over his shoulders. He jumped down off the dyke, crossed the stream and tried to scramble up the bank on the other side, slipping and sliding on the loose stones, just managing to keep his feet.

"Hang on!" he said. He had me in a fireman's lift, like I was a sack of potatoes, and I grabbed his jacket but it seemed to stretch in my hands, and I got hold of his trousers belt. Once he got to the top of the bank on the far side of the stream, he put me down, or rather I slipped to the ground. The villagers were still pursuing us, down from the dyke, across the stream, shouting and cursing, along with dozens of barking dogs. Then I heard a shrill wail. It was Rabbit. I suddenly saw Blindy with Rabbit in his arms, on the river bank.

"Run! To the car!" shouted the chief and gave me a shove. It was parked on the highway.

Meantime, he took a few paces towards our pursuers: "If you dare come any closer, I'll shoot!"

Monkey shouted: "He doesn't have a gun, you can see he doesn't, surround him! Surround him!" They rushed forward and someone flung a stone which got the chief on the right leg. He bent down. Baldy and Three-Lobes were the first to catch up with him, but when he really did pull his gun on them, they froze.

So did all the other villagers, except Bright's dad who came forward limping (he must have hurt his leg jumping down from the dyke), still holding the shovel aloft: "You fire if you want, you take a pot-shot at my old head, I don't want to live any more."

The chief spun on his heel and was hurrying towards the car when he saw that I hadn't moved. He gave me a push, I fell, he grabbed my arm and ran on towing me with him. Finally he pushed me into the car, got into the driver's seat and drove off, tooting the horn. But the villagers surrounded us, someone opened the door on my side and they dragged me out backwards. I was half-in, half-out, my shoes fell off, and my shoes and trousers came off.

The chief opened the driver's window and shouted out: "This is a police operation to rescue a kidnapped woman. I'm warning you, if you don't let go, I'll shoot!"

"He's got no bullets in his gun," shouted Monkey. "The local police never get bullets, they're just for show! Mother-fucker, if you come here rescuing kidnapped women, we won't have any wives left! Pull! Pull harder!"

Just as Monkey got to the car door, the journalist took an ashtray from inside and smashed it down on his arm. But Monkey grabbed the journalist's hand and sank his teeth in. The ashtray fell to the ground, where Three-Lobes picked it up and brought it down on the police chief's head. The policeman fired into the air and at the sound of the shot everyone scattered. Mum pulled me inside and the car door slammed shut. The policeman fired three more shots and the car began to move again. I looked out of the back window, to see the villagers still running after the car, but they were getting farther away and smaller and smaller until they finally vanished from view. The car picked up speed, we were going so fast now that several times it nearly overturned, and the three of us, my mum, the journalist and I, were shaken about, knocking our heads against the car windows and the back of the front seats. Mum vomited, and the journalist's arm was bleeding and he was gasping for breath, my legs were completely bare and Mum took off her jacket to cover them. I realised the coloured twine was still around my ankles.

I had escaped, escaped from the Blacks, escaped from the village, I had made the escape I'd imagined so many times, and now I had done it. What would happen to me now? I wasn't sleepy, I was too bewildered for sleep. I felt the car driving along the mountain roads through the night, and I fell into the black hole again.

Finally I made it back to the city, to the alley and the courtyard and our rented room. The pond was still there, and the drops of water on the lotus leaves still rolled back and forth. I watched as a frog tried to leap up onto the leaf and failed, even after two attempts. The landlord and Qingwen were so happy for me, they let off firecrackers to celebrate my return. That afternoon they took a fancy banner to the police station as a thank-you and pinned a big red flower to the police chief's chest. The next day, the city's *Evening News* published a lengthy report on the successful rescue of a kidnapped woman, complete with two photographs, of the policeman and me.

For a few days, the courtyard was in uproar, with a constant stream of people coming to photograph and film me. I was interviewed by local radio and TV, the morning newspaper and the business and finance news. I sat in a chair in the courtyard, while I repeated my thanks to my rescuers, over and over again. But what they wanted to know was how the kidnap had happened and about how poor and backward and uncivilised the place I'd been taken to was. Was the man I'd been bought by an old bachelor, a cripple, ugly and dirty? What was my child like, why had I called him Rabbit, did he have a hare lip? I hated their questions, I felt like they were pulling off my clothes, stripping me bare, shaming me. I said I couldn't remember anything, I felt dizzy. My head really was spinning, and I was seeing double, and finally I almost fell off my chair.

I refused to do any more interviews, and when more journalists turned up, I hid in our room and refused to come out. They poked their cameras through the window and snapped away, until I covered the window with a quilt. The interviews stopped, but still people with nothing better to do kept wandering into the courtyard, asking: "Which one's Butterfly?"

"What do you want with Butterfly?" demanded the landlord.

"Nothing, we just want a look." And they'd start poking around everywhere. If there were clothes hanging out to dry, they'd ask: "Are those Butterfly's? Why are there no nappies? We heard she was taken thousands of *li* away to a wasteland, and an idiot made her pregnant."

The landlord drove them out then, and after that he sat guarding the gate every day, refusing to let any strangers in.

I couldn't go and look for a job, go out trash-picking with my mum, or go and buy food in the market. I just sat in our room crying.

"Why don't you go back to our old village for a few days?" suggested Mum. But my little brother came on his summer holiday, and he said that everyone back there had seen the TV and newspaper reports, and knew all about me. I couldn't even go back to my home village!

I lost my temper when my brother asked: "However did you manage to get yourself kidnapped?"

"How could I help it? You think I wanted it? I did it deliberately?"

"So humiliating," he grumbled. "Not just for you, it made me lose face too!"

So we had a fight, and I got ill and stayed in bed for three days. There was a whining in my ears, like someone was crying all the time.

At first, I thought the whining was Mum telling off my brother, and he was crying, but then I realised it was Rabbit. I missed my little Rabbit so much. Who was comforting him when he cried? He liked sleeping on my breasts, he could only doze off when he was latched on to my nipple, was Bright managing to get him to sleep? When Rabbit drank the goat's milk, he often brought some of it back up. Even if Bright's dad managed to get the milk down him, would he know that? Who would make his clothes for him? When he cried for his mum, who would answer? At the thought of him crying, I cried too, great choking sobs and howls.

Mum tried to comfort me: "Butterfly, please don't cry, whatever happens, you and me, we're back together now."

I wailed: "I've got my mum back, but Rabbit's not got his mum! You've got your child, but I've lost mine!"

Mum developed an eye inflammation and in just a few days her eyesight got so bad she couldn't see properly and had to cover one eye with a hot towel. Still, she went out to talk to the landlord. I thought she must be borrowing money off him, because she'd said she wanted to buy me some new clothes and high-heeled shoes, and take me to get my hair permed. But around noon one day, he came to the door when she was rolling out dough for noodles and I was lying in bed, and said he wanted to introduce someone to me. It was the nephew of the tenant in the third floor east-side flat. He had never been married and he was a fine lad, though he limped a bit because he'd been run over by a car as a kid. If we married, he'd take me to Henan province.

Mum agreed to this: "The further away you go the better, no one will know anything about you there."

I got out of bed when I heard them talking. "Are you awake, Butterfly?" asked the landlord.

"I wasn't asleep."

"So did you hear what the landlord's been saying? If you're up for it, we can ask the tenant upstairs to get his nephew over and you can meet."

I went out of the room. "Why are you going out when I'm talking to you?" said my mum. I carried on walking, right out of the courtyard.

The alley was full of people coming and going, and when they suddenly saw me, they smiled at me without speaking, then turned and followed me with their eyes. A child came hurtling towards me, with a woman running after her. When the woman finally caught up, she cried: "Why are you making me run like that, eh? What a messed-up world we live in, look at her, kidnapped by bad men!"

I walked past the woman, ignoring her, not even looking. Behind me, I heard her talking to the girl: "What's kidnapping?"

"It's being sold by conmen."

"Sold to a kindergarten?"

"No, sold to the devil, right?"

I walked out of the alley and got into a taxi: "The train station."

I was back in the tunnel, and it was pitch-black, but I wasn't at all worried about bumping into the stones on the walls, I felt like I was riding on a bat, or I was a bat myself, flying along. At the far end, a pinprick of light glimmered, and when I reached that point, I got on the train.

By now, I knew exactly what province, county and township Spur village belonged to. It took a night and a day on the train just to get to the county town, and then there was a bus that took another day to get to the township, then it was a five-hour walk to Spur, unless you could get a ride in a passing car or on a tractor. I sat in Hard Class in the train, and there was a woman sitting opposite me, a short little thing, but lugging a huge bag. She kept trying to get it onto the luggage rack, but it was too heavy, so I helped her, and then she got out a couple of steamed buns and offered me one. I said no thanks, and she smeared chilli sauce on hers and tucked in. When she had eaten three buns, she got out an apple. I shut my eyes. At every station, the train stopped. Few passengers got off but lots more got on, until even the corridors were full. Then the train whistle blew and it started off again with a clanking of metal on metal, the carriages swaying from side to side. People's eyes glazed over and most of them nodded off, though four men opposite me were eating fried chicken, drinking beer and talking loudly. No one told them to shut up, maybe because the racket they were making made everyone else feel less lonely and bored.

One of them had made up a funny train song that he was very pleased with: "The train starts from Gansu with a 'Diddly-squat! Diddly-squat! Diddly-squat!'... Goes through Shanxi... 'Scabby... stingy! Scabby... stingy! Scabby... stingy!' Stops in Henan to top up with water, and leaves the station with a 'Skank you! Skank you! Skank you!' And finally gets to Shaanxi, 'De-dumb, de-dumb, de-dumb!... Poop... poop!'"

He finished with a long farty raspberry, and the carriage erupted in laughter. The woman opposite laughed too and asked me: "You don't think it's funny?"

"No."

"It's true, though, Gansu folk haven't a cent to rub together, in Shanxi, they're dead stingy, Henan is full of conmen and Shaanxi folk are just dumb, aren't they?"

But I just said: "Everywhere's the same in China."

I took my shoes off and sat cross-legged on the seat. The woman suddenly caught sight of my anklet twine, and her eyes shone.

"Where did you buy that?"

"It's home-made."

"Very sexy!"

I didn't answer her. The train rattled on and I got that whining in my ears again, it was Rabbit crying. I almost screamed his name but no sound came out. I felt like I was choking and grabbed myself around the neck and clawed at my chest.

The effort of suppressing my emotions made me sit up. The instant I opened my eyes, I felt the train disappearing in a puff of smoke and I was back in the tunnel, but this time it was being pulled apart like a cloud in the wind, and then it vanished. I was so confused, I didn't know where I was. A moment passed and my mind cleared: I was back in the cave, on the *kang*, I must have been dreaming, or maybe not... I clutched Rabbit tight in my arms.

When I went out of the cave, darkness had fallen. Bright's dad had dinner ready, millet porridge and steamed potatoes again. I served myself a bowl of the porridge and took seven or eight potatoes which I tucked away inside my jacket. I'm going to see my mum, I thought, and she won't have had dinner. I can give her the potatoes. The crows swooped down over the strip, then came down to roost in the pine trees, squirting their poop everywhere. I heard crying coming from the East Ridge again.

I had to meet my mum at the entrance of the village and decided to take Rabbit with me. I put new clothes on him and changed his nappy. When we went out of the cave, I saw Great-Grandad sitting on the millstone star-gazing. He hadn't done that in a long while, why tonight? And why was he sitting on the millstone, it was cloudy, there weren't any stars to see!

"Can you see the Eastern Well, Butterfly?" he asked me.

"It's cloudy," I said.

I looked up and there really weren't any stars at all, certainly not the Eastern Well. Then my gaze shifted to the patch of sky over the pine trees. No stars there either, then I thought I glimpsed one, but I looked again, and it had gone.

"Are you going to Rice's?" Bright's dad asked.

"Yes, she's giving me a piece of red flannel."

"You leave that baby behind, he's too little."

"Don't worry."

"What do you mean, don't worry? I'll look after him, give him to me, don't be long."

So I had to hand him over. Rabbit began to cry, and Bright's dad shushed him, crooning: "What's up little Rabbit? You've been crying all day."

I rushed away, and the dog followed at my heels.

As I was about to walk out of the alley, I said to the dog: "Go home! I'm only going to Rice's for a bit of flannel!" I chased it away and got to the village entrance as fast as I could. But there was no one there.

After a short while, the village boss appeared from the alley on his way for a drink. He shouted: "Three-Lobes, I'm going to Rake's house, you bring two bottles with you!"

Then he saw me: "What are you doing here, Butterfly?"

"I'm off to the store for some sugar."

"We're having a drink at Rake's, can you tell Bright to join us? We need to talk about the field swops."

"He's in the township."

"Not back yet?" And he stomped away.

I stood in the darkness. I couldn't see my mum anywhere. Maybe they'd seen the village boss come by and were hiding somewhere? I coughed. Surely my mum would recognise the sound. No one. I waited, and waited some more. It was very dark, like the night was blind, like I was blind. I still couldn't see my mum. I began to suspect Rice had been making it all up, but she wasn't that kind of person, why had she done that to me? She'd described my mother exactly! There couldn't be anyone else who looked just like her. Or maybe they were looking for another woman called Butterfly, there must be others with my name in this world, and they'd gone to look for their Butterfly. My legs ached from standing so long, so I hunkered down on my haunches, then sat, but the dew soaked through my trousers. I heard Rabbit crying, his high-pitched wails from high up on the strip clearly audible in the stillness of the night, and I heard Bright's dad yelling: "Rabbit!... Rabbit!" It sounded like he was having no success at calming Rabbit and was shouting for me.

Finally I gave up waiting. My mum hadn't come. Rice had got it wrong, she'd misunderstood. How would my mother get to a place like this? I turned around and headed back to the Blacks' caves. At first I looked around at every step, but when I got to the alley, I looked around one last time and couldn't see the village entrance any more. I leaned against the stone woman and cried out. The tears flowed down my cheeks, but they didn't feel like tears, they were like all the fluids in my body draining away, and I was getting thinner and then the flesh was falling off me. I stayed there a very long time, until I was so thin my clothes were hanging loose on me. Then I walked up the alley to the strip, feeling weightless, my body was gone, I was just paper, and the wind caught me up and plastered me onto the wall of the cave, then caught me again and stuck me on the other wall.

AFTERWORD

One day ten years ago, during a summer of no rain, I sat in a rented room in the south of Xi'an listening to a man from my old village as he poured out his story. He stuttered so his story came out in fits and starts. Behind the bed curtain, his wife was sobbing her heart out. There were a lot of mosquitos and I had to keep swotting them with the palm of my hand, though all I hit was my arms or my face.

"She's gone... she's gone back there," he said.

The scene is still vivid in my memory: he looked up at me, his gaze blank, and I was so stunned at the news that I sat silent for a long while. The 'she' was his daughter. She had dropped out of lower middle school and come with her parents to Xi'an where they were trash-pickers, but after only a year she had been kidnapped and sold. It took them three years to find her and with great difficulty they had managed to get the police to rescue her. But now, six months later, she had gone back to the village where she had been taken.

"It's demons who made it end up like this. Crazy demons!" he said.

His wife carried on weeping. My village neighbour suddenly lost his temper and grabbed a bowl from the table and threw it at the bed curtain.

"Fucking cry! That's all you do!" he yelled.

I didn't try to stop him, and I had no words of consolation. There was another bowl on the table with pickled vegetables in it, along with a colander full of steamed buns and a black plastic bucket that served as a plant pot, holding a small crab apple. They had planted it up three days after their daughter came back. My friend had called me over to celebrate with a few drinks, and I arrived just as the daughter was filling the bucket with earth. Now I pushed the bucket, bowl and colander out of the way so he wouldn't throw them at his wife, and gradually I found out what had happened. The press, TV and radio had all been keen to give extensive coverage to the heroic rescue of a kidnapped woman by the police. Everyone in the neighbourhood knew what had happened and who she was, so the daughter had been besieged and gawked at in the street. Rumours went around that the man she'd been forced to live with was dirt-poor and half-witted, and that she'd given birth to a child. She stopped going outdoors, or talking, and spent all day sitting motionless. My neighbour was worried she was either going to fall seriously ill or go mad, so he asked around for a prospective husband, the farther away the better, so no one would know about her past history. But just as they were talking to the matchmaker, the girl disappeared, leaving a note saying she was going back to the village.

This is a true story, one that I have never told until now.

The story felt like a knife in my heart. Every time I thought of it, it seemed to twist deeper inside. I had no idea where the village was that the girl had gone back to or how she'd been living for the last ten years. I was still in touch with my neighbour, he and his wife used to go back home every year for the harvest, and then come back to Xi'an for the rest of the year and work as trash-pickers. But his hair was thinning and he was getting frailer and more stooped. A few years ago, when I met him, he was still going on and on about how when they went to rescue his girl, she had been in a village on the loess plateau, blasted by winds, everyone lived in caves and couldn't even afford wheat buns. But the last few times, he never mentioned his daughter.

"Haven't you been to see her?" I asked him.

He brushed the question off: "What... what is there to s-see?"

He obviously didn't want to talk about it, and I didn't dare probe. Then I made a research trip to Dingxi in Gansu province, to Hengshan and Suide in Yulin prefecture, and Bin county, Chunhua, and Xunyi in the northern part of Xianyang prefecture. This was all loess plateau, and every time we drove along the ridge-top roads we would come across some woman coming back from digging potatoes, her face weathered and sun-burnt, bent double under the weight of a great basket, hobbling along bandy-legged, and I thought of my neighbour's daughter. In one village we passed by the strip in front of someone's house. It was piled high with farm tools of all sorts, and there was a donkey and a pig, a dog and a flock of chickens, and Chinese bellflowers and angelica laid out on the ground at the door of their cave to dry in the sun. A man was hunkered down eating his dinner, and there was a woman too, wiping her baby's nose and shouting imprecations at the people next door. She slapped her own behind and swore energetically at them. I thought of my neighbour's daughter then too. We strolled around the market and were driving on to the next village, when at the crossroads we came across a child trying to catch grasshoppers in a clump of grass, studiously ignoring his grandmother who was shouting for him. She put down the basket she had been carrying on her arm, and called: "Who wants some flatbread?" Still the child did not come, but the sparrows and crows and eagles did, and by the time the kid arrived with a grasshopper clutched in his fist, there was no flatbread left in the basket, only something that looked like a bone but was actually one of her teeth that had fallen out in the market. She had brought it home to throw up on the house roof. Then, too, I thought of my neighbour's daughter.

When I was young, death was just a word, a concept, a philosophical question, about which we had enthusiastic discussions that we didn't take too seriously, but after I turned fifty, friends and family began to die off one after another, until finally my mother and father died. After that I began to develop a fear of death, albeit an unspoken one. In the same way, when a short while ago cases of trafficking of women and children began to appear in the media, it felt as remote from my own life as if I was reading a foreign novel about the slave trade. But after I had heard what happened to the daughter of my village neighbour, it all became more personal; when I walked down the street, I stared at the passers-by, imagining which one was a trafficker. And if relatives came to visit with their children or grandchildren, I warned them to keep a close eye on the little ones as I saw them off at the door.

I was born and grew up in a village and didn't come to Xi'an until I was nineteen. So I thought I knew everything there was to know about rural life. But at the beginning of the 1980s, I had a conversation with a Women's Federation cadre, and she said research had revealed that sixty per cent of village women had never experienced sexual pleasure. I remember that my mouth dropped open in astonishment. Ten years ago, when my village neighbour's daughter was kidnapped, I paid a visit to the police, where I found out that they did not know the figures for the number of city women and children kidnapped each year (because it was hard to verify whether or not a kidnap had taken place), but proven, reported cases of people who had gone missing ran into the thousands. That astonished me too.

In fact, if you look carefully, every lamppost in every street and alleyway in the city, every signpost and every telephone box is festooned with Missing Person notices. Most of the missing are women and children, and most are apparently kidnap victims. And why do such incidents happen largely in the city (you hardly ever get notices like that in the countryside)? Kidnapping for ransom is understandable, as is theft of property, and even the theft of livestock and pets that are then sold on. But why does this barbarous practice of snatching women and children persist in our increasingly civilised age?

The recent transformation of China has led to the biggest migration of people from countryside to the city in history. Take Xi'an, for example: this is an ancient city but everywhere you see young faces, neatly dressed, with fashionable hairstyles, all taking cute selfies on their mobile phones, but all also talking in every conceivable kind of regional dialect. It is obvious that eighty to ninety per cent of them come from the countryside. In the building where I live, most of the rooms are rented out to young people like them. Some of them will actually put down roots in Xi'an and do well for themselves, but the majority drift from one job to another because they are badly paid, badly treated, or the job is too hard and they leave. But they won't go home, they would rather live on dry bread three times a day than return to village life. Once they have been in Xi'an for a year or two, they won't go back, especially the girls. The central government issues a discussion document at the start of every year, proclaiming that it wants to build new socialist villages, but the villages have no young people any more. Are they going to rely on the old folks who have been left looking after the children to build them? I have seen villages with smart new buildings, with signs reading 'Village Party Committee', 'Party Members' Recreation Centre', 'Medical Clinic' and 'Agricultural Research Station', but these are all in villages that are close to the city, with good land and within reach of highways. In remote backward areas, the men who lack the ability, the skills or the funds to leave, are left behind in the villages to scratch a living on the land. They have no possibility of marrying. I have been to villages made up almost entirely of wifeless men.

One man I met, crippled since he fell down a cliff and broke his leg installing electricity in the village, told me: "My family will die out because of me, and our village will vanish in our lifetime."

I could think of nothing to say.

Pandas are precious precisely because it is so difficult to persuade them to breed in captivity; conversely, the more despised and lowly the species – like rabbits, rats, houseflies and mosquitos – the faster they breed. Yet these despised and lowly men have no chance of breeding at all! The more something goes from being useful to being useless, the more it is considered art. So, in the city, all kinds of sex turns into 'art', while these village men remain wifeless and childless. I remember when 'scar literature' was fashionable, all of it bewailing the fate of educated youth sent to suffer the privations of village life during the Cultural Revolution. I was one of them, but I questioned why it was so wrong that young townsfolk should be sent down to rural areas, when it was apparently assumed that it was right and proper that villagers, including myself, should suffer poverty and hardship. Let me be clear: kidnapping of women and children is brutal and cruel and should be cracked down on. But every time there is a crackdown, the traffickers are severely published and the police are lauded for their heroic rescues, no one mentions the fact that the cities have plundered wealth, labour power and women from the villages. No one talks about the men left behind in the wastelands to wither like gourds on the frame, flowering once, then dying fruitless. These are the last villages in China, and the men are probably the last bachelors too.

This is the story of our age, is it not?

Nevertheless, I did not write this story for ten years. I did not know how to write it. How should I describe my village neighbour's daughter being tricked into a car, her struggles when she realised something was wrong, the beatings, the rape? How to describe how they threatened to disfigure her, to cut her kidney out, how she watched as the traffickers bargained over her and sold her? How to write about her mother who wept herself blind for three years, until her father heard about a trafficking hub in a small town in Shanxi province and spent a year slaving away in a brick kiln to scrape together the money to go and look for her, finally tracking her down, driving a hundred *li* of mountain roads by night, lying in wait for two days and three nights at the entrance to the village? How to write about their meeting, father and daughter, with him pretending that he was paying the bride a visit in order not to arouse hostility from the villagers; his trip back to Xi'an where he told the Public Security Bureau exactly where his daughter was, but they demanded that he raise the money for their trip because their budget wouldn't run to it; about how he went back to collecting trash to raise the money but was sentenced to six months in prison for stealing three manhole covers? How to tell the story of the girl's rescue: the villagers up in arms, the injuries to the policeman's leg and the father's head, before they finally snatched the girl back. How to describe how the girl came back to the city but was overwhelmed by public attention and longing for her baby, and returned to the village where she had been taken? I did not want to write the story of a simple kidnap. There have been far too many reports of criminal cases in recent years, some even more bizarre and cruel than kidnappings, such as the imprisonment and torture of people trying to present petitions for justice, domestic violence and terrorist attacks. What I wanted to explore was how the cities grew fat while the villages fell into destitution, what the village where my neighbour's kidnapped daughter ended up was really like, which bits had fallen down or washed away, whether the remaining villagers were timid or fierce, pitiable or loathsome, were they iced-up like snow-bound Mount Fuji or a live volcano that could blow at any moment?

That version of the story had a rich plot, with a bizarre ending, and I was full of indignation and grief, but after I had written ten, a hundred, several hundred pages, I had to stop. I was too anxious – I did not understand my characters or where I stood in this – for my novel to flow freely. If I held a rice bowl under a waterfall, how much water could I expect to catch? I knew I was innately curious, as if I hovered over life with a pair of chopsticks ready to sample anything. And I was sensitive too. When someone came to visit me, I sensed everything, the way ants smell out sugar. Eventually, I started the whole thing again. This story was like the rice straw used to tie up a live crab, I couldn't possibly use it to tie up bundles of garlic chives.

There are many ways of writing a novel but nowadays it seems to be the fashion to write violent, extreme narratives. Maybe that is what today's readers want, but it does not suit me. I have always thought that my writing was somehow akin to ink-wash paintings, painting in words, you might say. When I first started writing, back in the eighties, I was inspired partly by the Chinese opera tradition and the aesthetics of ink-wash painting, and partly by my growing awareness of Western contemporary art. And over the decades, these two sources of inspiration have become intertwined and have given life to my writing. Today, the land that former generations of writers, and I myself, have written about, as well as the familiar countryside that gave us spiritual succour, has been transformed beyond recognition. No matter how hard we look for it, it is gone for good; all our efforts to recapture it will just sound like delirious ravings. I once read an article by someone from Shaanxi, about how he missed his mother, she was the best at rolling dough in the whole world. After his article was published, he was swamped by letters from readers insisting that it was *their* mother who was the best at rolling dough! I'm no different. Every time I get sick and take to my bed, I long for mother's food, but my mother has been dead for many years, and no one makes food like that any more.

Whenever I find myself doubting how and what I'm writing in my novel, I step back a bit and go to an art gallery or attend a painting symposium. I find this benefits me greatly, and I make notes afterwards, both on my impressions and on the keynote speeches. Just before I began this novel again, I attended one such symposium and noted down some of the comments:

"Today's ink-wash painting must embody today's culture, society and aesthetics, it cannot turn its back on reality. Like other arts, painting cannot deny the fundamental changes in the relationships between humans and nature, between the individual and society, and between the self and the collective. If you only paint flowers and birds and scenery, it is as if the dramatic transformation of the last two hundred years had never happened, and you have just made something decorative, divorced from the era we live in. That said, ink-wash painting does not reflect the changes in society directly, it's not social comment, nor does it serve any ideology or concept. In fact, that was precisely the weakness of ink-wash painting in the twentieth century, that it saw itself as social comment rather than art.

"So what does it mean to relate this kind of painting to the modern era? And what distinguishes it from other art forms? The essence of ink-wash painting lies in 写意, *xieyi*, the 'suggestion' rather than the detail; that is, the talent of the individual artist, which is itself a coalescence of his or her lengthy honing of artistic skills, combined with self-cultivation, is revealed through the brush strokes. That is the core of this art form; *xieyi* is not concerned either with reason or with unreason. It is truth, not a conceptual idea. The artists' experience of themselves, their feelings, the society in which they live, and politics and religion, as well as their inner self-cultivation, meld together and form an indissoluble whole, a physical expression of their souls. The Western concept of the self is an atomised, individual self, while in Chinese culture, the self is one's personality, one's personal ideals, and has a collective and cumulative nature. In the West, the development of contemporary art has come about through the creative impetus given by an outpouring of pure individualism. This is the main wellspring of modern art, including post-modern conceptual art and installation art. But the driving force in China has been different: it is a construct of the ideal personality, a personality which has a collective and cumulative nature. We are not talking about a perfected self, but about a self that is constructed through an ideal collective and cumulative process."

The symposium speeches made me think of the words with which quotations from the Buddha open, in the scriptures: "So I have heard." So I have heard, indeed. And, having heard, I began to ponder many questions, such as: what is the ideal personality, what is the cumulative spirit of the community, and how to construct the individual through literature. I remember that I was reading some poems by Su Shi that evening, and it suddenly occurred to me that this poet was the very exemplar of the Chinese ideal personality, with his poems, his essays, his calligraphy and his paintings. Then I thought of the *xiaosheng*, the handsome young male role in Chinese opera. The philosophy and aesthetics of the Chinese people are most fully expressed in opera. Where did this role come from: the face painted and beardless, the character reserved and self-contained, a fine figure of a man, handsome and graceful? The type exactly describes Jia Baoyu in *The Dream of the Red Chamber*, Song Jiang in *Water Margin* and Tang Yao in *Journey to the West*. What Chinese aesthetic does this androgynous character reflect? What secret does it reveal about the Chinese cultural genes? Look at the Song dynasty writer Su Shi, able to write poetry and do calligraphy and painting; so good at everything he turns his hand to that the world loves him, yet how many people understand him? He suffered so many misfortunes and hardships during his life and yet there is no anger or sharpness in any of his writing. He overcame suffering, exile and criticism and was entirely at ease in his understanding of the essence of human life and the natural world, yet his texts are still regarded as empty and negative, or at best calm and optimistic. How lonely the wise are! When we write literature, especially literature nowadays, we are always lambasted for making our works too dark and their themes too critical. But in periods of great social transformation, there are many contradictions, conflicts, absurdities and anxieties so, of course, in the literature of the age, there is much unmasking, criticism, doubting and probing. The characteristics of the era define the writing of the era, the authors of this type of work must necessarily produce writing with these characteristics. But I also think that in our writings, especially novels, we write exhaustively about evil, but no one has ever written exhaustively about good. For a very long time, the chief protagonist of a literary work has always been pale and white. But why? Then again, when I read history books, I never understood why the people of the Qin dynasty esteemed black over all other colours – in the Warring States period, the Qin soldiers wore black armour, held aloft black flags, and stormed down like wolves or tigers and destroyed the Six Kingdoms before sweeping away again, and coming to an end after just two imperial reigns. Watching the footage on television, I see that the Islamic State in the Middle East also wrap themselves in black, and brandish black flags as they storm cities and territories. Yet in 20th century China, it is red that was esteemed: the flag of the Republic of China was red with a white sun, and the People's Republic of China is even redder, with its five stars. What is the relationship between black and red and a nation's character, and how does that symbolise our cultural genes?

During the long winter of 2014, I carried on making preparations for my work on *Broken Wings*, but I was still in a state of confusion. And I remained so all through the spring of 2015. Finally, when summer arrived, I took up my pen. I like working in the summer, the heat doesn't bother me, in fact I feel like a hot-air balloon, the hotter I am, the higher I fly. The jumble of thoughts of the previous winter, my inability to finish my new work, seemed to have nothing to do with *Broken Wings*. Instead, I smelled something in the air, something that I could bring into the story. It is like a pregnant woman listening to music so the baby will like singing, and sticking pictures of beautiful people on the bedroom wall so the baby will grow up beautiful. It's like people wearing a jade medallion around their necks because jade connects to the spirit, or a boxer having a tattoo of the head of a wild beast to make himself appear fiercer and braver. The nonesuch flower in this novel, like the real-life caterpillar fungus, begins with a small grub that hibernates in winter, then puts out leaves and flowers in summer; and when the plant flourishes and blossoms, then summer days are good.

As I began to write, it was not me writing, I was allowing poor kidnapped Butterfly to lament her fate in her own words. She has finished lower middle school, so she has a bit of education and social aspirations. She likes to sprinkle her speech with traditional sayings, she seems to know both everything and nothing. As she laments, who is she talking to? To me? To the world around her? The word for novel in Chinese is literally 'small talk' and this story is a very small talk, but it's not me talking, it's Butterfly. I originally planned to write 400,000 characters but after 150,000 characters, it was done. The reason may be that it's not a complicated story, or that I'm old and I wanted to cut her short, using subtraction rather than addition. But 150,000 characters is fine, and through me trying to get the whole process into it, and trying to escape from my former narrative habits, *Broken Wings* became the shortest novel I have ever written, and in so doing I was able to reap and enjoy the fruits of a different kind of experience.

Having completed this manuscript of fewer than three hundred pages, I said to myself: Your birthplace has determined what you are. It's like pottery glazes, on Jingdezhen porcelain it is blue and white, and on Yaotou pottery it is black.

I have been an author for decades, and have chosen any number of topics and forms, but with this work, I have written about myself, and only myself.

But a novel takes on a life of its own, it is both under my control and escapes my control. I originally planned it purely a lament by Butterfly, but as I wrote, other elements appeared: her baby grows in her belly day by day, the days pass and her baby becomes Rabbit, Butterfly's sufferings increase, and she becomes as pitiable a figure as Auntie Spotty-Face and Rice. The birth of a novel is like the clay figure shaped in the image of a divinity by a sculptor in a temple; once it is finished, the sculptor kneels to worship it because the clay figure has become divine.

On the morning of 15 July 2015, I remember the exact day, I put a final full stop to this text of 150,000 characters. We had a torrential rainstorm that continued till evening. It was the heaviest rainfall we had had all summer. I was waiting for family members to return from a trip away, and

my thoughts flitted here and there, like motes of dust. Then I thought of
these lines. In the first, Su Shi, exiled to far-off Hainan island, rejoices that
his protégé has succeeded in the imperial examinations:

> The azure seas can never break our bonds,
> Hainan's vermilion cliffs have pierced the unfriendly
>   skies.

The second line goes:

> When the birds and the trees are happy, how can we
>   not be?

GLOSSARY

dan - unit of weight, equivalent to one hundred *jin*

feng shui - literally, wind and water, also written *fengshui,* energy forces intended to harmonise individuals with their surrounding environment

jin - unit of weight, also known as *catty,* about one pound, half a kilogram in weight

kang - bed built of mud bricks

li - unit of distance, about half a kilometre

lingzhi - also known as *reishi* (Japanese), a kind of mushroom valued for its medicinal properties

mu - unit of area, ten *mu* equals about 1.6 acres

qi - also written *ch'i*, vital energy, life force

yuan - unit of currency

ABOUT THE AUTHOR

 Jia Pingwa (1952-) stands with Mo Yan and Yu Hua as one of the biggest names in contemporary Chinese literature. A prolific producer of novels, short stories and essays, he has a huge following on the Chinese mainland, as well as in Hong Kong and Taiwan. An early English translation of his 1988 novel *Turbulence* by Howard Goldblatt won the Mobil Pegasus Prize for Literature. In 1997, his 1993 bestseller *Ruined City* was first published abroad in French as *La Capitale déchue* (*Abandoned Capital*), translated by Genevieve Imbot-Bichet. It was published in English translation in January 2016, again by Howard Goldblatt, this time as part of the Chinese Literature Today Book Series. *Happy Dreams*, translated by Nicky Harman, and *The Lantern Bearer*, translated by Carlos Rojas, were published in 2017.

Jia Pingwa's fiction focuses on the lives of common people, particularly in his home province of Shaanxi, and is well-known for being unafraid to explore the realm of the sexual. *Ruined City* was banned for many years for that same reason, and pirated copies sold on the street for several thousand yuan apiece. The novel was finally unbanned in 2009, one year after Jia won the Mao Dun Award for his 2005 novel *Shaanxi Opera*.

ABOUT THE TRANSLATOR

Passionate about spreading Chinese literature to English readers, Nicky Harman has translated the works of many renowned Chinese authors into English. They include Anni Baobei's *The Road of Others*, Chan Koon-Chung's *The Unbearable Dreamworld of Champa the Driver*, Chen Xiwo's *Book of Sins*, Han Dong's *A Phone Call from Dalian: Collected Poems*, Jia Pingwa's *Happy Dreams*, Dorothy Tse's *Snow and Shadow*, Xinran's *Letter from an Unknown Chinese Mother*, Xu Xiaobin's *Crystal Wedding*, Xu Zhiyuan's *Paper Tiger and* Yan Ge's *The Chilli Bean Paste Clan*.

Harman has won several awards, including the Mao Tai Cup People's Literature Chinese-English translation prize 2015 and the 2013 China International Translation Contest, Chinese-to-English section. When not translating, she promotes contemporary Chinese fiction to the general English-language reader through the website Paper-Republic.org. She also blogs, gives talks, mentors new translators, teaches summer school and judges translation competitions. She lives in the United Kingdom and tweets as the China Fiction Bookclub @cfbcuk.

Lightning Source UK Ltd.
Milton Keynes UK
UKHW040828130219
337108UK00001B/25/P